the Threatening Throne

While Elisena began a protective chant, Tristan stretched out his hand toward the throne. Probably nothing would happen, he told himself. The power might not even wake without the sword. Magic could be dangerous, but he'd been raised on it. And, after all, he was the rightful heir to the throne.

He reached his fingers toward the socket where the lost sword should go.

The crackling jolt of power was akin to the unhappy effect of mixing magic with cold iron—only vastly worse. The shock of it lasted only for the length of time it took for him to be hurled violently backward off the dais.

He hit the floor and lost consciousness.

The Sword of Calandra

Susan Dexter

A Del Rey Book

BALLANTINE BOOKS • NEW YORK

A Del Rey Book
Published by Ballantine Books

Library of Congress Catalog Card Number: 84-91018

ISBN 0-345-29717-2

Manufactured in the United States of America

First Edition: March 1985

Cover art by Rowena Morrill

This book is for:

David and Sally, who kept me from growing up an only child.

Evelyn, who said *The Ring of Allaire* read "just like a book."

Elaine and Jeff, for love and support.

And Pippin, who sings while I type.

Contents

Weather~Witching

CALANDRA'S KING SAT near the top of Crogen castle's highest crumbling tower, picking dry flakes of yellowish mud from his sleeve ends—hardly a regal occupation for a man to indulge in.

But then, Tristan mused sourly, it was not at all out of character for this particular ruler, his own most unlikely self. He was in a foul humor, and between the intervals of temper, more depressed than he could remember being at any previous point in his life.

Toadstools! It wasn't *his* fault they had decided to crown him king! He hadn't exactly gone looking for the job; in fact, he had done a great deal to avoid it and would have done a great deal more if there had been the least prospect of success. That being so, Polassar had no one but himself to blame if those kingly trappings he insisted upon swaddling Tristan in only slid rapidly off again. Tristan would have been happy to have nothing whatsoever to do with the situation. He frowned at a particularly persistent bit of mud and scraped at it with his thumbnail. Failing to remove it, he sketched a spell over the dirt with his fingers and spoke a word of magic at it. Nothing happened, and Tristan swore softly. His fingers began to fidget again, restive as his thoughts.

1

Why should he be faulted—and so roundly scolded—for helping an old woman catch her runaway piglet by flinging himself on top of it? It had seemed a most natural and courteous thing to do at the time, if a trifle strenuous. His late master Blais had briefly kept a pig, and Tristan had learned enough from the experience to know that a successful runaway pig would mean an unpleasantly empty belly somewhat later for the pigkeeper. His response had been instinctive and hardly worthy of rebuke.

It wasn't as if there had been anyone else in the courtyard to witness the spectacular recapture, anyway. There had just been Tristan and the piglet's grateful owner—and Polassar, who'd stepped back out of the way rather than shifting himself to help, Tristan angrily recalled. Therefore, why a long-winded lecture on kingly dignity? What could dignity possibly matter when there was no one to see?

Well, you certainly can't be said to have lost the common touch. Thomas sniffed disdainfully and fanned his whiskers.

Tristan swore and would have turned away from the cat, but the decrepit state of Crogen's battlements left him scant room to maneuver at the spot he'd chosen. The margin of masonry between him and a sheer drop of some hundreds of feet was rather slight.

"Go away, Thomas," Tristan said in what he hoped would pass for a reasonable tone. It didn't.

We're a bit prickly lately, aren't we? Don't you like it here?

Tristan didn't, but that fact had precious little to do with the way he was feeling. The surface distresses and petty annoyances were unfortunately only symptoms of a far deeper ill. He felt justified. Events had, after all, been nothing like what he'd expected or desired, and if he had to live with matters anyway, he'd do so with little grace. Stubbornly, Tristan refused to acknowledge the least regret for his attitude.

"I can think of other things I'd rather be doing, Thomas," he said, still not relinquishing his close-cherished annoyance.

Such as? Thomas settled placidly at his feet and delicately licked a paw—unnecessarily. Thomas' fur was always immaculate and shone like well-polished wood.

Tristan sighed and leaned back against the stone for a long moment, eyes shut. "I don't know. I thought I did." He let himself think for a while, instead of fuming over Polassar, and his mind drifted back to happier times when his master Blais might have questioned him so. He started to relax, and some of his dreams, buried through many wakings and a lot of growing up, came back to him, freshly minted. When Tristan spoke again, it was more to himself or to Blais' memory than to Thomas, and his voice was gentler.

"There's still so much that nobody's found any answers for. Why can't wizards cross running water without half killing themselves in the process? There must be a reason and maybe a cure. And why should iron be poison to a wizard and not to anyone else? I'd like to work at finding those answers. I'd like to make a black rose," he went on. "I'd like to keep studying, learning—the way Blais did and would have wanted me to. But Polassar's got his own ideas, and everything I do is either wrong or unsuitable. He forgets I'm a wizard, not a king, however hard he tries to make me into one! What do I know about ruling or armies?"

Probably less than I do. You never did pay a scad of attention when Blais got onto the subject of government, as opposed to history, which of course was all glamor and heroism as far as you were concerned.

Tristan smiled ruefully. It had been four months since they'd left Darkenkeep's terrors behind a second time, and three scant weeks since Polassar had gathered what was left of his private army—after a noisy dispute with a lieutenant who'd long assumed him dead—and marched it to Crogen, forcing the castle to open to its new king. A heroic feat to be sure, Tristan thought acidly, reflecting on what they'd found within the ancient walls when he'd finally ridden in with his commander: gaping serfs, mostly aged and toothless—maybe they were just the slowest; squawking chickens; and the great courtyard itself filled with row upon row of just-planted pole-beans. Tristan smiled again, remembering how Polassar had been amazed far beyond his usually vast powers of cursing. Maybe Tristan wasn't the only thing disappointing Polassar. Was this the Crogen of half a hundred kings and a thousand songs? Tristan looked around and still wondered.

Crogen had proved to be a crazy quilt of masonry, towers and buttresses, walls and spires, cloisters and bridges, and courtyards, not to mention gardens, the remains of an orangery, dog kennels, mews, stables, barracks, and storerooms of all kinds and sizes, with no rhyme or reason to their placement. They just sprang up wherever there was room and sometimes where there really wasn't. Tristan got lost every time he poked his nose out of his own room. He liked to think of the process as making architectural discoveries, but it was still an embarrassment to him.

His ancestors—remote unknowns all—had been notable builders, though also notably dissimilar in their tastes. The most that could be said for the sprawling castle's coherence was that sixty of a hundred parts of it were hewn of the same stone—one which was locally and conveniently quarried. Luckily it weathered to a warm silver-gold pleasing to both its setting and a beholder's eye. The rest of the place ran eccentrically from white marble to red brick to carven wood, with a little colored tile thrown in. The whole was somehow more harmonious than a listing of its parts suggested—or maybe Tristan's eyes were just growing used to the place, so that he saw it less, past familiarity's veil.

Be that as it might, there was one thing about Crogen that still disconcerted him utterly. The fabled stronghold had no walls.

It never had, apparently. Traditional seat of Calandra's High Mages as well as its kings, Crogen had probably never been conventionally defensible. The buildings were walled and roofed against the weather; but without the magical defenses, Crogen could have withstood no attack more determined than a siege of raindrops. Polassar's capture of the castle had been accomplished by nothing more hazardous than a shouted order.

Tristan toed a crumb of mortar to the edge of the parapet and watched it fall. Crogen's buildings straggled up to the citadel's perimeters and stopped there, as if at an invisible line or a wall long ago removed. They huddled together, shoulder to shoulder as it were, edges touching to form a more or less solid boundary, but there were many gaps, and it was by no stretch a defensible arrangement. Some of the individual buildings were more or less fortified—there were the battlements and high parapets—but even Tristan recognized that those were more architectural conceits than anything practical. He thought of the great outward-sloping unscalable walls that Radak boasted. There was nothing at Crogen to match them, not even the token bit of battlement that he now stood upon.

They had come to Crogen, Tristan, Polassar, Polassar's incomparable lady Allaire, and Elisena with her ten magical silver rings, fresh from Darkenkeep—with its cold still breath-

ing on all their necks—and fresh, too, from the reforging of
the tenth ring and the still amazing discovery of the truth of
Tristan's heritage, to make what Elisena freely admitted was
a madman's gesture.

That, of course, was precisely why she'd chosen to make
it.

Their situation had been desperate, yet worthy of a certain
boldness of action. Had their heads managed to win out over
their high hearts, they would have fled to the safety of Lassair
castle, Polassar's own home. In fact they had done so, but only
briefly. They could have stayed there. It would have been
sensible. Often attacked though Lassair was, it was in a vastly
better state of repair than long-abandoned Crogen.

Polassar had argued hotly for remaining. After all, Lassair's
was the country he knew best, having fought over every inch
of it. It was logical that they stay there, if only to recover their
strength before going on to further battles.

Elisena had not agreed.

"Lassair is indefensible," she had insisted over Polassar's
protests. "It can never withstand another siege without repairs
that we shall have no time to make. Yet if we stay here, it will
look as if we intend to defend it. Whereas Crogen...No one
will take our presence there seriously. We'd be let alone, and
it's time we need now, more dearly than walls."

Time indeed: time to win over contentious lords, to convince
them that the unknown Tristan was their rightful king in place
of other claimants who'd been battling over the right to the
throne all their lives; time as well to build an army capable of
dealing with those lords who could *not* be so convinced; time
for Tristan to learn something of the nature of kingship and
accustom himself to it, not incidentally.

Tristan sighed heavily, wanting nothing less than that ines-
capable conclusion. His education was weighing heavier each
day.

It seemed to him that events had moved with an impossible
speed and a horrible inevitability ever since that evening when
he'd returned home to find his master dead in a duel of magic
and his master's legendary quest passed on to himself. He'd
followed Blais' last commands and faced both Darkenkeep and
the fearsome haughty hierarchy of the mages of Kôvelir, had
dared death many times without ever meaning to, and had
learned love, sacrifice, and a small bit more about magic and

its uses. Now, just when the climax of all that seemed about to be reached, things had stopped happening to Tristan if to no one else. At least, what was happening was not quite what he'd expected. Instead of being relieved at that, Tristan found he was only confused and uncertain and ultimately often bored under a thin film of apprehension. He sighed again.

Thomas swatted at him. *Isn't it windy enough up here?*

It was indeed. The breeze was cold and damp in Tristan's face and made his tattered cloak flap behind him. It wasn't all that long ago, he thought bleakly, that he'd promised Elisena he'd try the kingship her rings insisted he was heir to. He was baffled. How could bright hopes transmute to gloom in four short months? That surely wasn't all in his confused mind.

He thought of his having killed the dragon guardian of Darkenkeep and of how that insane, improbable deed had both reforged the tenth ring and won him Elisena—and this unwelcome kingship. He couldn't believe that he'd truly done such a thing, had a hand in it at all. The action and all the events close around it seemed a dim dream, remembered imperfectly, with its emphasis shifted and changed.

Tristan sniffed distastefully. His clothes still smelled of pig.

It had been inevitable, of course, that sooner or later he'd run up against someone who'd dispute his right to a kingship he personally didn't even want. But couldn't that moment have held off just a *little* longer? They might as well never have come to Crogen.

He didn't much like scheming, Tristan decided, or complicated strategies and political maneuverings, either. They made his head ache. He liked to take one day at a time, one after another in proper succession, and those days should by preference be spent uneventfully in magical pursuits. How, in the midst of this unwelcome quest for kingliness in himself, was he ever to find time for his magic? Was he to be only a king, and no more the wizard he'd struggled and studied so long to become? That wasn't fair—he'd worked so hard to make up for what he'd always supposed was his lack of any natural ability. And just when he'd come so close . . . Tristan wondered suddenly if any of this mattered, if he would survive long enough for it to matter. He was beginning to think not, but that didn't cheer him much.

"My lord is melancholy of late." Elisena had come to stand behind him, and he'd never heard her over the wind. Grown used to being so startled, Tristan didn't even turn around.

"Melancholy? That seems a light term for it. Are my eyes playing me tricks in this wind, or is that an army down there?"

He gestured at a distance-dwarfed cluster of men, tents, horses, and wind-whipped banners. The encampment was rather far off from Crogen, almost but deliberately not quite out of sight from the walls, but its existence on a formerly empty stretch of moorland was incontestable.

Elisena laughed, and the little crystals hanging about her face rang with her movement and with the wind.

"Galan will name it his guard, merely, when he plucks up courage enough and blusters in here to see what's going on. He'd have camped closer, I think, but having heard only that we hold Crogen, he can't have any idea how few of us there are here. He's wary of us still."

Tristan shivered, not only from the cold.

"So when he *does* find out . . ." He let the question hang. He hadn't had a chance to get to know Galan well, but nothing he knew suggested that Radak's lord would simply go home and leave Crogen in peace.

The wind laughed at them, smelling of the wet moors.

"I think," Elisena said, "that such cold, wet air as this should be most susceptible to rain-spells."

Tristan could just see the dark shape of her cloak out of the tail of his eye.

"Does that mean what I think it does?" He'd never even considered action, being fully occupied with depression instead.

"I'd be the last to object to Galan's being inconvenienced." A silver-ringed hand came to rest on Tristan's arm, and Elisena's hip pressed against his. "And as I recall, wasn't weather-witching yours and Blais' livelihood?"

So Tristan found himself upon the battlements again in just a few minutes, armed with a small bowl of fresh water, Blais' brass-hinged grimoire, and an assortment of small stones and feathers, all of them gray. Thomas crouched at his feet as they waited for Elisena to return.

Does she know that you're as likely to have it raining inside as out?

"I wish you hadn't said that, Thomas." Tristan was nervous enough about his magical disabilities without Thomas' putting mistakes he'd never even dreamed of into his head.

Well, you should have been practicing spells, instead of moping around up here just because Polassar and Elisena were too busy to nursemaid you.

Tristan glared at the cat.

"I was *not* moping. I simply like to be alone sometimes to think. And I certainly don't need nursemaiding."

Oh?

He'd have sworn the cat raised an eyebrow upon the comment.

"Where's Elisena, anyway? She said she'd be here by the time I got back with these." He gestured at the water and the book. "Oh, stars and comets! Now Polassar's coming. Just what I don't need."

Oh. Is that what all the stomping is? Thomas prudently wrapped his tail close about his paws, protecting every portion vulnerable to being trodden on by large, careless feet. *If he's not careful, he'll shake this whole rotten tower apart.*

Footsteps and the jingle of armaments drew closer, and Polassar's helmeted head poked into sight as he neared the top of the steep stairway. The rest of Polassar followed by stages: leather cap and gauntlets, brass and gold studding both, a longsword and a torso wrapped in a bearskin tunic that looked as if two large bears had been needed to provide it, and finally two very large, booted feet.

Polassar scowled at Tristan.

"Wizard, *will* you get back from that edge! 'Tis no less rotted than the rest of this poxy place."

Tristan shrugged. "It's safe enough." Nonetheless, he turned to obey; as he moved a large chunk of cobble broke away under his boot, making him jump back rather more swiftly that he'd originally intended.

"Aye," Polassar said. He pulled at his red moustaches, not quite managing to hide a grin behind hair or hand.

"Was there something you wanted?" Tristan asked pointedly. "Other than to see to it that I don't do anything so consummately unregal as splattering myself all over the courtyard?"

Polassar crossed to the parapet, keeping a prudent distance between himself and the gap in it.

"Nay, Wizard. Just up here for the view. Like yourself?"

"As a view, I find it somewhat lacking in aesthetic values.

For one thing, I can see a little too much from up here." Tristan went to stand beside Polassar.

"Aye." Polassar squinted toward Galan's encampment. "A most noisome clutter, to be sure."

"Then we'll see what we can do to change that," Elisena said blithely, ascending the stair in a sweep of skirts. She looked at Tristan. "Are you ready?"

Tristan nodded. So simple a weather-spell, under such favorable conditions, didn't really require the offices of two wizards, but he was glad of Elisena's company all the same. He was less happy when Polassar continued to hang about. Magic in front of an audience was difficult enough for him, and Polassar tended toward an unhelpful skepticism.

Best ignore it, though; speaking out now would be churlish and would distract him from his work as well. Tristan busied himself arranging the things he'd brought for the spell.

A long feather came first, the one that shaded from dark to a paler bluish color, very much like the cloudy sky overhead just now. That sort of overcast could persist for days if undisturbed, but with a little judicious prodding from a wizard the clouds could be persuaded to release their moisture on the spot. Blais' training began to rise to the surface of Tristan's mind, blotting all else out, though it had been a long time since he'd attempted any sort of weather-spell.

He made several practice gestures over the feather and then several more with it, glancing at the sky from time to time as he described the magical figures. Good. The clouds were a fraction darker than they had been and looked lower. Elisena stood beside him, the rising wind lifting her hair back from her face. She stroked several of her rings at intervals—not meddling with his spell, but seconding it.

Tristan relaxed a trifle. He'd performed this type of spell before often enough, though always with Blais' help. And those spells had always been done in time of drought, when the needed rain was consequently more difficult to realize. Now it was time for one of the stones. Whispering a chant whose words pattered like the first great drops of a rainstorm, Tristan lowered the pebble gently into the bowl of water. Tiny bubbles clung to the stone's surface briefly, then left it and rose through the water. Tristan spoke a short inversion spell, did the summation, and waited.

Thomas fanned his whiskers curiously. Polassar looked apprehensive, then puzzled. Clouds moved majestically above their heads, on the way to other parts of the realm and beyond.

Toadstools! It hadn't worked—and he'd been so careful, doing more of a spell than was strictly needed, just to be safe. Seconds ticked by, and Tristan knew he was going to have to ask Elisena where he'd gone wrong—in front of Polassar, who'd doubtless laugh, or say he was even less a wizard than a king.

Tristan turned and opened his mouth to speak. The last of the breath he'd been holding came out first.

And the rain came down like a silver sheet. They were all soaked to the skin by the time they'd fled down the stairs and across two open courtyards to reach the shelter of a corbelled archway.

Galan

WHEN DO YOU expect this to stop? Thomas asked, sniffing at a puddle which had overflowed a windowsill and now decorated the floor, wetting the rushes. None of Crogen's windows were still glazed, and most lacked shutters as well, though Polassar had men at work on that. When the wind was right the rain found its way past the hangings easily. After three days, things had grown rather damp; Tristan decided he might just as well have accidentally invoked the storm indoors after all.

"I don't know. That spell's *supposed* to be self-limiting, but—" Tristan's voice trailed off uncertainly. He began yet another frantic search through the grimoire's weather section. Thomas jumped onto the table's dry top.

Polassar squelched through the doorway.

"Wizard—"

"I know. I *know*." Tristan didn't even look up. "I'm sorry about all the mud and I know it's making things impossible for you, but I'm getting to work on a counterspell right now. It just takes time. I want to be sure I get it right."

Good idea.

"Nay, 'tis not that. We've got company on the way. Where's the Lady?"

"Elisena? Haven't seen her all morning." Tristan shut the book on a page of sun-spells, none of which had worked when he'd tried them earlier, and sighed. "I hope she's somewhere dry. What sort of company?"

"Unwelcome." Polassar turned to leave the room just as Elisena entered. There were cobwebs on her skirts and a smudge of something dark just above the tip of her nose. She was grinning broadly despite that, but her face stilled when she saw Polassar.

"Galan?" she asked solemnly. Polassar's helm dipped in assent. "What rotten timing. I have something to show you, Tristan, but it can wait—had better, now. How near is Galan?"

"He'll be hammering at the gate in five minutes, unless his horse mires down first." Polassar gave Tristan a glance. "Don't suppose you could manage—"

Tristan spread his hands helplessly.

"I'm afraid we can't count on mere mud to stop him," Elisena said. "Is he alone?"

"One rider with him."

"That will be Reynaud." Elisena turned, extending a hand to Tristan. "You may conduct Galan to the Great Hall, Polassar. And send Allaire to me first, if you will."

"We'll receive him now? Like this?" Tristan was almost trotting to keep up with Elisena as they passed along the rose marble cloister. He noticed mushrooms underfoot.

"There's no time to receive him any other way. But trust me."

"I do, but—" he broke off as they made a dash through the rain and reached the Great Hall. A gutterspout carved in the likeness of a chanticleer crowed cold water all over Tristan. He swore, slipped, and fetched up painfully hard against a door whose wood was too damp-swollen to permit it to open with the easy push he'd tried to give it.

"This spell has definitely gotten out of hand," Tristan said unnecessarily, shoving at the door with his shoulder. The sound of the rain changed from a splashing to a drumming as they passed under a roof.

Thomas was waiting for them inside—dry.

Tristan stared at the cat. *"How did you—"*

There are ways of getting about this place, if you're small and observant. And I am not a wizard's cat for nothing.

Elisena had moved past them and now stood in the exact center of the drafty hall, gazing upward. Behind her was Crogen's throne, squatting among shadows on its low dais. Once, Elisena had said, the royal seat had been covered with beaten gold and silken cushions, but it had long since been stripped and looted back to the bare rock it was originally carved from—rock and cobwebs.

A fit symbol for his kingship, Tristan thought. It looked as if the roof might be leaking directly over it, which seemed fitting as well.

"It might be better to receive Galan somewhere else," Tristan suggested, watching the falling drops of water splash against the floor. "This will hardly create an impression of strength."

Fresh torches had been placed in the wall brackets, at least. Elisena gestured them alight, her magic defying the rain. More of the room sprang into view.

Eighty feet above their heads, cobwebbed oak rafters crossed. Tatters that might once have been banners hung from them. Tristan mentally questioned the motives of builders of a room so dwarfing to ordinary mortals—also a room so impossible to warm. The air was still so wet that there were haloes about the witched torch flames.

"Where else?" Elisena asked. "The kitchens? No, this will be all right. I can do a great deal with it." She bent her head over her rings, briefly. "What this room must have been, once—"

It echoed now, a vast inner space that once had rung with the deeds and laws of kings, with music and the clash of arms, the hiss of torch flames, and the laughter of fair women. Now empty, dark, barren, and maybe haunted. Tristan looked about, puzzled at the images springing into his mind.

"The world is made of light and shadow," Elisena said. Her words might have been conversation as much as a spell, her voice remained so ordinary. "Every thing, every creature, every magic. The arrangement is all."

She lifted her left hand, gestured elaborately. Five of her rings flashed upon her fingers, dazzling Tristan's eyes; when the glare had faded he could yet make out an afterglow, the ghostly outlines of a tapestry upon the wall behind the throne. He blinked rapidly. There was no tapestry there, yet still he saw it.

"We can alter the arrangement." Elisena's fingers continued

to weave, and shadows shaped themselves or drew apart into complex new patterns about the wisps of light she flung to them. Tristan thought he made out tall many-branched candlesticks, high as trees almost, and as his eye traveled up them he was further drawn to the nebulous banners that now hung from the ceiling. He saw the Falcon of Westif, recognized the Silver Hart of Amrein. There were other sigils renowned in legend but so long unseen in the world Tristan knew that he could identify them only from his studies. A *glamour*, Tristan realized of a sudden, recognizing that most spectacular and difficult of all the major categories of spellcraft. Clothing an empty room in its memories was one thing; making those memories live for any eyes that entered the room was more difficult than the actual physical transformation of lead into gold. There was less in the way of raw materials to work from, and the spell required a finer hand.

He glanced down and saw that the floor had changed as well. Its stones now ran with light and seemed less broken, less pitted. Tristan's eye traveled along them, across the room. In a far doorway stood Allaire, the finest ornament any king's castle might boast and far finer than Crogen deserved. Carvings upon the doorposts framed her, but she enhanced them rather than the other way round.

Allaire had found, somewhere—maybe at Lassair—a gown of pale velvet the color of sea foam. Its pile had been carefully plucked away in a faint design of flowers about the neck and at the ends of the long hanging sleeves. The style was antique— Tristan supposed it would have to be, there having been no lady at Lassair since Polassar's own mother had died—but Allaire could hardly have noticed or minded if her gown was no longer the latest fashion. No more did Tristan. He smiled as she walked toward him, appreciating the delicate play of the gown's soft blue-green against the pale shades of her skin and hair. Silver would have set the colors off further, but Allaire wore no rings now, and no jewels of any kind save one white pearl that hung in the hollow of her throat, its chain tether as fine as spider silk.

Tristan supposed he was as little in Allaire's thrall as any living man could hope to be, but still she seemed to stop the blood in his veins and the breath in his lungs in sheer awe of her. She glowed like a shadow revealed by the absence of shadows. Doubtless her presence helped greatly in Elisena's casting of the glamour, which might have been why Elisena had sent for her. Allaire seemed multiplied into all those ladies Elisena must once have had waiting attendance on her, or would have had at the court in Crogen—a useful bit of propaganda, a mark of status.

Allaire was beauteous beyond words—but Elisena's smudged nose was dearer to him. Tristan turned back to her.

Elisena's flickering gestures still made a clear sight of her difficult to catch. Allaire stood quietly, not questioning, as words pattered around her. Tristan glanced from one woman to the other, then, startled, looked down at himself.

Some of the wayward glow was attaching itself to his clothes, turning the shadows into darkest velvet, the few highlights into lustrous silver embroideries so that he seemed to be garbed in robes wondrous fine yet strangely indistinct. He was royally dressed, Tristan thought, as his mouth opened soundlessly. She'd even altered his shoes, adding ridiculously long points to the toes. He could still feel his old boots underneath and clung to that familiar comfort amid the dizzying splendors. He recognized the purpose of the spell belatedly.

"I think we are ready to receive Galan now," Elisena said.

Galan had not exactly put on weight during his convalescence—but the proud planes of his face had lost a good deal of their former definition. A casual observer might have been tricked into believing that Galan had lost, along with his left eye, a measure of the force of will that drove him, but it was not so. Radak's master was its master still and master of himself as well. His right eye turned on Tristan as he entered the hall, and the gentling effects of illness and pain were burned away from his face, replaced by hatred.

"Well, my lord, why are we so honored this day?" Elisena's stance was quiet, her manner superbly assured. Boldness won her the first round, but Galan was not slow to counter the move.

"Curiosity, lady." He shook water from his fine cloak and looked about at the room's shadows, either wary of traps or simply suspecting that he was being deceived. A dark wolfhound stood at his heel, dripping and shivering. Thomas hissed at it. "Curiosity and many tales."

Reynaud had entered a half pace behind the dog, his manner impassive, unimpressed. A black cloak fell to his feet in such supremely elegant folds that Tristan felt as if his own brown wool garment was only an old blanket, and he was sure Reynaud could see the sham beneath Elisena's spell. Reynaud was also, unlike Galan and the wolfhound, absolutely dry. Not a drop of water, not a spatter of mud, not the slightest dampness or stain spoiled his cloak. Considering the weather outside and Galan's sodden state, it was certainly an impressive display of magic.

Equally certainly, Galan could not have noticed Reynaud's condition yet, for he'd hardly be pleased that his master of magic had not included him in the spell. Tristan wondered what that said about the relationship between the two. Reynaud nodded to him casually, even as Tristan thought that, and took up his place beside and slightly behind his master, well clear of the growing puddle forming about Galan's boots.

"I have heard much about your doings here, lady, and Polassar's, and even"—Galan flicked another venomous glance in Tristan's direction—"his."

Tristan swallowed hard and hoped no one else would see his discomfiture in the chancy light. Elisena at least had *memories* of protocol to draw upon for guidance, and Allaire might naturally carry herself like a queen, but he had nothing except a shaky suspicion that he would better serve his own cause by disappearing than by standing here now. Tristan didn't know if he ought to speak or what he'd say if he did.

Galan's eye now fell upon Elisena's hands. She was letting her rings glow softly, Tristan noticed, probably to draw Galan's attention more to them and less to the illusions of the hall, as well as to offer the man tacit proof of their right to hold Crogen.

"I see that some of the things spoken are true," Galan said. "How strange that there should have been a connection between you, daughter, and this lady. How little we suspected it when she first came to us, a homeless wanderer." He favored Allaire with a look and a chill smile. She looked daggers back at him, then spoiled the effect by taking a half step closer to Polassar. "Well, these high matters are beyond my understanding, doubtless. I have long been ill."

There was no need for Galan to gesture at the patch over his eye. Already it struck at Tristan like an accusation. Memories seared him; he recalled the escape from Radak and Galan's plottings, a desperate fight, strange treacheries, and Thomas' lucky blow in his defense, which had cost Galan the eye. Tristan wondered at the strong taste of guilt on his soul. Galan would have had him *dead*, not merely maimed. Why should he be so quick to accept blame for the whole episode?

"I have heard, lady, what amounts to a declaration of war." Galan dropped a hand to his sword hilt. His hound grew more attentive.

"Then you have heard wrongly. We wish only to live at peace with all. Even those who camp armies at our gates." Elisena's voice rang on the air like little drops of silver striking a stone floor.

"Indeed? I had heard, for instance, that Polassar of Lassair was no longer involved in the safe and harmless work of undertaking ancient quests, but had taken a young wife, given the appearance of abdicating his supposed right to our throne, and instead backed a puppet king."

Polassar made a strangling sound, as soon as he had worked his way through enough of the rhetoric to appreciate the insult fully. He groped blindly for the hilt of his longsword, and Allaire clung to his arm in restraint. She was barely able to force him to subside.

Galan nodded.

"Your clumsy moves will put an end to petty rivalries and raidings, Polassar—by fanning the situation into open war! You've disturbed the balance of power here—"

"Would that be the balance you've been engineering, with yourself at its fulcrum?" Elisena inquired sweetly. She held her chin up, her head like a fragile flower on her white neck. That was a danger sign, as obvious as a man's squaring of his shoulders or the loosening of a blade in its scabbard. Tristan wondered if Galan had ever been observant enough to know that. He nearly smiled his own appreciation of it, then stilled his face hastily back to sober propriety.

Galan colored first; he drew his lips back in what might have passed for a smile. "You are too shrewd, lady. Very well then, let us be open and discuss this situation sensibly. You see, I have come here unarmed and unescorted as a token of faith; you need not fear me."

"Accompanied by your master of magic, who is proof against any threat to your person? Greetings, Reynaud, if belatedly."

Reynaud inclined his head.

"May we parley then, lady?" Galan asked sharply.

"Of course, my lord." Elisena inclined her own head. "I would fain sit and discuss high matters with you, but the only seat in this room is the throne, yonder, and there is only one among us with right to sit there."

"I will grant you, lady, you have moved swiftly and cleverly, with master strokes I would not have expected of you." Galan poked a gloved finger at her. "But I think you will find gathering other lords to support you difficult. This charade of lost heirs to the throne is hard to swallow, too complex for belief. Why not simply throw in with Polassar's claim to the kingship, if you've the desire to play at politics?"

Galan's manner was vastly insulting, at once familiar and contemptuous. Tristan's palm itched, and he was hard put to remember that he carried no knife and that all which now remained of his sword was wrapped around Elisena's finger, where it still made a formidable weapon. The wolfhound leered at him, its red tongue lolling. Its eyes were a disconcerting light blue, as if it were some witch-made beast.

Elisena's tone remained unruffled.

"Tristan is king by birth and right, Galan. You can neither alter that nor deny it."

"So I must perforce accept it? Lady, if you had searched the length and breadth of Calandra, you could scarcely have arrived at a more unsuitable candidate for your schemes."

"Perhaps so." Elisena's rings flickered. "But there was no question of searching the land for an heir to the throne. Tristan is king by right, and that fact can no more be hidden than the rainfall can." As if in response, falling drops drummed on the roof over their heads.

"*Right?* You speak to me of *right*? Lady, I have as much right to this throne as any has! A royal line as old as ours is apt to be confused and disputed, and this has caused us ages of war and grief. But I never yet heard that there was peasant stock mingled with the blood of our kings!"

Polassar made another strange sound, and Allaire returned her hand to his arm in alarm. The wolfhound snarled.

"There is proof of his right," Elisena said calmly.

Tristan's right hand clenched involuntarily, as if to hide what he considered an incriminating mark. There was no sign just then of the glowing crown upon his palm, but he knew Elisena could reveal it at will. Tristan felt he could scarcely bear to see it again. King or no, however he might have thought he'd accepted his fate, the sight could still unnerve him.

Galan seemed informed of the mark as well. His half-gaze flickered to Tristan's fisted hand.

"Any proof you offer with those rings or any other magic is suspect," he said coldly. "And I think you will find that I am not the only lord who will doubt it."

It was impasse, as both players sought and failed to find a checkmating move, an unanswerable argument or an unarguable answer. The wolfhound's panting became the only sound in the room.

Reynaud spoke from the shadows.

"In any case, such discussions are meaningless." He looked directly at Tristan. "If you intend to rule this land, then you must rule it from Crogen in the *fullest* sense, having been duly crowned with *all* the proper ceremonies. And I submit that you cannot do that, or you would be so crowned already, and there would be no army outside your gates nor any need for the one you are trying to assemble."

Elisena seemed to be viewing Reynaud with a great deal more alarm than she had honored his master with.

"I believe you will find that you lack one ingredient of those needed for the crowning ritual," Reynaud went on. "And if you intend to rule from Crogen, then you had best be certain that you have the royal sword. All the 'right' in the world will avail you naught without that blade."

He turned to Galan, black robes swirling dramatically. The scarlet-and-gold workings on the clothes beneath glowed softly in counterpoint to his words.

"No need to waste more time here, my lord, and risk a chill. It is not for nothing that Crogen was abandoned and let fall to ruins. Usurpers *cannot* rule from it."

The Proof

"WIZARD? DID THAT viper speak true?" Polassar queried.

Tristan could only shake his head absently as he watched Elisena gazing speculatively at the throne. Reynaud's words, true or not, seemed to have tangled in the hall's shadows so that they hung there before Tristan's puzzled eyes. His clothes were his own again, at least. So much of the glamour had gone already.

Galan would be back, of course. He'd felt out the situation in his most masterly fashion, and was setting up his next move now, doubtless. The game he played would be complex; only the most subtle reasoning could account for his attempt at parley when he'd the numbers at hand simply to sweep them out of Crogen altogether. Surely his spies would have told him so. Galan's enmity was obvious, and there was no hope of reconciliation.

Of course Galan might simply be afraid of Elisena. Her rings were an unknown quantity even to Reynaud, who seemed privy to so much else. . . .

Tristan crossed to stand by her side. Elisena looked up from her scrutiny and wanly smiled.

"I had a surprise for you, but it certainly wasn't this."

"Then what he said *is* true? About a royal sword? It sounded so handy, I was hoping he'd made it up to suit the moment."

Elisena's face shadowed once more. "Reynaud was more right than he may have known, and too right to be guessing. I should like to know how he knows as much as he does." Her fingers reached out to brush the arms of the throne. Swirls of silver about her fingers caught and held the light.

"I knew the crowning would involve certain spells. This is carved from the living rock Crogen is built upon, and a great deal of the power of the kingship comes from it." Her fingers left snail-trail traces of silver light behind them, briefly. "The power that will mean the difference between ruling here or merely struggling to beat off rival claimants all your life. Magics about it have grown layer by layer, age by age—not the work of any one High Mage, but of all of them. The spells are deliberately and exceedingly complex." She frowned at the throne again.

"Is it written anywhere?" Tristan asked, thinking of a tremendously powerful grimoire, perhaps hidden somewhere inside Crogen. He couldn't recall having seen a book anywhere in the castle, but he hadn't truly expected to. They were lucky to have even a roof over their heads after so many years of Crogen's abandonment—and a wizard would never abandon his books.

"No." Elisena's crystals rang as she shook her head. "The spells have grown up around the throne slowly, as different mages each added their personal touches to the ritual, and I doubt that it was ever *intended* to be set down. The High Mage would have known the ritual, when the time of a coronation came. He was probably the only person who did know the full spell—who could be trusted to. Still, a lot can be read yet from this tangle of magic, and I've been worrying at it for the past week. Parts of the last knot wouldn't come undone—the parts touching the sword, I'm led to suspect. That's why I know Reynaud spoke true, even if he only meant to frighten us. And I don't like it."

Her eyes had emptied, Tristan noted with alarm, as if she was no longer quite speaking to him. Since Tristan didn't feel he was quite understanding her, he supposed he and Elisena were even.

They were also alone. Polassar had thought it wise to be sure Galan had truly quit Crogen and decided to safeguard the departure with his own eyes. Allaire had gone with him to shield him against mischiefs born of his own rashness. The hall was still, save for the drip of water. The glamour continued to fade, its edges curling in.

"One of the last touches added to the spell was the sword—the king's own blade, I would think. No mere ceremonial weapon would suffice. A stronger crowning was needed in a troubled time, and that would have been when Nímir was first starting to make his power felt. The High Mage keyed the spells to the sword, and now no crowning can take place without it. It would appear that the fabric of the great spell can be added to at will, but not subtracted from."

"Are you sure?" Tristan whispered, hardly knowing his own voice.

A spell like that could get awfully bothersome after a few kings, Thomas pointed out. *A crowning could take a week, by the time everyone got their bits in.*

"I have been studying these spells for a fortnight and wondering about the sword's role for half that time, though I wasn't sure it was a sword. I thought it might be another ring." Elisena smiled, unexpectedly. "Did you think I was only inspecting the kitchens all day long? I have been searching out the spells—and more. There was something I knew had to be here and better hidden than anything else in the realm except these rings and you—the Regalia."

Tristan looked at her questioningly.

"You see, I knew the High Mage would have hidden all those things that had any real value before the start of what he must have seen as the last great battle," Elisena said. "He'd have left plenty here to be looted, so that none would think to look for the rest; thus he saved those things that really mattered to him. And what better seal for him to have set on these treasures than the rings which he himself had made?" She lifted a hand, and rings flashed.

"I was coming to tell you about it when Polassar announced Galan. I've found the Regalia, everything we need for the crowning—except there is no sword there. Anywhere."

She led him behind the throne and paused in a cobwebby space before the wall. Tristan thought she might have been counting off paces. Certainly Elisena measured handspans carefully before settling on a certain bit of wall for closer attention.

"A secret passage?" Tristan asked with interest. Dust tickled his nose. Lichens tapestried the wall.

"There's hardly a wall in Crogen that doesn't have at least one of those," Elisena said blandly. "This is something more."

How delightful. Thomas squeezed between Tristan's boots, worming his way toward a better view.

Elisena raised a hand and slowly, with conjuring gestures, folded the fingers of it until one ring alone was clearly visible. Tristan supposed at first that it was the Kingstone, seeing a flash of blue from the ring's center, but then he noticed that the ring was on the wrong hand. This stone also was blue, but cut to a longer shape and bound by a twist of silver like a rope around its edge. Elisena pressed the stone against the searched-out spot upon the dark wall, and spoke several soft words. She touched her tenth ring to the spot when the first ring had been withdrawn. There was a creaking sound, very faint.

Tristan leaned closer, the better to observe. Thomas stepped prudently back.

Elisena flipped her hand over, put her palm to the wall, and pushed. A six-foot section of stonework higher than Tristan's head slid obediently back with a lot less grinding and scraping than seemed proper.

Something inside the opening glittered. Tristan was briefly, unpleasantly reminded of the treasure heaps they'd seen in Darkenkeep. Glitterings in the dark spoke of pain to him now.

"Have you got your crystal handy?"

Tristan nodded, and Elisena must have felt the movement of his head beside her own. He produced the crystal, fumbling in his haste, snatched it safely out of midair, and lighted it with a word and a nimble twist of his fingers. For once, the spell worked on the first try.

The dark rolled back before the little light, and they were looking into a small recess. Standing in its middle, if he *could* have stood there—it was packed too full of objects for him to do more than speculate—Tristan could have touched all five walls without stretching unduly.

"Go on," Elisena said. "None has more right to enter here than you. It's your castle."

There was just room for them both, close to the right side wall. Several rolled carpets took up a lot of the scanty floor space, and in each back corner stood a great candlestick shaped like a serpent twining around a fruit tree. Some half-burned candles remained in the sockets. Elisena lighted them with a touch of one of her rings.

"When last these burned, the king was on his throne receiving word of my capture by Nímir." She stared into the white flames as a cat might have done, as if seeing that day. Then she blinked her silver eyes, shedding the troubles and memories as casually as a duck sheds water, and fell to explaining the symbolism of the candletrees to Tristan.

His eyes adjusting to the candlelight and his perception sharpening, he saw that upon one a snake climbed a tree full of fruit and flowers while upon the other the serpent struggled at a bare tree's base, sloughing off its old skin, awaiting renewal. The sense of the symbolism needed little explanation, once the artistic abstractions were understood and the curves and texture given meaning. The reference to a new king succeeding the old was obvious.

Tristan nudged a rolled-up rug with a boot toe.

"What's this?"

"The carpet kings walk to their crowning on. Royal feet don't touch the common ground on such an important day."

Thomas sniffed derisively.

Elisena unrolled a few feet of the carpet and let Tristan see, worked in silk upon an unfaded scarlet, the strange animals, flowers, mountains, and rivers.

"All Calandra's here, in miniature." The pile was knotted and clipped, not embroidered as he'd at first thought. The individual threads were fantastically thin, impossibly many. Elisena stroked it appreciatively.

"I'm supposed to walk on *that*?" Tristan was horrified. The mere idea of doing such a thing struck him as rankest sacrilege.

"Well, it's only for one day." She managed a bright smile. "I doubt you'll wear a path on it."

"My boots will be honored," he said, still wondering.

"You won't be wearing them." Half a step took her to a wooden chest, carved with sun-guarding griffins. "There are these. More suitable, I think you'll agree."

Elisena held up scarlet slippers, their soles worked with runic patterns in tiny seed pearls. Then she proceeded to lift an astounding array of garments from the seemingly bottomless chest: undergarments of finest linens, shot with gold threads, a white robe stitched with a starburst, doeskin gloves, and finally a great robe of cloth-of-gold which could not even be lifted entirely free of the chest. Every mage in the kingdom must have vied to fashion the coronation accoutrements. Or perchance the articles had been accumulated bit by bit, like the coronation-spells.

There were magic signs on every possible surface, inside and out, in lines, circles, arcs, and pentagrams. Tristan recognized some symbols and several of the incantations. He could guess at the power of those he could not read.

"The proper crowning of a king is no light thing here," Elisena said unnecessarily. "The king himself is but one ingredient in a vaster spell."

There was a circlet of interlaced silver, set with a great emerald of which wondrous tales were told, and a scepter of silver also, deceptively plain until Elisena turned it in the light and Tristan saw that it was entirely covered with one lengthy, runic power-cantrip.

Every article in the room was shot through with magic to its very core. The Maristan kings had not wielded magic themselves—until now—but their mages had wrapped them closely round with it. Tristan wondered if he might not be better suited to this kingship than he'd suspected. It would be nice to think so.

He turned the circlet over in his hands, wondering about that and about the ceremony Elisena had ferreted out. What part—and how great a part—did the missing sword play in it? If it was as vital as Reynaud had said—it was properly Elisena's worry, not his, but still—

"I think these may interest you more."

Tristan let the thought go, and looked up at her. Elisena was opening another chest smaller and less ornate than the one which had held the clothing. It was filled with closely packed scrolls, and there were a dozen others like it along the back wall. Tristan's eyes widened.

"The records of the kingdom, and beyond to when our people first came here from over the seas. Valuable, once we've the time to read them slowly enough not to go blind."

Tristan was already bent over one scroll, having squirmed closer through the precious clutter. He unrolled the parchment slowly, fascinated as the past rose around him like a rich perfume, the writing before him still black and clear as upon the day it was penned. He chose one of the histories next, by chance, and stayed with it longer, marveling at illuminations, caressing the fine leather of its cover. There were bound books tucked among the scrolls as well, their rich bindings still supple. He'd nearly forgotten the peculiarly wonderful odor of old books well kept.

"Take that one with you, if you like."

Tristan glanced up and was surprised to find the candles all guttering and his eyes smarting with strain. His back ached, as did his cramped legs. He smiled apologetically at Elisena and discovered that his face felt unaccustomed to the movement.

"How long—"

"An hour and a bit. I'd not the heart to disturb such pleasure—not when I remembered how long you'd been away from Blais' books," she said indulgently. "And I was further reviewing the spells. A different angle can be useful."

Tristan looked about dazedly, his fingers curled unnoticed within the partly closed scroll, marking his place.

"You're still sure there's no sword here?" The room looked fuller than he had remembered it, as if Elisena's spell-questing had brought other, hidden things back into the range of his sight. That might be only the candles' flickering, he supposed, as they gave up their last light.

Elisena nodded solemnly. "I hadn't expected it to be, truly. It was the king's own sword, and it belonged with him, as did the crown—the ceremonial one, that is, the one for show, not the circlet. You'll note there's no crown here either, though that doesn't matter to us—the power resided in the circlet, and that's what would have been used during a crowning. There's more magic woven into it than there could have been in the crown, which was intended solely to impress the impressionable. There's little of that sort here."

Her gaze swept the room. "These things, though—they're all the trappings which wouldn't have been in daily use and which could have been safely locked away without anyone's missing them—anyone such as the king, who might have wondered at his High Mage hiding treasures just before a battle that there should have been no question of his winning." She gave the objects under discussion still another look.

"I am satisfied that the sword is not here, but I'm still not sure how critical that is to the spell. I wish I could be, but it's just too difficult to judge. Come out here now; I'll show you."

She waved a hand to dismiss the candles, which snuffed

themselves one by one as Tristan got stiffly to his feet. Elisena shut the panel on the darkness, and Tristan could almost feel the High Mage's still puissant enchantments closing about the door again.

Elisena led the way to the throne again and lighted its surface brightly with her rings. Tristan followed awkwardly, his knees still giving him trouble.

"You can see that the throne's been here longer than Crogen itself. Those carvings are more weathered than you'd expect indoors. Yet this whole place is also better preserved than you'd expect, after being abandoned so many lifetimes. Magic preserves and magic lingers."

"Why was it abandoned? What was Reynaud hinting at?" Tristan asked, thinking dire things.

"I'm not sure. Things got so complicated after the last king died—shifts of power, usurpations, wars, and sieges, which you can read about the same way I did. I wouldn't be very surprised to learn that this place was simply unlivable, with the land around it ruined in all the fighting."

"Reynaud made it sound like something more than that," Tristan insisted, "by what he left unsaid as much as anything he did say."

Thomas sniffed. *That was to make you curious—as if you needed it.*

Elisena stepped onto the dais and beckoned Tristan to join her.

"He might have meant this." She stared down at the throne.

"There's power; I can feel it too," Tristan said. The air all but hummed, though he saw nothing untoward and heard nothing.

"Yes. So you can understand why a real kingship might be impossible without such power, no matter how many of the lords you manage to unite or how much support you get from them. This is something more than that, something outside civil strife. The circlet as opposed to the crown, you might say. Here a crowning means more than just a solution to political problems. And it concerns the fight against Nímir."

Tristan felt an irrational touch of chill. "But I thought the rings—" That matter was done with, surely. Once Elisena's last ring had been placed upon her finger, Nímir's defeat had been assured. Tristan said as much tentatively.

"The rings were meant to be linked to the power of Crogen,

as my marriage was meant to link Calandra and Esdragon. The sword alone was not enough of a weapon, nor were the rings. They were made to be joined. I don't know if we can ignore that." Elisena leaned over the throne, peering at the right arm of it. "See. Here."

Tristan looked. The silver caught his eye first, as it caught the torchlight. A worn circle of runescript was inlaid into the stone. It bounded a circular hole in the stone itself, a hole about the diameter of a big walnut.

"What's that?"

"As nearly as I can learn, that hole is the spot into which the hilt of the royal sword was plunged when first the spell was spun. A bit of the living heart of Crogen, of Calandra itself, attached itself to the sword. Now, during the crowning, the hilt of the sword must rest once again in the hole." She pantomimed Tristan holding a sword upright before him.

"And then what happens?" Tristan asked warily.

"I don't know. It would appear to have been a very private experience, probably having something to do with imprinting the king to the throne and vice versa, with the sword as the link between them." Elisena gazed at the clear crystal that hung from her thumb, but apparently it told her nothing, for she shook her head impatiently.

"What I don't know is just how vital that link is. The rings and the throne are kindred powers, and I have found already that the rings can channel the power of the throne to some extent. It's possible that you will be able to do the same, even without the sword, if you know what to expect and take it slowly. It could be dangerous, even so."

"I imagine it would be." Tristan looked at the throne once more and at the circle of runes burning in the rings' light like white fire. He couldn't see anything inside the hole—he wasn't even certain of the shadows. Power was there, definitely.

"The High Mage spared no compassion for usurpers. I think it likely that if someone attempted a crowning not knowing about . . . that, the power might well flow through *him*, rather than being safely channeled. Such a crowning would not only be useless, it would likely be fatal. That's probably what Reynaud was referring to."

Tristan continued to stare at the circle, which seemed to have taken on a different form even as he watched it. It was

no rune circle now, but a coiled dragon, quiet yet not sleeping,
its long claws winking, its thin wings partly furled along its
back. Powerful. And venomed. He blinked, and the circle
became an inscription once again.

"*We* know what to expect," Elisena said, most softly. "It
should be possible to test the spell safely. You're the rightful
king. You bear the mark of that right. That may make a difference."

Tristan could hear his own blood sighing softly as it passed
through his ears.

"I want you to try," Elisena went on, as he'd known she
was going to.

A risk, she says, a gamble.
"One we have to take, Thomas."
The cat switched his tail. *We do?*

Tristan shivered. Elisena had gone to fetch some herbs which
she said were necessary to the spell, leaving him alone in the
throne hall with Thomas. The rune circle was still glowing,
though the rings that had lighted it had gone with Elisena. It
was the only light in the room. Tristan found that disquieting.

"We don't have the sword, Thomas," he said more reasonably than he felt, wondering if he might be over compensating
for his rapidly failing nerve. "It's not here, and there's no time
to try to find it. Even supposing Galan is nervous about at-
tacking us before he knows what the rings can do, he won't
hold his hand forever. And if Elisena's right about Nímir . . ."

*I suppose it never occurs to you that there's the tiniest
chance of her being wrong, just once, someday?*

Tristan was forced to admit that it had not. Both Elisena's
confidence and her competence overmatched his own, which
inspired trust. And surely Elisena would never have suggested
this test if there weren't a strong possibility of its success. If
it *were* possible to tap into the power of Crogen without the
sword, they'd all be better off if he tried. That was his sole
reason for volunteering to do so; but all the same, Thomas had
a valid point.

*Just feel it, she says. Touch it, get to know it—without
waking it, of course. As if it were a sleeping kitten or something
equally harmless! Well, you can get to know fire, but it will
still burn you.*

"I saw Blais handle fire once, Thomas, with nary a blister to show for it, either." Tristan smiled. Thomas hissed, irritated beyond speech.

"It sounds possible, Thomas."

It sounds insane. Have you finally taken leave of your senses totally?

Tristan stopped listening to him. He had no choice. Fear was already starting to blacken the edges of his mind, like some deadly frost. And he felt, somehow, that this test would be useless if he weren't able to summon up some deep, unquestioning trust in the throne, in the power behind it, and in his right to be there, to attempt this thing. Most important of all was a blind trust in himself.

His breathing slowed and deepened. Thomas grumbled on unheard. Tristan eventually let his senses expand a little again and was thus not taken by surprise when Elisena bound a twist of hellebore flowers about his waist as a protection against harm. Her hands left him and rested lightly upon the throne.

"I can sense it," she said. "The power seems . . . quiescent. But that's no guarantee."

Tristan agreed. "I'll be careful." He felt almost drowsy and lifted himself back to full awareness sternly.

He thought obediently about the throne and the fabric of the magic of Crogen. It was vital that he understand whatever was about to happen and learn as much as he could from it. He stretched his hand toward the socket. Elisena began intoning a chant. Her hands wove silver in the air about him.

Gently. Lightly. It was absurd for him to be so nervous, almost flinching away, as if he expected a physical contact. Probably nothing would happen. The power might not even wake without the sword. Maybe it was set up that way. He had nothing to fear. Magic could be deadly dangerous, but he'd been raised on it, after all. This was nothing so new.

The socket looked like a hole burned through the day and into the night. Tristan thought he could see stars in it, like those he saw in Valadan's eyes. It might be nice to touch one, and they seemed to be within reach. What might a star feel alike? Like a candleflame, only cold? Or like ice melting on his fingers, so cold that his body was deceived into registering heat? He welcomed the curiosity—it made this insanity easier to continue and canceled fear. Tristan reached his fingers into the velvety dark, probing impossibly deeply, seeking a star. He found one.

It felt at first akin to the crackling jolts he'd sometimes gotten from touching metal in cold dry weather or a little like the unhappy effect of magic on cold iron, only vastly worse than either. The shock lasted just for the length of time it took for him to be hurled backward off of the dais, to hit the floor and loose consciousness of the pain.

His senses seeped back gradually, so that he was struggling to sit up long before he was really aware that he was doing so. It was several moments after that before his muscles began to respond reliably. His legs trembled whenever he tried to move them, and the room swam, waves of light and dark alternating. *Everything is an arrangement of light and shadow*, Tristan repeated to himself inanely.

His ears rang. It took him a while to realize that part of the noise was Elisena speaking to him.

Her face was the color of new milk, her eyes huge.

"Are you all right?"

Tristan wiped the back of one hand across his nose. "I've felt better." His fingers were bloody. Thomas mewed at him, too concerned for I-told-you-sos.

Tristan couldn't stand for a distressingly long while; when he finally managed, he promptly overbalanced and would have fallen but for Elisena's throwing an arm around him. He was bruised from tumbling onto the stone floor, but he supposed that he was lucky. If he'd been seated on the throne instead of standing before it, he would have been trapped in it instead of falling back, and would certainly have died. Tristan tried to say as much, but he couldn't get intelligible words out. Elisena fumbled distractedly with a pouch of herbs, and her hands fluttered passes in front of his face, doing little more than increasing his dizziness.

There were tears on her own face, unheeded. Her misery made Tristan quite forget his own and any anger he might have expected to feel over her having coerced him to test Reynaud's theory and her ideas with his life. He wobbled to the edge of the dais and sat down, trying to concentrate on controlling his shivering.

He thought he had succeeded, but the shaking didn't stop.

It was only then Tristan realized that the trembling wasn't wholly his own. Elisena clutched his hands tightly.

"Tristan, I'm sorry." Her teeth closed on her bottom lip, released it again. "I truly never expected such a severe reaction. If Reynaud hadn't warned us—"

"I'm not sure he meant to." Tristan steadied his voice with an effort. "At least now we know why Crogen was abandoned."

The Spelled Candle

TRISTAN WOKE AT evening—or rather, he finally let himself be wakened then. Thomas' energetic use of him as a back scratcher had become difficult to ignore. Also there was something tickling his nose, which elaborate eye-crossings revealed as a small feather.

For a canary, Minstrel certainly could moult an incredible amount of plumage when the season for his doing so came. Tristan sighed, swiped the feather away, and heard Minstrel cheep apologetically. Thomas pounced on his moving fingers with delight.

Tristan sat up, pulling the cat onto his lap. He felt fairly well now, better than he had expected to. Elisena had put him to bed with heaps of blankets, numerous draughts of herbs, and a great deal of concern, which would have been most gratifying if he'd been in shape to appreciate it.

Well, you can't say I didn't warn you.

Tristan smoothed the fur on Thomas' back.

"Any suggestions on what we do now, Thomas?"

Yes. Get something to eat. You slept all night and all day, and I've been guarding you with commendable dedication, at great inconvenience to myself. He reached back and licked a few stray hairs into place. *Unless you'd rather watch me eat that mouse that thinks it's hidden under the bed?*

"Thank you, no. Now that you mention it, I'm famished myself."

Tristan considered staying warmly tucked in his bed while he tried to magick some food up from the kitchens—and remembered that his last such attempt had been far from successful, though memorable. When a mug of ale arrived out of thin air without the mug, the event could be either inconvenient or messy, depending upon the particular circumstances. That time, it had been both. It would be better to take himself to the food.

Neater, anyway, Thomas agreed.

Crogen by night was a vast improvement over Crogen by day. The torches along the passageways discreetly hid far more than their light revealed. A pair of Polassar's men-at-arms flanked the bottom of the stair. They both saluted and seemed puzzled when Tristan absently failed to respond to it.

He stared about himself instead, in the middle of the cobble-paved courtyard.

"Thomas! It's stopped raining!"

Oh, really? I was wondering why I wasn't getting wet. The cat hoisted his tail and headed for the kitchens.

Those kitchens were in excellent repair now, since Polassar's men liked to eat well, even if Polassar himself paid no especial attention to meals, either on his own behalf or theirs. Tristan had no difficulty slipping inside long enough to grab a loaf of new bread, a chicken leg, and a horn of ale—all unnoticed by the kitchen boys and the few guards lolling around the firepit and tending to a spitted deer by giving it an occasional prodding with a spear butt. He didn't even need to risk magic to avoid being bothered.

Not that he usually was bothered. Half the time, Polassar's men paid him not the least attention, unless he chanced to be in Polassar's company. Simple clothing and an unassuming manner went a long way toward making a man disappear into the background.

That suited Tristan well. It made getting around the castle smoother, less troublesome. And getting lost was less embarrassing. He tucked himself into a dim corner out of sight of the kitchen crew and spread out his looted dinner.

"Chicken all right with you, Thomas?"

It might as well be. As long as I stick with you, I'll never acquire a taste for anything better. And mind those bones.

His own hunger and Thomas' assuaged, Tristan made his way to Elisena's stillroom, rightly supposing that he'd find her there. Looking for her among her herbs was always a safe choice.

He found Polassar as well, his commander's helmed head brushing the bunched herbs which hung drying from the low ceiling. Doubtless those explained his not having removed the bear-helm. He had a couple of his captains with him, apparently reporting on Galan's strength.

"I suspect Galan hasn't so large a force gathered here as he'd like us to think." Elisena fingered a bit of orrisroot absently as she spoke, crumbling it into a silver mortar. "He can't be holding back only from fear of the rings. His numbers may be equal to ours, but he holds the inferior position, being outside Crogen. Such walls as we have are still walls."

"Lady, his ranks swell like the Est in flood. And these few bits of brick will never stop him, if he's determined to breech 'em. I've not the men to hold this heap properly." Polassar was in his proper element, commanding. His face might look as grim as his words warranted, but he was contented enough under it.

"Such fortifications as we have will at least delay him." Elisena set the pestle carefully back into its mortar. "And can he know what support we may have been able to summon? Or how many of the old magical defenses we can call back into service? No, I think he's bluffing, Polassar, though I'd hesitate to call that bluff, since our position's no stronger than his, in truth. He's giving us a few days, I think, to let fear grow in our hearts, second thoughts take root—to let me see things *his* way. That's why he's let us see so much of his army. I think he'll be back to talk again before he joins battle. That's ever his way."

"For a man with his force of arms, he's witless chary of battle." Polassar looked scornful.

Elisena smiled. "That's because battle's a risk. There's always an element of chance, however slender. Galan's no gambler; he only wagers on certainties. Which at least gives us time."

"Time for what, Lady?" Polassar's broad face was puzzled

now. "You have some plan for dealing with this?"

His captains nodded happily, full of confidence in their witch. There were rust spots all over their armor, despite their best efforts to keep the stuff polished. Tristan thought about the rain and felt a twinge of guilt, as well as the reminder of failure.

"We'll let that wait till Tristan joins us," Elisena answered, finally. "He should be in on this—"

Tristan cleared his throat.

Polassar jumped, while Elisena extended a hand to Tristan calmly, as little surprised by him as he ever was by her.

"Come in, you're just in time. Has Thomas been taking care of you?"

"Oh yes." Tristan let himself be guided to a chair, while the captains were dismissed, and motioned impatiently for Polassar to sit as well. He'd crick his neck for sure if he had to sit long, looking up at his tall general. "Yes, he's seen to it that I got him a good meal, so all's well. What's the news here?"

"Galan seems to be staying put." She gestured, yielding the tale to Polassar.

"Aye. My scouts report that horsemen come and go from his camp like fleas on a stray dog, but he's made no move in any direction with his army. His men are still drying their gear," Polassar added with a grin.

Shouldn't have let the rain-spell lapse, Thomas criticized from beneath the table. *Now he can use his bowmen.*

"He's vulnerable out there," Tristan offered hopefully.

"Not to us, Wizard. I haven't the men, not even if I pull in the garrison from Lassair."

"He may have Lassair attacked as a diversion," Elisena said. "We should be prepared for that possibility." She left the question unsaid, but it was plain enough—what would Polassar do if his home were attacked to divide his loyalties? Was he harboring some mad plan which he hoped would save both Lassair and Crogen?

"May he have much joy of it, Lady! 'Tis not much there that I'd regret losing. All I value is here." Polassar waved a hand at the room, setting bunched herbs swinging about his head.

True or not, it had at least been gallantly said. Tristan turned a bottle full of dried feverfew blossoms over in his hands, watching the loose petals sift back and forth against the glass.

"So," he said. "Galan's staying. What are we doing?"

"I think what Galan said about us having tipped the balance of power is true," Elisena said. "And I don't believe he's ready for the type of all-out war that might ensue if he attacked us now, with the lords torn between us, him, and their own personal ends. Some of his plans have been long a-making. Complex, devious, and perhaps at a very delicate stage just now. Perhaps." She took the bottle away from Tristan, to stop him fidgeting. "I think that's why he's here personally, to feel out another solution—one that will make less trouble for him. He may elect to wait us out, or try to starve us out, if he can do that without provoking fighting."

"I'll not make that easy for him," Polassar rumbled.

"Also, there's Galan's health to be considered," Elisena went on. "He nearly died of the wound when he lost that eye. I think it's moving him to a caution beyond what he'd ordinarily consider. He truly does not see as he once did. He's shaken. He'll be wary of further chances."

"Your rings don't tell you anything about his plans?" Tristan asked, wondering how much of her theory might only be wishful thinking.

"No. Reynaud knows how to guard him too well for that. He knew me a long time, and it helps him, even if the rings are strange to him." She gazed at her folded hands and the weight of ensorcelled silver on them.

"So, our options are much the same as Galan's," Elisena continued. "We wait, and gather what support we can, and hope he leaves us enough time for it—hope that we profit more from the waiting than he does."

After a while, they discussed the sword.

It might literally be anywhere. They established that none of them had heard of any legends attached to it. It was simply a blade carried into battle by the last king, and all knowledge of it ceased with that climactic battle. The king had been slain that day and the kingdom plunged into a disorder from which it had never recovered. The sword might have been stolen, destroyed, carried off, lost at the sea's bottom, or captured by Nímir. Tristan shivered at the last suggestion, remembering the heaps of arms among the other treasure he'd seen hoarded in Darkenkeep. If it lay there, the sword was gone for good.

They had, at best estimate, a few days before they must

expect another contact with Galan. A real search for the sword was patently impossible in such a short span of time, if they had any expectation of success.

Still, Tristan insisted, it was equally plain that they were crippled without the sword. Even in the unlikely event that they found some way of outwitting Galan and of uniting the kingdom, there remained the ultimate question of Nímir. If they needed the sword to use in the fight against him, or needed the power of a crowned king, then they needed it, and avoidance now served no purpose.

"And there are all those records you found," Tristan went on rapidly. "There *may* be some information in there, if not about what happened to the sword, maybe at least enough about the sword itself that I could work up a seeking-spell for it. Now I know that it will take time to comb through those records. I know you don't have leisure for it. You'll be busy, and so will Polassar trying to drum up what support you can for us, and shoring up our defenses. But you'll admit that there's very little *I* can do to help you with either of those efforts. In fact, you're likely better off if I *don't*." He waved a hand at her fledgling protests. "So let *me* look for the sword, and you two tend to the rest. It's only fair, and it won't be any worse than searching for Allaire was. I can do it."

Fine high words, Tristan thought sourly, regretting them more heartily with each passing instant. When he'd set out upon his quest for Allaire, all unknowing that it would lead him to Elisena and his own strange destiny, he'd at least known where to begin looking. There had been volumes written on the search alone, mapping the way and eliminating blind alleys extensively. Of the sword, he had not the slightest hint of prophecy to guide him. After four days, he still hadn't.

He did know more about his kingdom than he might ever have wanted to know. He'd read legends, histories, rolls of tax collections, and censuses. He'd found the same incidents described by several separate observers, which was illuminating in some ways but mostly pointless, as the incidents described were hundreds of years out of date. The books seemed to have been dumped into the chests in no particular order, which made a careful search even more vital, if he wasn't to overlook the very thing he sought.

Tristan read about his remotest ancestors, a plague of wyverns, several accounts of ship construction, a description of a state visit made by a duke of Esdragon, several reports of famines and floods, and an inventory of fabrics for the queen's gowns. He finally found a mention of a crowning, which at least had some small bearing on his task. Unfortunately, it had taken place far too long ago and told him nothing. He finished everything in the first chest, and began on the second.

By the time he'd gone through five chests, a week had passed. He couldn't have finished even those few chests if he hadn't begun routinely skipping all of the census reports.

He lost track of and interest in Polassar's and Elisena's projects. Tristan sat all day in the little room where he'd ordered the records put. He read, thought, and finally concluded that he had as much of a grasp of the situation as he was likely to get and enough to begin composing his seeking-spell. He turned to Blais' grimoire then and rested his eyes on its familiar script.

He worked out the formula with great care, checking and triple-checking, scratching out old formulae, and scribbling in new ones. He finally assembled his materials and set to work.

He was half tempted to rub Thomas' fur for luck first. His magic was still ticklishly unreliable, in spite of all he'd been through and learned, and the old habit of behaving as if it were going to fail, of covering for that possibility, was hard to break. Lower expectations meant fewer disappointments, but Tristan knew he couldn't afford to fall into that kind of mood now. He desperately needed all the confidence he could muster.

To be sure, there was much to be nervous over. This was by far the most complex spell he'd ever tried, on his own or otherwise. The incantation alone was an ornate masterpiece of shadings of meaning and shadings of tone and inflection; the fingerplay would have done a great dancer no disgrace. It was an ambitious spell, no mistake. Tristan had learned a great deal more than he realized since his apprenticeship had been so abruptly and violently ended. Blais would have been pleased and perhaps not at all surprised.

Preparation, execution, summation, and all, the spell ran for six hours, and Tristan was near to fainting by the end of it, both from exhaustion and from his breathing of the burned herbs he'd been using in the tightly shuttered room. He sat on the floor amid a pattern of stones now disarrayed, blinking and trying to come back to himself.

"Thomas?" His voice was hoarse with much speaking, and Tristan wished he had the strength to conjure up a bit of wine. "How did it sound to you?"

Fine. The unicorn should come strolling in here anytime.

"Unicorn?" Tristan started to jump to his feet, horrified. If he'd made a mistake in the very base of the spell . . . It was just like him, to get so lost in the details of the spell that he misconstrued the very roots of it. So many little twigs to attend to that he was blind to the trunk of the tree itself. . . .

Sit down, I'm teasing. It was all right. More than all right, it was a neat piece of work.

Tristan leaned his head against a table leg, too weak to heave the nearest object at Thomas, as he was sorely tempted to do. He felt dazed still, breathless, as he awaited the spell's outcome. Minutes ticked by, measured by his unsteady breathing.

And nothing happened.

No sword materialized out of the air. No clue to its whereabouts insinuated itself into Tristan's mind. There was no blinding revelation, no glorious fulfillment of the spell. No sword. Nothing.

Tristan bit back a sob of frustration, and struggled against an overwhelming desire for sleep. He might have known it wouldn't work. . . .

Well, there were still more books to read in search of the sword.

And in his tent, as his cockatrice banner snapped and chattered in the wind, Galan spoke with Reynaud, his master of magic, ending a lengthy discussion and resolving it in his mind.

"Just put him in my hands. I care not how. Only that, and name your price. Whatever it may be, it will be granted you. I so swear."

Tristan translated laboriously, as the flickering of the candleflame caused the black words on the gray page to waver and shift form. It was bad enough that this tongue should be one he was not especially proficient with, without the eyestraining necessity of using these special candles. But without their light the ensorcelled book could not be read at all. In other lights, no matter how sorcerous, its pages were blankest white. And he had to finish his task before this last candle guttered out, because there were no more of them, so far as he knew. He scribed the words down as fast as he could make them out, their meaning to be puzzled over later.

The . . . blade, that must be. *The blade where fire like water runs* . . . poetry, possibly. But "blade"? That might mean something. He had learned to be alert to even such slight references.

Will . . . when moon and king to Cathlein come.

Cathlein? Was that a place? Or someone's name? It had a familiar ring; he'd heard it before, Tristan was sure.

The greenish light of the candle cast ghastly shadows over his face, which looked bad enough without such help. Tristan hadn't eaten in days, unless Elisena had remembered to force food on him, and as for sleep . . . So now his never-handsome face was hollowed out at odd places, made odder still by the light shining upon it, and his nose looked longer and sharper than ever, with less face behind it. His eyes were red-rimmed and itchy, refusing inconveniently to focus on the page in front of him. Tristan sighed and scrubbed at them with his fingers, till he was distracted by a more pressing kink in his neck.

In a short while he'd have another grinding headache, no doubt. It wouldn't make his task any easier, but he was too stubborn to quit. He'd already used some of Blais' more potent brews—as much or more than was safe—trying to keep himself alert and functioning long past his natural limits. Elisena was rightly worried about him—she'd been by some two hours before, taken one look at him, and said sternly that no one expected him to find the sword all by himself, killing himself in the process. Then she'd gone to bed, after extracting a promise that he'd follow shortly. But he was still at work as the night grew old.

Tristan knew himself to be irrational, obsessed. That no longer mattered. He'd work around it, and for now it served to keep him at his search. He was afraid that, if he slept, he'd have forgotten the key to this cipher when he finally woke—if he even did wake before the week was out. And this book certainly *was* promising, if difficult. The best he'd found thus far, with its references to swords.

Enough. What did he have so far? He carefully scribed it out, the quill's scratching counterpointing the crackle of the candlewick as it burned.

> *The blade where fire like water runs*
> *From the well beneath ancient Crogen's throne*

The words leaped easily from the page to his mind. Definitely a spell at work here. The back of Tristan's neck prickled.

> *Risen will be in full moon's light*
> *When moon and king to Cathlein come.*

Tristan started awake, staring at the words he'd set down. The pen lay beside his hand and the ink had dried on its tip. He must have fallen asleep while he wrote, which hardly surprised him, but those words . . . he thought dazedly about automatic writing—or was it automatic translating? Tristan shivered. His left foot was still asleep, more stubborn than the rest of him.

Full moon's light, hmmm. Tristan rubbed his ankle slowly. A fine magical precedent for that one. Darkenkeep itself was best found by moonlight, and the light of the full moon was an important ingredient of many spells.

Cathlein still tugged at his mind. He *knew* this—place. It was a place, he was sure. Something connected with Valadan. He wondered if any of the books within his reach contained maps to jog his memory.

The answer struck him with almost the force of a physical blow, because of course he'd known it all along, and had been too tired and thick-brained with overwork to realize it. The field of Cathlein was the spot where the armies of the King of Calandra and the Duke of Esdragon had finally met, after avoiding each other for weeks in a struggle for advantage of either ground or numbers.

The delay had served both leaders—their armies were matched nearly to a man when they finally met, and that terrible day and night had seen two armies devastated and the king and the duke dead at each other's sword points. It was after that doleful battle that Nímir had driven Valadan away and imprisoned him.

The sword would have been there with the king—in his hand, no doubt. What more logical place for it to have been lost, overlooked perhaps, or inadvertently buried—unrecognized or its importance unrealized by the shocked survivors left on that field? And why shouldn't a magic-linked blade reveal itself at certain times, under correct circumstances? Again, it was only logical.

Tristan got up, his cramped legs still protesting, and walked to the window. The moon hung in the sky like a coin, silver now but tending soon to gold, for it would set within an hour.

It was full tonight. But by tomorrow's night it would be on the wane. Was this timely finding of the verse the working of his spell at last, then?

The hour was right—the only time it would be until the moon came full again. They couldn't wait for that, surely. The king was ready, and Valadan certainly knew the way to Cathlein and could get him there by moonset.

Tristan yawned, then winced as a pain shot through his jaw and down his neck. It was just his usual luck, to have found a spell that wouldn't keep till morning.

He went out so quietly that Thomas, sleeping by his chair, never even heard.

A Trap Sprung

CLOUDS FLUNG SWORD-SHAPED shadows across the moon. Tristan might have taken that for an omen, but he was more occupied with hoping that the clouds wouldn't obscure the moon altogether. Cold and damp, the night air fanned his cheek. Valadan moved rhythmically under him, his hooves making little noise on the still soft earth.

The stallion had made no protest at their abrupt departure. Maybe he'd been as eager to get out of Crogen as Tristan suddenly was, the fresh air revitalizing him. He seemed to soar through the night, rather than merely running over the ground. They'd long since left any semblance of a road behind and taken to open country; they might have left the ground behind as well, for all Tristan knew.

Moorland it was, grass-covered and rolling. The few trees they passed huddled in lines, like dark slashes in the gray fabric of the grasslands—dismal enough, but Tristan did not care. After days of inaction and frustration, just being in the open air was exhilarating. He was glad to be out in the night.

The ground rose before descending again. Valadan slowed and halted.

Cathlein, the stallion said, and pawed savagely at the turf.

44

* * *

At Crogen, Thomas stirred and stretched, wakened doubly by the ending of a dream concerning impossibly fleet-footed mice and the abominable stink as the last of the special candles dissolved into a puddle of spent wax. He reached a paw out toward Tristan's ankle, ready to claw a mild protest over the stench and beg for a window hanging to be lifted. The ankle wasn't there.

Thomas came fully awake in an instant, already on his feet. His whiskers twitched.

Despite his alarm, he half expected to find Tristan fallen asleep in the antechamber, where he might have gone for a breath of fresh air, but Thomas wasn't greatly surprised when the room proved to be as empty as the one he'd just left. He *was* amazed that Tristan could have gotten out without tripping over his own feet or otherwise wakening him.

Fine time of night to go wandering off. He's probably catching his death of cold somewhere, or I will be, looking for him.

Tail lashing, Thomas sprang to the tabletop and sniff-inspected the book open there. Its pages were blank now, which was proper—but something about it didn't smell right. Not just those foul candles, either.

It wasn't something Tristan would have noticed, human-dull as his senses were—any more than he'd noticed a nebulous difference in the hand that had written certain passages upon the page. The ink wasn't visible now, so Thomas didn't notice either, but he *did* find that this one page had a smell subtly different from all the others, as if it and no others at all had been handled, though most carefully handled.

Thomas sniffed again, leaped from the table, and set off at a run for Elisena. He was not alarmed, not quite—yet. But this matter required further investigation.

The field of Cathlein spread before Tristan, mottled with moon-cast shadows like tarnishing silver. Valadan shuddered beside him, then dipped his head and pawed the ground again, fiercely. Chunks of wet grass flew.

"What is it?" Tristan asked.

The delicately modeled head lifted, wide nostrils drinking the night wind. The stallion's ears pricked.

I have not been upon this spot since the battle here, Valadan said. He continued to make little nervous movements with his hooves. He had been calmer going into Darkenkeep, Tristan thought.

I would rather be elsewhere now. There has been much death here. The land remembers it too clearly and speaks of what it knows.

Of course it would be painful for him, Tristan thought, ashamed that the horse's pain and grief at the loss of his last master on this spot had not occurred to him.

"Would it be easier if you waited farther off?"

I cannot leave you alone here. There is an evil about this place.

It didn't feel evil to Tristan, though he respected Valadan's judgment. The night wind was cold, but it was only wind.

"Will you hear me, if I call? Can you go just that far, and still feel easier?"

Valadan dipped his head in assent, reluctantly, Tristan thought. He patted the stallion's smooth shoulder.

"Then go off a little way. I'll shout when I need you."

Elisena had been working long and hard with her rings, in addition to doing all she might to sway such minor lords and knights as Polassar had been able to contact to their support. Her days were filled with emissaries, her nights with excruciatingly carefully worded letters of supplication. In the course of that, she'd neglected herself nearly as thoroughly as Tristan had; but being a little more skilled with herbs than he was, she'd held up far better. Still, she was shocked that she'd become so engrossed by the work that she'd failed to notice him working himself into an obvious state of nervous exhaustion. His appearance that evening had frightened her.

At least she'd convinced him to rest. She hadn't expected to succeed, though she'd ordered him to bed as if he were a child. Tristan had a stubborn streak, which never manifested itself at the best of times. He stirred beside her now, and she reached out a hand to soothe him.

Thomas licked her fingers apologetically.

Lady? I'm sorry, but I think you should come.

She lighted her rings slightly by reflex and was startled to find that she was alone in the bed except for the cat crouched beside her. The bedding was undisturbed, save for the spot where she lay.

"Oh. Can't you get him to bed either?"

He's not here. Anywhere. Thomas' eyes glowed like two little moons.

"Not here?"

I had a quick look in the stables on my way here. Valadan's gone too. You'd better come.

In minutes, Elisena was as wide awake as Thomas and stood beside him peering at the blank-paged book.

"This is what he was reading?"

Yes. But the candle's gone. You need it to—

"I know." A gesture, almost automatic, with one ringed finger, and there was a crackle of flame about the blackened bit of wicking. The candle burned again, more unnaturally than before, its light unwholesome as ever. Elisena's lips opened softly.

"You're right, Thomas. There's something *very* odd about all of this. This bit of text doesn't relate at all to the rest, and the script is different, though it's been faked very cleverly. It's plain enough if you're looking for it, but if someone was counting on Tristan's being too tired to notice—"

I don't read that tongue. What is it?

"A trap, Thomas. And I can make a fair guess as to the hand that laid it."

In ten more minutes, they'd roused Polassar and waved a frightened-looking Allaire back to her bed, while Polassar yawned and swore at the cold floor and tugged his boots on. He was still fastening up his tunic as Elisena showed him the book.

"I'll take your say for it, Lady. The page looks blank to me. What does whatever you saw mean?"

"It means that someone wants Tristan at a certain place at a certain time, alone. Given those circumstances and the way they've ensured them, I don't think they mean him any good."

Polassar scratched his chin, adjusted his hastily donned clothing further.

"You are sure he's not here? Asleep in a corner somewhere? This stone heap could swallow a man with a better sense of direction than the Wizard's got, and he's not been much himself, lately."

"He's not here, Polassar. Thomas searched before he came for me, and I looked, too, before I woke you." Her control of the rings was still imperfect—might always be, Elisena feared, since she could never hope now to have the tutelage of the

High Mage who'd made them for her. Her seeing-crystal had showed her only the dark, empty stable and gave her no clue as to where Valadan had gone, where he was now—or even more vitally, where *Tristan* was. He was not in Crogen. That was certain, and her heart needed no rings to tell her so.

"There's a hand behind this, Polassar, and it takes no great feat of divination to see whose. I think, much as we mislike it, we must extend an invitation to Galan, and welcome him into Crogen."

Now where, on all this broad battlefield, among the tussocks of grass and the tangles of berry bushes, might he expect the sword to be? Tristan scanned the vista, eyes straining to pick up some moonlight glimmer where no moonlight should be, which was the closest his imagination and experience could bring him to what the sword's manifestation might look like.

A blade flashed by the side of his head and into the tail of his sight, the moonlight gleaming on it, before the sound of its passage through the air reached his ears. Tristan flinched away instinctively and turned half around to see what the movement was.

His reactions were slow. Part of his mind was still registering that the shape had been like a sword blade when his eyes were running over the dark-clad figure now in front of him, the blade in its hand. He heard a hiss of displeasure over the missed strike, which told him, before he had time to wonder, that this was no phantom. Then the blade was coming in again, silent as a shadow. He almost stood staring while it spitted him, but fencer's reflexes took over; Tristan jumped away just as the point sliced through his jerkin and scored his ribs.

He reached for his own sword, remembered as his fingers closed on empty air that he'd never yet replaced the blade so wondrously lost in Darkenkeep. He didn't even have his table knife at hand; he'd left Crogen in haste, never dreaming he'd need arms—not with Valadan to protect him.

He opened his mouth to call the Warhorse, but knew it would be useless. The shout died in his mouth as another shadow shape came at him from the left. He thought he made out others as well, in all directions. No more than a half dozen, he thought, but couldn't be certain. He dared not look at anyone of them long.

His first attacker was holding off now until the others joined him, sure of the kill and willing to wait for it. Tristan leaped at the man—actually *past* him, swirling his cloak out madly to strike the man in the face. The billowing fabric made an excellent prop for a confusion-spell, and Tristan used it to good advantage. He swirled it continually between himself and his attackers, trying to hide himself in an enlargement of the shadows the cloak trapped.

He magicked with a speed and variety inspired by desperation, but was only marginally successful. At most, he was able to confuse no more than his attackers' aim. He couldn't gain enough distance to retreat properly, and there was nowhere to hide. Tristan slipped and fell, catching a kick in the side as he went down and barely gaining his feet again. Panting, he whirled the cloak yet again with one hand, his free fingers working passes to keep up the illusion.

He could only see three men now, and suspected that the others were fanning out, hoping to get behind him. Tristan wished desperately for even a small bush or a lightning-blasted stump, anything he could firm up into a more convincing illusion. Why hadn't he ever bothered with Blais' invisibility-spells? Well, all right, Blais had forbidden them to him—they were unreliable and dangerous if botched—but that had been a long time ago. He should have been practicing practical things like that.

One man had moved slightly too close. Maybe Tristan could get the sword away from him? Armed, Tristan thought he'd stand a far better chance of holding them off until Valadan could get to him.

The blade came questing in. Tristan leaped back, intending a feint, followed by a probably senseless attempt to wrestle the sword out of its wielder's hands. He jumped back—

Into nothing.

He fell, his cloak flapping about him like broken wings, as his arms and legs flailed uselessly at the air. There was a crackling sound, and something stabbed and whipped at him. Then Tristan hit the ground, flat on his back, and whatever moon and starlight there was winked out.

Wind stirred Galan's silver cockatrice banner fitfully, so that the bird seemed to shake itself and settle its feathers. Inside the tent beneath the banner, Galan faced his master of magic.

"Well? Is it accomplished?"

Reynaud considered the night sky, as if the mottling of stars and pewter-colored clouds above could give him answer. The gold-and-scarlet workings on his garments sparkled. He let the tent flap fall back into place presently and turned to Galan.

"By now? Yes, if the men you sent were as good as you say."

"Excellent. That witch will be easier to deal with in this moment of surprise and shock, I think, and I'll handle Polassar in my own way. When this difficult interview is over, you'll have your price—if you're still certain you wish to terminate your service with me."

"I have not been home in a long time, lord." Reynaud's sharp face was calm, unreadable of anything more than the open meaning of his words, as usual.

"It's your mistake, sorcerer. You could have claimed a high position here. You've earned it."

Galan turned uncomfortably away, fingered a map which lay rolling itself up upon a table. A man accepting less reward than his service warranted was an anomaly not to be trusted, and he had never been comfortable trusting Reynaud in any case. Ridding himself of the man safely would be difficult, but he'd do it. He wondered if Reynaud expected that.

"At least I shall be in a position to dispense with your services, but I'd be easier if you'd stay." Stay where he could be watched. "No? Well, I've never yet met the man who claimed to understand you." Galan's lips twitched into a smile. "Let us answer the lady's summons now."

Tristan lifted his head dazedly. He couldn't, for an instant, fathom where he was or how he'd come to be there. His heart was hammering, and breathing hurt. He was distinctly sure that he'd fallen, but it was too dark to see where he was, and he couldn't remember what had happened.

The moon found its way out from behind a skein of clouds, and memory came with the light.

He was lying on stony ground, but the lacy darkness overhead wasn't sky. It was a tangle of thorny bushes, which had broken his fall, even if numerous painful bits of them were embedded in him now. He must have stepped off the edge of a gully or gone near enough to the edge that the soil had crumbled and pitched him over.

He'd fallen right out of sight, better hidden thus than by

any of his spells, and fortunately had been only briefly stunned by the impact. Tristan felt bruised and scratched, but thankful that everything still seemed to work, after a fashion. His fingers found a tender lump on the back of his head, and passed it off as unimportant.

His would-be assassins were beating the bushes for him already, as a huntsman would for a fox gone to earth. They weren't being particularly subtle about it. Tristan could track their progress quite clearly by sound alone. Doubtless they assumed the fall had knocked him out or crippled him.

They would know he hadn't moved. The crackling bushes would give him away, too, when he tried to get up. There was no use his trying to slip past them.

Bars of moonlight slanted between the branches above him, shining as bright as silver sword blades. Almost without thinking about it, Tristan reached for one.

The spell he spoke was not one he remembered hearing or seeing. It seemed to come up out of the night itself, the darkness and brightness of it. Sword-obsessed as he was, the spell was no great wonder. The blade solidified beneath his fingers.

Tristan wasted no time in admiring his creatiôn, or wondering about it. He gripped the hilt tightly, and stood up to face his ambushers.

He didn't really want to kill them—just beat a fast retreat to Valadan. But the blade wouldn't let him do otherwise. It seemed possessed of a savage will all its own and it was quicker than he was.

The first man he met happened to be a master swordsman and a seasoned streetfighter, but he got in only one feint and a badly aimed slash that nicked Tristan's forehead before the moonbeam blade had sliced through his heart and one lung. Tristan jumped free of the body as it sagged into the bushes, dragging at the sword because he couldn't seem to let go of it. The noise of the fight would certainly draw the others.

What could be swifter or lighter than moonlight? The blade seemed sharper than mere steel and longer than it should have been. Its light dazzled and made of Tristan an invincible hero-figure. He blocked another cut at his head and thrust out automatically. A man fell, and another was caught on the backhand. That still left at least two more, and Tristan could see only one, which meant trouble. He swung about.

Then Valadan came leaping from above, like an embodi-

ment of the spirit of the night. Hooves flashed as bright as the
sword blade, and what they fell upon did not rise again. Tristan
found himself surrounded only by bodies.

He leaned abainst Valadan's shoulder, weak with reaction.
The stallion's mane blew against his face, and clung to the
blood there.

"Who were they?" Tristan asked finally.

There may be markings on them. Valadan was full of re-
morse that he had not sensed the men earlier. His head hung
low.

Tristan stroked the horse's neck.

"It isn't your fault. They knew I'd be here. And they must
have known you'd be nervous here and planned for it—known
I'd send you away. Otherwise, they wouldn't have chosen open
ground like this." He swallowed, tasting blood.

"Nothing was left to chance. I begin to think that bit of spell
that led me here wasn't half so providential as it seemed."

He knelt gingerly beside the nearest body. There was nothing to identify the man by his outer clothing—he could have
been a peasant or an outlaw—but upon his innermost tunic
was a badge. Tristan drew the man's own dagger and cut it
free.

He held it up to the moonlight. It was spotted with blood—
black in this color-empty light—but he could still make out
the device: a cockatrice, that venomous bird which so aptly sym-
bolized Galan, the man who'd chosen it.

Tristan cursed himself for a hope-blinded fool.

Galan's hand in this had to mean that the clue was false,
and he should have expected that Reynaud's skills would be
put to some such use, which had to be what had happened. He
felt sick.

He searched all the rest of the bodies, just to be sure, but
there was no doubt in his mind. Tristan sent the dagger flying
out to bury itself in the bushes and put a foot in Valadan's
stirrup, wincing at the pain of a wrenched ankle.

"Crogen," he ordered tightly. "As fast as you can."

An Accomplished Fact

"MOST FATHERS WOULD have been quit of you when you left the house that had sheltered you all your life, amid such treachery and turmoil," Galan said reasonably. "But I've more tender sensibilities than most, perhaps. I—"

"Is that why you named me changeling and bastard in front of your lords?" Elisena asked coolly. "Spare me your fatherly attentions, Galan. You are father to nothing more than the outer shell of this last body Nímir placed me in—and possibly not even that. I should greatly prefer to think not."

"You addled wench! How do you dare, in your situation, to speak to me so?" Galan's face had gone a most unhealthy color, and he now dropped all fatherly pretense, Elisena was pleased to note.

"You are here because I summoned you, Galan, and for no other reason than to answer my questions," she rapped out. She stroked her rings gently. "Now. What have you done with Tristan?"

"*I*, lady?" Galan smiled, regaining a measure of control.

"You deny any knowledge of his whereabouts?"

"I cannot do otherwise, lady. Those magic rings of yours will tell you that I speak the truth."

Elisena glanced down at her linked hands. The weight of the warm silver was as comforting as a shield in her hand, but she might have preferred to hold a sword.

"Perhaps. But if you speak the truth, it is because you have been careful not to know exactly what was done. Thus, though I might truth-read you, you would be blameless." She sighed. "He worked through you, did he not, Reynaud? The act has your stamp all over it. I should have guessed, or anticipated you. Now. *Where is he?*"

There was a pounding in his ears. Tristan wasn't sure if it was the echo of Valadan's flying hooves or the beating of his own frightened heart. He knew that he could barely breathe, either from apprehension or his inexperience with Valadan's full magical speed. He'd only been able to complete the trip because his need, his desperation to get back to Crogen, had overridden all lesser considerations.

He left Valadan in the courtyard and made his way silently to the Great Hall. The moonbeam sword was still in his hand, unnoticed. Crogen looked deserted, as if Polassar had deployed every man in his command to join a search. Would they have missed him yet? Tristan found his knees were trembling. Whatever was going on, he was eerily certain that the danger didn't extend to himself alone, that it was here, waiting, in Crogen. He was frantic to find Elisena.

Aha! Thomas said, from somewhere at his feet. *Now things begin to get interesting.*

Tristan controlled an impulse to yell with surprise.

What are you going to do with that thing, anyway—use it for a nightlight?

Tristan eyed the blade, then the sinking moon. If he expected to get any use out of this thing, he'd have to make haste. And he wanted to use it—the sight of it had just put an interesting idea into his head.

"Fill me in, Thomas. What's happened?"

She's got Galan in there. Sent for him. He's explaining how he doesn't have the faintest idea what happened to you. She's worried sick, he added. *Why didn't you wake me before you left?*

"I'm sorry I didn't. But I think I wasn't meant to." *Galan,* he was thinking furiously. As if he'd needed further proof. It suited Tristan's anger well that Galan should be here in Crogen.

"Thomas, let's go hear what he has to say. Is there somewhere I can do that without anyone seeing me?"

Learning my tricks, are you? All right, come on. But watch where you point that thing.

"Galan, what have you done with him?"

Galan raised his right brow. The left was mostly obscured by his patch, and it was difficult to tell if it moved.

"Lost your scarecrow king? That's hardly any concern of mine, but since you ask me, I'd say it's likely he lost his nerve and ran for it. What else can you expect of a peasant? I daresay he'll turn up—if you look low enough. Certainly he was low enough when you found him."

Elisena's expression never altered, but it took all her strength to restrain Polassar's wrath by mind alone. Galan untouched was insulting and growing bolder than was bearable, but Galan beaten to pulp would tell them nothing. And there was Reynaud to consider. He stood impassive beside his master, his eyes cloaked in shadows.

"Galan, I am not half so helpless as you deem me. I suggest you make me an answer *now*."

"I'll answer you thus, for the good of this realm. I acknowledge the power of those rings of yours—to do otherwise would hardly be sane—but you cannot rule here alone. You are very young, you lack experience and will need guidance, and Polassar is acceptable to very few." He leaned closer, as if to exclude Polassar altogether. Reynaud kept his place.

"Now, you have made a great mistake, but I think it can be neutralized. He's made it easier for you by running off, don't you see? You're free to consider the matter I attempted to propose to you earlier, without embarrassment. I will act as regent for you. I am willing to overlook much undaughterly behavior, we can work together now—"

Elisena's silver hands rose before her as if on puppet strings, the swirls and coils of silver flaming on them. The ancient glories of Crogen woke in the shadows around her like a lightning flash, limning her face uncannily. Her features might have been carved of stone. Slowly, slowly, she forced the hands back down, as if the rings had reacted to a portion of her will to which she would not grant dominion.

Reynaud had stepped back a pace, and Galan paled, if only briefly. Then the werelight dimmed, and torch flames alone lighted the group again, more normally.

Tristan entered the dark antechamber cautiously, fingers first as his hand crept around the doorframe, feeling his way, trying to shape the room beyond by touch.

Don't go any farther unless you want Reynaud to see you. He's sharp-eyed. You can hear, at least. Mind you don't trip over the furniture.

"Are you prepared to make me an answer, Galan? Or must I bring this power to bear on you?"

Galan glanced at his master of magic, who seemed now quite unperturbed. Well, if Reynaud wasn't worried—he wished he knew just how far he could rely on the man's protection. Was Reynaud aware of his own limits? Did he overestimate them, as some men did, or was he perhaps blind to them? Oh, Reynaud would pay for exposing him to this doubt.

Anger warmed him. How dared the girl speak to *him* so? What did she think she was, to give herself such airs over a few paltry trinkets? Polassar's support alone was not enough to back her; she was surely bluffing, making a show to suck the nerve out of him. Well, she'd fail, then.

"Galan?"

"Lady, enough of this wrangling! Your peasant is, by now, beyond any help you could hope to give him. I present you with an accomplished fact."

It was a glorious moment for an entrance, and Tristan made the most of it. It was a move Thomas himself would not have been shamed by. With the glowing moonbeam naked in his hand and his forehead still bleeding from the forgotten gash, Tristan half stalked, half limped into the hall.

Galan's startled, furious glance at Reynaud left no doubt of their respective guilts, but Tristan reached inside his jerkin and pulled out the handful of badges anyway, flinging them at Galan's feet. Even in the uncertain light of the sword, the bloodstains were visible on the silver cockatrices.

"I very much resent being forced to kill total strangers just to stay alive myself," Tristan said. "It's wasteful and unnecessary." The moon-sword glimmered dangerously in his hand.

He lifted its point toward Galan's throat.

"It wasn't in your best interest to provide me with such a lesson."

Dickon

TRISTAN LET THE sword fall. It hit the floor without the characteristic clatter of steel, and its light went out, leaving only the afterglow of a stamped-on firefly. Tristan resisted an impulse to giggle. If the moon had set just a couple of minutes earlier, before Reynaud and Galan had quit the hall—

Polassar made a noise of consternation from behind him. He stooped past Tristan to recover the blade, came up empty-fingered.

"Wizard? What have ye done with it?"

Tristan didn't answer, which was enough of an answer. Elisena said something swiftly, to clarify matters for Polassar.

"Then that wasn't the witched blade? But I thought—"

"I hope Reynaud thought so too," Tristan told him tiredly. "Anything that puts a little fear into him is fine with me."

He hadn't moved yet, except to let go of the illusory sword. Better he didn't try—his knees still felt wobbly, with no prospect of becoming less so.

Elisena took his arm firmly.

"Sit down. You look as if you're going to faint."

Tristan managed to stop swaying by a vast effort.

"I'm sorry. I'm worrying you."

"A trifle, yes. Are you hurt anywhere else? Other than that

cut on your head?" She had somehow gotten him as far as her stillroom. Fortunately there hadn't been any stairs to tackle, which might be why she'd brought him there. Tristan didn't know. He didn't remember walking. He found that a bit unnerving.

He let her settle him onto a bench and shivered convulsively. Deft fingers probed at his forehead to sponge the dried blood away.

"Well, at least it's not deep. A scratch. Is there anything worse?"

He sighed. "No. This is just the first time I've stopped to think about what happened—and almost happened." Tristan shut his eyes. "I am probably bruised black all over and I think I got kicked in the ribs once, besides being scratched there too. There are definitely thorns in my backside from falling through a bush, and I'd really rather not sit, but I don't remember any other swordcuts. I'm sorry I scared you."

"How did you *expect* me to feel?" Elisena's fingers were gentler than her words as she stroked some sort of ointment around the now cleaned cut. "Finding you had vanished, with Galan's men all about . . ."

Tristan winced doubly from the implied reproach and the sting of the medicine.

"I didn't think how it would look to you. I didn't think about anything."

"A good case could be made for that, yes." Her fingers sketched a pass of healing over the salve.

"I was expecting to be back with the sword before you woke up. A nice surprise." He winced again. "I know, that sounds childishly stupid."

Children have more sense than you do. Thomas curled up in his lap.

"I wasn't expecting a trap," Tristan went on doggedly. "I didn't know those books could be tampered with—and I wanted to catch the moonlight. That was supposed to be important." He stopped, aware of how miserably inadequate that sounded. It had been a stupid move, there was no denying that, or excusing it. He'd been blind, easily led. He'd never have done such a thing in a fencing match.

"I just wanted," he heard himself saying, eyes shut, "some way out of this."

It almost found you.

"Beware easy solutions." A ring brushed his cheek, a butterfly's touch. "Finding the sword is not *that* important."

Tristan was too beaten to protest.

"No lectures," she went on. "It's done, and they would serve no purpose anyway. The experience was lesson enough, I think."

Tristan had to agree with that, but his depression only deepened. He'd had his fill of searching without clues for something that might not exist anymore, and his dashed hopes were leading him toward an apathy he couldn't afford. He felt very old.

Elisena put a cup to his lips. Tristan drank, because it seemed easier than resisting.

"There. Sleep. This will help—it's a very old wine, brewed in ways no one remembers any longer."

A few minutes later, he was lying down, feeling the light weight of a blanket from his throat to his toes. His awareness of anything more was limited and frightening. He seemed to be losing control of his thoughts as well as his body. Tristan fought free of the heaviness of the wine.

Shamelessly, he begged Elisena not to leave him there alone, because it seemed she might, and suddenly the dark, even with the wine's softening, seemed more than he could bear. He felt like a child, but he asked anyway.

Elisena sat down beside him.

"I won't, if only for fear that you'll leave *me* again if I do."

Something warm dropped on his cheek and cooled there. Tristan struggled to get his eyes open and succeeded, but could barely focus on anything. *Her* eyes looked enormous, pools of silver dripping more silver. Another tear hit his cheek, and her fingers gently brushed it away.

"You would think," Elisena whispered, "that I might at least have mentioned that I was glad you were still alive."

Thomas was occupied in the midst of a sunbeam, batting an ensorcelled dandelion puff back and forth between his paws. That it was magicked was plain enough—an ordinary dandelion would not have stood an instant of such play.

Tristan was seized with an unendurable desire to levitate the puff out of the cat's reach, before Thomas realized he was awake. He crooked two fingers, examined their position carefully, then lifted his hand and silently mouthed a word.

The dandelion flew to tatters in Thomas' face. The cat hissed.

"Sorry." Tristan looked at him sheepishly. "Toadstools, you'd think I'd know better than even to bother."

Thomas grumbled to himself, and pawed a bit of fluff off the tip of his nose.

Tristan sat up and yawned.

"I wonder what was in that wine?"

You didn't need for there to be anything in it. You had a week's worth of sleep to catch up. Is everything still working? Other than the magic, of course. That seems perfectly normal.

Tristan stretched a little, experimentally. He had a lot of sore muscles.

"I think so. Thomas? Did I really order him out of Crogen?"

Don't you remember?

"I was hoping I remembered it wrong."

You were very regal. Polassar should be pleased. Of course, it was a very impolitic time for you to go all decisive—and when you told Galan not to come back to Crogen until he could back up his words with something more than hot air—that might be considered rash.

Tristan put his head in his hands.

"Thomas, tell me I'm dreaming all this. *Please.*"

Thomas nosed silently at another stray bit of dandelion fluff.

In a few minutes, when he'd run recent events around and around in his head till he was dizzy and sicker of them than ever, Tristan decided he ought to find Elisena. He'd expected to see her before this, since he'd slept the night—or however long it had been—in her workroom. But if she wasn't coming to him, he'd best seek her out.

He came across Allaire very shortly. She was waiting just outside the stillroom door, somewhat nervously, but a vision nonetheless. With her questing days over, she had more leisure for those arts she knew best, and their application showed, as did the usefulness of the maid she'd brought with her from Lassair. Her beauty had redoubled since her renunciation of the rings, rather than suffering from the loss of their special properties. She took Tristan's hands, and, despite his preoccupation with heavier matters, he was agreeably dazzled by the white perfection of her smile.

"You'll be looking for Elisena." She made music of the words.

He nodded.

"She asked me to wait for you, and see that you got some food. It's in the kitchens, if you'll come now."

She was rather pointedly trying to steer him away from something, and none too subtly either. Tristan halted.

"I don't understand," he said uncertainly. "Doesn't she want to see me? I know she was angry, but I thought that was all straightened out."

Allaire shook her head.

"Elisena said I was to beg your pardon for her, but that something unexpected has happened. She doesn't want to be disturbed for a while. She's quite sorry."

Tristan was still inclined to think that she simply didn't want anything to do with him for a while, which was baffling. Elisena had been very tender the night before—unless he'd dreamed that? And such swings of mood as this craving for privacy would seem to indicate weren't like her.

It was childish of him to feel hurt or disappointed. Had he needed just the sight of her that desperately, so that he couldn't wait just a few hours more?

He could barely swallow his breakfast—and sitting down to it wasn't easy either—but Allaire babbled on so brightly that she seemed not to notice and made it easier for Tristan to hide his discomfort. He didn't mark many of her words until he heard something about Polassar's having had the quest for the tenth ring set to music by his bard. Tristan was surprised to learn that Polassar kept a bard—the man didn't seem sensitive to poetry. But then, how else were a hero's deeds to be remembered?

"So he gave Geffroi much silver, in fee to set it all to fair music."

"He would," Tristan said, acerbic and unthinking. Allaire's maid, who was perhaps a bit more perceptive than her mistress, giggled. Allaire looked at the girl sharply, and Tristan recovered himself before she turned back to him. "Ah, that is, he *should*. Somebody's got to see to that sort of thing. You certainly deserve a song—and Polassar of course, being a hero and all. I—"

"It's all lies, of course," Allaire said matter-of-factly, and then it was Tristan's turn to stare in surprise. "It's gallant, and he means well, but none of it's true. Such sentimental drivel—having heard this song of Geffroi's, which everyone exclaims so prettily over, I shall suspect every other song I hear of being gold spun over the common clay, and not an honest job of it at that. But you must never suspect Elisena's feelings for you, or doubt them. Ever."

Tristan had to fight to get a bite of biscuit and honey safely swallowed before it choked him. "Does it show that much?" he asked, trying to be humorous and revealing his misery instead.

Allaire looked at him, her blue eyes deep enough for a man to drown in, their concern sweet as balm and nearly dripping from them. She might never have loved him, as perhaps he might never have loved her as he'd thought he did at the time, but it was plain she'd never been so indifferent to him as Tristan had thought either. "Yes."

She'd meant to comfort him, having seen through his distraction as through glass, and Tristan was a little comforted, but not sufficiently. He went off by himself as soon as he could manage to, still depressed and worried. He might have been more comforted if he'd been worrying only about Elisena, but unhappily that wasn't the case. Solitude was no salve either; he still fretted. Tristan thought he needed something to do, precisely so he wouldn't have so much time to think.

He would have returned to his search of the records, but somehow he couldn't face those again or trust them so soon after his failure. Odds were Reynaud wouldn't be able to fool him again and wouldn't even try, but still—Tristan wandered around looking for Polassar for a while and was finally told that his commander had ridden out on patrol and wasn't expected back till nightfall. After that Tristan just paced aimlessly.

It was just sun-high. He should have stayed with Allaire after all—he might have tired of her prattling, but at least he wouldn't have been stuck with hours of self-torment, wondering what was going on that he either didn't know about or wasn't being trusted to know about.

That's not rational, you know. No one's persecuting you. Except possibly yourself.

Tristan sighed, surprised that Thomas had stayed with him

so long. "I know. It's just that I feel so left out. There's nothing for me to do here, yet there's so much that's begging to be done. And the one time I manage to take some kind of action, it blows up in my face." Tristan fiddled with a loose brick in the wall, wondering if it might by a key to another of the secret passages. It seemed not.

There are dozens of things you can do. I'd think you'd be happy to be bored, for a change.

Tristan smiled wanly. "It will pass. I hope. I'll try not to be so impossible."

He found a bench on the sunny side of a courtyard, sat down carefully, and began to do finger exercises. If his magical control was even worse than usual, Tristan decided he'd no one to blame but himself. He'd neglected the basics of his craft sadly, and a wizard couldn't do that with impunity. Not with magic. Not for long.

The practice helped more than he'd expected it would. Tristan got pleasantly engrossed with working the stiffness out of his brain and fingers, so much so that he didn't even notice that he wasn't alone any longer. He was startled when he looked up to see that a figure wearily shouldering a pack had appeared as if conjured in the courtyard in front of him.

Wherever the man under the pack had come from, he'd walked a long way getting to Crogen. He was literally travel-stained, his clothes showing more mud than color. He was all brown—hair, eyes, skin, and the homespun-and-dyed cloth of his jerkin and breeches. His shirt might once have been white; now it too was dust-colored.

He halted when he spotted Tristan sitting by the wall, hesitated, and then approached, venturing a shy smile.

"All right if I join you?"

Bemused, Tristan nodded. This was definitely not one of Polassar's men, then—though he hadn't really thought so.

The boy—on closer examination, he seemed very young; the gray in his hair was only dust—shrugged out of his pack, which looked heavy enough to contain all his worldly possessions and a brother's besides. A longish bundle clanked as he set it free of the rest.

"I swear, I never thought Falkerry was so far from everywhere else in the world!" He sat, breathed deep, and leaned back against the sunlit wall, eyes closed blissfully. Tristan and Thomas exchanged amused glances, unseen. "Good thing for me that they say the captain of the guard's out on patrol—I'm not up to facing him yet. Not till I can feel my feet again."

Maybe he was one of Polassar's scouts? But the mention of Polassar's name drew a blank, although the offer of a drink from the ale jug Tristan had swiped from the kitchens earlier certainly did not.

"Has there been fighting here already? Thank you, that damped the road dust down wonderfully—a dry throat's a plaguey thing. I mean, were you in a battle?"

He gestured vaguely at Tristan, who realized finally that he must be sporting a fair crop of bruises on his face by then, besides the bandaged scratch on his forehead.

"No," he answered, embarrassed. "It was something private."

"Oh." The boy looked faintly disappointed. "I thought you might be one of the soldiers."

"Sorry, but not really."

"I just thought maybe you could help me. That's why I'm here, you see. I want to join the army—to serve the King."

"The King?" Tristan asked, startled. "How'd you hear about *that*?"

"News travels." He took another sip of ale, and then he politely passed the jug back. "Even to Falkerry, sometimes. Not often, but sometimes. The market was buzzing with it. All about a king who was at Crogen to be crowned—when's the last time you heard of *that*? And he was going to unite the lords and stop all the petty fighting and throw out the lords who treated their folk like beasts bred to bring them tax monies. I hadn't heard that one before either, but it sounded like a fine thing to me, and I imagine he's going to need all the soldiers he can get to work such a wonder, so here I am. My father was furious, of course, but it's not the harvest season and the planting's done, so he couldn't find an excuse good enough to keep me. And here I am."

"To serve the King?" Tristan repeated stupidly. Had Elisena's attempts to gain them the support of the people come only to this? At least it was a response, but . . .

"To serve the King. Is that why *you're* here?" the boy asked brightly. "Even though you're not a soldier?"

"More or less." Tristan heard Thomas snicker. "You're a farmer, then?"

The boy looked aggrieved. "My *father* is. I'd liefer be a

knight, if I can work my way up so high. I don't know if I'm very brave, but I've heard luck has a lot to do with military matters, and I've always been lucky. War's a wonderful way of advancing one's station, by all I hear. Why, there's Halrin, the miller's son. He took service with Baird of Amrein, and now he's captain over ten archers!"

He looked rapturously up at the sky, patently seeing visions of similar glories pertaining to his own future. Then the boy sobered, looking back at Tristan with an expression of nearly comical seriousness. "Of course, I don't expect to start very high. I don't have any what you'd call battle skills. You don't learn much like that while farming. But I've got my own sword and I can use it a little; I learn very quickly. Surely they'll take me?"

He sounded as if the fear that he might not be accepted into the army had been long considered, though hoped against. Tristan hesitated, knowing that Polassar, who'd take any sword that came along, would certainly accept this boy's, no matter how clumsily it was wielded; he was wondering how he might engineer things so that his commander would refuse it. A farmer's son—maybe an only son—and perhaps all of sixteen, with admittedly no skill at arms, wouldn't last three minutes in a serious fight, dreams of glory or no.

Reminds me of you, Thomas said, *when you used to beg Blais to let you go on a quest to prove yourself—of course that was before you actually had to go on one*.

"You don't have to say anything," the boy said sadly. "I can see what you're thinking, clear enough. He'd want more experience, this Polassar. He must be pretty rough, if he's the king's own commander."

"He can be." Tristan half smiled.

"Well." The boy got to his feet, grimacing a little from tired muscles and maybe tired bones as well. "That's as it should be. All I can do is try. And if he won't take me right away, maybe he'll let me hang around until I can pick up the things I need to know. A soldier's got to start somewhere. Maybe you'll put in a good word for me, if you know anyone who's got my lord Polassar's ear? Dickon of Falkerry, that's me."

"Falkerry? Where's that?" Tristan couldn't place it on any of the few maps he remembered seeing, even the ones Polassar kept pulling out to instruct him upon military matters.

"Where the Fal meets the sea. In Esdragon," Dickon went on, when Tristan must have still looked blank. "Dickon of Falkerry—that has a proper soldierly sound, doesn't it?"

Tristan sighed inwardly. Doubtless the boy was now entertaining himself with visions of being knighted for valor on the battlefield. *Of* Falkerry, as if it were some great lord's demesne and not a nearly nameless accumulation of huts and fishing boats at a minor river mouth!

Dickon hefted the pack again, waved at Tristan just before he disappeared through the archway.

Tristan looked down to find Thomas watching him like a basilisk.

Aren't you going to tell him who you are?

"No."

You don't think that's a bit cruel? He's entitled to an answer to his question, even if it's no. And he's entitled to know whom he was asking it of.

"Why? Frankly, Thomas, I'm tired of every person I happen to meet twice kneeling to me. Polassar still does it half the time, and I keep looking behind me to see what important person's there. It's rather nice just to talk normally to someone."

You exaggerate. And he'll get offended and go home.

"That's exactly what I'm hoping he'll do, Thomas." Tristan looked at the empty archway.

It is? If you'll pardon my noticing, you've hardly got such a vast army here that you can affordably turn men away.

"An army won't begin to solve my troubles. And I don't like the idea of children getting killed over a kingship that I don't even want."

Children? Most men count themselves grown at that age. You did. And it wasn't all that long ago.

"He might just as well be. A farmboy with the mud still on his boots and great big stars in his eyes!" Tristan rolled his own eyes despairingly. "Why am I bothering explaining this to you? He seems like a decent boy and he surely deserves a chance to live a little while before he gets himself killed. If he doesn't get any encouragement from me, maybe he *will* give up and go home, which is where he should have stayed."

That's patronizing.

"Maybe. I'd rather think of it as compassion for the least

of my subjects—just part of learning to be king." On that note of self-righteousness, Tristan tried to start his exercises up again. Thomas was having none of it.

It's an excuse. If you want to be softhearted, fine, but don't pretend it's something else. The cat's paws left precise tracks in the dirt as he stalked away.

Tristan watched him go, tapping his index finger against his closed lips. He hesitated. However right Thomas might be, he just wasn't in the mood to abet any more useless waste. The tapping stopped, the lips parted a little, almost into a smile. Perhaps . . .

Tristan walked through the archway himself. Yes, almost certainly . . .

He bent down and plied his belt-knife carefully. In a few moments he had dug all around the edges of a bootprint Dickon had left in the soft ground where a puddle had lain. The impression was so clear, Tristan could even make out the mark of a roughly patched hole where the sole had been walked through. He wiggled the knife blade underneath, working slowly lest the soil crack.

Gently he levered the chunk of dirt up, balancing it on the flat side of the knife as it came free. At last he had it—a perfect bootprint and a little of the surrounding soil. Tristan glanced around the courtyard.

Ivy, some dead, some still stubbornly green, cloaked a wall. Tristan walked over to it and swept the curtain of leaves back with one hand. Behind it, at the base of the wall, the dirt was dry as old bones, untouched by rains or dew.

He laid the bootprint tenderly there and said words over it. At last, satisfied, he let the ivy leaves drop back into place. The bootprint, shielded from weather and prying eyes, was quite safe.

And as long as it remained so hidden and until it turned back to dust and lost all resemblance to Dickon's boot, Dickon himself would be as good as invisible to any guard captain he chanced to approach. He wouldn't be truly invisible, his outward appearance might not alter even slightly, but he'd somehow and most certainly be overlooked and ignored, exactly as easily as his ensorcelled bootprint would be. Tristan smiled proudly at his handiwork.

Thomas would certainly have disapproved, but it seemed

the only way. Tristan knew he hadn't the ease of authority to accomplish this end in any other, more prosaic way—at least not so quietly, without fuss. No guard captain would do his bidding in this without question—after all, he had no reason for refusing Dickon's service that wouldn't sound mad to Polassar or any of his soldiers. But the magic would do very well.

The Cold Stars

THE DOOR'S WOODEN panels were bound to each other with intricate ironwork, ostensibly practical but flagrantly decorative—a smith's show-off piece, no doubt of it. Tiny, round-headed nails studded and punctuated the work, nine hundred of them, in fact, as if to make the work magical by number even though it was worked in magic-thwarting cold iron.

Tristan knew perfectly well how many nails there were—he'd had ample time to count them. He'd been waiting outside the door for a good four hours when Elisena finally opened it. Since he knew she was inside, whereas Elisena had no idea whatever that he was outside, Tristan saw her face before she had time to set it along lines of normality.

"What's wrong?"

She jumped—actually and incredibly, she jumped, losing every shred of self-possession and composure. Then Elisena spoke so calmly as to make Tristan misdoubt his own eyes.

"How did you know where I was? I asked Allaire not to tell you and then I moved again when she'd gone."

"I know. I had Minstrel fly from window to window till he found you."

"But Minstrel's moulting." She eyed him askance.

70

"He can fly a very little, if it's important enough." Tristan explained patiently. "This was. Are you all right?"

Elisena shivered, but Tristan couldn't quite touch her, because she didn't seem disposed to permit it yet. She held herself so carefully, in such reserve that he was unable to guess how to proceed, having gotten this far.

"I've been trying to see into Nímir's heart." She held up her left hand. The once clear crystal that hung from her thumb was white as a drop of milk now—or white as ice. "I hope it will clear again, eventually, but for now I can do nothing. He holds it too tightly." Her voice was bleak, and exhausted.

"Nímir? Couldn't we just take one thing at a time, and not borrow more trouble when we're already richly blessed with so much of it?"

"No."

That seemed a little final. "Is that all you're going to say?"

"I—I hardly know what to say."

Elisena unbent at last, with a sigh that seemed to dissolve her bones, and reached out for Tristan's hand. Yet she recovered swiftly enough that her silvered grasp was firm. "I wasn't sure—I could tell myself that it wasn't true, but I knew it was, and it wouldn't go away just because I wouldn't look. I had to be *sure*, and so I had to be alone today. I wasn't trying to shut you out. I thought you'd sleep longer—"

"You should have waked me. Then you could have had the use of your own workroom, instead of—" Tristan reached past her and pushed the door open. The room revealed was dark and dusty, devoid of all furnishings. The dust on the floor was much disarranged, as if someone had first paced, then sat there. "I thought so. Were you in there all day? And you scolded *me*! Now come along. It's cold here."

She looked at Tristan closely for the first time. "Are you still afraid that I'm angry with you?"

"You have a right to be," Tristan said, accepting it. "I'll admit that I was stupid and irresponsible."

"I gambled to test the crowning-spells, and nearly paid for it with your life. And you never said one word about it. Not one single word. Yet you think *I* have a right to be angry?"

As she gestured, the whitened crystal swung and captured both their gazes. Elisena fixed her eyes on it, hardly seeming to breathe.

"Tristan, tell me truthfully—does it seem to you that it's

colder here than it should be?" Her tone was very far from calm, and the words tumbled out in haste.

"Cold?" He remembered that there'd been ice on the puddles in the courtyard two mornings ago. Probably this morning as well, for the sun had shone only fitfully. "But after all it's nearly winter," he added reasonably, even as he thought of it.

Elisena caught her breath, but the noise was surprisingly like a sob.

"Tristan." Her voice trembled, just barely. "I had such dreams last night, they made me start to think, and then I couldn't rest until I'd searched out their meaning... The time's not what we thought; we got all turned around in Darkenkeep. I was a fool not to have remembered what is possible there. So I didn't suspect till this morning, and you wouldn't at all; you're too used to the weather being chancy. But I've asked around and I've searched my rings, made them answer me. It's not winter. It's spring here now. Or it *should* be."

Tristan disagreed with her findings rather strenuously, but there was no avoiding the truth, once Elisena cataloged for him all the things that had convinced her. Even if he'd been so confused in Darkenkeep that he'd totally forgotten how seasons were apt to shift and time pass erratically while one was inside, there was plenty of people about who knew what the proper season was. Minstrel was shedding his feathers at what Tristan had blithely assumed to be the wrong time of year, and those cursed pole-beans...

While he and Elisena talked, walking through Crogen, both of them too restless to go indoors even though it was dark, mealtime and past, the air seemed to grow a lot cooler. My imagination, Tristan thought, knowing it had to be, but suddenly he was less sure of that. His turned ankle ached. There was no breeze. The air itself was chill, brittle as glass.

"This is not winter, but Nímir will move against us now. He knows where we are. We can't hide, even if we chose to. There's no reason to expect him to hold his hand, and now the rings alone aren't enough to stop him."

Tristan shot her a quick glance, even though he couldn't see much in the dark. "But the legends, the prophecies—"

"Say only what *might* be. And they were written a long time ago." Elisena's voice was bleak. "When I remember how confident I was, how I boasted that my captivity had taught me how to use my rings—what a magnificent piece of self-delusion!"

"What about the other wizards here?" Tristan asked hastily, alarmed as much by Elisena's state of mind as by her arguments. He'd never seen her frightened before—not like this.

Elisena shook her head slowly at his question, and looked long at her rings.

"Do you know of any mages left in Calandra capable of joining this fight?"

Tristan considered. Now that he thought of it, it seemed to him that none of Blais' friends had called for a very long time before Blais had died. The memories he had of them were vivid, but they belonged to a child, and a small one at that. If those wizards had disappeared, or had been slain too, if Blais had known of it—that might be what had prodded his redoubled pursuit of a quest Tristan had seldom heard him speak of. Yet mages traveled a good deal. Even he and Blais had, during the crucial seasons of planting and harvest, working the weather for pay and for the land's life. Those other mages could still be around—there must be mages everywhere, weather-witching, or else nothing would ever grow in Calandra. He said as much, and Elisena agreed.

"The wizards have done well, saving as much as they have. Their achievement is the greater because not even the oldest of them can remember what the land was firsthand, can truly know what they're trying to preserve. Yet how many of them still live? There's no way to find them; the old guilds and leagues are all dissolved. Those who live work alone and in the dark, hardly knowing what they do, and I fear they'd hide from the likes of us as readily as from Nímir."

Tristan worked his way through what that meant.

"So we're back where we started. You said before that we'd need the power of Crogen's throne behind us, as well as the rings. Which makes sense anyway, since that was the original plan. Married to the last king, you'd have had both powers at your disposal if things had gone as the High Mage meant them to."

He sighed. "If I'd had the least bit of luck in that test, if there'd been the slightest feeling about it that it was something I could master if I went about it the right way, I'd try again.

But all I learned from it was that, without the sword, I'm wrong, king-mark or no. The throne knew right away and it didn't waste any time showing me."

"That's not your fault."

"No. But it doesn't help. It just means, plain and simple, that we've got to get that sword."

Very neat, all problems solved. And it's such a little thing. Thomas materialized at Tristan's feet, slick as if he'd been gifted with invisibility.

"There's this, too," Elisena said. "I don't believe it's an accident that Galan showed up as quickly as he did. I think we can see Nímir's hand in that as well."

That led to many new lanes of thought, none of them pleasant. Tristan broke the troubled silence.

"The records here are useless. There aren't any recent—if you can call something that long ago recent, anyway—recent enough to mention what happened to the sword after the battle. If there ever *were* any, they'd have to have been written after the battle, and the High Mage seems to have sealed that room before the fighting started. Whatever records might have been made have probably been lost. I thought if I read enough, I might get a feel for the sword, or the time it came from anyway, enough to work out a spell to call it, but it seems not." Tristan toed a loose cobble, aimlessly.

The stars overhead were bright as diamonds and looked as hard. Tristan had had plenty of time to think, as well as count nailheads, while he waited for Elisena. This seemed the moment to speak of that.

"I'd thought about the records the mages should have in Kôvelir, though they won't be much more use for the same reasons. But I want to go there anyway."

You do? Thomas left off batting at a grass stem that had thrust up between the paving stones.

Elisena's lips opened with a question, though she did not speak.

Tristan held her hand, tracing and retracing the little roundness of bone that poked up on the outside of her wrist, as if memorizing the feel of it was vital to his very life. She seemed suddenly so fragile, though he knew she was surely stronger than he was, even without her rings. Yet her bones seemed as thin—and as dear—as Minstrel's. And Tristan knew without doubt that she was no more beyond being hurt than he was, or

Polassar, or Allaire. The rings ensured vulnerability more than safety.

"We have a little while before Galan can raise the kind of army he'll feel safe behind," Tristan continued awkwardly. "He can't do it alone without arousing quite a few of the lords against *him*, so he'll have to make alliances with them, which will be complicated and take up his time. You and Polassar will be doing the same thing, of course, but again you don't need me for that. You might be better off without me."

"What are you saying?" Elisena's brows lowered forbiddingly.

"There's something else in Kôvelir besides the records in the Library. Something I didn't pay much attention to at the time, but now I wonder—did you ever see those cards Crewzel had? The ones her husband made?"

"I knew she was a card-reader."

"The pack she has is unusual. Those cards have a way of revealing unexpected things, doing things they shouldn't be able to do. There might just be something that will at least put me on the track of the sword. You know the proverb: 'If the door's locked, try the window.'"

I thought that was for thieves.

"It's better than just sitting here waiting for the snows to cover us," Tristan finished lamely, wishing Elisena would make some response. It was clear that she thought this just another of his ill-wished and badly thought-out schemes.

"Alone?"

"Valadan can get me there quickly and safely. And Thomas, of course. I think it's worth a try. We don't have many other options."

"No," Elisena said and looked long at the whitened crystal. "We don't."

A Journey Begins

TWO MORNINGS LATER, Valadan was saddled and waiting at Crogen's rear gate, the exit least in view of Galan's army. Tristan walked toward the horse with some last-minute additions to his pack, settling into his new clothes as he went.

You could have picked something more interesting than gray, Thomas suggested.

"What, black? I'm not Reynaud; I can't carry off that style." Tristan ran his fingers over the close-woven wool of his breeches. At least they were whole and not patched anywhere. Who cared if they were drab? "Besides, I'm trying to be inconspicuous."

Who better?

"And I'm partial to gray."

You should be. It doesn't show the dirt.

"That won't matter. I'm taking along a couple of new spells for cleaning."

It will matter.

Polassar came striding up in nail-soled boots that prompted Thomas to spring for the safety of Valadan's back. The man had mellowed a bit—but not very much—since he'd first been told about Tristan's plan; his speculations as to how much room Tristan had in his head for crack-brained schemes had been audible all over Crogen. His disapproval went unmasked still.

"Wizard? Have you got enough sense to be careful without needing to be told?"

Tristan grinned, knowing Polassar would tell him anyway. "I think so. I'll be all right."

Polassar threw his head back, scanning the sky. "There's snow in that wind."

"I hope I'll be in Kôvelir before it hits." Tristan nodded toward Valadan. "Take care of yourself. And good luck with the army."

The army reminded him of other matters. Tristan had met Dickon once more, hanging about the drill yard. The boy's face had been long as he'd described his inability to connect with anyone empowered to sign him up. He remained hopeful, though, even if he had to go to the King himself. If he could just find the King. Had Tristan perchance seen him?

Tristan had few qualms about what he'd done. Men on a single basis wouldn't do Polassar much good anyway—what he needed were whole companies, trained and accustomed to working together. One lone and unskilled soldier was useless and would come to no good end. Tristan considered that he might have had trouble convincing a captain to *let* the boy enlist. In any event, the thing was done, and he suspected that Dickon might even now be packing up to head home. Surely polishing other men's weapons wouldn't entertain him much longer.

Polassar had come to him early to give him a small bag of money—all that there had been in Lassair and what he'd somehow won in gambling. It had seemed a lot to Tristan, more than he could ever need. But Polassar had been apologetic at the smallness of the amount.

Now Elisena came to see Tristan off, a bundle of herbs in her hands as she tried to pretend that his was a casual leave-taking and that he wasn't going into any danger at all. Allaire had spoiled that pretense, though, by refusing to watch him leave. She'd hugged Tristan hard just before breakfast, cried tears all over his new jerkin, and then locked herself away somewhere.

"I don't know why everyone is fussing so," Tristan said, tying a saddlebag closed. "You're apt to have more trouble here than I could find if I went looking for it—which I won't do. I should be worrying about you."

You mean you won't be?

The herbs were lemon balm—he could smell them now as Elisena twisted the stems in her hands, apparently without realizing it. She noticed them, as the scent reached her, too, and flung the mangled leaves away. Tristan took her juice-perfumed hands.

"If you should need me—"

"I can reach you, if I must. Pay particular attention to mirrors; I can send messages in them—they're backed with silver—in an emergency. But I don't expect to need them. And beyond the Est it will be difficult to track you. It's hard to see over all that running water. So do as Polassar says and be careful."

"Is Nímir—" he hated to ask about that; he was sure she was keeping a great deal about that problem from him, feeling however wrongly that it was her private battle.

"Nímir is not quite ready to take up arms, I think. It may be difficult for him to warp the seasons the way he has done, taking all the little concentration he allocates to us to maintain his snows."

"To *us*?" Tristan felt he'd missed something, as he nearly always did when Elisena spoke of an enemy that she knew far better than he did.

"What little has been learned of Nímir suggests strongly that he doesn't concern himself with Calandra alone. There are lands on the other side of Channadran as well, and I suspect they're feeling his power now. That would explain his leaving us relatively alone for such a long time. If he'd pressed his attack at all, neither of us would be here discussing this! Nímir's plans are as complex and shifting as the snows of the Winter-waste, but even he can't attend to everything at once. Thus he's made the errors that have allowed us to survive this long, even with all the odds against us."

She stroked Valadan's nose, and Tristan remembered that the horse had tasted Nímir's power as no one else but Elisena had and lived to reflect on it.

"Philosophy," Elisena said, shaking her head. "We should be more practical." Valadan lipped at her palm, seeking the slice of apple she offered him. "I think Nímir must direct his attacks with precision to be successful now. That is attacks—as opposed to mere holding actions to keep the advances he's made. Those nearly run themselves—like Darkenkeep. He's a long way off for complete control on a grander scale, so he needs to know exactly what he's doing. Our only hope is that we can move before he can turn his full attention to us. Glaciers move slowly. Perchance Nímir must also."

"Just so he doesn't move while I'm gone."

"You won't be away that long." They'd agreed that he had two months, a sevenday more than that at the very outside. By then Galan would certainly have returned, and Tristan would have to be back, sword or not.

"Tristan—" Elisena gripped his arm, shattering his thoughts. "I think you'll be all right. Nímir knows me of old, and he knows Crogen, but he's seen little of you. You're something new; you don't fit any of the patterns. I don't think he quite knows what you are, or how to touch you. So he's blind to you, to whatever you do. But 'ware stabbings in the dark. He can be uncannily accurate."

Tristan looked around. The sky overhead was the color of a dappled horse's belly, and there was nothing in the landscape to warm the scene. A frosty wind came up out of nowhere, tore all feeling from his face and fingers, and whistled away again, as swiftly as it had come.

Tristan almost wished for rain. It would make for miserable riding, but better that than the snow that seemed imminent. The grass was still green in spots, but the bare bones of the leafless trees were as gray as the sky, and the wind rippled the grass like a cold hand stroking a bed-fur.

It seemed the sunlight was always ahead of him, just out of reach. Though he rode always toward it, the shadow of the snow clouds seemed to ride with him, so that Tristan felt as if he was darkening the whole world, merely by riding through it. He resisted the urge to look back, mostly because he feared to see the snow drifting in his wake. Better simply to suspect it.

It's too soon for winter! He wanted to scream his protest. And now, when he had to leave Elisena alone... He'd have considered turning back, to stand beside her against Nímir's forces, but that wasn't possible. He reminded himself that this trip had been his idea. Without the sword, he was just about useless to her. Yet—

She can take care of herself. Thomas popped his head out of the saddlebag. *And I'll take care of you. Now let's get going.*

They'd been riding two hours, and weren't even at the Esdragon border yet. Mounted on a horse endowed with magical speed, Tristan should have done better than that. He'd let his mind wander too often and too long.

"Valadan? How fast can you get me to Kôvelir?"

I could raise the city in an hour, but you would hardly know your own name when you got there. If Valadan felt Tristan's urgency, he gave no sign of it. His stride was as regular as a dreamlessly sleeping man's heartbeat. *My full speed can be disquieting.*

"I'll risk it," Tristan said recklessly. "Let's go."

You lack the experience needed to make that judgment.

"But we've got to—" Tristan heard the heat in his words, noticed the dryness of his mouth. Such useless fretting did not move him one inch closer to Kôvelir, but it would quickly exhaust him, or worse. "I see. And the last time I ignored your advice, at Cathlein, I nearly got killed. All right. As fast as you think is safe." He swallowed. "But hurry!"

That's one of the things I like about you, Thomas purred. *Always so calm and reasonable, and never the least bit impatient.*

Vanished Hope

THERE WAS GOOD fishing to be had at the mouth of the Est, where river met sea and waters mingled. Plenty of boats put out from the Esdragon shore to tap the riches daily, and Tristan had little trouble buying himself a passage on one. He was lucky to be well ahead of the weather following him, or the boatman might have asked an even more outrageous price than he did for the trip across to Kôvelir.

Passage directly to the city would have meant a hefty dock fee, Tristan learned. He agreed to be dropped a little way outside the city instead. They were in midstream by the time the subject came up, and he'd have agreed to any suggestion put to him. Maybe the landfall would mean a shorter trip— one heartbeat shorter would have been enough. Running water and wizards did not mix, and if Tristan had needed any reminder of that fact, he got it the moment the fishing boat left the Esdragon shore.

The trip was a nightmare, though it took place in broad day, and was best forgotten. Tristan rode into the city in a daze, drowsy and fuzzy-headed. Sleep was over-tempting, and he unwisely let Thomas convince him to snatch a few moments' rest in a convenient doorway. The cat promised faithfully to wake him after only an hour, and Tristan *did* want to be fresh when he presented himself at the mages' Academy, as Thomas suggested solicitously. At least he'd like to be able to remember why he was there.

He'd agreed, and thus found himself dismounting before the rune-covered gate of the Academy at sun-fall, hours late, still groggy from sleep, with a kink in his back from the narrow doorway. To perfect the moment, a chilly rain had begun to fall.

It always seemed to be raining in Kôvelir. Tristan sneezed violently and shivered. He hadn't been able to get warm, no matter how he'd tried. A couple of his fingers were blistered from the spell remedies he'd attempted.

Great raindrops splashed the cobbles as he walked toward the gate. Thomas mewed plaintively from Valadan's saddle.

"No." Tristan answered testily. "If you'd done as you promised, we'd have been here before this started. If you were sleepy, too, you could have said so. And I'm getting just as wet as you are."

But you can take your clothes off to dry them. And I said I was sorry. Thomas burrowed despairingly back into the saddlebag.

Valadan flared his nostrils and blew noisily, then shook rainwater out of his ears. Under his hooves, a line of cobbles bore runes inlaid in silver, part of a circle of magic protecting this innermost of Kôvelir's nested circles. Tristan pulled at the bell. It was shaped like a bird, and set up a lusty chirping.

The noise kept up for a great while, then ceased. Tristan waited a moment more, pulling his cloak closer in a nearly useless attempt to keep rain from running down his neck. He rang the bell again and waited yet longer. He was beginning to suspect that unexpected visitors who lacked a knowledge of the lock-spells were far from welcome with the mages, when the small panel set beside the gate finally creaked open. A face appeared in the opening, frowning.

"Go around to the service entrance, can't you? You fellows have got to remember you're not allowed the use of this gate." The portal began to close before the man's lips had dropped the last word.

"Wait!" Tristan nearly thrust a hand in to stay the man. He thought better of it—he needed all his fingers for his magic,

after all. The urgency in his voice had some effect, though—
the man gave him a disgusted look.

"What are you here to deliver, anyway?" he asked exasperatedly.

"Myself," Tristan answered. "I'm here to see Master Cabal."

Tristan had supposed, on his one previous visit to the city,
that the porter he'd met then, one Howun, had been the most
discourteous spokesman the Academy could boast. He was
wrong. The present porter laughed in his face now.

"Master Cabal, is it? Get along with you and next time leave
your mad ideas in the alehouse where they were begotten."

Tristan stared desperately. He needed to see Cabal in particular, not solely because Cabal was the only mage in the
Academy whom he knew personally, but because Delmon was
Cabal's apprentice; if anyone knew where Crewzel and her
cards could be found, it would be her son. Without the boy,
he might be days locating her—wasted days.

"Please, I know he'll see me, if you'll just take him
word—"

"Master Cabal's not receiving visitors at present, certainly
not tradesmen who haven't the courtesy to attend on him during
business hours."

"He'll see me, I tell you." He had to hope that, anyway,
but Tristan couldn't imagine Cabal personally turning him away.
"Please, just take him my name: Tristan of Calandra."

The response the name produced was absolutely incredible,
not from the porter, who looked no more impressed than he
had previously, but from the bell by the door.

The silver bird lifted its wings, swelled the feathers at its
throat till they looked like a silver-furred ball attached to its
neck, and burst into full song. The notes rose and fell, echoed
each other, and were soft or strident by turns; they varied
endlessly yet repeated major themes—greeting, gladness, welcome.

The song was not unlike Minstrel's, which Tristan was used
to hearing, so he was not so much surprised by the song as by
the porter's reaction to it. The man's eyes were round as coins,
staring first at the bird, then at Tristan. His mouth worked.

Lest the song be mistaken for anything other than welcome,
the main gate flung itself back upon its hinges, almost with a

flourish. The porter made to snatch at its handle to drag it closed again, then checked himself. He was still struggling with his tongue.

"This is not possible... It would seem Master Cabal *does* wish to speak with you. Most irregular. I'll have to report—"

"Do what you like," Tristan said reasonably, "but I'm not waiting out here while you do it. And neither is my horse." He whistled to Valadan, who politely came closer and let Tristan take his bridle to lead him inside. The porter gave ground as if he'd never seen a horse before.

The portal closed softly behind them, leaving the corridor rather dim. Tristan sighed, fished out his crystal when he saw the man making no move to produce a torch, and lighted the stone. The porter jumped as the light bloomed around him. Apparently he hadn't considered that Tristan might be a wizard, too.

Maybe he thinks you're a master in disguise, Thomas suggested. *What was that all about with the door?*

Tristan shrugged. The man was motioning him nervously toward an archway, silently, as if afraid of giving offense with his words. Probably he was mentally reviewing what he'd already said to this suddenly mysterious and possibly dangerous stranger, weighing what punishment he must expect.

"If you'll wait here, sir?"

Tristan passed through the archway, looking about. The court was open at its center, and the rising water of a fountain contested with the falling rain. Tristan sneezed again. At least they weren't being rained on anymore, but he'd have appreciated a room with a fire.... Valadan pulled free of his hold and began to browse about, sampling potted herbs and doing a great deal of snorting until he found something he considered edible.

Thomas got busy too, fluffing and licking as he tried to dry his fur. He hissed and showed claws when Tristan tried to help out with a bit of dry cloth.

Tristan jerked his offending fingers back, startled.

You were rubbing the wrong way. Thomas began to lick his right forepaw furiously.

"So were you. I don't see what difference—"

"Master Cabal is not receiving visitors at present. Who are you to think of disturbing him?"

The voice came from the archway, which was no longer empty. Tristan straightened up and turned around. He recognized Howun at once. The light was poor, but Tristan's memory wasn't. By the look on his face, Howun remembered him too. Of all the people in Kôvelir to run into—

"*You?*"

Tristan nodded cordially.

"How dare you—"

Tristan's heart sank. It had been too long a day, and he simply wasn't up to this sort of unnecessary scene. He squared his shoulders and looked Howun in the eye.

"I've come to see Master Cabal, Howun."

"And were told he isn't receiving visitors. But you saw fit to force your way in here—" Howun's narrowed green eyes were set off nicely by the scarlet silk of his robes. If possible, those were even more ornate than the set he'd worn the first time Tristan had met him. Tristan's own homespun wool was clotted with wet road dust and stained with seawater. The contrast was acute.

Tristan choked back another sigh, set his jaw and decided to assert himself. If he was going to get to Cabal, he'd have to fight his way past Howun first, and the man had a lot of past insults to pay back.

"Well, Howun, I can show you Master Cabal's private rune— will that satisfy you that I know him? As to my forcing my way in here—the door was opened for me, I might assume by Master Cabal's orders. Now, I will wait upon Master Cabal's convenience gladly, but I've no intention of waiting on yours, in the street and in the rain." He advanced on Howun as he spoke, punctuating each sentence with a step. Tristan had long ago noticed that highhandedness in others woke a corresponding arrogance in himself, a fault he didn't attempt to curb now, as Howun didn't seem disposed to appreciate the value of a civil answer.

Behind Howun's shoulder, the porter was babbling out the story of the bell and of the gate that had opened of itself. Howun was scornful.

"Why should Cabal set such a spell? He'd hardly concern himself with a street beggar, even now—"

"Maybe he wants to talk to me," Tristan offered mildly. "Why don't you just ask him?"

Howun spun upon him with a snarl starting to twist his

lips, then arrested the movement. Someone else had joined the porter just on the other side of the arch. The man's voice was pitched so low that Tristan couldn't catch a word of the conversation; he doubted that Howun could, either. Apparently the man's mere appearance had commanded Howun's attention and his sudden silence.

The newcomer's robes offered an answer; they were black— barren of ornament, but still the highest rank a mage of Kôvelir could earn. He carried a staff, its tip glowing faintly as he looked from the porter to Howun.

Howun cleared his throat. "Master Bleyvr. I'm sorry you were disturbed by this. I was just sending this fellow away— or trying to. There was no need, really, for Alric to send for you too."

Bleyvr raised a brow. His face was that of a crow, or as near as a man could come to that, all nose and bright eyes; it might in some circumstances have been friendly or downright merry, but the expression on it now was forbidding. "It was Master Cabal who sent me to conduct this gentleman to him."

"He's *expected*?" Howun's eyes opened with shock.

"Obviously. Why else the spell upon the door and its mate in Cabal's chamber? He wished to know at once when Tristan arrived." Bleyvr lifted a hand to Tristan. "Come. Don't keep him waiting."

There was an apprentice waiting to take Valadan to the stables. Tristan let the horse go without a qualm. One of them, at least, should be warm and dry and at his ease. He followed after Bleyvr, as Howun stalked away.

The halls of the Academy were deserted. By the few noises Tristan heard, he supposed that most of the apprentices and journeymen were at their evening meal, taken communally. The division between the public rooms and the masters' private ones was obvious when it came. All sound died away, save for the two men's footfalls.

Tristan had been to Cabal's rooms once before and he knew they still had some little way to walk. He cleared his throat hesitantly.

"My thanks for the timely rescue, Master Bleyvr." The man had spoken not one word since they'd left Howun and he said nothing now. "I hadn't expected such opposition," Tristan added lamely. Bleyvr still made no reply.

When they'd reached Cabal's chamber door, though, he

turned and put a hand on Tristan's arm for emphasis.

"Understand, I am permitting this only because Cabal is so insistent upon seeing you. And frankly, this is the first thing in too long a while to engage any part of his interest. I presume your business is important, but you will be wise not to overstay. He tires quickly."

With that, before Tristan could speak the smallest question or betray his confusion by more than a blank look, Bleyvr's staff prodded the door open, and Tristan was thrust inside.

The room was Cabal's private workroom as well as his sleeping chamber. That much was made plain by its furnishings. There were books and curios everywhere. A table littered with bound volumes and glass retorts stood before the fire, which was well built up. The room was stifling hot, and the equipment was grimy with disuse.

On the far side of the fireplace was a great bed, its embroidered curtains only partly drawn back. Cabal lay in the center of the bed, propped up on a mound of pillows.

"Master Cabal? I—no one told me you were ill. I thought all the fuss was just because you were so busy—" Tristan crossed the room hastily, barely noting the small, rich rugs that jeweled the floor. He didn't know whether to feel foolish or anxious.

Cabal's face was alarming, though not from any expression the old man intentionally wore on it. The entire left side of it was drawn down, like a waxen statue half melted. The eye on that side was lusterless and looked blind. The room smelled of stale burned herbs. A bitter scent, Tristan thought, with rising anger that no one had thought to prepare him for this.

Cabal's words halted him at the foot of the bed. The old mage spoke softly, but clearly enough. The drooping corner of his mouth slurred his speech but little.

"Well, so you've finally come back. Took your own sweet time about it."

Tristan was not sure what answer he was meant to make. It might have helped if he'd known the question. Confused, he said nothing, and Cabal lifted his right hand slightly, to wave away concern. The gesture augmented the feeling, rather than the reverse that was intended. Firelight flickered across the old man, giving his face the only color it had.

"Ah. This is naught. Even wizards age and must suffer the consequences of that. Sit down now."

Tristan dragged a chair close to the bed, glad of the minor distraction of movement. Again Cabal beat him to speech.

"It gladdens my heart to see you again." The lopsided smile was nonetheless clear in its intent. "You were so full of doom that last time, I feared—"

It was impossible to guess that Cabal had once been nearly as tall as Tristan and broader of shoulder or that the powers at his command had been awesome even in a city of magic. The fires of that magic were dying down and the man shrank in upon himself like a coal in a cooling brazier. The change was beyond what mere age or sickness could have wrought. Tristan, watching, knew grief, and thought with some surprise that Blais' untimely end might not have been so tragic after all. There was worse ways to finish a life and a career. Feeble and fickle his own magic might be, inconvenient and distressing, but Tristan didn't think he'd relish the emptiness it would leave behind in him if it ever went from him utterly. Looked at so, it was amazing that Cabal was even still alive.

Tristan's face must have made his thoughts plain.

"You mustn't distress yourself," Cabal insisted. "My leech here tells me that I'm much recovered. And Bleyvr is the best herbalist in the city."

Tristan made some sort of soft, proper reply and then went on into small talk and presumably correct responses to whatever Cabal was saying. His thoughts needed a lot of rearranging and, therefore, most of his attention. He'd come prepared to tell Cabal the truth about Blais' quest and how it had finally been fulfilled. Cabal had been a student here with Blais and, besides being curious about an event long a mystery to him, he could have been of real help in the search for the sword.

Now there was no question of any such thing. If Cabal thought Tristan had abandoned his master's quest for the present, Tristan was content not to inform him otherwise. If the mage assumed that Tristan had come back to the city to further his magical studies, that was fine too. Tristan let himself be invited for a light supper and resolved that he'd simply talk to Delmon on his own and locate Crewzel the same way. Then he'd see what he'd see. That pinned all his hopes on her cards, but they were the reason he'd come to the city in the first place.

Bleyvr did not sup with them, but appeared at the door from time to time, sometimes bringing tea or medicines, often merely glancing at Cabal before disappearing again. Tristan supposed he was guilty of overstaying the little welcome the man had given him, but he saw no help for the situation. He kept an eye out for Delmon. The supper hour was surely over; the boy ought to be in attendance upon his master, or at least put in an appearance before going to bed. It was odd that he hadn't been around earlier.

The opportunity to slip a question about the boy into the conversation naturally came soon enough. Tristan propped Cabal on pillows, lighted fresh candles when he was bidden to, and fetched and poured from a wine flask Bleyvr had left. Any of those tasks should have belonged to an apprentice, though Tristan smiled when he asked, to show that he did not resent doing the services himself.

"What's happened to Delmon? He won't suspect you're breaching his contract by taking me in?"

Cabal's face furrowed with concern. "I truly wish I knew. He's not here. He's gone. Run off."

"Gone?" Tristan asked, horrified. "What, you mean back to his mother?" That would scotch a promising career—apprenticing to Cabal had certainly been the chance of a lifetime for Delmon and had promised to free him from Kôvelir's streets. It was a chance Tristan wouldn't have expected the boy to toss away.

Cabal shook his head. "I don't know for certain, but I doubt it. Just before I fell ill, the boy came to me asking to leave the Academy. It's against our rules, and he hadn't been here long enough to have regulations bent for him. He'd only been here for a few months. I was forced to refuse him, but I did ask if his mother needed him. He has no other family. I could think of no other reason for him to want to leave." Cabal swallowed a last sip of wine, to ease his throat. His hand wavered, so Tristan took the cup and set it back safely.

"Thank you. I couldn't let the boy go, but I thought perhaps I could offer the mother some aid, something beyond what he could have hoped to do. I asked if she were in need of him, and Delmon said he thought so, because she'd disappeared."

"Disappeared? How did he know? Did he say anything else?"

"Not a great deal. It wasn't a very plausible story. And frankly, a child raised in the streets like that—he had a good heart, but he dissembled as naturally as a man breathes. It turned out he'd been visiting his mother when he was supposed to be at private practice. He could slip out of the Academy easier than water through a sieve."

Cabal shut his eyes a moment, then continued. "One of those times, he couldn't find her, and he was worried. I forbade the boy to go, but I intended to make inquiries myself. Then this happened—" Cabal gestured vaguely at himself, as if his growing old had been a surprise to him, a matter he'd absent-mindedly overlooked. "I suppose Delmon must have thought no one else would help him, and I couldn't, of course. By the time I was able to notice that he wasn't there, he'd been gone for days."

Gone—and more urgently, Crewzel vanished as well! Tristan felt as if he'd just run head-on into a stone wall. Again he moved and spoke by reflex as Cabal and Bleyvr talked of setting a guest room aside for his use till his own could be got ready. Bleyvr agreed to make all the necessary arrangements, and someone's yawning apprentice was summoned to conduct Tristan to the room. Tristan hardly recalled bidding Cabal good night. He paced the tiled floor of the room nervously, unable even to attempt sleep. Thomas watched him from the bed.

Tristan was alarmed as well as disconcerted. Crewzel had a formidable personality; any harm which would dare befall her was apt to be of a most serious nature. And something *had* happened. Nothing could have made Crewzel abandon her son willingly. Nothing, unless . . . Images of ice rose unbidden. But what could Nímir want with Crewzel?

The room was chill, as if the fire in the grate had not been lighted long enough to warm more than the air. The walls and floor still breathed cold, despite the hangings and rugs that decked the room. Tristan had an instant's vision of himself back in Darkenkeep. His every step might tend in that direction, wherever he thought he was really going. Such was Nímir's subtlest and most terrible power, and Tristan was keenly aware of his awesome vulnerability then, a helplessness that had nothing at all to do with ambushes by Galan or Reynaud. Their overtures seemed harmless by contrast with the vague shadow that he sensed looming over him.

If he turned to look at it, of course, it would have vanished, like Crewzel. *Night fears*, Tristan insisted sternly to himself, and childish ones at that; but he jumped in alarm at the sound of coals tumbling over in the fire. He was still unsettled from his journey, no doubt, and the aftereffects of crossing the Est, the passage over running water. And then there was the unexpected factor of Cabal's illness, which altered all his careful plans.

He was probably safer in Kôvelir, amongst the mages, than anywhere else in the known world, Tristan reminded himself—assuming his fears had any basis at all. Tristan thought of the things Elisena had said about Nímir not knowing precisely what he was looking for. His hunted feeling persisted and deepened. He remembered the day he'd come home to find Blais gone forever, the way the cottage had felt then. There had been danger in the very air.

Why should Crewzel vanish just when he was on his way to consult with her and those strange cards? Was there a connection?

Still, wasn't he rather conceited to think Nímir would personally trouble with him at all? Surely the most he'd need to face would be underlings; their master would never bother . . .

Thomas regarded him from the bed, stretching himself lazily upon the fox-fur coverlet.

Your humility's astounding. Considering the harm you've done him by accident alone—

Tristan turned away. There was a danger in seeing Nímir's hand everywhere, he supposed. The chronicles and prophecies could lead to such conclusions easily and thence to despair and hopelessness. It had happened to mages before, by some accounts, and even led to suicides. Better maybe not to dwell on Nímir's all-powerful aspects, but leave oneself the freedom and will to act.

That's fine. Very sensible. Of course you see his hand nowhere, and that's a worse danger. You're so trusting.

"We're safe *here*, Thomas." Tristan swept a hand out to indicate the room, plain but comfortable; the door and the small window were both securely closed with bolts and spells.

Oh. Then you're wearing a path on that rug because you need the exercise. I see.

And if his fondest hopes were true, Tristan admitted, then why had he not felt safe telling Cabal about his business in the city? It wasn't courtesy or misliking to burden an old, sick man. That hadn't held him back. It had been his way of protecting someone who could no longer protect himself from a very real danger.

You know, don't you? Why he was expecting you, why he was so glad to see you and not surprised at all? And all that about a guest room tonight, till a room can be got ready?

Tristan looked crossly at the cat. "Don't play games, Thomas."

My memory's better than yours, it seems, though that doesn't surprise me. Or are you still mixed up from crossing the river? The last time you were here, Cabal wanted you to stay, to study with him. You couldn't, so you told him you'd come back when you could. And now you're back. Do you see yet?

"See what?"

You just got yourself apprenticed again.

Toils and Tribulations

NEXT MORNING, WELL scrubbed and nearly rested—he had finally slept toward dawn—Tristan presented himself at Cabal's door. Bleyvr met him and offered a breakfast which Tristan declined. There had been oatcakes and some excellent dates left outside his door, and Tristan had disposed of them before coming to bid Cabal good morning.

Bleyvr nodded his head to indicate the inner bedchamber, volunteering that Cabal was undergoing a therapeutic massage. It would be some little while before he would be available. Tristan would not mind waiting?

Bleyvr's manner was far more cordial than on the previous evening. Tristan supposed that he must somehow have passed some unspoken test, but he didn't know whether to be glad of it or not. If it meant that Thomas was right, he foresaw no end of problems. He wished that learning of Cabal's illness and Delmon's disappearance hadn't rattled him so—he needed to remember exactly what Cabal had talked about, and Tristan found that he couldn't. His perceptions of the evening were badly skewed. Only a few events stood out with anything like clarity.

"Master Bleyvr, I'm not really sure I ought to be here—"

"Ah, but he's asked for you already." Bleyvr was using herbed steam to weave bracelets and collars for the treatment of joint-evil. His nimble fingers caught the mist as it rose from the boiling pot, twisted and twined, and cast spells with great skill. "He talked of you a great deal, after you'd retired last night."

That would account for Bleyvr's friendliness, then, Tristan supposed. He watched the pungent steam rising for a while, noting the little magicked coils of it already lying in the coffer at Bleyvr's elbow.

"You certainly seem to do him good—I've felt for the last week that Cabal needed to talk with someone other than myself, but he's sent every other visitor away. I wonder if you might convince him to show you some points of fingerplay? He needs to do the exercises; it will help strengthen his bad hand. But he resists me when I suggest it. He's never been a man to accept orders gracefully, so we must perforce outwit him."

Tristan's misgivings were deepening by the moment. He'd only come to tell Cabal of his intention to spend the day searching the city for Delmon. It looked as if Cabal and Bleyvr might have other plans for him. . . .

Told you so. Thomas was examining a bag of herbs by the skirts of Bleyvr's robe, hoping it might be catnip. He had not been as pleased as Tristan to breakfast upon dates, and felt his sufferings deserved compensation.

"It hurt Cabal greatly, to learn his apprentice had run off that way. After all he'd done for the boy, a little loyalty was not unreasonably expected. With his sickness, he cannot get about, though he's recovered enough to need some diversion, some part of a normal life to return to—but he has no one here to instruct. As his physician, I would prescribe another apprentice—Cabal needs one and even he knows it. He also knows he can't expect to live long enough to begin again, even if he had the heart to. He can't hope to finish a child up to journeyman. You, though—you're half-made already, you he can hope to make a difference to, and your being here will help him as well. I mistrusted you at first, Tristan, but I have seen my error and ask your pardon for it. I'm glad you chose to come back."

Tristan began to wonder if he might choke on the guilt rising up in him. Why couldn't he have seen this coming last night, hours ago when there was still a hope of straightening the mess out?

"Did you come here expressly to study with him, this time?" Bleyvr asked casually, adding another pinch of herbs to the boiling water and nudging Thomas gently away from his feet.

"It . . . wasn't my original intention, my lord. I'm glad you think I can help him, but I don't want to disappoint Cabal. I won't be able to stay here more than a few days. It would be better to tell him—"

Bleyvr raised a brow. "It would be better to let the future care for itself. There are few things certain in this life; it doesn't do to assume too much too soon. Come. Cabal will be ready to see you by now."

Try as he might, Tristan couldn't free himself from the chains of Cabal's expectations and Bleyvr's assumptions. Cabal had it firmly in mind that he'd come back to complete his studies; telling him otherwise seemed both needlessly cruel and increasingly impossible. The only safe course Tristan could chart was to go along with the scheme as best he could.

Tristan resigned himself to hoping that he could open the subject more reasonably in a few days, when Cabal should be stronger. Even one night had made an obvious change in the mage. Surely a few days would serve even better. In the meantime, he'd continue his quest as best he could—in the Library by day, in Kôvelir's streets by night. There were certain advantages—Kôvelir's fabulous mages' Library could well lead him straight to the sword.

By the end of the first week, he knew it wasn't going to work.

Even his worst fits of pessimism had not prepared him for the magnitude of the disaster. He was, after all—at least on his good days—fairly confident about his magic. Tristan knew he was patient and painstaking. And he had a good grounding in all the basic magics. Blais had seen to that.

The program Cabal had set out for him, though, was anything but light or basic, and Tristan had committed a grave tactical error in agreeing to it. The work was exacting and required serious attention that Tristan couldn't give it. He studied all day with Cabal; then at night, when he was presumed to be polishing what he'd learned, he was instead searching the streets for Crewzel.

Cabal set him tasks and problems and expected to see results. Tristan spent most of his night hours honing his memories of Crewzel and her favored haunts. She had been wont to work all night and sleep the days away, so he never slipped back into the Academy much before dawn. He got precious little sleep, and his magic suffered doubly from his exhaustion and the lack of the stringent practice it required. However, the magic's suffering was as nothing when contrasted with Tristan's own.

He was scorched and singed from various candle-illusions. His fingers were chapped from waterwork and blistered from continuous practice with the cup-and-ball trick. Sorcerous juggling had given him one badly bruised toe. When the carpet he'd been flying had rudely split, he'd bruised another sensitive portion of his anatomy even more severely. He kept tripping over the hem of the full-skirted robe custom forced him to wear, and that made him appear quite graceless, besides causing a lot of potions to be spilled.

He'd been stuck halfway through a shape-shifting for a good hour. His head ached continually from the eyestrain he got poring over crabbed runic handwriting in bad light, and on one of his nighttime rambles, he'd caught cold.

Well, it served him right for trying to cram two full-time occupations into one set of days. He could study or he could find Crewzel and the sword, but not both. It was getting harder for him to decide which he ought to do. Tristan daily felt more and more trapped and he was too groggy to see a way out of his situation, if there was one.

The lesson of the day was mirror reversal—useful, Cabal had said, for checking one's fingerplay, a skill Tristan could profit from. Tristan's skepticism did not alter the fact that he was going to have to demonstrate the spell to Cabal in less than an hour.

He'd set up the mirrors, aligned them with finicky precision, worked out all the charms, and said nearly the last incantation. Maybe *this* time—

Thomas slipped into the room through the barely cracked door, jarring it open so that it creaked loudly as he passed through. Tristan started at the sound, lost his careful concentration, and felt his control of the mirror slipping. He tried to get it back and made the mistake of glancing at the mirror as he did so.

The room seemed to be dissolving, dividing in two, turning itself inside-out. Tristan felt the sharp stab of a headache behind his eyes and he flung a hand over his face to shut out the room, because it seemed that its walls were wavering, as well as their reflections within the mirror. He stumbled back to sit on the bed and almost missed it. His fingers were terribly cramped, and the muscles in his arms were quivering and jumping clear up to his shoulders.

The bed bounced lightly as Thomas leaped up onto it. Tristan bit back a groan, let his hand drop, and opened his eyes. Thomas rubbed against his fingers.

Any luck?

Tristan took a deep breath and forced the room to steady the rest of the way. "If I could do that to someone other than myself, I'd think it was marvelous. What about you?"

There are houseboats anchored in one of the bigger canals.

"Houseboats?"

Like barges, only people live on them.

"Live on them? Out on the water?" Tristan shivered reflexively. "Why would anyone want to?"

Presumably because the rent's low. It's the only part of the city the mages don't tax, because there's nothing a wizard can do with running water. Anyway, it occurred to me that if someone had taken Crewzel there, there's no magic could find her. I went a-looking today.

"And?"

Nothing. Not a sign. They like cats there, though. The waterfront's a fine place for a cat. Pity I see so few of 'em, with you.

"How I do crave a pipe of good tobacco! But Bleyvr is set against it, so there's no hope for it. I think he's secretly delighted at this chance to wean me from my pipe."

Bleyvr caught both his name's mention and the speech, looked up, and smiled. It did wonders for his face, Tristan thought.

"That's the thanks I get for letting you have the perry wine— now you grieve for your pipe. 'One exception leads to excesses,' as the maxim goes."

"Oh. Poor Bleyvr's taken offense, Tristan."

"Perhaps he simply doesn't like smoke. I saw a simulacrum in the city today that he'd appreciate—the smoke circled back into the pipe after it left the mouth, so one pipe of tobacco would last a week."

"In the city today? I understood that you were doing mirror-work—the formulae we discuss yestereven. Your practice should have brought you to the question which I was going to answer with your lesson tonight."

Uh-oh. A nasty slip, one Tristan hadn't intended. The perry wine wasn't good for his discretion. "I *have* practiced, Master. I was just in the city for a few hours." For once, that was true. He'd come back early.

"'The practice of illusion requires more than the illusion of practice.' I know I haven't forbidden you the city, Tristan, but you'd do well to remember that saying. Your work is here. What were you doing in the city?"

As a Master, Cabal had the right to ask that, and Tristan had the duty of answering.

"Sir, I've been trying to find Delmon. I know the places he used to live in with his mother. I thought he might have gone back to one of them."

"Since you're alone here, I assume that he hadn't?"

Tristan shifted uneasily in his seat. "No, my lord. I didn't find him."

"No, nor will you. A search has already been made. There's just no trace of him."

"I'll try again, when I have a free hour. There are other things I want to try—"

"Forget about the boy and attend to your studies!" Cabal snapped. It seemed Bleyvr was right, the pain of the desertion went deep. The old man seemed to make an effort to soften his voice before he spoke again. "I appreciate the trouble you've taken to find him for me, Tristan, but it's been time wasted. I can't condone more of that, even if you don't agree with me on the matter."

Tristan took the admonition to heart, but he didn't abide by it. He was back in the streets that very night, once Cabal was safely abed.

He wandered through the craftsmen's circle, emptied now by nightfall, save for the folk that lived there. By day, the place was jammed with armorers, fullers and dyers, silkweavers, potters, glassblowers, silversmiths, and enamellers. Farther on, past the wine merchants, his nose informed Tristan that he'd reached the butcher's quarter, close to the poulterer's. Beyond lay the markets, where by day there were colorful fragrant hills of raisins and peas, dates and barley, baskets of almonds and apricots, and mountains of wheat, lentils, and figs.

He had not, save for one brief stroll very early on in his search, troubled with the section where the goldsmiths worked near the houses of the wealthier merchants. There was small reason to think he'd find Crewzel there—or Delmon for that matter. No, Crewzel had always worked the torchlit squares of the Second Circle, that section too close to the stockyards and warehouses of the outer circle for better folk to dwell or the Watch to care much what went on there. Rich clients Crewzel had seemed to have, but they'd always come to her in secrecy. Small chance any one of them could tell Tristan anything about her, even if he'd found by chance the right person to inquire of.

Tristan paused, listening to a young boy play upon a flute of antelope bone. The tune was unbearably sad, as was the glimpse of the blind white eyes between the child's lashes. He moved on.

Is this supposed to be a systematic search? I mean, are you risking disobeying Cabal because you have some sort of plan?

Tristan took no offense. Thomas was quite right. Aimlessly wandering the streets, hoping to catch a glimpse of Crewzel, was no fit way to proceed, but it was what he was reduced to. He knew all too well that a month or a year of such searching might bring him no nearer to her than he was now; and even if he found her, there was still no guarantee she'd lead him to the sword. No, he'd have to try something else. Besides, his feet were aching, and the charms he'd tried had only made his blisters worse.

Therefore, the next day he did not slip out of the Academy the minute Cabal released him to practice, but instead went to the Library and spent many hours bent studiously over books and scrolls. No one bothered him, or noticed that every volume he chose or searched out pertained not to magical theory, but to swords.

Telekinetics was one branch of the Arts Magical that Tristan had never ventured out upon. He wasn't certain he was ready for it even yet and thought Cabal might have given him the lesson as a punishment—or a warning. Levitation needed very solid magical groundwork; maybe, Tristan thought, he was meant to see how wobbly his own was, so that the experience might spur him on to greater diligence.

The three eggs revolved slowly in the air, as if almost frozen there while being tossed by an invisible juggler. Tristan watched them gravely, trying to fine-tune his control by turning each in a different direction, moving them this way and that. There was a brass bowl of fruit upon the table from which the eggs had just risen. Tristan lifted the fruits one by one and thought that he might just be able to get the bowl up too. His fingers wove carefully for a heartbeat or two, then made a graceful drawing gesture as Tristan rotated his wrists to bring his hands palms up.

His wrists ached as if he were actually holding something heavy. Tristan saw that the table had lifted a couple of inches, following the bowl. Did he dare try for it? Tristan decided he ought to, since he wasn't sure how to set the thing down without dropping everything else, too.

He was surprised at the ease with which the table rose, once he'd amended the spell to include it. It seemed as light as a bag of feathers. He hadn't expected such mastery of a new spell so quickly. Why, with any luck he'd be able to levitate *himself* by day's end, and that should properly impress Cabal. Maybe even earn him a little respite.

Enjoying himself, Tristan began to move his floating objects about once more, setting a pomegranate into orbit around the still revolving eggs. He recognized tension in his shoulders and made himself relax, drawing what might almost pass for an easy breath. His magic was actually working the way it ought to. It had been so long since that had happened, and it felt so good. . . .

Without warning, vertigo took him, blurring his sight, making his ears ring. It was too much. The mental legerdemain was exhausting, impossible to maintain if Tristan so much as thought about what he was doing. He'd better get rid of something, to lighten the load on his concentration before he strained something or before the whole mess fell apart.

It was already going, the table falling fastest—and going to make a terrible noise when it hit! Tristan didn't know who had the rooms on either side of his student's cell, but he did know that neither room was empty. Someone could easily hear his crashing humiliation, and come a-running. He could bear that even less than his spell's failure.

All that flashed through Tristan's mind as he jumped for the table, his fingers no longer spell-casting but merely snatching. It wasn't that big a table. He could catch it.

His spell might be breaking up, but Tristan was by no means free of its web. The movement of his hands had no effect on the table's rapid rate of descent, but the thing began to turn over as it fell, in response to Tristan's changed position, moving as a magnet will when repelled by another magnet.

Tristan was too close to note that intriguing aspect of the disaster until there was no longer time for him to jump clear. The table's edge fetched him a sharp blow on the head as it went by, and Tristan reached the floor at the same moment the table finally did, partially under it.

The eggs splatted down around him, one by one.

Did you do all this by yourself, or did someone break in here and ransack the room while I was out?

"Oh, very funny!" Tristan dabbed gingerly at the left side of his head with a wet rag. He had a largish lump just above his ear and he still felt sick to his stomach.

What happened, then? Were you still working on that levitation-spell? Thomas sniffed delicately at a bit of dried egg.

"Yes." Tristan dipped the rag back into the basin of water, groaning as the small movement involved made the room seem to spin.

What were you lifting?

"The table."

Mmmm. I wouldn't have said it was that heavy. Oh. Dropped it on your head, did you?

"Leave me alone, Thomas."

Obviously, that's ill-advised. Look at the trouble you get into. Are you really hurt, or just grumpy?

Tristan flung the balled-up rag at the cat. "Go *away!*"

Tchh. I can see that must be pretty painful.

Tristan felt his anger ebbing away. Sustaining it just plain hurt too much. Despair was easier on his aching head.

"It was just so stupid, Thomas. I *had* it! I swear I did. It felt so right, and that stuff went up as easy as could be—and then it just let go. I couldn't hold onto the spell."

*You probably shouldn't have tried to. That's why you got
your head smacked. You look terrible. I think I could get Bleyvr
to follow me back here, if you think—*

"No! I don't want anyone else to know about this." Trying
to stop Thomas, Tristan got halfway to his feet. Staggering for
balance, he managed to reach the edge of the bed, and collapsed
across it. Thomas sprang up beside him, licking at his cheek.

*I'll get Blais' salve for you, at least. And once that's on,
try to sleep. You were up all night conning that spell. No wonder
your concentration's bad.*

"I can't sleep. It's nearly sunfall. Cabal will expect me to
show him this spell right after dinner, and I've got to get this
mess cleared up first. Not that I'm sure I could do this again
if I *could* concentrate on it." Tristan shut his eyes tightly for
a moment and then sat up. "It's all beside the point. None of
this is getting me any closer to Crewzel or even Delmon."

At least you're getting a good education.

Tristan sighed. "Wrong again. I'm not. I'm just picking up
enough to fool Cabal, a little flash and polish that doesn't even
go skin-deep. There's no time for anything more, if I'm going
to find Crewzel. And even this little doesn't work half the
time." Tristan rubbed his head again and winced.

Sure you don't want Bleyvr?

"No. I mean yes—not unless he knows where Crewzel is.
Or the sword. I'm not hurt, Thomas, just tired out and sick of
all this. Nothing works anymore—"

Tristan made a sweeping gesture with his left hand as he
spoke, and a fallen candlestick righted itself as if it had been
attached to his fingers with a string. The candle dropped back
neatly into the socket. Tristan stared a moment in astonishment,
then moaned and fell back onto the bed again. By the time
Thomas finished locating Blais' salve, Tristan was fast asleep.
The cat took the bed-fur in his teeth, and his tuggings as he
settled it around Tristan did not disturb his master in the slightest.

Tristan supposed he was nothing if not resilient. The last
thing in the world that he felt like doing was confronting Cabal;
but when he woke, he got up at once, washed and salved his
face, and did what he could to disguise the edges of the bruise
that had strayed into easy view. He brushed dust and lint off
of his clothes, happy that at least his hands weren't shaking.

Though he'd missed two meals by then, he wasn't hungry, but he wished he might have slept longer. Lack of sleep tended to make his hands twitch—not helpful to a wizard.

Thomas watched concernedly from the fireside, as Tristan carefully righted the table in the conventional way.

You'd be well advised not to lift anything heavy tonight, he said.

"It wasn't the weight, Thomas. I just lost my hold."

I meant in case you got under it again. A dropped egg's messy, but at least it won't knock you out.

"Oh."

No offense, but you're not exactly exuding confidence.

Tristan feigned astonishment. "I'm not?"

If you could get him started playing chess, Cabal might not want to see what you learned today.

Tristan ruffled Thomas' fur. "I don't play chess that well, Thomas."

He might have been tempted to try the stratagem anyway, but Cabal didn't offer him a game. Tristan thought at first that Cabal might be angry because he was late—in truth, he *was*, by over an hour—but he thought he saw something else in Cabal's face. Bleyvr's expression held a hint of watchfulness, a concern that had been ebbing over the previous days. Apparently Cabal had had a bad day. And nights were generally worse for an invalid.

Cabal ignored Tristan's attempt at conversation, curtly signing him to begin his lesson. Tristan stepped slowly to the center of the room, thankful that for once the chamber wasn't all that well lighted. Blais' ointment had done a fair job on his head; that and sleep had left him feeling a little better. There was an ache at the base of his skull, though, that was pure tension, and he knew that he was very pale.

Cabal offered him no direction, so Tristan chose to warm up by snuffing and lighting the candles in the pentagram holder on the table behind him. He wondered if Cabal noted the skill it took to work sorcery on objects out of the wizard's line of sight. He got no comments, no praise or criticism, either. He'd have to do without guidelines, then. Tristan shrugged mentally, not daring to do so physically.

The candles were nothing, mere trifles. The perilous levitation was still to come. Tristan swallowed hard. He couldn't collect his thoughts—there was a very real possibility that his mind would go blank of the spell the moment he was called upon to use it.

Tristan lighted the last candle once again. The room was still dim and oppressively hot as well, for the brazier had been too lavishly stoked. His headache got worse, and he could feel sweat trickling down between his shoulder blades. It was no use his telling himself how well and easily the levitation-spell had worked before. Tristan remembered the spell's conclusion just as clearly, and the whole formula was now firmly linked with pain in his mind. Even if he refused to let himself dwell on such thoughts, those memories were enough to ensure failure.

Time was dragging by; he had to get on with the business at hand. There was a brass bowl on the table by the brazier. Tristan decided to direct his efforts at it. He flexed his fingers so nervously that one of his knuckles popped loudly. Cursing that under his breath, Tristan made the magical cat's cradle of his hands and began to work through the fingerplay. He was a beat behind on the incantation and had to correct himself.

It did no good. The bowl did not lift by so much as an inch, but sat obstinately, reflecting the candleflames—unwaveringly reflecting them. Tristan couldn't even make the bowl tremble. He tried every variation he knew or could extrapolate of the spell, and none of them had any greater effect. He began to wonder if the bowl might be nailed to the table.

He worked so hard that he forgot about Cabal, about Bleyvr, and about Thomas watching from under the bed. He was utterly alone with the magic, striving with it, struggling, and it might have been made of quicksilver for all the grip he could get on it. The room was as black as night, as if all the candles had gone out when he switched his attention to another magic than theirs. The brass bowl gleamed from far away, tiny as if it had been at the end of a tunnel. It was the only light Tristan could see—with his concentration so finely directed, there was no reason he shouldn't be able to lift the bowl. He should have been able to melt it, had he chosen to, or unmake it utterly.

The room lurched, twisted around him, and there was no light at all for a moment. Tristan gasped for breath, waiting for the room to come back. It did so, slowly. There was no way for him to tell how much time had passed.

The bowl was still on the table.

"Tristan, this is most discouraging."

Huh. Fat lot he knows about it. Thomas' eyes gleamed.

"I wonder what explanation you're going to offer me? It's an advanced spell, but you had ample time to prepare—if you chose to use your time for magic."

Tristan opened his lips. They felt stiff, as if he'd bitten them till they bled, and he still couldn't seem to draw a breath that would quiet his lungs. The hot air was thick with herbs and the fumes of the wine Bleyvr had poured and was mulling over the brazier. Whatever their intended value, they were doing him no good. Tristan wanted very badly to sit down but he dared not unless he was invited to—it would show a lack of respect for Cabal, which he certainly didn't wish. He wondered what it would signify to Cabal if he fainted, which he felt like doing.

"Can it be that, having been your own master for so long, you find yourself unwilling to submit to another?"

Tristan's head jerked up. "My lord, no! It's just that I—"

"I'm afraid your protests only give weight to my theory, Tristan. I've heard too many excuses."

Tristan looked at Cabal, shocked.

"My lord, that's not fair. I came to *you*—"

"And can you say that you have applied yourself to the studies I've given you with the total dedication they require? You may have half blinded yourself to that truth, Tristan, but I think you're too honest to lie to me. You have let yourself be divided and distracted, and your work shows it. All too well."

Tristan shivered mentally under the attack, because there was much truth in what Cabal said. It *had* been a long time since he'd had a master to answer to. Maybe that showed more than he'd thought. Cabal's accusations might be unfair, since he had no access to salient facts that Tristan had refused to give him, but none of them were completely untrue. Tristan had never intended any arrogance, but he suddenly saw that his behavior might well be so construed. He looked down at the floor, contrite.

"What do you suggest, then, my lord?"

"A revision of your attitude is certainly in order. And do not slight the groundwork I have been trying to instill in you. You may be far ahead of others your age in some things, but

you are far behind in as many more. Whether you can catch
up is up to you. Keep your mind to your work. And get some
sleep. You look half dead for lack of it."

"Yes, my lord."

Tristan was surprised when Bleyvr offered him a cup of the
hot wine, before giving one to Cabal. He took it with wordless
gratitude, but found he could barely swallow. There was a
lump in the way, as if a fist had somehow lodged in his throat.
He hoped he wasn't sickening with something that might keep
him bedridden, unable to continue his search. The cold had
been bad enough. He coaxed a sip down, eventually, and looked
up to find Cabal watching him.

"Tristan, why do I feel that nothing I've just told you has
made any lasting impression?"

The winecup slid free of Tristan's slack fingers and slipped
splashing to the floor at his feet. There was nothing he could
say. He couldn't voice a denial, not with Cabal seeming to
suck his very soul out through his eyes. How the man could
know of his secret intransigence—know that, yet not the true
reason for it—

A voice interceded softly. "Cabal, it grows late."

"Aye, late indeed, Bleyvr!" There was more heat in Cabal's
voice than the comment warranted. "Mayhap too late. I was a
fool to think otherwise, it seems. Tristan, be so good as to take
yourself out of my sight for a while."

The look Bleyvr gave Tristan was part sympathy, part plea.
He doesn't mean that the way it sounds, it said. *His anger's
directed at himself, because deep down he thinks the failure's
his.* Tristan, however, saw nothing of the look. He scarcely
saw anything, as he turned and stumbled from the room.

Thomas tried to restate Bleyvr's plea, from his own understanding of the situation.

He's old, and he's sick.

"I know that, Thomas."

*Then don't take what he said so to heart. He doesn't un-
derstand your situation, and half the things he railed at you
about frustrate him as much as they do you. How much magic
have you seen Cabal work, since we came here? You know
how you feel—how much of that must he be feeling too?*

"I know that also. He's angrier at himself, for being sick,
than he is at me. It still hurts." A tear slid down his nose,

hidden by shadows, Tristan hoped. He felt sick or mortally wounded, his whole life gone out of his control, ashes all around him.

He was furious with Cabal for tricking him into this, angrier still at himself for letting it happen. He'd wasted precious time and hadn't even a little magical skill to show for the days and nights of toil—nothing but a nasty headache and a rawness in his throat to match the sickness in his belly. He wondered if he'd ever manage to cast a spell straight again—or even no more crookedly than he usually did—or if the scars of this night would haunt and maim him for the rest of his life.

No, he *hadn't* been applying himself to the magic, not till this last day, this terrible night. He'd never intended to, because he'd assumed that he'd find Crewzel before he reached this pass. He'd never seriously expected to master any major skills, proceeding in such a halfhearted fashion. Why then was he so disappointed when things turned out exactly as he'd thought they would?

Back in his room, Tristan picked up his cloak and brushed ineffectually at an old stain near its hem. He sighed, gave up the job without essaying a spell, and fastened the garment around his neck.

You're not going out? Now?

"One last time. I don't expect to find Crewzel, but I can't stay here thinking. I've got to get out."

It's late.

"You don't have to tag along."

Shape you're in, how would I dare otherwise? Have you given up sleep as a penance, or what?

"We're going home tomorrow. That should cheer you up. Just as soon as I talk to Cabal—if he'll see me."

White-Frost

TRISTAN WALKED PAST the beggar child and saw she was selling—or attempting to sell—glowworms to light late travelers home. It was nearly dawn. Trade, far from being brisk, was nearly nonexistent, and the girl's thin voice had long since taken on a note of despair. Soon she'd have not even the hope of a customer to warm her.

Tristan found that her pitiful crying of her wares seemed to echo in his ears for an absurdly long time. Suppose Delmon had become one such as that child—a child alone in this vast, hard city, where life was rough enough for an adult? Tristan almost went back and had to remind himself sternly that there was nothing he could do for the girl, even as a surrogate for Delmon.

He couldn't even manage to take care of himself, and she'd probably just be frightened of him and run off. Tristan didn't think he could bear that last humiliation atop all else. His discouragement was such that when he slipped and turned an ankle painfully, he barely marked the incident, but just limped on, trying to be more careful of the wet cobbles. Thomas wasn't with him to lend his nightsight. The cat had long since deserted him in search of more interesting company.

Cabal's words kept ringing through Tristan's head, harsher each time than when he'd first heard them. A few more hours, and he'd have to face more such words, fresh ones, when he told Cabal that he was quitting, going home. Tristan groaned at that, though the pain in his foot had not moved him to an outcry.

He hated to seem even more inept than he was. The course he'd chosen to follow had made that inevitable, but it still shamed Tristan, for he thought it made Blais appear to have been a poor master indeed, able to instill not a scrap of discipline in his apprentice. And Blais had had enough to contend with, without that charge as well. Tristan knew firsthand what it was like to struggle along with a quest you could admit to no one; not only was it painful not to get the least bit of help, but the loneliness of having no one to talk to freely was a heavy thing. And Tristan could imagine what he'd been like for Blais to have as an apprentice. That was an even heavier weight.

Could he, Tristan wondered, have been somehow hoping that Cabal would find means to cure his magical disabilities, even without his own aid? Was that a secret motive behind this quest to the city, one he'd never admitted even in the most hidden depths of his longing? Was that where this pain welled from, that old wound of frustration reopened by hope?

He felt tears on his face again, squeezed out of him by injustice. Often he'd longed to take Cabal into his confidence. He could have begged the man's not inconsiderable aid, besides gathering an understanding which would have been a balm more soothing than Blais' heart-made salve. But always the promised time had been a day away, a day after which Cabal should have been stronger, better able to tolerate the shock of the news. That day, of course, that existed outside of all calendars, for it had never arrived.

The sunward sky was pink, but night still held sway in Kôvelir, particularly indoors, away from the open sky. Tristan found his room empty—Thomas wasn't back yet. Having made sure of that, Tristan blew out the taper he'd lighted. He didn't want to see the room or to have any of the magical paraphernalia reminding him of what was past. He doused the light, and lay down on the bed to wait for morning. Despite his contrary intentions, he slept.

The fire banked in the grate still shed warmth into the room, but touches of cold pricked Tristan often. He snuggled underneath the bed-fur, but the chill still found him and tangled with his dreams.

He dreamed of Darkenkeep, though he strove mightily not to do so. Tristan found himself walking its mazy ice corridors again in search of something, as he had once searched there for Allaire. He was wading through bones—at least six thousand-and-four sets, he remembered crazily, and that was only counting the bones of the wizards, not those of the heroes and the would-be thieves.

In the dream, the object of his search seemed always just out of his sight, around the next bend or behind an ice pillar. He moved toward it gladly, then seemed to lose all understanding of what it was he was looking for. That was common enough in dreams—Tristan knew that even in his sleep. One sometimes skirted just on the outside of the desired object without ever quite being able to see it. He'd often dreamed of books in that way, of volumes full of wondrous things, only to have the pages overflowing with secrets go blank as he began to wake or looked too closely at them in the dream. But here the thing was out of reach of his mind as well as his fingers.

He kept trying to master the dream, which meant that he wasn't very deeply asleep, for he was confident that such a thing was possible as well as desirable. Darkenkeep's cold stung his face, but Tristan kept pressing on, toward something—it might even be the sword, he thought with a thrill. He was almost there. . . .

Tristan woke up with a shiver, to find that morning had come and he seemed to have been transported to fairyland overnight. His blankets and furs were covered with a fine dusting of frost and ice crystals. So was the rest of the room.

The carvings on the bed and the chairbacks were delicately highlighted with frost. The few books he'd brought to the room had the carved-out titles on their spines further picked out in white. The sheepskin before the fireplace was crusted on the ends of its fur, and bold feathers of frost crept up the brass andirons. The fire must have gone out very early, for what was left unburned of the logs was frosted as well, atop a layer of ashes.

Tristan's eyes widened. He stared at his cloak, hanging on a peg by the door, embroidered now with what looked to be a forest of ferns or perhaps the work of a very deranged spider.

Hoarfrost? *Indoors?* With the windows closed?

The early sun made diamonds of the floor, but did nothing to melt the encrustation. That shouldn't be.

Somehow, Tristan didn't much like the idea of touching any of those crystals with his bare feet or fingers. Thomas agreed wholeheartedly. Snow-crystals that didn't melt at the touch of the sun might be capable of even weirder things.

What were you dreaming last night when I returned? You were tossing around so, I'm surprised you're not black all over, but I didn't know you were working magic too.

"I can barely work spells awake. How could I asleep?" Tristan kept his voice low. "All I remember is that I was dreaming." His breath was freezing in front of his lips.

Tristan bethought himself of his stones, finally, and was very glad to see that he'd left them and their carven carrying-box beside the candle on his nightstand, almost within arm's reach. Drips ran down the sides of the candle—ice, not wax.

With a great deal of care—and a crumb of the levitation-spell he wasn't aware of using—Tristan was able to ease the box closer and flip its lid open. His firestone lay on top, and the other contents of the box were free of frost, though he thought he saw a few minute crystals beginning to take hold after he'd lifted the firestone out. The tip of his nose felt frozen as well.

Tristan put the stone on his palm and extended his hand into the sunlight. The light was waning—either the sky outside was intermittently cloudy, or the frost on the windowpane was thickening.

There were all manner of applicable spells—if Tristan wanted to incinerate the room and its furnishings. He'd have to be careful and gentle. He glanced at Thomas, hoping for a suggestion.

Don't look at me. It's the phases of the moon my eyes are supposed to mimic, not the sun.

Tristan recalled a spell used during the spring planting, when a gentle warmth was needed after the seeds were put in the ground, to induce them to sprout. What worked for a field should work well enough for a small room. And it was the only spell of that kind that he could recall by heart, without consulting a grimoire he couldn't reach.

Tristan moved his fingers into the path of the feeble sunbeam, turning the firestone, letting it absorb heat from all sides to bolster its own latent heat. He visualized soft and warm living things, chicks and puppies, Elisena's hands, the gentle heat of Minstrel's feathers, as he slept one-legged upon a finger, sunbeams falling across his face, tickling his nose, and the damp warmth of a sun-kissed garden. His fingers made passes sluggishly. It was a sleepy sort of spell. Tristan's eyelids drooped as he finished it.

The fire crackled into life, and the candle lighted itself. Tristan was so startled by the reaction that he dropped the firestone, which struck a spark from the flagstones. The frost was gone. The candle hissed as a drop of water boiled out of the melted wax.

Tristan couldn't begin to explain the incident, so he simply washed his face—no need to dress, as he'd slept in his clothes—and set about packing his few belongings. There was no sense in wasting more time, once he'd accepted his defeat. The frost—well, that was a curiosity, but its interest for him had already passed.

Thomas refused to sink into such gloom. He rolled about in the sunlight, stretched himself, and had a leisurely wash. Evidently his solitary prowl in search of a less doleful companion than Tristan had been successful. He fairly oozed contentment till his sun got blocked.

Tristan had crossed to the room's single window and stood before it staring moodily out. The window was narrow, so not much light got past him. Thomas twitched his whiskers in annoyance. He got up, stretched again, and went to rub himself against Tristan's ankles.

Tristan paid him no heed. It was still too early to think of going to Cabal; he had hours of time still to kill. It seemed a waste, even though he could trust Valadan to get him back to Calandra far sooner than his pride would wish. No matter how long he avoided facing defeat, the moment of truth would still arrive all too soon. He was seriously considering simply leaving —it would serve Cabal right if he just vanished, like Delmon. Tristan reminded himself that Cabal's misunderstanding was not wholly the man's fault.

Having the sulks again, Thomas thought. *He needs a bit of fresh air. Or some good news.* He made an inquiring sound, but Tristan didn't react.

Are you tired of your search yet?

"No, of course not!" Tristan snapped.

Oh. Then you might care to hear about last night.

"If it's about the supple young cat you spent it entwined with, you're wrong."

She was supple enough, though, as it happens, that wasn't her main interest for me. Thomas leaped to the windowledge. *You sound jealous.*

Tristan very pointedly turned back to the window. Thomas stretched out a paw to tap his wrist.

"Thomas, I don't need this. We'll be going soon, but till then I'd appreciate a little peace and quiet."

Thomas crouched upon the sill, wrapped his tail tidily about his feet, and yawned.

Fine. Just thought you might like to know that cats see a lot more than you unobservant humans do. There are thousands of cats in Kôvelir, and they're all in close communication with each other—another thing you two-legged fools don't go in for. Still, it's probably just a rumor about that ginger-haired woman, the one that went off with the dark man who hates cats.

"*What* man who hates cats?" Tristan asked exasperatedly.

I thought you weren't interested? Well, they don't have a name for him. More like a bad smell than anything else, even a description. But the feeling I get is that he does nasty things to us, too horrible even to mention, and that's why the cats here remember him. They were glad when he went, but they couldn't understand why she would go with him. I've got to admit I don't see her going against her will. She just went with him.

"Who? Crewzel? What makes you sure it's her?"

I talked to the cats in the neighborhood we stayed in before. As I said, the lines of communication are quite good. She's at a fishing village a few miles outside the city. There are always lots of cats in fishing villages.

Mist and Bitter Herbs

TRISTAN'S HEART WAS as heavy as if it had been hung with iron chains, and his thoughts were as troubled as so much cold iron would have made them. He hadn't seen Cabal and, much as he'd dreaded the meeting, having avoided it had not brought him relief. Much the reverse.

He'd gone to Cabal's rooms, and been turned away—not by Bleyvr, which he might have expected. With Bleyvr he might at least have left a salving message, but the man at Cabal's door had been a stranger and one who seemed most preoccupied and anxious. Behind him, in the outer chamber, there had been voices unfamiliar to Tristan, voices whose low murmur had had worrisome implications.

It seemed very likely that Cabal had had a relapse of his illness, but Tristan hadn't stayed to find out. Even if he could have gotten to Belyvr within a few hours, his presence would have made no difference, and he dared not let the trail to Crewzel grow cold while he waited.

Tristan told himself that he wouldn't shoulder guilt about that or about Cabal's illness itself. There had been signs of what was coming even before the past night's disaster. He didn't truly think his ineptness had pushed Cabal beyond his limits. More probably, the oncoming attack had made Cabal irritable and impatient. Tristan didn't believe that anything he'd done or not done would have mattered much—or at least so he desperately told himself.

And, remembering his dreams of Darkenkeep and the uncanny frost that had followed them, he thought it best to get himself and the baleful influences that seemed to dog him out of Kôvelir as fast as possible. That might be the only aid he could hope to give Cabal.

The cottage was visible at intervals through the heavy mist, which presently curled like a serpent about the bases of the black trees, so that those trees appeared to spring from the mist rather than the earth.

"Thomas? Did you hear something?"

No. Should I?

"I don't know." Tristan looked back the way they'd come. "I just thought—"

That's unusual enough.

Tristan shrugged. The road behind him was empty—or had been, when he'd turned round. But he thought he'd heard a whisper of wind, unlikely as that was in the fog, though the leaves on the trees were as still as sleep now. Nothing—maybe.

Tristan jumped violently as cold rainwater dripped down his neck from a branch above, and Thomas forbore to scoff at him again. Indeed, the cat moved with more caution—even anxiety—than Tristan had ever noticed before. Thomas had treated Darkenkeep as an adventure, and nothing in Kôvelir's benighted streets ever gave him the slightest pause, yet now he hesitated and kept close.

Nothing in the village of Morsk had prepared them for this. Valadan had brought them from Kôvelir without incident in good enough time to satisfy even Tristan. The way wasn't long, though the roads were in poor repair. They'd reached the village before sunfall, even after a late start—though only by a little.

Morsk was a fishing village, and there were still plenty of folk about its cluster of circular huts, despite the evening fog. A woman gutting pilchards for drying was willing to give Tristan directions to the cottage where the "strangers" lived. She even, when Tristan seemed anxious not to disturb the wrong folk at the supper hour, confirmed that there were just the two of them, a dark man who spent a lot of time walking the beaches, though he did not fish, and the woman who wasn't seen much at all. Yes, the woman's kerchief-covered hair had been red, almost certainly. No, no child with them.

That "dark man" could have been anyone, one of Crewzel's more secret customers or more happily a new husband. Yet somehow a name kept coming to Tristan's mind, and a more sinister explanation. He'd never met the man by day, or seen him undisguised. But his name had been Cheris, and they'd met twice, quite briefly, while Tristan was in Crewzel's company. The second of those times, Cheris had tried to kill him.

Tristan knew no more about the man, but he was willing to bet that the featureless dark figure Crewzel's cards had shown might well be disliked by cats. And come to think, there'd been not a single cat in the village.

Rotting leaves squelched underfoot as they headed up the steep slope toward the cottage. Once there came a sound that was more like a shriek. Tristan jerked his foot up in alarm, peering for a sight of some fieldmouse or other small, mangled creature, but there was nothing under his boot save a clump of greenish fungi, indented where he'd trampled it. Tristan's skin prickled. But even supposed plants *could* feel pain, as Blais had always insisted and he had always privately doubted, they had no voice to express hurt, had they?

The fungus was nearly the only living thing to be seen. The light was failing, making Tristan squint uneasily through the mist. He put his hand on a wet tree trunk. It might once have been an apple—shriveled brown fruit lay on the ground beneath it, skins cracking and oozing unpleasantly—but the tree was plainly dead, as were all the rest they'd passed. Thomas shrank back against Tristan's boots, not for the first time.

"Thomas? What's the matter?"

Nothing. Keep going.

A fresher stink than the fungi, a different sort of decay, led Tristan off a step toward where Thomas had lately been. He found a rusted cauldron, a heap of wood ashes, and a smaller stinking pile of matted hair and bones.

"Thomas? What *is* this?"

Thomas stood close by him, also looking. He spoke dully.

They say there is a bone in a black cat which will make a man invisible if he holds it in his mouth. Only, to get the bone, you have to boil the rest of the cat away. Alive. Or alive at first.

* * *

There was more, besides: a snake's skeleton, seemingly tied into a knot; a framework of sticks onto which a hide had been tacked for drying—but the thing on it had been a whole rabbit, not merely the pelt; piles of burned herbs about the cottage and patterns of stones with brownish stains on such edges of them as the rain and dew had not been able to reach; and herbs growing, wormwood, nightshade, and mandrake, all gone to seed and, beyond that, to rot.

Maybe dropping in unannounced wasn't such a good idea.

Tristan was at a loss. Magic could have a dark, cruel side, he knew well, but this was beyond all reason. What sort of magic did the painful deaths of small, harmless creatures make? And what sort of man would use it?

He thought of the magical things so dear and familiar to him: cantrips, tisanes, and tinctures; retorts full of strange-colored smokes; black-lettered pages faintly burned at the edges; chants smooth as honey on the tongue; herbs with bitter smells and bright promises; Blais' fingers moving in passes as graceful as a dancing girl of Sis-Kemper; Thomas, stalking velvet-footed over grimoires and manuscripts, his paws glittering with surplus magic; and Minstrel's songs, gold notes overlaid with sweet silver.

Tristan felt ill as much from the comparison as from the stench of decayed wormwood. He kicked the caps off a small stand of death-shadow mushrooms and stepped up to the cottage door.

The room in front of him was dim, full of cobwebs and deserted, but there was another door hard by the hearth which would open either onto another room or into the stairs to the second story. Tristan opened it—and found himself standing outside once more. The door slid out of his grasp and sagged closed, barely missing Thomas' tail.

Funny—the cottage had looked to be bigger than a single room. Tristan went in again and peered about, seeing no sign of life or any bootprints in the dust, save his own. And where was the access to the second floor? He saw no ladder. He might have thought he'd missed it in the darkness, but there was little enough in the room to hide it.

On an impulse he went around and tried again. He found himself, predictably if a bit unnervingly, back outside again, instead of inside the cottage. Tristan nibbled at his lower lip, surer of his judgment now. It was a fairly common type of illusion, a species of confusion.

Still, it held up well, being a solidly crafted illusion, if not a terribly original one. Tristan tried the door a good dozen times, with various opening spells, and the image of the room never wavered; the second door always opened upon the yard— the *front* yard, come to think of it. One of these times, he might well meet himself coming out. Thomas agreed that might be unpleasant.

Then the spell varied itself, as if in response to Tristan's tampering with it. He opened the front door for the thirteenth time and found himself out among the bare trees, with no cottage in sight. The door, his last hold on reality, whipped away again. Tristan picked Thomas up carefully in one hand. This might be more serious than he'd anticipated.

Every direction he tried looked a good bit like the others, enough so that they were identical in their uselessness. Tristan couldn't recover his bearings at all. He shivered. If this were Cheris' work—but Valadan had given him no hint of any present danger. The stallion wasn't visible now. Hopefully he was only hidden by the darkness.

It might be that his crystal could literally shed some light on this. Tristan drew it out and spoke the words needed to light the bit of stone, and some others to alter subtly the properties of its light. The crystal glowed like a star in the mist, but revealed nothing of the illusion's workings.

Tristan took a couple of steps, aiming to gain the edge of the trees. This was only a simple confusion spell, but effective for its very simplicity, and easy to maintain. If its wielder could keep it up long enough, Tristan knew he could easily starve where he stood, unable to leave, even if he finally chose to.

He strode forward, tripped over a root that apparently wasn't as illusionary as it looked, and pitched forward. Hampered by the crystal in one hand and Thomas in the other, he fell right to the ground before he could catch himself. On the way down, he cracked his head hard on something that wasn't even there and felt a momentary disorientation, besides the pain of the blow. He was lying on the ground. Just for an instant, Tristan had been sure he wasn't doing that at all, but was upright and leaning against something—something that his confused fingertips insisted was a doorframe. Very odd.

"Thomas, lend me your whiskers."

My what? Are you all right? Thomas squirmed in his hands.

Tristan held the cat closer to what looked like the ground and felt otherwise. "Close your eyes. And then tell me what you feel."

Thomas fanned his whiskers, rather alarmedly, then again in surprise.

It's a door. Open. But—

"Don't open your eyes." Tristan shut his own, and concentrated on remembering that he was standing upright. He fingered the edges of the wooden frame to make certain that it was a door and not a high window. A splinter snagged his finger, and he swore under his breath. His fingertips continued to describe the frame to him.

He reached through it with his foot, until his toe met with an obstruction. Tristan knelt to examine that more closely. His fingers said wood, about the height of a stair-tread—and sure enough there was another such behind and above the first.

Tristan began to ascend the stairs, eyes still tightly shut. He didn't like to wonder what might happen if the illusion took over again. He still remembered that inside-out mirror trick with painful clarity.

The flight was narrow and steep, as was to be expected in a cottage of this type. There were only ten steps to be climbed, and Tristan was heartily thankful that they were steps and not a ladder, which would have been even more common in this type of building and much more difficult to climb. An absence of further obstacles told him he'd reached the top—or at least he hoped he had. Risking all, Tristan dared to open his eyes.

He was in the open doorway of a dark little room, and there before him was Crewzel, bent over a globe of glass which she was misting with her breath at intervals, as she read the incantation that kept up the illusion. She'd never heard him on the stairs, so total was her concentration, nor did she see him in any of the tiny, carefully angled mirrors. Her candle was a mere stub, shedding little light, and Crewzel's brow furrowed as she squinted and read.

Behind her, Tristan could see a window; out through it, he could see Valadan in the dark yard below, revealed by the occasional flash of his eyes.

"That must be tiring," Tristan said to Crewzel. "You can stop now."

Crewzel let out a shriek like a trapped mouse, not at all the sort of sound Tristan would have expected from her, somehow. The glass ball rolled onto the floor and smashed, releasing a puff of pinkish smoke. Tristan looked at Crewzel.

She was thin. Her breastbone jutted out sharply from her chest, and Tristan could see the fabric of her gown jerk as her heart beat beneath it. Crewzel's hands flew up to her throat as if to prevent her breath's leaving her, but it had already done so. She hadn't even straightened when she saw him, but hunched over further, as if to protect herself.

Tristan took a step toward her. He had to duck, under the roof's steep slant. Cobwebs tickled at the end of his nose.

"Why the games?" He gestured at the window and the unobstructed view of the yard below. "You could see it was only me. It wasn't that dark when I got here." Surely she hadn't forgotten him so swiftly.

"For your own sake," Crewzel answered hoarsely. It took Tristan a moment to realize that she was answering his question. "So go—now, while you still can." Her cheekbones threatened to burst through her pale skin.

Tristan stared at her, then at the room, hoping it might tell him what she did not. He saw a table, littered with stale food crumbs, a three-legged brazier, a tiny pile of charcoal, and a shallow clay lamp with a twist of thread for a wick. It smelled as if it burned lard.

There was nothing else—no books, no rug, nothing to sit on but the one low stool Crewzel had by the window. There was a pile of straw in the far corner, with a blanket spread atop it. Cool air sifted through holes in the thatch; rain surely would do the same.

"I don't understand—"

"Then you've lost what's left of your shallow wits." Crewzel snapped. "It's simple enough—I'm asking you to leave."

There was a flash of Crewzel's old spirit in her tone, but it flickered and died as Tristan watched.

"That's a little abrupt, don't you think? I just got here. And I've come a long way to see you." Tristan bent to set Thomas on the floor. This wasn't at all the reception he'd expected, even though he'd taken her by surprise.

"If you go now, you can still get a good night's travel in." Crewzel took a step toward him. "I can't say it any plainer. Get *out*. Or is that too difficult for you?"

"You don't even want to know why I'm here?" He'd taken

an involuntary step back and had to stop himself from taking another, remembering the stairs.

"No." Her breath came fast and shallow.

"Well, if I might ask, what are *you* doing here?"

Crewzel didn't answer, if she even heard. She'd spun to the window again and was peering out of it intently.

"If you're still here when Cheris comes back, I won't answer for it! And I expect him at any moment." She pulled a shawl that was more tatters than cloth closer about her narrow shoulders.

"Cheris?" For an instant Tristan had thought she was for some reason afraid of him and hiding it with the promise of her man's imminent return; then he realized that her fear was more likely *for* him. Cheris was a rough customer and had shown murderous intent before. "Then you really are here with him. But why? I thought you—"

"Don't pass judgment!" she snapped.

Tristan spread his hands in front of him, as if to fend the words off.

"I'm just surprised. You never seemed that fond of him."

She made no answer to that. Crewzel turned away from him instead, uncertain in a way he'd never seen her. "Please go." It was a genuine plea, something else he'd never had from her, and delivered in a whisper that seemed to be all the voice she had left.

She's crying, Thomas noted.

"I'd like to understand," Tristan said. "Make me understand and I'll go. But not until I'm sure you're all right."

"Why shouldn't I be all right? I have a man to look after me now!" And Crewzel laughed.

"Cheris? Do I offer congratulations, then?"

Crewzel laughed again, unnervingly, but said nothing.

Tristan groped for some sort of understanding. "Are you afraid he'll mistake my being here? Surely you can explain to him—*I* can explain to him—"

Along about then he became aware that Crewzel was sobbing rather than laughing, as she settled among her ragged skirts in a heap on the dirty floor, together with the bits of broken crystal.

It took Tristan the best part of an hour—after he tossed his confusion away, to be examined later if need be—to calm Crewzel enough to get sensible talk out of her. The bones of her hands felt bird-light when he held them. Thomas helpfully fetched a few small items from Valadan's saddlebags; with bread and wine, they had a meal of sorts.

Tristan had suggested going to the ground-floor room, where surely there would be more in the way of comforts if the decay there was the illusion he suspected it of being. But Crewzel grew so agitated when he mentioned it that her terror nearly undid all his careful soothing. He wondered aloud why she preferred the real disintegration above the stairs, and she surprised him by responding.

"That's his workroom down there—which I wouldn't enter even if he permitted me to. It's bad enough hearing what goes on down there! I don't want to *see*—" Tristan hastily made her drink more wine, holding the cup to Crewzel's mouth when her hands shook too badly to manage it.

"You'll think me witless," Crewzel finally went on. "To know what he's doing and yet be able to live with it so long as I don't have to see it. It's hypocrisy, but—" Her head drooped. Tristan pulled a leaf stem free of her tangled red curls. He understood all too well.

"No. I saw the—things—outside. I'd rather not have seen them myself."

Crewzel nodded against his shoulder. If she glanced out the window at all, she could scarcely have failed to note some of the things in the yard. "Once I was sure he had a child with him. I told myself that it was only a cat, that they always sound like babies crying, but I couldn't truly believe it. I didn't have the courage to look."

She seemed rational enough now, maybe ready to talk to him. It might even be safe to ask questions. Tristan thought he might as well try. Of course, Crewzel might have been making perfect sense all along, and he might have simply failed to understand her.

"Why do you stay, then?" he asked carefully.

Crewzel shivered. "What else can I do, *now*? If I were going to run, I should have done it at the very first. He's woven too many holds over me now—like a spider, tangling his prey in his sticky threads. I never should have let him bring me here. It's not like the city—I can't hide here, he'd find me in five minutes. It's too late to run."

"Maybe I shouldn't ask," Tristan murmured, "but how—"

He needn't have asked. She'd been about to speak of it anyway, it seemed.

"He wore me down. He kept after and after me, and he started talking about love, and one mad, bored moment I listened to him. And when I'd listened that once, I'd given him the key to my ear. I was lost in that minute, and too stupid to know it. I don't exist anymore. He's eaten my soul. It wasn't even me he wanted, as it turned out," she added bitterly. "It was the cards—only them."

Crewzel drew out a leathern case from among the folds of her skirt, and turned it over in her hands. There'd been an arcane design tooled onto the case once, but it was doubly secret now for being so worn and blackened.

"But he can't work them—" Crewzel laughed harshly. "They show only black for him, or only himself. Unless I work them. I can read them for him, a little. Not as well as he'd like. It's not what he wants, anyway, because he'd like to dispense with me. How it galls him that he can't."

Tristan kept quiet, fearful that, if he interrupted with any comment at all, she'd go silent on him again. The cards were the whole object of his long search for her, but he felt no thrill of joy at seeing them at last, he was so troubled by Crewzel's state.

"He thinks I know how they work," Crewzel said and she laughed again. "But I don't, and no one believes me. Giffyd was drunk when he made them, didn't understand them himself. So how should I? My wonderful inheritance!"

"Why stay here then, if he treats you so?" Tristan asked again. "You're not chained to him." She might be more disposed to sensible solutions now. He discounted many of the earlier things she'd said. There were no signs of sorcery or of any magical hold on Crewzel, only that oldest and strongest sort of binding which had nothing to do with magic and very little to do with love, though it often went under that name.

"You'd think I'd have an answer for that, wouldn't you? But the truth is I don't. When he's not here, I tell myself I'll run, but when he comes back I'm still here, despite all, no matter how he uses me."

Thomas made a disgusted noise.

"Do you love him, then?" Tristan asked, wondering how she could, unless she was unsure even of her own feelings.

But Crewzel had always been very self-sure.

"*Love?* What does love have to do with anything? I loved Giffyd and he got himself killed, but I'm still here, alive." She fiddled distractedly with her mug. "Love's no surety. Besides, no one could possibly love Cheris. You have to know a person to love him, and the more I come to know Cheris, the more I marvel his own mother didn't drown him at birth like a deformed kitten . . . Why are you here?"

Tristan blinked at her abrupt shift, then collected himself. Crewzel wasn't, he realized, absolutely rational yet. Whatever Cheris had done to her, it had affected her deeply—understandably. Tristan would have to take great care, since it was obvious to him now that her moments of normality were neither permanent nor consistent.

He gambled that one would continue for the few minutes he needed to speak of all the strange events in his recent life, and that he'd have time as well to tell her those things about Allaire he'd been unwilling even to hint at before. If he was to have Crewzel's help, she'd need all the information he could give her, whether she believed it or not.

He couldn't tell if she did, quite, though she accepted his every word without question. Tristan wished that the wine hadn't been necessary to calm her. She might not be questioning because she wasn't attending to anything he said. She drank continuously as he talked.

At last, though, he was able to answer the only question he hadn't touched on yet—the only one she'd put to him. Just in time, probably. The wine was nearly gone.

"I'm here to have my fortune told. As you started to tell it once in Kôvelir. I wish now I'd let you go farther then." The room was much darker now, the candle nub faltering its last. A wind played in the dead herbs of the garden below, stirring strange scents. Valadan whickered, but apparently the sound was only a horse noise, nothing of import. Valadan had been uneasy ever since leaving Kôvelir and more than usually watchful. In the mist, he sounded far away.

Tristan kindled the brazier, as much for light as warmth. Crewzel spoke, when she finally did, to his back.

"You? A king? Well, I suppose you might as well be. You're not much of anything else, are you?"

She might be surprised. Thomas abandoned his sentry post on the windowsill, and crept close to the brazier's heat.

"I may be a dead king, if you can't help me." Tristan added more bits of charcoal to the little blaze.

"You don't travel in much style for a king."

She might be drunk, or merely skeptical. Best to ignore her less rational statements until he was sure. She might only be baiting him, Tristan thought. That was ever Crewzel's manner, her way of dealing with any strangeness. He needed to remember that. She'd always been tricky to handle.

"I'm a king with no qualifications beyond a rather unusual childhood, and a wizard who can't cast a spell straight," Tristan agreed pleasantly. "Why give myself airs?" He smiled disarmingly over the flames.

But he'd lost her again.

"You want me to read for you?" Crewzel fumbled with the cards, so clumsily that Tristan could easily have taken her for a sleepwalker, despite her open eyes. "Why shouldn't I read for you, when I've read for the likes of *him*?" she went on shrilly. "Sit you down, sir."

Tristan started to touch a hand to her arm, whether to offer comfort or to gather her up and drag her away to safety and sanity, he didn't know. But Thomas stayed him with a firm paw on his wrist, until finally Tristan understood. Break this mood now, painful and strange as it was, and he might never get a reading or learn what he'd sought so long. Crewzel swayed close to some breaking point; better by far to harden his heart, to let her play this scene out, and gain what he could from it. After—

Her hands seized his wrists with a grip a falcon might have envied and slammed his hands down onto the unshuffled pack of cards. She prisoned his eyes with her gaze, and Tristan wondered how even Cheris could bear one of her readings now. Crewzel had become as strange as Giffyd's cards, a part of them rather than merely a user of them.

Fortune

"I SEE FIRE for you—a circle of white fire. And ice. A great deal of ice. A destiny you might prefer to avoid, but cannot run from. I see you chained."

Tristan nodded, and his ankles ached as if they were indeed shackled with iron. The card in his fingers now, held carefully over Crewzel's palm-up hands, showed a circle of runes very like the one on the arm of Crogen's throne. Surely it was the same, except that Crewzel or the cards saw them flaming as they perhaps would during the crowning. There were incredible colors there, some even that he had no names for. Tristan shifted on the floor, winced, and carefully picked a long splinter from the heel of his left hand.

"Have you a question?" This was the next and the final stage of a card-reading, after the peek at both past and future. Tristan nodded again. As far as he was concerned, the previous part of the reading had been unnecessary. He knew his past, and the cards' view of the distant future had been inconclusive, as such readings were bound to be.

"Then take up the pack again." Crewzel gathered the elaborately laid-out cards together and put them back into his hands as a pack, leaving only the circle card lying on the boards between them. "Speak your question."

"I am seeking the royal sword of Calandra, the King's Blade," Tristan responded. "It is mine by right, and I would claim it. Where is it now?" The cards felt curiously heavy in his hands as he shuffled them slowly—cool as stones and as weighty. There was no guessing what Giffyd had made them of. They were too heavy for ivory and they did not feel like leaves of metal.

At Crewzel's silent direction, he laid out the cards once more, face down. First five cards, ranged into two rows which crossed one another at right angles so that the central card belonged to both rows or neither. Another card was then laid crosswise atop the center. Light spilled from its edges.

Crewzel flipped the top card over. It was the circle again.

"Yes, we know *that*," she said impatiently, and reached for the bottom card.

Jewellike, impossibly precise and tiny, figures moved— armies of men, horses, and weapons, in a silent dance of colors and light, like a window into the past or a dream. Tristan leaned close.

The action and the scene varied, from battlefield to throne hall to other places he had no means of recognizing, and faces changed, flickered, and shifted into one another bewilderingly. But one thing remained constant. It seemed as fine as the flash of sunlight upon a strand of spider's web, yet it was unmistakable—the sword, by the side and in the hands of the kings of Calandra.

"Yes, but that's past. Where is it *now*, he wants to know," Crewzel murmured crossly, flicking another card over.

The leftside card showed them a robed mage making passes with his hands over an unsheathed blade. Tristan stared hard at the scene, knowing the information would be invaluable to Elisena. Even if he didn't grasp the spell fully, she should be able to extract whatever he saw from his memory. He watched intently, not even blinking until Crewzel tipped the righthand card over.

At first Tristan thought the card was whitely blank and started to question Crewzel as to its meaning. Then the steam cleared away, and the smith drew the new blade from the quenching-trough. It was perhaps the finest edge he'd ever put on a blade, as the pride in the smith's face showed. Light and water ran from the sword as he gripped the tang that would serve to anchor the hilt.

Laying the blade aside, the smith shrugged into a jacket of furs, for the mountain air was chill on his bare torso, even with the smithy fire so near. Behind him, through a wide-open door, Tristan could see a steep dirt road, flanked by great cedars. Higher and farther beyond still were hillsides where more of the trees were distance-blurred to a peculiar blue-green. Only in Kinark did cedars grow to such a size and in such profusion. They and the swords whose forging they overshadowed were the twin glories of their land, told of in a hundred songs.

So. The sword was one of the fabled blades of Kinark. It had traveled a long way, but Calandra had been far more open to trade in former days under her kings. And a king would want and could afford the finest blade available. But where was this sword now?

The central card beckoned. It held whatever answer they'd get, just on the other side of its elaborately limned back. Crewzel's thin fingers slipped beneath it, caught a corner, and slowly, deliberately eased it over.

The card's face was black. Not merely blank, but as dark as the underside of a rock lifted up to reveal the crawling things beneath.

Tristan was about to speak when a stair tread creaked, just outside the door. He would have put it down to his imagination, but Crewzel reacted startlingly. She stiffened all over without stirring a hair or uttering even the slightest exhalation of her breath. Then, with a movement as smooth as a flame leaping, she whipped the cloth from the pallet on the floor and flung it over the brazier.

Tristan's heart thudded. Thomas, all alertness now when it no longer mattered, stood close. Some of the scattered cards glowed feebly. By that faint light, dimmed as Crewzel feverishly gathered the cards to her, Tristan saw her lips move, soundlessly.

"Cheris."

No second footstep came. He knows I'm here, Tristan thought, searingly angry that he hadn't kept a better watch. But he'd have thought Valadan—

The air was deathly still. Tristan could scarcely breathe, even when he finally dared to try. Crewzel gestured abruptly at the door, at the side where it was hinged to the frame with leather thongs. Tristan supposed she intended him to hide there, shielded by the door, to slip past Cheris in the gloom produced by the stifling of the brazier and gain the stairs. Tristan doubted he could move so quietly. And if he did, what would happen to Crewzel?

What if he has a torch?

That question had occurred to Tristan too. He would prefer to try the window, but from this height he couldn't guarantee he'd land on his feet like Thomas. The cloth was scorching now; he could smell it. What was Cheris doing? What foul spell was a-making as he tarried outside the door? Tristan's eyes strained through the dark. Toadstools! What was Valadan doing? How had Cheris got this far unannounced?

As if to a cue, the black stallion screamed a warning. Valadan reared above the low mist, hooves at the ready, yet too panicked to fight and too loyal to flee. Now Tristan's ears caught the sound that had rendered Valadan oblivious to all commoner perils.

The Hounds of Nímir! Once again they were on Tristan's trail!

Nímir possessed no servant more dreaded, more deadly. Silent, less visible than the wind, dauntless as no earthly dogs could be, they were not truly dogs at all. They were beyond any hope of imagining or understanding; the very thought of them was a terror sufficient to kill. They must have trailed their quarry all the way from Kôvelir, or perhaps farther, and now the hunt was ending.

Cheris was harmless by any comparison. Without hesitation, Tristan swept Crewzel and Thomas close to him and blanked his mind of all magic as he wrapped his arms about them. There was no chance this time to seek the aid of any of his stones or to speak the briefest cantrip. What hope of success he had must come from within himself. He remembered how emptied he'd felt when his magic had failed him in front of Cabal and embraced that void fervently.

The door began to open. Even in the gloom, Tristan saw the tips of black-gloved fingers, the toe of a pointed black boot. He let the sight go, along with memories of a silver-hilted knife which had fought even without its master's hand on it and the sights and scents of evil in the yard below. He became as still and silent as the table beside him—but no more silent, for that would give him away just as readily. He fought to include Crewzel and Thomas in the deception as well. Neither of them resisted him, Crewzel mostly from shock. Tristan buried her face against his shoulder, hearing the rustle of the lashes of her open eyes against the cloth of his jerkin. She made no greater sound. Wind banged the door below against its frame.

They weren't hidden from Cheris. But it was no longer Cheris they had to hide from. Cheris, not understanding, seeing only what must have looked like the feeblest attempt at a shadow-confusion, chuckled. The door opened a crack farther.

As it did, there was a great swirl of wind up the stair, followed and revealed only by a smell of ice and fouled snow. Cheris exclaimed something unintelligible and took his hands from the door to fling them up in front of his face. He was hurled back against the frame with a crack of splintering wood. He might have screamed—if so, the wind took the sound. Dust, sucked from cracks in floor and walls and the thatch of the roof, coiled about him.

Tristan's ears popped painfully. His eyes watered till vision was hopeless. The wind shrieked and ripped about him, impossibly cold, and his lashes froze to his cheeks.

The gale's scream rose until it was pitched beyond sound. When it died away, satisfied, the three by the table were quite alone.

Seemingly far away, a black horse's mane tossed in a normal night breeze. Stars picked out odd glitters in his eyes.

The Hounds came bidden to seek a sorcerer, Valadan said, snorting. *And they have found one to carry back to Channadran.*

the Road to Kinark

FOR A MOMENT Tristan stayed where he was, on the floor, feeling Crewzel's heart beat raggedly against his own. One of his feet had gone to sleep; he thought he might fall if he tried to stand too soon. And his knees felt none too sure, either.

The coals had finally burned through the cloth over the brazier. Flames licked the cloth briefly, consuming it. Thomas, the pupils of his eyes expanded so that no green was left around them, stared at Tristan.

There goes one of my nine lives—aged away.

"*Enough!*" Crewzel exclaimed, writhing out of Tristan's arms. She staggered to her feet, whirling off balance toward the door. "Kill me, I'd welcome it! But you won't frighten me to death." She stopped, swaying, before the empty doorway.

Tristan felt for the pouch at his belt, drew out his crystal, and lighted it. He rubbed at his ribs, which were elbow-bruised.

Crewzel shoved her tangled curls away from her face, distractedly. Her hands shook.

"Oh, stars! Where has he gone? What's he going to do this time? Tristan, get out of here— *no*, stay. He'll have something waiting for you if you try to leave. He'll do to you what he did to Giffyd. We've got to think, make a plan. Why's he so quiet? What's—"

She walked blindly into the table, upsetting it. The accident barely staunched her words for an instant as she stepped over the mess.

"The waiting's worse than anything he does. He knows that. He builds his power on it. He's like a cat ready to spring, but holding his hand, holding his hand until—"

"Crewzel—" Tristan didn't think he had her attention. He set the crystal on the floor and rose. He took hold of her shoulders to stop her wandering and make her look him in the face. "Crewzel, it's all right. He's gone."

Her head shook violently.

"It's a trick, I tell you. He's probably waiting right outside the door—"

"No," Tristan said gently. "No. He's gone." Then, knowing that her weeks with Cheris would have amply schooled her to believe any evil, even one that a lowly card-reader would never in normal life have run foul of, he told her what the Hounds really were.

When he'd finished, Crewzel drew a deep, deep breath. Then she laughed. It was a long time before she quieted.

"They took him in preference to you, because he was just what they were looking for? Oh, that's too rich—he deserved it too well. And Cheris always wanted to be renowned!" Her eyes glittered in a way that hardly seemed healthy, and Tristan wished he could settle her down and convince her to sleep. He wondered if he should coax her to leave the cottage and if he could take her to the village and put her under a less memory-tainted roof. That might be his best course.

"But you've made me break a vow, Tristan—one I never expected to break in this life or the next." Crewzel was still laughing.

Tristan only looked at her, puzzled but patient, wondering what was coming next.

"I'll hardly be able to dance on his grave now, will I?"

Try as they might and did, they could not set up a pattern of cards again that showed the sword. Crewzel's cards were as stubborn and contrary as Tristan's own magic ever was and showed naught but stray flashes of fortunes that could have belonged to anyone. Once the answer had been laid out before them; and only once would it offer itself.

That final card, so promising and so silent, haunted Tristan's dreams, but he couldn't turn it over in his sleep, and Crewzel never found the pattern when he was awake. In the end, he gave it up as a hopeless task and decided to make the most of the little new information the cards had given him.

He had not known that the sword was a Kinarkan blade. He might have suspected so, but there would have been no way before to make sure of the guess. Tristan was sure now, having probed the cards' version of events to his own satisfaction by questioning Valadan. The stallion's memories of that last great battle might be painful, but they were vivid. And they all tallied with what the cards had shown. Valadan did not know of the sword's forging, but there was no reason to expect that the cards would be true in all else and false in that.

It was a Kinarkan blade, then, forged with a skill that was older than Calandra itself, a skill straight out of legends, often mentioned in magical works. Tristan had made notes aplenty during his hours in the mages' Library, and the name of Kinark appeared in them time after time.

Unbreakable, one hastily scribbled note said. It had meant little at the time, hence his nonchalance in jotting it down, but now the notation greatly comforted Tristan. He'd been worried that if the cards could not reveal the sword's present location, it would be because the blade had been irretrievably lost. He remembered all too well the field of Cathlein sinking into cold marshland and knew how quickly a sword might rust away to nothing if left behind there. A lot of swords might meet that fate, but a Kinarkan blade surely would not.

Tristan flipped through his notes again, tapping a reed pen thoughtfully against his teeth. They were in the village, where he'd managed to rent a room for the two of them and where they might have a fire and decent meals. He wouldn't have been able to pass another night in that cottage, even if Crewzel had insisted on it, which she hadn't. There was nothing there for her but nightmares.

The move had been good, Tristan thought. Crewzel seemed better; certainly she slept like one deprived of rest for weeks and ate when he coaxed her to. He, too, appreciated the warm sun and the salt tang of the harbor that the wind brought along with the cries of the gulls. It had been a day of peace, good for thinking. For a few hours, he'd forgotten to be anxious.

As if that relaxing had opened some door in his brain, an inspiration began to seep through to the surface of his thoughts. Something in what he'd been reading or had read of at even greater length in Kôvelir, attracted his attention as the answer he'd been seeking with such desperation.

Thomas was also enjoying the warm sun, enjoying it with shut eyes and a contented smile curling up the corners of his mouth. When Tristan leaned forward over his notes, he blocked the sun neatly, if inadvertently. The smile faded from Thomas' lips. One green eye opened in what would have passed for a scowl on a man's face. The cat considered moving, after glaring at Tristan produced no response. But the idiot was sitting on the windowsill with his books—the room provided no chair, and Crewzel was fast asleep on the bed. Thomas was sure that if he moved, Tristan would only shift back into the light again, unthinking.

When Thomas complained, Tristan merely noticed that the cat was awake. Thomas thought he seemed excited. Not natural. On such a warm, mild afternoon, after luncheon, the proper attitude was one of a comfortable drowsiness that wouldn't trouble a sleep-seeking cat overmuch. He steeled himself, wondering what could be coming, misliking it even before he knew.

"I keep reading that Kinarkan blades are half alive—and not just in fighting. There are dozens of legends recorded of lost swords popping up at their place of forging years later. No explanations, just the legends. I—"

You mean like salmon going upstream to spawn?

Tristan stared at him in genuine puzzlement. Maybe he'd been talking to himself? Whatever, he went on with it. "It might just be that Kinarkan smiths recognize their work and know a sword when it comes their way again. Really good craftsmen are like that. Blais could always tell his spells from anyone else's."

Thomas shut his eyes. *Especially yours.*

"Or maybe it means that Kinarkan blades are special enough to be treated well, not disappear into the general mass of old weapons. Kings' blades get treated better than a commoner's, I expect, and passed down rather than buried."

Or they might just be legends.

Tristan was tapping his pen against his knee now. Thomas sprang for it, got it, and batted it across the room under the bed. He stood in the sun at Tristan's feet, looking up.

"They say cats can find their way home from almost anywhere. Want to test *that* legend?" Tristan asked.

I take it we're going to Kinark?

* * *

They were, but only the two of them. Crewzel, invited, refused to join the party. Tristan wasn't happy about that, Thomas knew, though he probably didn't crave her company so much as he felt guilty about leaving her.

Thomas thought he need not have scrupled so. Crewzel might still be pale and silent at odd times, as if she didn't quite trust herself, but it was no question of her health that held her back, nor was there any doubt that her old force of will had returned to her. She refused Tristan's entreaties with a dismissing shake of her head, saying he had a sword to look for while she had a son, and neither search was likely to lead to the other. She wished Tristan luck, but she wouldn't go with him. From that point she would not budge.

So they took a little too long buying provisions, that Tristan might salve his conscience by ensuring that at least Crewzel wouldn't go hungry before she got back to Kôvelir—if she even intended to start her search in that city, which was by no means certain. Thomas had a great deal of work to do, making sure that Tristan tended to their own needs as well as he did Crewzel's. He was prone to forgetting that *they* were the ones riding into the wilderness, while Crewzel was returning to civilized lands. The last time Tristan had had charge of provisioning a quest, they'd all gone very hungry indeed, and Thomas had no wish to repeat the experience.

He nagged and prodded; it was slow work, and it was late in the day when they finally took leave of Crewzel. Not that that mattered, given Valadan's abilities, but old habits die hard, and Thomas would have liked an earlier start, if they had to start at all. It would have meant more hours asleep in the saddlebag, before nightfall came and he had to go to work seeing that Tristan made a decent camp.

Dark trees closed around them. They were moving down the coast, just a mile or so in from the sea, on a trade road of sorts. Eventually the cart tracks would strike another road which ran out of Kinark, if any of Tristan's maps were correct. They'd be in moorland by then, but just now they were surrounded by forest.

Tristan rode along listlessly, his shoulders slumped, his thoughts amply veiled in gloom. He paid so little attention to his whereabouts that he never noticed Valadan slowing his pace from a gallop to a trot, then on down to a sedate walk, and didn't recognize the stallion's consideration. Valadan snorted.

It was growing dark. Night fell early under the conifers, and Tristan was by no means alert enough to avoid being swept out of the saddle by a low-hanging branch. An hour before, a deer had wandered across their path, her coat red with the sun's last light, and had paused in startlement to gaze at them before she vanished soundlessly. Tristan had never even seen her.

Thinking too much, Thomas suggested acidly. *Anything for the sake of misery.* Tristan gave no sign that he'd heard the harsh judgment, either.

He was too preoccupied with fretting about several matters at once. It took him a lot of miles to sort his feelings out, more to form conclusions. He decided that he wasn't truly worried about the Hounds still being on his track. They might not realize their mistake for a long while and they'd take longer to find him again after that, since they clearly had little idea of what they were after. Tristan was more bothered about riding into the unknown, as he now was. Always before, he'd had clear destinations and definite people to contact, even if the search hadn't been as simple as it had sounded. Having a direction as well as a goal had at least given him a starting point.

Concern for Crewzel kept surfacing, too, mostly as a sharp reminder that this was the second time in less than a week that he'd run out on someone who needed him. That thought led him back to Cabal and to a wound barely scabbed over and certainly not healing. Over and over, Tristan remembered that last evening and the last things Cabal had said to him. He knew there was only one way Cabal could interpret his disappearance; he knew it would hurt the man—hurt a man already sick almost to death. And there was nothing he could do to remedy the situation. Tristan quivered under his own assault.

The way to find something was to look ahead, not back. He might as well be standing still or back in Crogen, waiting to freeze to death, unless he could shake himself out of this mood. Tristan lifted his head and blinked his eyes. He was amazed to see that it was nightfall and to find himself under trees that blocked the moon and starlight.

Valadan snorted at him, amused in spite of himself. *Yes, a long way.*

The dark was close, for the road cut deep between two hillsides and was not very wide. The needle-covered slopes seemed within arm's reach on either side.

The slopes were covered with trees, too, where the soil

conditions permitted or where there were rocks to anchor roots.
Sometimes the rocks failed their promise. Valadan slowed and
clambered carefully over a tree which had fallen athwart the
trail. Tristan stood in the stirrups to help the maneuver and
then peered ahead into the blackness. He couldn't see far, but
he thought the trail curved sharply a few paces ahead. They
should be thinking of stopping, though it would be nice to find
a place with fresh water near, and that might be difficult in the
dark.

I smell smoke, Thomas said.

"Out here?" Tristan sniffed. Indeed, there was the scent of
wood smoke. Thomas was right. "Another traveler, maybe?"

Valadan snorted and paced around the gentle curving of the
road. The path wandered from its course to avoid a stray out-
cropping of granite, and beside the rocks was the yellow glow
of a small campfire.

One man, no horse, Valadan observed.

Tristan considered a moment. There was no reason to be
wary of another solitary traveler like himself. And this night,
any company was preferable to his own. "Shall we stop here,
then?" he asked Thomas.

Why not? It will save you the trouble of gathering firewood.

Tristan dismounted and led Valadan closer, limping a little
as his legs got used to carrying him again. He stumbled over
a leaf-hidden boulder and saved himself from pitching forward
by jerking Valadan's reins. The horse whinnied and pulled back
angrily. Tristan supposed he'd have done the same, had he
been a horse. He apologized, slipped Valadan's saddle off, and
watched as the stallion began to search for grass.

Thomas regarded him sardonically. *Very good. Now our
audience knows he doesn't have to be afraid of you either*.

Tristan hefted the saddle and his pack and ignored Thomas'
grumbling. When he was sure he was within easy hearing, he
hailed the man, who had undoubtedly been watching all the
while.

The offer to share fire, food, and companionship that night
was well received. They exchanged names. The stranger was
called Jehan, and his accent wasn't one Tristan could readily
place.

Tristan set his pack down and untied its laces. "Empty
country," he ventured.

"Aye. Trade season's not started yet; the weather's still too chancy." Jehan had a youngish face, fair and a trifle red about nose and lips, either from cold or drink. His hair was dark, and both it and his short beard were tightly curled, a characteristic not often met with in Calandra. Tristan thought he'd seen hair like it in Kôvelir and tried to place from where such folk had come. The man's clothes gave no hint of his origins— a rough jerkin that might once have been green, breeches never of any especial color, and a leather coat made from a sheepskin turned wool-side in. Such nondescript garb clothed most of the common folk of the world and was not much different from what Tristan himself wore.

"Are you bound for Kinark too?"

"Nay, I've just left it, bent for Kôvelir."

"Maybe we can trade news of the roads, then. I've never been to Kinark before; I'd like to know what to expect. The customs, for instance—"

They'd agreed to pool food, getting a more varied meal thus than either of them could have had alone. Tristan had contributed cheese and a bit of fresh fruit—bought only because the price was irresistibly low, for fruit didn't travel well, and it was a wonder it had come to the fishing village at all. Jehan had snared a rabbit earlier; it was spitted over the fire. Tristan had herbs of all sorts with him, some useful for cooking as well as magic, so he began to minister to the rabbit with dried thyme and powdered rosemary. A pine knot burst and flared as he leaned over the spit, washing his face with heat and light—more light than had played over it previously.

Jehan made an inarticulate noise. As Tristan looked up, thinking the man had choked on a bit of cheese, Jehan sprang across the fire, scattering logs, rabbit, and hot coals unheeded in his wake.

Tristan wasted an instant wondering how he'd walked so blindly into such madness. Then reflexes took over. By the time Jehan reached him, Tristan was on his feet, backing out of the man's way. At that, he was barely in time, scarcely out of reach of a pair of big hands that were bent on throttling him. He had no time to protest, but he tried.

"What are you—"

He got no further. Jehan found a grip on his knees as he dodged away, and Tristan fell heavily. The impact jarred the breath out of his lungs, and the magic Tristan started was perforce a silent one, a desperate amalgam of shadows and smoke from the torn-up fire. Being a wizard had its uses. He'd work a confusion to enable him to slip out of Jehan's fingers like a trickle of smoke. He'd—

The fall must have jarred his wits loose as well as his breath. The spell was marvelously effective, but Tristan confused himself so utterly that he scarcely knew where he was. He thought he'd succeeded, until the smoke started him coughing.

When the air cleared, Tristan found himself staring at his hands incredulously. There was a length of hempen rope wrapped three times about his wrists and clumsily knotted twice. Another cough almost choked him, and Tristan wasn't sure if the tears that blurred his sight came along with that or with the chagrin at his spell's arrant failure.

Jehan's back was to him as the man rummaged through his baggage—probably looking for more rope, Tristan thought. Anger flared. He could probably get free without recourse to magic, but he was in no mood to waste more time. Tristan began another spell—more carefully thought-out this time— moving fingers that were fast growing numb from the tightness of the rope.

He whispered a word, and the rope obligingly loosened itself a trifle. Good. Tristan grinned in relief. The first spell might not have worked, but this one would. With another word, he sent the rope's ends snicking free of the first knot. Jehan was still occupied.

The rope was quivering eagerly, wonderfully responsive. This was easier than if he'd been unpicking the knots with his fingers. The rope ends hissed free of the second knot. As they did, plainly unraveling of their own accord, Jehan finally located his spare bootlaces, turned around with them ready, and caught sight of the witched rope in action. His jaw dropped. His eyes widened.

Tristan grinned a trifle smugly. Let the fellow see that he was no one to be trussed up and robbed like any common, hapless traveler!

The knots were gone. All he needed to do was get his wrists free of the triple wrapping of rope . . .

Overconfidence was a marvelous—and dangerous—thing. Tristan wasn't the least bit concerned with Jehan. His magic was working perfectly, and he couldn't resist savoring that, watching the rope uncoil itself. Indeed, he needed to do so to guide the spell. He started to move his hands apart, still smiling.

Jehan's fist caught him squarely on the side of his jaw. Tristan would have been wary of a knife or a sword, and he could have made some shift to defend himself from either, if he'd kept his wits about him. With his attention divided so between his spell and Jehan and distracted by pride, as well, Tristan's reflexes simply weren't adequate to protect him against something as immediate as a blow from a fist. His teeth met with a force that astonished him, shredding a bit of his bottom lip that got in the way.

The blow sent him sprawling sideways to the ground. His shoulder hit dirt. His head hit an upthrusting tree root, and there was an abrupt gap in Tristan's memory of events.

Jehan

THERE WAS A confusing throbbing in his head and a smothering weight on his chest. Tristan stirred as much as he was able, which was not much. He opened his eyes and was dazzled by firelight, which sent a bright stab of pain through his skull. The heat of the fire brushed his face. Tristan tried to turn away from it; he discovered that he could only move his neck and that it also hurt.

The weight on his chest resolved into the stranger, or his knee, anyway. Tristan wriggled, trying to get free. For all the good it did him, he might as well have lain still. He struggled harder and was rewarded with a rough shove which slammed him into the ground again. The fire-lighted branches overhead spun crazily.

His head cleared again as Jehan finally took his knee away. Tristan drew a painful breath and noticed that his hands were tied again, behind his back, this time. Tristan's fingers flexed in panic, uselessly. Then he remembered Valadan, and drew a shaky breath of relief. The stallion would be near; the grass he'd been heading for couldn't have been so far away as all that. He would be back, and Thomas was somewhere about, presumably. Surely they'd see that he got out of this mess.

Have a nice nap? Thomas' fur brushed the back of his neck. *You had to show off, get loose while he was watching you, didn't you? You pick the worst times to get vain about your magic. And you do get yourself into the oddest situations. He's probably the only traveler for leagues about this place, and within ten minutes of meeting him, you've charmed him so that he couldn't resist knocking you over the head and tying you up. How do you do it?*

Before Tristan could make Thomas an answer, Jehan returned, a rag in his hand. He noted at once that his prisoner had regained his senses again. He strode over and jerked at the ropes roughly to test the knots. They held. Thomas leaped for the cover of the shadows beyond the firelight.

"Aye. Warlock you may be, but you're like enough to ordinary folk in some ways. Your cursed magic's not proof against everything an honest man might use. And you need your hands for it. You're almost safe, once they're bound."

How does he know you're a wizard? Thomas' eyes gleamed green and unnoticed under a nearby bush. *That little spell was never enough—*

How indeed? But there wasn't time to wonder. "This isn't necessary," Tristan said unhappily. "What harm have I done you? If it's my money you want, just take it. It's in my belt-pouch." Jehan was right enough about his hands. Even if his head cleared quickly enough to let him shape the spell he needed, Tristan doubted he could have worked it again while unable to see the knots. Thomas had made a good point too—how *had* he gotten into this? It had happened so swiftly that Tristan couldn't begin to imagine anything he might have done differently, except to have kept on riding. How had he provoked this?

"What harm?" Jehan's hand moved toward his face. Tristan flinched back, sending sparks of pain shooting through his head again. But Jehan did not strike him; he caught hold of Tristan's chin in a viselike grip while he brought his own flushed face near.

"What harm, sorcerer? You have the brass to ask that? For a fortnight and a half, I've had no sleep that your face did not invade, and now you play me innocent? Half-mad I may be, but 'tis your doing, so don't waste your false ignorance on me!" Jehan shoved Tristan back onto the ground. "Maybe you thought 'twould make better sport to watch me close while you played your game, but it's not so safe as you supposed. I've got you now."

Tristan looked at him blankly. "But I've never even seen you before tonight. How can I possibly have hurt you?" He was beginning to be more than nervous, wondering where Valadan was. He was afraid of what might happen if he tried to call out. The stallion ought to have returned of his own accord by now, surely. He couldn't be unaware of what had happened.

Another sort of fear began to tickle at Tristan's spine. Only a great danger, such as the Hounds, would have lured Valadan off. Could they have found him again so soon—helpless, tied up like a chicken?

"You deny you're a wizard?" A brand flared in what was left of the fire, washing one side of Jehan's face with scarlet, making him appear grotesque and fearsome. Tristan thought he would have preferred both sides to stay hidden.

He tried to keep his apprehension out of his voice when he answered. "No. Of course I don't deny it. It's an honorable calling. I don't know how *you* knew it, though. I—"

"Who but a wizard could witch a man's dreams?" Jehan's teeth glinted in what might have been a smile. Perhaps he was pleased, then. He was twisting a bit of cloth between his hands, Tristan noticed, wishing he hadn't seen it; it looked unpleasantly like a strangler's garrote.

"You keep talking about dreams. What kind of dreams?" Tristan felt himself to be at a terrible disadvantage, lying on the ground as he was, with his head splitting, the salt taste of blood in his mouth, and all feeling already gone from his fingers. He might easily be debating for his very life here and he didn't even know why. Certainly he wasn't in any sort of shape to be doing so. He could hardly think straight. But if he could get the man talking—

"I am here," Jehan said with exaggerated care, obviously feeling the explanation was unnecessary, "for the sake of a dream that has robbed me of all sleep and peace these three sevendays and led me farther from Kinark than any sane man should go. And yours is the face in those dreams—the master of them. But they'll stop now. Oh yes, they'll stop."

How? Tristan wondered. He knew better than to ask. He wasn't responsible for the dreams, but if Jehan thought killing him would ensure an end to them . . . Tristan tested his bonds, surreptitiously, he hoped, but Jehan noticed and kicked at him. It was not an especially hard kick, but it was painful and the last straw to prick Tristan's patience.

"Toadstools!" he burst out angrily. "Do you seriously think that if I could work a spell to trouble your sleep miles and weeks away, I'd be lying here tied up like a sack of meal right now? Wouldn't I have recognized you? Either you've got the wrong wizard, or there's something going on here that neither one of us understands!"

That was perfectly logical. Jehan seemed to think so. He considered the point a long, thoughtful moment. Then, moving faster than such a big man ought to have been able to, he whipped out the rag he'd been playing with and used it to gag Tristan firmly and very thoroughly.

"I'm not as ignorant of your tricky ways as you maybe expected, sorcerer," he said, as Tristan twisted his head futilely, choking. "Thought you could play with me as you liked, didn't you? Well, you've overreached yourself. You're in my hands now."

And with that and no further ado, he crossed to the other side of his fire, turned his back, and settled himself for sleep with apparently perfect confidence.

Tristan stared at the man incredulously, but he never moved. This was no trick. In a few moments Jehan was snoring gently.

Tristan felt clearer headed, and realized only then how muddled he must have been before. He gave himself a mental shake. He'd missed some simple, important point in the exchange, surely, one that would explain all of this. He *must* have done so. If he could just think . . . He'd better call Valadan.

He tried once to twist his head and spit the gag out, but the pain that shot through his bleeding mouth and bruised face suggested he not try the move again, at least not without carefully weighed consideration. Well, maybe he could contrive to get his hands free; it felt as if the flesh of his wrists had swollen about the rope, but Tristan worried at it anyway, hoping he wasn't simply pulling the knots tighter. His hands were magic-toughened from years of difficult spell practice, strong, supple, and used to exotic contortions. He didn't doubt that he could get loose if Jehan stayed asleep long enough, though he might lose some skin in the process.

Something jabbed his wrist. Tristan tried to swivel his head around to see what, but all he accomplished was a shifting of his gag so that it dug even more nastily into the corners of his mouth. Maybe whatever was there was sharp enough to sever the rope, if he rubbed against it.

Hold still. Thomas' claws hooked into his wrist yet again when Tristan wasn't able to obey swiftly enough. Its source explained, the pain was almost welcome.

Then, with barely a flicker of movement and not the slightest sound of hoofbeat or jingle of his bridle, Valadan slipped into the clearing. He positioned himself between Tristan and Jehan watchfully.

And about time, Tristan thought without charity.

You want to learn to duck, Thomas said helpfully. *Or better still, there's that personal-protection-spell. A truly useful article, that, and the cantrip's not at all difficult to pronounce. Keeps little inconveniences like this from happening.*

Tristan rolled his eyes and jerked his hands urgently, containing his scathing retort until a more appropriate occasion should present itself. The ropes bit into his wrists and he swore, muffled by the gag.

Have you loose in a minute, Thomas promised, and set his claws to work on the ropes again. *You could save yourself a lot of bruises if you'd only learn patience*, the cat added.

Another unwise attempt on Tristan's part to assist with the rope-slicing got his left wrist deeply scratched. He sucked at it while he used his right hand to work the rope from his ankles. His fingers tingled painfully, as if they weren't grateful to be free.

Sorry, Thomas said, not sounding so.

Tristan's legs weren't so benumbed as he expected, nor as bad as his fingers. He managed to get to his feet without making more than a little noise, and Jehan didn't stir. Valadan guarded him closely, just in case.

Thomas sprang to the stallion's back.

Come on. Saddle up and let's get out of here.

Tristan rubbed at his left knee, watching Jehan as intently as Valadan did.

What are you waiting for? Thomas' tail tip twitched violently, and Valadan started as partially unsheathed claws pricked his back.

Tristan knew he could—should—slip away then. He could be halfway to Kinark by morning, far enough to be safe from even a madman's pursuit. But if he did that, he'd go without answers or an explanation for the feeling that seemed to be rooting him to this spot. He told himself it was something more than curiosity.

If he did go, there was no guarantee that Jehan wouldn't simply follow him, bent on revenge for his mysterious dreams. They must be terribly strong, for Jehan seemed no easily frightened simpleton. And a madman on his trail as Tristan moved into the madman's home country was a complication he couldn't afford. Yet that wasn't the whole truth or the real cause for his tarrying now. He still watched Jehan, who was in truth worth the watching.

Jehan was no longer slumbering peacefully. The man had rolled over onto his back, making Thomas hiss with alarm. He wasn't waking, though. His lips were faintly twitching under his beard, and the furrows Tristan had noted before on his forehead had deepened as if freshly carved there.

Come on, Thomas pleaded.

"Not yet, Thomas." Tristan didn't take his eyes off of Jehan. The man's eyelids were quivering now, unless that was a trick of the flickering firelight. Was this one of the dreams he'd spoken of?

Thomas hissed something rapidly about idiot wizards and the ill-fated cats that followed them.

"I'll watch myself, Thomas," Tristan said reassuringly.

You should have done that before. What do you think you're doing?

"He tied me up and then went straight to sleep," Tristan said, wonderingly. "He never even tried to rob me, Thomas."

Maybe he just likes ropes.

"He understands that wizards use their hands and their voices for spells. He did what he could to make sure I couldn't use magic on him and then went to sleep."

He tied you up so he could get a good night's sleep?

"I think so. Thomas, I need to know why he thinks that."

Maybe he's just crazy.

"Maybe. But I can't chance that or ignore this. Some very strange things have been happening—and he comes from Kinark, which just happens to be where we're going, Thomas!"

This is the road to Kinark. Where else would he be from?

Tristan paid no attention.

At least tie him up.

"No." The man's distress was plainly intensifying. The

nightmare had him. "He's afraid of me already, Thomas. If he's going to tell me anything, he'll have to trust me first."

Idiot. He's twice your size.

"All the same." If he wanted information, he'd do well to look as nonthreatening as he could. Tristan moved a little closer to Valadan, though, as a concession to the sense of Thomas' advice.

You're not just going to wait here till he wakes up? I didn't think he hit you that hard.

Tristan fingered his head. His skin was tender at one spot, and touching it hurt, but the skin was whole, and he thought the bone beneath it was likewise sound. He hadn't expected to find evidence of a serious injury. He felt fine, except for the fading headache. Thomas wouldn't know that, though, and was therefore alarmed.

"No. It's nothing like that, Thomas. Really. I'm all right—just curious. I want to know why he jumped on me like that. I want to know what he thinks I've done to him. If he's just crazy, then we'll leave him, but I think there's something more here. Look at him. He's certainly dreaming now."

Jehan was flailing about with his arms, as if he struggled to hold some invisible thing away from him. His head flopped from side to side. Tristan could hear the man's teeth grating. Jehan's knees jerked up; then he let his feet fall back, as if he were some great puppet idly played with. A whimper escaped him. It would be only a matter of moments before his thrashing finally waked him.

Jehan woke abruptly, distraught at first, the dream still half on him. Then his blank look shaded away to anger as he plainly supposed that Tristan had dared plague him with nightmares, even while held prisoner. When he spotted Tristan standing free beside Valadan, his face shifted again—to fear.

Jehan came to his feet, nimbly snatching a smoldering brand from the fringes of the fire. He stood swaying, holding the wood like a club before him.

Tristan wondered if he might not have more to fear from Jehan's terror than his anger.

"Easy." He spread his own empty hands placatingly. "Calm down. I'm not going to hurt you, but I'm not going to let you tie me up again either."

Jehan backed away a step. Valadan detached himself from Tristan's side and stepped to cut off the man's escape. He moved as easily as a fire-thrown shadow, and no normal horse could have shifted so quickly, far less as silently. Jehan recognized that and whimpered again, a lost sound.

"I just want to talk to you," Tristan said. "Stand still and he won't bother you. I swear it."

"By what?" Jehan managed to stammer. "You think I'd trust anything *you* cared to swear by?"

There was only one thing for it. If trust had to be earned, then earn it he must. Tristan waved Valadan away with all the authority he could muster and sat himself down on a fallen log within Jehan's easy reach. Thomas was alarmed beyond any comment now.

"Sit down," Tristan suggested.

Jehan didn't move. The stick in his hand was trembling, and there was a muscle jumping like a fish at his jawline.

"Well? I was under the impression that you wanted to talk to me about something. I'm not going to run away, so you may as well start."

Jehan didn't answer.

"Nothing to say after all? That surprises me—I can see you're having trouble sleeping."

Jehan replied with a strangling sound, but Tristan was glad to hear rage in the sound. He could deal with anger easier than unreasoning fear, which was why he'd spoken arrogantly enough to provoke it.

"No," he said, as Valadan tossed his mane and took a step toward Jehan. Thomas flattened his whiskers back and hissed, though Tristan wasn't exactly sure at whom. "Put that thing down. I don't want him—" He gestured at Valadan. "—to misunderstand. I don't want to see you hurt."

"You haven't cared about that before this!" Jehan snarled. Apparently Tristan's mildness had made him bolder—but hopefully not rash. Tristan thought he had very little strength left for more fighting.

Tristan tried again. "You keep saying things like that." He gave his head a shake and decided he'd better not do that a second time. "Can't you understand that I don't have the slightest idea what these dreams you keep mentioning are? I've never set eyes on you before tonight and I should think I'd remember you!"

Jehan flung the brand away violently—fortunately not toward Valadan.

"Then answer me this! Why is your face in my dreams?"

"I don't know. But I want to find out. That's why I stayed." Tristan pointed at the log Jehan had been sitting on before.

Jehan eyed him warily.

Tristan sighed and tried yet again.

"You must admit that if I really am behind the dreams, then I've behaved very carelessly with you now. Does that make any sense to you?"

Jehan gave that a moment's consideration. At least the man was thinking now.

"No." The answer was grudgingly given.

"Then trust me," Tristan said. "Let's talk. I'm as baffled by all this as you are—I only set out on this journey today and now I find that the first person I meet has been dreaming my face for weeks. I'm a wizard, yes, that's true, but this is outside my experience."

It crossed Tristan's mind to wonder if this might be Elisena's work, a sending-spell gone awry, perhaps, but this had no feel of her. Her spells didn't go wrong, and she'd bade him watch mirrors, not men. He could make no other guesses about the dreams.

Jehan settled nervously on the ground, across the fire from him.

"All right. A truce, then. But try no tricks."

Tristan spread his hands again. "You have my word. Now. Describe one of your dreams. The one you just had should be fresh in your thoughts."

The dream had begun, Jehan said, as harmlessly as all his dreams did. He was at work in his forge. He interrupted the tale to explain that he was a blacksmith—not an uncommon calling in Kinark, certainly. In his dream, he was at work in his forge, comfortable and contented, pounding out a bar of iron upon the anvil.

It was in his mind that the bar was to be made into a ploughshare, a fine sturdy piece fit to serve for years in the rocky soil of the mountain valleys. Yet, glancing down at the anvil, he saw that the white-hot bar was longer than a ploughshare—longer than it needed to be. Indeed, it was a sword-blank. He recoiled from it in horror, but could not wake.

That required a little explanation, Tristan thought; but when pressed, Jehan would only say that he did not follow the trade of the swordsmith. He was a blacksmith only, a repairer of cauldrons and mender of hinges. He made farm implements and naught else. Maybe, Tristan speculated, there was some craft law against weapon-working by those who hadn't attained the necessary grade. Jehan grew agitated when he asked, so they had to leave it at that, with the man trying to turn away from his anvil.

Yet something in the dream kept dragging Jehan back to that anvil, where next he beheld a spider spinning threads of silver about the still-glowing blade. It was as if he were also entangled by the threads. "The blade must be tempered. The work must be finished," a voice then said behind him. Jehan turned away from the voice and the anvil; but no matter where his eyes fell, the sword shape was there. Behind it was a stranger's face, the face whose stern commands broke all his dreams—Tristan's face. In agony, Jehan picked up his tools and went to work.

"Well? What does it mean?" Jehan asked when the tale was finished.

Tristan wished he knew. He'd never been particularly good with dreams, even his own. He couldn't understand why the dream was so alarming, but he could hardly say so to Jehan. He stared into the fluttering yellow-white flames of the camp-fire, trying to order his thoughts.

In ordinary dream parlance, the riddle looked simple enough. Something that attracted was yet feared. It might be a sword. It might not be.

"You don't know, do you? All the way from Kinark, to make the face in the dream tell me why he's cursed me with it—*and you can't answer the riddle!*"

Tristan looked up hastily as Jehan exploded to his feet, ready to get to his own feet if necessary for prudence's sake. Beyond the fire, Valadan made as if to rear, then subsided.

"Look," Tristan said quickly, "there are people you can go to about dreams. There are spells, herbs—there's no reason for you to have suffered so long, or to have come so far. There must be—"

"Do you think I didn't *try*?" Jehan asked, eyes rolling. "Spells are no use, as I've learned over and over. I've been to dream-sifters. They can't help me. I've come for an *answer*. I can't do anything else. I can't sleep for more than a half hour." He sagged back to the ground, all the fight gone out of him. "And the dreams are starting to come when I'm awake, now."

That was probably because the man wasn't sleeping. It was a wonder he'd held on as well as he had, Tristan thought.

"I'm sorry," he said. "I'm trying."

Jehan picked up the wineskin and took a long pull at it. "Aye. I know." He looked at Tristan, seeming calmer—and contrite. "You're doing your best, and that's more than I've any right to expect, after the way I used you. Are you sure you're all right? I blacked your eye a bit, I think."

Tristan remembered not to shake his head again. "It's all right. I'll fix it later."

Jehan looked baffled. "Fix it? Oh. Wizardry, I see now. I'm thick tonight. I haven't slept—" he passed the wineskin to Tristan, letting his words trickle to a halt.

The dream-sword could literally be a sword, or it might only represent something else, some other conflict. Any dream-reader could have told the smith that, and probably had. Obviously it hadn't helped. Maybe Jehan had cheated himself of a cure by refusing the explanation, Tristan thought. But *his* face? Why and how should that be in Jehan's dreams? That piece didn't fit into the puzzle at all.

"Do you think this could be a sending from some other sorcerer, then?"

Tristan shrugged. "I suppose it could be, but I don't think it is. There's no feel of that kind of magic about this, Jehan. Oh, maybe a taste of it, but nothing like the malevolence there would have to be with a sending." He began to rummage in his pack and found a bit of blank paper and a pen eventually. The ink bottle still hadn't surfaced.

"There's a mage I know in the city—a master, a very great healer. He might be able to help you. I know you say you've been to dream-sifters before, but Bleyvr's really good. If anyone can help you, it will be him. I'll write his name out for you, so you can find him—if I can ever find the poxy ink—"

Still, he doubted even Bleyvr's skill could stop the dreams. Dream roots ran deep and grew tangled; Jehan's might be beyond anyone's untangling. It was a pity. Tristan might, given more time and a better beginning, have liked the man.

The moon was long down. Tristan was aching for sleep and

could well imagine how Jehan felt after—what, nearly a month?—of such nights. He took another sip of the thin, sour wine he'd bought in Morsk and passed the skin to Jehan again. Maybe drink would bring a sound sleep, though Jehan would surely have thought to try that early on.

Jehan's sleeve slid back as he reached for the wine. Tristan noticed a scar on the underside of his left wrist, bigger than the little burn scars any smith sported on arms left unprotected against flying sparks and popping coals. The scar was very pale against the surrounding skin and diamond-pointed.

Tristan let his breath out softly, remembering tales read of strange rites of initiation and of life-long vows sealed by the quenching of a blade's hot tip in a smith's own blood.

"'A mender of hinges,'" Tristan repeated dully.

Jehan had found a wedge of cheese on the ground by his feet and brushed the ashes off of it. The rabbit was long since charred past any hope of edibility, so he broke the cheese in half, offering a share to Tristan.

"You're a swordsmith," Tristan said sharply, ignoring the food. "Or are you going to tell me you got that scar by random accident?"

Jehan started and tugged his sleeve down to cover the mark. Done casually, that might have defused the question, but his furtive look gave lie to his answer. "You're mistaken. It's just a burn. I got careless. It happens."

"You were only careless to let me see it. Why did you lie to me about something so important, when you expect me to unsnarl your dreams?"

Jehan looked away, breaking the deadlock of their eyes. "It's not what you think. You don't understand our customs—"

"That's a famous one, though. And wouldn't it be rather difficult to get that sort of burn in just that place by accident? I'm no fool, Jehan. I know what that mark is. And I don't think you can disclaim either it or your trade so lightly."

Anguish stamped Jehan's face as he turned to Tristan again. He dropped his eyes to the ground. "It wasn't a lie. I don't follow that trade now."

"But you did. I thought those vows were unbreakable." His anger was making him question like a lawyer, Tristan thought. What sort of a game did the man think to play?

"Mine *are*! And stronger than *this*!" Jehan struck his wrist with bruising emphasis. "And stronger than the dreams, too."

A smith from Kinark, dreaming of swords and dreading those dreams so that he'd left his home to wander the roads? The smiths of Kinark *never* did that, for so famed was their work that they had no need to go in search of customers. Folk came to them, whatever the cost and inconvenience. A Kinarkan blade was reckoned to be worth the price. He had been right, Tristan thought. There was something odd here.

He remembered the ill-fated seeking-spell he'd worked up for the royal sword. It would be the most bizarre working of a spell he'd ever heard of, Tristan thought, but he ought to be well used to such by now and not so surprised. It couldn't be chance that brought this meeting with a swordsmith when he so needed one's guidance. It couldn't.

Jehan sat with his hands clasped, trying to still their trembling, staring at nothing. Tristan took care to make his voice gentle when he spoke again. He was responsible only for the dreams, not Jehan's reaction to them, but still he felt a pang of guilt.

"It's no wonder the dream-sifters haven't helped you, if you've been no more honest with them. This riddle's hard enough, without working blind. Never mind." Tristan prodded his pack with one toe. "I've got some herbs here, something that will make you sleep deep enough that you shouldn't dream. They'll only work for a couple of hours, but they'll give you a little rest."

He set a little pannikin on the fire, poured wine into it, and added the powdered herbs. Jehan watched dully, without hope. Tristan thought perhaps he ought to be glad not to be burdened with Jehan's true story. It looked to be a crushing weight, whatever it was.

"There. That will be ready in a few minutes. While it steeps, we can talk. I told you I was bound for Kinark. I didn't tell you why. I'm looking for a sword and I need a swordsmith's help. You can think of it as my leech's fee."

Tristan told Jehan the sword's history, and how it figured in Calandra's desperate situation. He did not mention his own part in the story, except to say that he'd been sent to seek the blade; he had learned a little about it in Kôvelir and discovered that it was a Kinarkan blade. Trust was fine, but it only went so far before it became foolishness. Tristan noticed that Thomas looked a little relieved at his discretion.

"So I thought," Tristan said, "that if I went to the spot where the sword was forged, I might be able to follow it outward from there. That's not too much to hope for, but it's the only road open to me—unless those legends *are* true, and the swords have a way of returning to their forging place."

"Seems like a lot of trouble to go to just for a ceremony," Jehan said.

"It's a bit more than that. The crowning can't rightly be done without it. What do you think about the legends?"

"Ah. Truth to tell, I never heard that one before. People say a lot of crazy things. They'll believe anything. And then some fool writes it down and it's taken for gospel forever. I've never had a blade of mine come back to me, except once, and that one was . . . broken." He hesitated over the word. Tristan was puzzled. He'd thought the Kinarkan blades unbreakable. Another false legend, maybe. Another hope gone.

"Some folk, now, they'll bring a blade back to be refitted, if the hilt's bad, or they want a new edge put on and won't trust such a costly weapon to ordinary craftsmen. Maybe that's what started the talk. But I can't see where that will help you find your king's sword for him."

Tristan's spirits sank. This trip, then, was a waste, but he couldn't be certain of that till he'd completed it and had to go home without the sword. If Kinark had no answers for him either—

He stared at the fire, which was paling as dawn's light woke colors from the trees around them. The wine would be ready; he'd better give it to Jehan and try to get some rest himself.

The flame-warmed air shimmered like magic between him and the trees. Through it, Tristan saw snow falling like great feathers at Crogen. Deceptively harmless-looking, the fall could cover the land to the depth of a man's waist in a day. Then the freeze would come to lock the accumulation in, after fierce winds had piled up great crushing drifts.

Tristan could half sense the storms building over the Winterwaste—that shifting barrenness mirroring Nímir's ever-changing, ever-deadly plans and desires. Storms would break soon and were more to be feared than any army Galan could raise. But for those storms and the power they were beholden to, he'd have let Galan have Calandra with his blessing—whatever that might be worth.

A Sane Decision

TRISTAN DANGLED HIS line into the stream, trying to make his thoughts slow and cold, like those of a fish. The glare on the water's surface mirrored his face lopsidedly back at him, distracting him from the spell and hiding the pebbled bottom from his sight. Tristan squinted past the reflection. He needed to find a deep, still pool. That was where the big fish would be waiting for an eddy of the current to bring its dinner to it.

His hook was silver. Tristan's thoughts went down with it through the water, sinking, sinking. Silver bubbles of air clung to the hook, but they broke away now and rose to burst at the surface. This water had come a long, long way since it had been but melting snow on the branches of the cedars in the mountains near Kinark. Still, it was not particularly old, since water transmuted so easily and often—not so old as the great trout that waited, gills gently fanning, upon the pink and gray pebbles a few feet from Tristan. The fish was hungry, though not ravenous.

Tristan thought like a hungry fish. That was relatively easy for him, because he was awfully hungry himself. Unlike the fish, however, he couldn't wait for his meal to come to him. A dew-jeweled dragonfly regarded him from a mossy rock that stuck up out of the water near his face.

He paid out the line carefully, letting the hook—thought-fully baited with a bit of rabbit fur—drift to where he thought the fish might be. He hadn't slept much, and a good solid breakfast would be very welcome. Trout would be perfect.

Running water negated magic. It was difficult to keep a feel of where the hook was and much more so to induce the fish to bite at it. Tristan leaned closer, hoping to see the fish, or at least the flick of a fin, to tell him in which direction the fish's mouth lay.

The water smelled of snow. Tristan felt his mind swept all at once back into Darkenkeep, helplessly, with his horrified eyes still wide open and fixed blankly on the streambed. Caverns of ice rose around him, pillars like great icicles, walls of crystal that were only frozen water, purer or fuller of rare poisons than most. Tristan whirled and ran frantically the way he thought he'd come, slipping on the slick floor, hoping desperately that he wasn't far from the entrance, if the portal still existed.

He went around mazy twists of corridors and ducked through openings both great and small, his hands flung out to hold him up, to fend off low-hanging icicles that threatened his eyes. He skidded, nearly fell, and slammed into a wall instead.

But no matter. There was a door in front of him, finally. Tristan tugged it open and plunged through, into the open air—Crogen's Great Hall, where a throne of ice awaited him.

Tristan cried out and turned to run again, only to lose his footing once more and crash to the frozen pavement. He lay still, feeling his hot tears to be the only warmth in all the world. Something as wet but colder slapped his face.

Lucky one of us knows something about catching fish.

Tristan opened his eyes, and the trout's tail smacked his cheek again. Thomas pinned the thrashing fish with both front paws and administered a killing bite to the back of its head.

Tristan pushed himself up, shivering. His fishing line was wrapped around both his ankles several times—small wonder he'd fallen. His clothes were soaking, so that first fall must have been straight into the stream. He disentangled the line with great care, his fingers trembling.

Want to talk about it? Thomas' fur was wet too. He shook himself like a dog.

"I wish I knew what to say. I wish I knew what that was." Tristan tried to stand, clutching at a sapling as his knees gave way. His boots slithered on mossy rocks.

It was pretty violent for a daydream. Thomas took hold of the trout's tail and offered it to Tristan. *Maybe some breakfast will help.*

"If Jehan's wide-awake dreams are anything like that one, I can understand why he was ready to kill me to make them stop. There wasn't even a shred of warning." Tristan considered letting go of the tree. Not quite yet, he thought. His legs weren't ready to support him.

What did you see? Thomas asked gently.

"Darkenkeep." Tristan shuddered, and the tree quivered. Leaves fell into his hair. "Only it turned into Crogen. It was awful. I think it was what will happen if I don't come up with a sword."

It was also cruelly unfair. He was prepared to be wary of winter's little traps—of the icicle forming daggerlike on the ceiling above his bed, the freezing fog that might take a lone traveler unawares, or the patch of slick ice in the middle of a long flight of otherwise safe stairs. But this instant and total loss of control over his own mind—or even merely his eyes—was against all reason. If it were Nímir's work and not merely some bizarre product of his exhausted and desperate brain—where did that leave him? How would he ever know whether or not Nímir was clouding his mind again as once before and twisting his judgment?

If you can think to question, he's not.

That sounded right, but even if it were, was it entirely so? Tristan released the sapling and staggered forward a couple of steps. There was just no way to be sure. Hagridden, he started to make his way back to the campsite where Jehan slept by the ashes of the fire.

Darkenkeep went right along with him, only a little less clearly this time. Tristan could see the real trees behind the walls of ice well enough to avoid bumping into most of them. He wasn't hallucinating this time—he simply couldn't shake the dream. A sending from Nímir or not, it had aptly mirrored his worst fears, and that alone ensured that it would stay with him. He might not be able to sift Jehan's dreams with any accuracy, but Tristan had no trouble understanding his own.

He had no reason whatsoever to think that the sword he sought still existed and there were very pressing arguments for its destruction—the silence of Crewzel's cards, for one thing. Nor did Tristan have any reason to suppose that a swordsmith could lead him to the blade. Jehan had given him that proof.

He was no less ignorant of the sword's fate than before, after weeks of searching, and he had less reason to be hopeful about the search's outcome. To think otherwise was an indulgence in self-delusion.

There simply wasn't time to ride all the way to Kinark, just to convince himself of something he already knew. No. The dream convinced Tristan of that, as nothing else could have. There was no point in going on to Kinark.

Yet if he did not go there, where would he go? Back to Calandra, as he longed to? Back to Elisena, empty-handed, knowing the doom that would spell for all of them and for the land itself? No! He couldn't.

The sound of Jehan's snores reached Tristan's ears briefly, then broke off as the man apparently woke. Well, at least he could travel with the smith on to Kôvelir and see that the man got to Bleyvr—do some good for someone, while he still could.

A smith. A swordsmith of Kinark. And little more than a day's ride away, lay the city where every commodity in the known world could be found, along with every magic and all the raw ingredients for the maddest idea Tristan's brain had ever hatched. The idea was insane—but it meant he could go home with a chance, at least, a last toss of the dice.

Thomas crouched low behind the doubtful safety of Tristan's pack. It was a good thing that Valadan was on the scene as a moderator. He might be needed, but even the stallion couldn't guarantee that a hapless cat might not get trampled in the brawl that might ensue.

Tristan had begun the mess, walking up to a still sleep-fuddled Jehan and announcing that he'd been on his way to Kinark to look for a swordsmith and that, now he'd found one, he wasn't going a step farther. Jehan's reaction was predictable, loud, and more violent than even his performance the night before had led Thomas to anticipate.

"Forge a sword for you? Aye, when unborn babes speak from their mother's wombs, and such unnatural acts become commonplace!"

Tristan was quietly insistent. He looked awful, worse than one sleepless night could answer for, but he was implacable. Jehan offered to go back to Kinark to see that Tristan got whatever help he needed or help from another smith. No, Tristan said, with as much finality as simplicity in the one word. No. And so they wrangled on.

"You don't understand!" Jehan shouted finally, raging with frustration. "I *can't* forge another sword! I'm not a swordsmith now."

Tristan didn't know enough of Kinark's customs to draw much of a conclusion from that, but he tried. Smithing was a craft like any other. It would have its rules. He thought of the mark Jehan tried to hide.

"Are you saying you broke your vows?"

"They broke *me*!" Jehan sobbed. It was an appalling sound. Jehan heard it himself, seemed shocked, and scrambled to his feet.

Tristan moved to intercept him, only to be shoved off his feet before he'd had a chance to get properly on them. Jehan vanished into the trees.

The smith didn't get far. Valadan loomed in front of him, fixed him with his star-shot eyes, and Jehan collapsed to his knees, weeping.

Tristan didn't blame the man. He'd looked into Valadan's eyes a couple of times himself. He knelt hesitantly beside Jehan, afraid to touch him yet.

The sobbing continued and eventually became words, at first a few at a time, then a rush of sentences.

"I had a brother once. Younger. I was a stripling when he was born. I raised him. Our parents died of a fever plague when he was still small, leaving us alone. It was hard, because I was learning the sword craft, and that brooks no rival. I could take no wife to help us, but I never regretted it. He was my family, all that was left to me. He was everything I wasn't, couldn't be. Light. Laughing. He made my life whole.

"And when he was sixteen, he decided he would go off to war, because he had only the gift of fighting with a sword, not the seriousness needed to craft one. He wanted to find his own way, which was proper, and it was time. He was almost a man. He was as tall as I was. He had a company to fight in, friends who would teach him the things a soldier must know, and I let him choose from all my blades, and take the one that suited him best. I made him armor and I sent him on his way. Two months later his friends carried him home to me. Dead, with the blade—the blade of my forging—broken beside him."

Jehan gulped a steadying breath of cold air and added quite unnecessarily:

"I will never forge another blade."

Tristan led the smith back to the fire and set more herbs steeping. He was wobbling on his feet—tension and lack of sleep were beginning to take a real toll. He fastened his mind firmly on Jehan.

"You don't know why the blade broke—or when," he said gently, offering a cup of the herb brew.

Jehan slapped his hand away. The cup went flying off into the trees, spewing tea. Sighing, Thomas went to look for it.

"My blade failed him! I don't need to know any more."

Small wonder, Tristan thought, that dreams of swords drove the man nearly mad. Jehan wasn't far from coming unhinged now; he was, in fact, wavering at the border of that dark country, swaying and staggering. Talking might do him good, if it could be carefully steered—Tristan hoped he had enough wits left to manage that. This needed the healer's touch of someone like Bleyvr, but there was no one else handy. Jehan might not make it to Kôvelir.

"The dreams." Tristan tried again. "They don't come without reason, and I don't think they're only concerned with guilt. I never believed in destiny—if I ever thought much about it— till I got in its way and was nearly trampled by it. But I've been told I have a destiny and I think you figure in it."

"No." Jehan stood up. Valadan lifted his head, and the smith sat down hastily, angrily. "How did he happen to let me tie you up before, anyway?"

"I don't know." Tristan smiled ruefully. "Maybe it was a punishment. I don't always understand him."

"There's a lot you don't understand. You want a sword forged, and not just any blade, but the finest Kinarkan work, a sword to have a magic laid on it, a sword that can crown a king and save a kingdom."

Tristan nodded. It was nicely put, better than he could have done at that point.

"And you still ask, after what I just told you? I think I must have loosened your wits, after all."

Tristan frowned. "Why?"

"You never saw my neighbors' faces, but I should think

you can imagine them, all the same. One of my blades was broken, shattered like an icicle—a blade that should have been my best, if my own brother carried it. No one was ever so bold as to say it, but I knew right enough what they were thinking. What kind of smith crafts a blade that poorly? I am a smith, aye, but not in Kinark. They never said that either, but I knew it for true."

So, the man had lost both his family and his trade at one stroke—or one shattering. Tristan thought he did understand, but he wouldn't let that get in the way. It wouldn't do Jehan much good and it wouldn't get him a sword.

"We don't have to go back to Kinark," he said, as if that might have been the problem. "We could work in Kôvelir as easily—"

Jehan looked at him hotly. He was still hurting, but his guard was going up again. "Let me go."

"Why?" It was time, Tristan thought, to push. "Are you any more miserable facing this than running from it, always looking over your shoulder, knowing it's back there before you look? Besides, you wanted me to make the dreams stop."

"I don't think you can." There was pure suspicion in Jehan's tone, not the least vestige of hope that Tristan might play on. He was forced to opt for honesty.

"No. You're quite right. But I think *you* can, if you have the courage to work through this. Forge a sword, for yourself if not for me."

Valadan nuzzled at Tristan, wanting the space between his ears scratched. He was no longer blocking Jehan's way or even looking at him, no longer on guard at all, but Jehan never stirred.

The smith was still sitting so, chin on fist and eyes fixed on the trees, when Tristan woke.

He hadn't intended to sleep. It wasn't wise, and Tristan wouldn't have thought it quite that necessary either. His weakness surprised him. He'd gone without sleep for longer periods before. He had no recollection of dozing off; one minute he'd been sitting beside Jehan, lost in thought, wondering what further argument he could offer, and the next thing Tristan knew, he was lifting his head from his folded arms and blinking at the reddish light of the falling sun. His head throbbed briefly.

He was mildly surprised to find Jehan still by his side, but it was better not to question. Tristan got groaningly to his feet and made his way down to the stream. The water seemed colder than before, but that was welcome—and for the moment Tristan was too thirsty to fear a recurrence of his nightmare.

Thomas crouched on the speckled gravel beside him, lapping delicately. A last drop clinging to his whiskers was fastidiously swiped away.

Now what?

Tristan dipped out a handful of water and scrubbed his face with it. His eyes ached; he hadn't had nearly enough sleep.

"I don't know." He was fresh out of solutions and not convinced he had the right to press the issue, anyway. "I'm not sure I'm enough in my own right mind to deal continually with people who aren't in theirs." He stopped speaking to rinse his face again. He needed to shave too, but wasn't awake enough yet.

"At least I knew Crewzel. But *do* I have any right to ask this kind of thing of Jehan? How do I know I'm not doing him a lot of harm?"

You think too much.

"I can't think at all. That's the trouble. Everything's all fuzzy."

Mind like a sieve, Thomas agreed pleasantly and began to groom himself.

Hooves rattled on the stones as Valadan made his way slowly down to the water. He drank. The stream rippled softly around his legs, as if it enjoyed the touch. Tristan watched the colors shift and blend, almost hypnotized. He leaned his face against Valadan's warm neck, finally, and shut his eyes.

He could hear the stallion still drinking. The water gurgled down his throat, past Tristan's ear. Careful, Tristan warned himself. You're falling asleep again. If only sleep could give him the answers he sought, instead of offering yet more questions.

Still, he had not dreamed while he'd been sleeping the day away. He could probably sleep safely even now, unlike Jehan, who knew neither rest nor peace. And that was as much Tristan's fault as anyone's—if, as he half suspected, his seeking-spell for the sword had been the spark that set Jehan's mind smoldering. Jehan might have dreamed of swords in any case, or those dreams might have lain unwaked at the bottom of his mind all his life. Tristan couldn't be sure, but the intrusion of his own face into the dreams made him feel responsible and sick at his helplessness.

He had no right to ask such a pain-fraught thing of Jehan; but having gotten the smith into this fix, Tristan had a moral obligation to get him out of it, if he could, especially when Calandra's fate rode on the toss of the dice as well. He couldn't let mere exhaustion or uncertainty sway him from that.

Valadan lifted his head at last, pearls of water dripping from his muzzle. His eyes sparkled in the twilight. Tristan returned his gaze and let himself be swallowed by the stallion's eyes. There might not be comfort for him there; perhaps there would only be a stern prodding toward the task before him. But he could hope at least to gain strength to carry him through the next few hours. That wasn't too much to ask.

His tiredness dropped away. Tristan felt quite fragile, as if the least stress would set him shaking, but his mind seemed a touch clearer. Moving with exaggerated care, he filled the empty wineskin with water and walked back through the trees to Jehan.

The smith drained the skin, drinking without pause. Still he said nothing, and his gaze was distant. Tristan spotted a fallen branch a few yards off and dragged it back, to begin building up the fire once more, before night fell. He cleared the old ashes away and gathered tinder with a brief summoning gesture from his lefthand fingers, not really thinking about it. Dry twigs and bits of grass swirled into a tiny pile beneath his fingers, carried by their own diminutive wind. Tristan scooped them together, still not really noticing them or wondering how they'd gotten there, and took out his firestone.

You know, when you forget to expect to fail, you're really much better at this, Thomas pointed out. The fire crackled to accent his point.

Night fell. Tristan makeshifted a griddle out of a flat rock, mixed oats and water together with a dab of honey and roasted the resultant cakes over the fire. He found he was hungry. Pity it was too dark to try for another fish.

He handed Jehan a warm cake. The smith took it and stared at the broken pieces in his fingers.

"A flawed blade would be no use to you," he said, as if they'd been discussing the subject for all the past hours.

Tristan shrugged. "No man would bear that mark if he

weren't a master swordsmith. You've judged yourself too harshly." Trying to coax a straying bit of batter back to the center of the griddle with his magic, Tristan let his fingers stray a trifle too close to the coals. He yelped and stuck the blistered tips into his mouth.

"Anyway," he managed to go on, blowing on the fingers, "I'm not such a great shakes as a wizard that I should judge anyone else's proficiency at his craft." He sucked on his fingers again.

"You'd trust me where I don't trust myself?" Jehan wondered.

"Oh, yes. That may be foolish, but still—sometimes things can work out in the most surprising ways. The only thing is, you have to risk it, first. If you don't try, nothing happens."

Jehan looked pained.

Don't you think that's just a touch oversimplified? He's not stupid.

Tristan flushed a little, but Jehan, of course, hadn't heard Thomas. The smith coughed into a closed fist.

"I have tried to make this decision sanely," he said at length. "But the more thought I give it, the more certain I become that it may not be. If I choose now, that choice comes after too many days without real sleep, and my thoughts are as clouded as bad glass. Yet if I sleep, I will surely dream; and after another of those dreams, I would promise anything to anyone who could offer me hope of ending the dreams. I have tried from the first to do what seemed right—I put down the tools of my trade, I gave up my forge, I left my home, and none of that helped at all with my grief; then the dreams came, and it did not help with them either. I think there is no doing right here now. I have done all that I can think of to do. I can die, I suppose, but I wonder if that is a real answer?"

Jehan leaned upon his fist once more, then gnawed upon one large knuckle. "I took to the road seeking an answer, and 'twould be cowardice to turn back without one, even if I end my life. So I will do this thing you ask, Tristan, and may Calfr who forged the lightnings have mercy on us both."

Chance Met

THEY RODE TOWARD Kôvelir as the morning mist lifted and moved all day at what Valadan considered to be a slow pace, lest Jehan be greatly unnerved. It was plain that he found a horse that could carry two men and a small anvil without complaint disquieting enough; there was no sense risking magical speed as well. Knowing a beast had magical powers and actually being confronted with those powers could be quite different matters.

Sun-fall found them within sight of the city at last—rather a long sight.

"We'll camp," Tristan said. "No use trying to get the gate-keepers to open up for us. It will be dark by the time we can get there, I doubt they would let us in once they'd shut the gates for the night." He glanced back at Jehan. "Are you still sure we can find all the things you'll need in there?"

Jehan raised his curly brows.

"In the Wizards' City? If we don't, I'll suspect the very foundations of the world. The legends say there's something of everything in the world in Kôvelir. If it doesn't come there naturally, the wizards bring it there, just to keep the legend honest."

They didn't have Elisena there, though, Tristan thought. He missed her, abruptly, the scent of herbs and spring that clung to her, and the jingle of the crystals in her hair. If all went well, he'd soon be back with her. It couldn't be soon enough for him. He felt lonelier than he had at any time since Blais' death.

The wolf star was rising, with a glow and a glitter as silvery as Elisena's ten rings. Tristan stared at it till he saw it even with shut eyes, then stumbled off to gather firewood while Jehan arranged their camp. Leaves crackled under his boots.

You worry too much, Thomas said, scrambling after him. *She's very capable.*

"More than I am. I know. But I don't like leaving her alone. And she's facing a more immediate danger than we are."

"Are you sure about that?"

Tristan let the branch he'd just picked up drop onto his toe, tripped over it, and only saved himself from falling by blundering into a tree trunk. He clung to the rough bark with both hands, whipping his head frantically from side to side. He couldn't tell where the voice had come from. He couldn't see anything in the gloom under the trees, nor hear anything more, with his blood singing and surging in his ears. He dropped a hand to his belt, seeking his dagger, and couldn't find it.

"Oh, aye, I was surprised to see you here too, but I think I'm handling it better. Isn't Kinark in the other direction?" One of the shadows seemed to have moved a little.

"Crewzel?"

"If I'm not, you're in trouble, aren't you? If you're still looking for your knife, you lost it while you were dropping that chunk of wood on your foot." She stepped out of the trees, hitching her skirt up with one hand. "Well met, if unexpectedly." Crewzel bent suddenly; rising, she tapped Tristan on the chest with his dagger's pommel.

"But how did you find me?" Tristan was astonished, though he felt there ought to be a far stronger word to match the feeling. When *he'd* been searching for Crewzel, she'd been nowhere to be found. And now, in literally the last place he'd expected—

"I wasn't even trying. I was just stopping here for the night and heard your voice. Thought my ears had gone bad." She bent again and began to stroke Thomas, who purred and uncharacteristically let himself be lifted up into her arms. "You didn't answer my question, unless you were too frightened of voices in the dark even to hear it—what are you doing here? You said you were going to Kinark."

Tristan wondered dazedly if she thought he'd lied to her. But Crewzel would hardly have been so tactful about such a suspicion.

"As luck would have it, I didn't have to," he said. "Not all the way. Some of that destiny you're always talking about met me on the way, and now we're both bound for Kôvelir. His name is Jehan. He's a smith."

Crewzel sighed. "Wonderful. Has he got any food? It's all very well for you to smile—what have *you* got to be gloomy about, larking about on that great enormous horse, while I've spent these past two days wandering in the wilderness?"

As she flounced past him, and as they passed through the relative brightness of a clearing in the forest, Tristan noted bits of straw tangled in the ends of Crewzel's curling fall of hair, and doubted she'd spent those two whole days walking. She'd hardly have gotten this far. After all, this was a traders' route. Tristan rather suspected that haywains plied it frequently at any season this close to the city. Such would willingly offer a traveler a day's ride in return for the promise of a prosperity-spell or a fortune-telling. Wandering in the wilderness indeed! Why, Crewzel even wore a necklace of strung raisins among her other beads, such as merchants carried for quick snacks along the road.

Tristan grabbed up convenient bits of wood as they went and just managed to have an armload by the time he'd guided Crewzel back to where Valadan and Jehan now waited. Crewzel settled herself wearily by the fire and virtually ignored both her introduction to Jehan and Tristan's brief recitation of her history.

Jehan gave her stares aplenty, though, both then and all through their hastily scraped-together meal. Certainly he'd a right to his surprise and curiosity. Crewzel sighed and rubbed her bare feet.

"I should have taken you up on your offer," she lamented. "Even though you were going in the wrong direction. You got turned around soon enough, and I'd have saved myself a dusty walk."

"Tomorrow you won't have to walk." Tristan could hardly repress a smile. He tossed a few hot stones onto the bread baking at the fire's edge. Unleavened, it wouldn't rise, but the stones would bake it faster, giving it heat from both sides at once.

"One of us will," Jehan pointed out. "No horse can carry three."

Valadan snorted deprecatingly.

"It would be a bit crowded, anyway," Tristan agreed tactfully. "It's not far now; we can both walk. And once in the city, we get to work." He'd been practicing his spellcraft upon the spit that was roasting a rabbit for their dinner. With only a little concentration, he could turn the spit without physically touching it. He was mildly elated with his accomplishment, and the scent of the roasting meat improved his humor even more. If this kept up, he would even be able to stop worrying for a little while.

"Work, hey?" Crewzel's hand snaked out and caught a crisp morsel of rabbit. "Never a moment's rest with you."

Tristan grinned and gave the spit another turn. He bespoke the fire until it burned more brightly. "No. Want to hear about it?"

"Not unless that's the price of the meal." Crewzel snatched a bit of bread and began to gnaw at it.

Tristan told her anyway, still feeling optimistic about the project. Somehow that seemed easier in the flickering firelight—at least easier than speaking the whole thing through in broad daylight would have been. In the dark, all things were possible, however strange.

Crewzel waved one hand at him. Then both.

"No more, I beg you. A wizard setting himself to work cold iron—you *are* going to need my help! I suppose next you'll turn my own words against me and say we didn't meet by chance."

Sleight of Magic

TRISTAN EASED THE shutter-bolt open, hoping fervently that the rusty metal wouldn't complain loudly. But the goose grease he'd stealthily worked onto the metal the night before had done its work faithfully, and the bolt slid over with a click, its action just stiff enough to catch two of Tristan's fingers painfully.

He dared not curse, even under his breath, lest he inadvertently utter some magical word while in physical contact with cold iron. Tristan could feel Thomas crouching beside his feet on the street cobbles.

"Never mind smirking," Tristan whispered angrily. "Get up there and make sure that room's still empty!"

Thomas vaulted onto the wooden sill and nosed the shutters open. Whiskers a-twitch, he peered in.

"Well?" Tristan prodded.

Just a minute! The fire's out, so it's hard for even a cat to see. Thomas' tail jerked angrily. *Thought so. A dog. A big one.*

"Toadstools! Do you remember any good quieting-spells?" It was too dark to read anything from Blais' grimoire.

Better not. That's a smithy, remember. Lots of iron lying about. This is a quiet time of night, and pyrotechnics would be pretty conspicuous.

Tristan swept the alley with a hasty glance. They dared not linger in the open too long—there was no innocent reason for being there, if anyone should see them. Fortunately there was no moon in the sky at this hour.

Everything in the world might be found in Kôvelir, so Tristan had found no trouble in locating the tools that Jehan needed in addition to the hammer and anvil the smith carried with him. But Tristan's funds were running low, even with Crewzel helping him bargain in the secondhand markets, and he still had to find and pay for the special water Jehan needed. If Jehan's guess as to its cost was accurate, there would barely be enough left to keep them eating after travel provisions were exhausted. There was not enough to purchase the bellows Jehan would need.

That meant that Tristan had to steal the bellows—his reason for lurking in the dark street outside a forge. He'd found a smithy boasting two bellows—a patched pair set aside and not yet sold, but already replaced with a new set. There would be no hardship to the smith because of the missing implement. And Tristan could return it when the job was done.

But he misliked stealing. Crewzel would have laughed if he'd confessed such nice scruples to her; she had led a far rougher life, and such things mattered little to her, so Tristan hadn't spoken of his dislike while asking her tactical advice. But the crime ate at his conscience, all the same. He would be happy when this night was over. Probably he'd be a wreck, as well.

Or maybe in jail, Thomas suggested unhelpfully. *There's definitely a watchdog.*

Tristan stretched, got his chin onto the windowsill, and looked down his nose into the smithy. He couldn't see a thing.

It's asleep, Thomas said. *On the far side of the firepit.*

"The *far* side?" Tristan slid back down, scraping his chin unpleasantly. He rubbed at it and thought, trying to remember clearly what the forge had looked like when he'd visited it in daylight. He'd seen so many forges while searching for the bellows. Their layouts all blended in his mind.

"Maybe if I'm very quiet?"

You'll never in your life be that quiet. And the dog's too close to the bellows.

"Is it chained?"

I don't think so. But the smith probably lives upstairs. A couple of loud barks and you'd have him to worry about, too.

Tristan spread his hands. "I don't know what else to do." He fitted a boot toe into an irregularity in the brickwork, heaved, and gained the windowsill. Now to let himself down inside. Jumping would be too noisy, and the window was just a little too high to make this easy.

Thomas joined him on the sill, purring thoughtfully.

Good, Tristan thought. The cat could see better in the dark than he could—maybe that would help him reach the bellows more quickly. Thomas scanned the room again. His tail twitched.

Might work. I can't see any chain. When you get inside, crouch down as low as you can, right under the window, and don't move, whatever you do. When the time comes, grab the bellows and run.

"When's that?" Tristan started to ask.

Thomas slapped him across the lips with a paw. *You'll know. Get down.*

Tristan dropped and dutifully crouched on the brick floor. He felt silly. The dark of the forge seemed to breathe softly around him, though he couldn't hear the dog. Gradually his eyes adjusted to the tiny amount of light that the unshuttered window admitted. Overhead he heard the *scritch* of Thomas' claws. Then a soft meow.

Something stirred in the darkness beyond the firepit.

Tristan's eyes widened as the mastiff prowled straight toward him, its nails clicking on the bricks. Surely Thomas didn't think he was hidden here! He'd be seen the moment he moved, and probably sooner. Tristan shut his eyes, afraid they might reflect what light there was and give him away right then, but he couldn't bear the blind suspense for more than a dozen heartbeats. He heard Thomas call again.

The dog's head came up sharply. Its dewlaps slapped against its neck.

Was he supposed to try to slip past while it watched Thomas? Tristan wished the cat had elaborated just a bit on this brilliant plan, or that he hadn't acceded to it so readily. His leg muscles tensed uselessly.

The mastiff sniffed wetly. It would smell him long before it saw him, Tristan feared. And which would come first—the fanged attack or the howled alarm? How should he escape either one? He would have been frozen in his place, if he hadn't been trembling so.

The dog hadn't seen him, though. It stood a scant three feet from Tristan's face, following Thomas with its eyes while its great nose worked and its lips quivered. A rumbling, almost too deep-pitched for Tristan's ears, came from the mastiff's chest.

Then, having whetted the beast's ire sufficiently, Thomas yowled like an uprooted mandrake, arched his back and stood tall upon the sill, legs stiff and fur bristling. The mastiff leaped. Its hind feet landed on Tristan's neck and back, slamming him face-first onto the bricks, as the dog hurtled through the un-shuttered window after Thomas. Sounds of the chase receded down the alley.

Tristan dragged himself over to the bellows, then back to the window, moving mostly by instinct. He blundered into something that went over with a clatter, then heaved himself over the sill and managed to crawl into a patch of shadow before a tinderbox-flicker and candlelight appeared in the windows above the smithy. By the time the questions, shoutings, dog-callings, and cursings began, he was several alleys away, feeling at a puffed lip. His neck hurt, not to mention his face or his ribs.

Tristan hoisted the bellows farther up into his arms and wondered where he was supposed to rejoin Thomas. He wondered how the cat had intended to lose the mastiff, and if he'd succeeded yet.

Two greenish points of light appeared at a level a foot or so above his boot soles.

The things I do for you! Thomas grumbled.

Crewzel viewed him with considerable disfavor when Tristan finally crept through the door of the empty former stable she'd found—or if you took Crewzel at *her* word, was renting to him—for the forging operation.

"How you escaped the Watch is beyond me," she scolded. "You're about as stealthy as a troop of armored cavalry. I heard you half the street away."

Tristan dropped the bellows onto the floor, where the partly inflated skins made a soft *whuff* as they settled. He made no further comment. He couldn't have been so noisy as all that, for Jehan was still sleeping placidly, rolled up in the pelt of a long-wooled sheep.

Crewzel touched his face. "Tchh. What did you do, trip

over something in the dark? Wool-gathering, likely," she added disgustedly.

Tristan sat down and reached for the earthen mug he'd left tucked in the fire's embers, hopefully kept warm that way. The tea inside was awesomely strong and stung his split lip. Tristan winced and set the cup aside, wiping tea off of his chin.

"No," he finally said. "There was a watchdog we weren't expecting."

Crewzel scowled.

"You *should* have been expecting it! You could have had a sleep powder ready. Did you expect they were going to make it easy for you?"

Tristan supposed that he'd only have accidentally inhaled such a powder and put himself to sleep. He said so.

"You'll never make a master thief at this rate," Crewzel insisted.

"I don't need to be! We've got all the tools now, unless Jehan thinks of something else." Tristan rubbed the back of his neck and grimaced again. The mastiff's claws had left either welts or cuts there.

Crewzel bent close to see. Over Tristan's protests, she began to smear a smelly ointment of her own concocting over his skin. She dragged the evening's tale out of him bit by reluctant bit, saying finally that he'd probably deserved worse.

"Not one bit of sense," she grumbled. "Go to sleep. He'll want you in the morning, and if you really don't want him to know where you got those, you'd better not look like you've been up all night."

Tristan stretched himself out on the floor carefully, finally finding a position which pushed neither his bruised face nor his wounded neck into the scratchy bedding straw. He heard the rustle of Crewzel's skirts, then, as his eyes closed, the ceaseless slap-slap of her cards, being endlessly gathered up and laid down.

For a sword, they would need a great quantity of charcoal, and not an ordinary sort. Therefore Tristan had, at Jehan's direction, purchased half a load of oaken logs from a lumber-yard.

Jehan patted one of those logs as they finished chopping the last of them into handy, unrecognizable chunks. "Good Bralorn

oak. Must have cost a fortune here. It's dear enough in Kinark—
and it grows there."

Tristan didn't like to remember what the oak had cost. He
wiped sweat out of his eyes. And all so it could be chunked
and burned. He knew it was necessary, but still he felt a tickle
of outrage. He mentally counted the coins he had left. There was
no need to panic yet, but Tristan suspected there might be soon.

He thought they were ready to begin stacking the log-chunks
for the charring, but Jehan was wandering about the stable,
randomly touching bits of equipment—grindstone, bellows,
anvil, hammer, and exotic tools whose use was beyond Tristan's
best guessing. The smith might have been merely checking a
mental inventory, assuring himself that nothing vital had been
overlooked, but his expression was curiously blank. Tristan's
spirits sank.

Jehan's grim resolve to work through and out of his personal
troubles seemed strong enough, and his pledge was equally
binding, but neither of them had truly been tested yet. A strain
seemed to grow as each new bit of equipment arrived—whenever Jehan could no longer pretend even to himself that he
didn't know what work he was about to undertake. Tristan
watched anxiously, then decided it would be best not to be
seen doing so.

He shivered. A wizard who barely dared touch cold iron,
he thought, and a forsworn swordsmith who'd pledged never
to make another blade—how dared they attempt this thing?
And for such a crucial, special sword at that? Jehan had a right
to be nervous.

Jehan lifted his hammer, stroking the ashen handle. He
shuddered.

Tristan, unable to bear more witnessing of Jehan's fears or
rehearsing of his own, grabbed an armload of wood and staggered to the charring pit beside the stable's rear door. He went
back for a second load and began to stack the stuff in the pit.
As he'd expected, his ineptness speedily drew Jehan's full
attention.

"No! Not like that. Here—" Jehan took a chunk of wood
out of Tristan's hands and began rearranging the others to suit
himself, shouldering Tristan away. The smith was frowning,
but at least he was normally engrossed in his craft, and anything
was better than that senseless look he'd been wearing. Tristan

grinned to himself, picking a splinter out of the palm of his left hand.

"All right. But you'll have to remember, I'm no hand at this. Wrong kind of background. Not many wizards hang about forges." Only a very powerful mage would attempt to master the wild magic that cold iron and normal magic made together. An "enchanted" sword more likely had only an ensorcelled hilt, usually silver, which had been worked upon well away from the blade. Spelling the iron itself was difficult, dangerous, and so unpredictable as to be pointless. Runes cut into the steel helped only marginally.

"Seems funny to send a man who can't touch cold iron after a sword," Jehan said. "Even if you were just supposed to find one, and not forge it. Is it truly poison to you?" He and Tristan had discussed the matter briefly, days before, because Tristan thought Jehan was entitled to know the extent of the help he could expect to have.

"Only when it's coupled with magic." Tristan set his arm-load down as he was bidden. "It's not as bad as all that. Don't worry. You'll have another pair of hands available whenever you need them, clumsy though they may be."

They finished the stacking. When all was to Jehan's satisfaction, they covered the pit over with chunks of sod cut the night before in an abandoned courtyard. The moist dirt had a springlike smell to it, despite having come from ground only a little removed from a city street. Tristan thought at once of Elisena, and his sight blurred as his eyes grew moist.

Jehan dug draft holes around the base of the pile and a larger chimney hole in its center. Using his knife and a few sticks of wood, he made a nest of shavings and kindling inside the chimney hole and lighted the pile with a ceremonious flourish, having struck a flint to his elaborate fire-steel. Tristan could have done the job as easily with his own firestone, but it wasn't necessary to involve magic at this stage—and maybe not desirable either. The smith would know best about that.

"Now," Jehan said, drawing out his pipe and lighting it with a burning twig plucked from the chimney hole, "once that gets going, I'll cover the chimney and block the drafts. Then it just smolders for three days or so. I'll keep an eye out to see it stays lighted and get the anvil mounted proper and the firepit made."

"You're sure that's enough oak for the charcoal we'll need?" Tristan fretted. It had better be. He couldn't buy more.

"Oh, aye, if we're careful with it, for but the one blade. It usually uses ten or twelve bushels a day to keep the fire going, but I think we'll do some better than that. Charcoal burns hotter than wood and slower, so you don't need as much. It will last."

I imagine he knows what he's doing.

"I didn't mean that, Thomas. I just—"

Crewzel came into the yard and the conversation, her steps dragging. She coughed at the smoke rising into the air and frowned.

"That will bring visitors," she pointed out.

Tristan nodded and started shaping a spell to render the smoke invisible, or at least less noticeable. The smoke did diminish, but more because Jehan had taken a spade and begun filling in the draft holes than through any agency of Tristan's magic. Tristan shrugged and stopped working.

Crewzel sank down on the bench beside him, not troubling to arrange her multicolored skirts which billowed over Tristan's feet. He had thought to ask her how her day had gone, but he hardly deemed it wise or necessary. Crewzel reached into her bodice and plucked out a tightly stoppered bottle. She held it out to Tristan.

"Ask him if he can tell if this is really Istron water."

"Istron water?" Tristan asked delightedly. He'd searched all over the city in the course of his other questings, trying to locate this supposedly vital ingredient of the forging process, without the slightest success. "Where'd you get it?"

"From a trader. He's selling it for medicinal purposes. I pride myself on my expertise in delving out magical frauds, but the smith had best judge this one himself." She jerked a thumb at Jehan, who was still giving the pile of wood and earth a close scrutiny.

Jehan tasted the water, a drop on the tip of one finger, and began to consider.

"How many can you get?" Tristan asked of Crewzel.

"Twoscore bottles that size. I told the trader I wanted to bathe in the stuff. To cure the megrims."

"Just *finding* this should have cured them. It's real. Sweetest thing I've tasted since I left Kinark." Jehan stoppered the bottle and clapped Crewzel on the shoulder.

"I'd liefer have wine," Crewzel said, sidling away.

"You shall," Tristan promised. "Jehan, what is so special about this, anyway?" Tristan would never have placed such importance on the mere water used to quench the hot metal. Any oil or water would have done, he thought.

"Traces of minerals," Jehan informed him. "They combine with the steel, lend it strength and resistance to corrosion. That's why our blades last long enough to become legends. And I've heard that this water makes the swords more amenable to magic, but I don't know if that's true."

Tristan nodded. "I've heard stranger tales than that." He should be glad that Kinarkan smiths didn't quench their swords in blood. Some smiths did, or so he had read. "Does every smith in Kinark use water from the same spring, then?"

"River. And yes, we do and have done since the properties were first recognized."

Tristan glanced up at him sharply, struck by an unwelcome thought. "Are you sure the particular blade we're talking about was made after that discovery?"

"Oh, aye. The water was in general use then." Jehan seemed perfectly at his ease, now that he was caught up in discussing his craft. He puffed carefully on his pipe. "Beyond that, I can't tell you. Smiths are always willing to experiment within the bounds of tradition. I told you this wouldn't be easy, if you recall."

One more gamble, Tristan thought, misliking it. But he'd come this far—

He watched the little tendrils of smoke still escaping the draft holes to rise into the sky. The air above the pile shimmered with heat already.

"How long does it take to forge a sword?"

Jehan loaded his pipe freshly and lit it anew. "I've known smiths to labor a year or more on a blade before they were satisfied." Then he grinned as Tristan blanched. "But it's a fool who drags a task out that long, not a perfectionist. I'd say a fortnight till all's done. Less, with luck."

Still, that cut things very fine, finer than the sharpest sword could have done. Tristan had barely three sevendays left out of the time he and Elisena had agreed upon.

"When do we start, then?"

"These coals will be ready in about three days. By then I should have the rest of the things in order, and we can make a start." Jehan twirled the bottle of Istron water about in his nimble fingers. "Now that this is taken care of."

Thomas reared himself up against Tristan's leg and sniffed the bottle.

I hope you have sense enough not to drink any of this stuff.

"Oh, I don't know, Thomas. It doesn't seem to have hurt Jehan any. He's grown to rather a good size, wouldn't you say?" The smith's head nearly brushed the cobwebby ceiling of the stable. He was bigger than Polassar—taller anyway, though slim except for his massive shoulders and arms.

Your nose is all that you could depend on to grow, Thomas said, squashing Tristan's envy.

Crewzel sat, isolated by shadows. She had not spoken ten words since returning with the Istron water. Tristan dished up a bowl of stew for the evening meal, but she would touch nothing. He thought perhaps to tease her out of the mood and made up a very ornate story about his escape from the watchdog, but it fell horribly flat. He tried again, another story with similar effect. Nothing availed, so he gave up reluctantly.

The meal over, Tristan fetched out Blais' grimoire and worked for a while on committing the personal-protection-spell more firmly to his memory. Thomas had acidly suggested that course again after the incident with the watchdog. The spell wasn't difficult, as the cat had promised, but it had to be letter perfect and used instantaneously to be effective. Tristan had most of it learned, but he kept mixing inflections on the final two similar words whenever the grimoire wasn't right in front of him. Tristan sighed. His concentration was poor. Crewzel's non-critical silence oppressed him.

He called her name, finally, somewhat urgently. She looked at him blankly, then turned away once more—an enigma, Tristan thought, as every person he met lately seemed to be—utterly beyond his comprehension, with untold private torments locked behind the eyes. Then, staggeringly, he realized that every person now central to his life had been a total stranger to him less than a year before. Life's unpredictability could be very bewildering. Tristan felt cold and lonely.

Maybe Crewzel felt the same.

"No one's seen Delmon at all?" He hardly needed to ask; the answer was without question. His words hung dismally in the air between them.

"Jehan says we've got three days before the charcoal's ready. He'll be busy, but he won't need me until then. So, for three days, you've got another pair of eyes."

Make that two. And mine are sharper. Thomas flicked a bit of straw between his paws.

Stolen Oranges

"IT'S NOT AS if he weren't used to taking care of himself," Tristan said, watching an auroch's hide being stretched for drumheads. "There's that to be thankful about. I've never seen a more self-reliant child."

"How many children have you known?" Crewzel asked sarcastically.

Tristan sighed, careful to do so quietly. "Not many, I'll admit. But he's better than I was at that age. More used to the world, better with his magic. And after Cabal worked with him, the magic should have come along even more quickly. I stand by what I said. Delmon can take care of himself."

"He'll never be the layabout his father was, but the boy's scatterbrained enough," Crewzel said.

Tristan blinked, perplexed. "Excuse me, but I thought you said you loved Giffyd."

"I did." Crewzel raised her head. "It didn't blind me. He wasn't the most practical man I've ever met. Kind, yes. Loving, yes. But never practical." She sighed. "It didn't matter. I knew I could have done better without him, but it wouldn't have been the same. It hasn't been."

The silence could not become more uncomfortable without

becoming unbearable. Tristan cleared his throat hesitantly, then went on as if he'd not been interrupted.

"Just because he hasn't gone back to the Academy, that doesn't mean that anything happened to him or even that he's not still in the city." The auroch's hide boomed dully as it was further tightened. Four men tugged at it, their combined strength barely equal to the task. "And even if he's not still looking for you, there are plenty of marvels in this town to detain him."

"I should just follow *you* around the city," Crewzel said angrily. "Anything that fascinates you is bound to attract Delmon!"

Tristan swung around and caught hold of her wrists.

"Crewzel, we *will* find him! I swear that. Why can't you believe me?"

She glared at him, eyes narrow. "I don't think you should make promises you can't keep. You mean well, but you'll only be hurt when you disappoint yourself."

"We'll find him! Unless you know some reason why we shouldn't."

She tugged her hands away. Freed, they began to twist the beads tangled about her neck. "I just keep thinking... what if he *did* find me? Suppose Cheris—"

Tristan dismissed that with a wave of his hand, wondering how safe he'd have felt doing so if he hadn't personally seen Cheris carried off.

"Cheris would have told you. He would have enjoyed telling you far too much to keep quiet about it. Now hush. We *will* find him. Look. Oranges." He turned her around toward the fruit vendor. "Let's have some fruit. It's past sun-high; you must be as hungry as I am."

As they inspected the rosy-golden globes, Tristan went on:

"I can always go to the mages. They may have a skilled seeker here—they ought to. And Delmon was a student of theirs; surely there's some help they can give us."

Even while he spoke, Tristan knew the words shaped a lie. There'd be no help from the mages. As an outsider he could hardly expect help. Cabal was too ill, and if his sudden disappearance had upset Cabal, there'd be small use in Tristan's going to Bleyvr for advice, either. Tristan wished, not for the first time, that he'd taken time to make a few friends during his days at the Academy. But his only close contact with anyone there other than Cabal and Bleyvr had been with Howun—

hardly a decent avenue to pursue, if he wanted help.

What help did he really expect anyway, when no one had given Cabal any in the same matter? Tristan couldn't understand that now, even less than when Cabal had mentioned it to him. To be sure, wizards were a solitary lot, not much given to friendly gatherings or mutual assistance, and they could be jealous of each other—but surely not here among their own brotherhood?

Tristan lifted his eyes from the fruit stand, drawn out of his thoughts by a flicker of movement. A child's hand reached stealthily up from behind the concealment of the piled fruit and plucked another orange from the heap. Then, as the child slipped away into the crowd, Tristan caught for the barest instant a clear sight of him. Small and bird-quick, his face turned away but crowned with a thick familiar clump of dark hair, the child wore a bright blue tunic—a tunic such as Tristan had noticed apprentice magicians wore here.

Tristan started walking rapidly through the crowd, hardly seeing the people he elbowed aside, his head lifted to see over them. He moved faster and faster, dodging about as the traffic made necessary, around carts and wash-laden laundresses, almost under the hooves of a team of dray horses, past a snake-dancer, and away from Crewzel's shouted questions. He lost Thomas, too, as he began to run. He steered well clear of a mailed and helmeted swordsman, a-bristle with blade, dagger, and morningstar, posted by a curtained litter. The blue of the tunic was always just vanishing around a corner or behind an obstacle.

Hanging lengths of bright-woven gauze brushed Tristan's face like cobwebs. Bells jangled by his ears as he collided with a tree of wind chimes, and he left the shouts of irate merchants and some few tumbled wares in his wake. But he was closer to the child now. He could see a ragged tear in the tunic's hem and many stains, as if the garment had been slept in often.

The boy looked back over his shoulder, a reflex of his street life, perhaps. He saw Tristan, then whirled and began to run. The oranges stuffed into the front of his tunic banged against his chest.

"*Delmon!* Wait!"

Shouting the boy's name had no effect. If anything, the child ran faster, dodging and squirming through openings in the crowd so narrow that Tristan couldn't follow without bruisingly widening them. They ducked under the edge of a chandler's awning, past soft candles still forming, and perilously close to a steaming cauldron of molten wax, out onto another street.

The boy dove under the arm of a massive carter who was supervising the loading of sacks of rice onto his wain. Tristan wasn't small enough or so lucky. He crashed hard into the man's side, bounced off, and fell atop a heap of the rice sacks, half stunned. The carter turned slowly toward him, scowling dimly.

Tristan got to his feet, grinning apologetically, desperately hoping to escape a beating and very afraid that he wouldn't. The carter took another step toward him.

His smile felt strained, but Tristan kept what there was of it on his face as he felt for an opening in the press of the crowd behind him. He had to wait until nearly the last second, before the man closest to him decided it might be prudent to move out of the way of the brewing fight.

"Sorry," Tristan offered, knowing that he must look like an idiot. The carter's forearm muscles bulged as his hand slowly, deliberately fisted.

Tristan turned and ran. If anyone had still been in his way, he'd have been well trapped, but he was lucky now and then thrice lucky to be able to put a flock of noisy sheep between himself and all pursuit. In the narrow street, the flock jammed the way to near impassability, and Tristan barely made a way through them, but desperation lent him agility.

Then he took to the alleys, choosing those where the angle of the sun ensured the blackest shadows.

Crewzel caught up with him there a few minutes later. Tristan didn't think she saw him at first—before he recognized the source of her footsteps, he'd been holding his breath so that no one should track him by his panting—but she turned when the breath-holding started him coughing.

She dropped down beside him and clamped a sweaty hand over his mouth, careless of his choking.

"Have you gone mad? Half the merchants in this circle want your hide for sausage casings! You left a swath a bull in a pottery shop would have cause to envy!"

Tristan twisted his head away from her hands. "I almost had him!" he said angrily.

"Had whom?" Crewzel stared at him.

"Delmon. Who are *you* looking for?"

Crewzel continued to stare.

"Delmon? Tristan, that wasn't—" She giggled. "I thought you were just trying to get the oranges back. What a sense of honor, I thought, a chase like that over two poxy oranges. And you such an accomplished thief yourself!"

"You mean it wasn't him?" Tristan put his head wearily into his hands. The cough had mutated into hiccoughs. "Are you sure?"

"Think I don't know my own son?"

"No wonder he ran from me then." Tristan's knees felt rubbery when Crewzel tugged him roughly to his feet. He could feel various bruises too, gotten and ignored during the chase. "I must have frightened him half to death, whoever he was."

I'd say the way he got rid of you more than made up for the fright, Thomas said. *Such delight on such a small face. Lovely to behold.*

Entangled in Dreams

DURING THE NEXT three days, Crewzel grew less and less like herself and became more and more like the stranger Tristan had found in the cottage outside Morsk. They'd been everywhere and seen bits of the city that Tristan suspected even Crewzel had never crossed before. Her guard of cynicism had fast been worn away. She couldn't always keep up the brittle cheerfulness that had made Tristan sometimes forget why they were walking the city. Her silences had deepened as the hours fled by.

Everything in the world could be found in Kôvelir. But it was a terrible place to *look* for something, especially something as small and mobile as a small boy. Crewzel and Tristan sought in craftshops and markets, chophouses, booksellers, apothecaries, and among the teeming ranks of street-hawkers, but turned up nothing—not even rumors.

They seemed to have exhausted all avenues of search, and Tristan was at a loss as to how they might further proceed. He had scant leisure to brood on the matter, for the charcoal was by then ready. As the forging process got underway, there was also Jehan's unsteady state of mind to contend with.

Tristan was so anxious about so many disjointed matters

185

that he hardly knew precisely what there was about Jehan that bothered him. When the sun had barely risen, he watched sleepily as the smith buried a sharp steel knife in the dirt between the doorposts—edge up, to cut any evil that might attempt to gain entry. Tristan didn't know if that was Kinarkan custom, an essential part of forging, or just some new superstition of Jehan's. Still half asleep, he was disinclined to guess.

The smith moved about the stable absently, touching his tools, picking up some and laying them out in new patterns, though he'd hardly need most of them yet. He gave the bellows a squeeze, testing the strength of the forced flow of air.

Watch him, Thomas advised. *He doesn't need all those things arranged just so right now—he's only going to light the fire.*

Jehan burrowed into a leather bag and brought to light a fat stick. He took up his knife and began to cut shavings from the wood, letting the yellow curls drop into the center of the firepit. The tang of cedar reached Tristan's nose. Another tradition, perhaps.

He's still not totally committed to this. He's more than half hoping he won't have to go through with it and that he'll find something to prevent it or some way around it.

Tristan risked a whisper to the cat.

"But Thomas, he said—"

I heard the whole discussion. Thomas patted Tristan's lips shut. *Mark how his hands shake. He's nervous, and I think it's because his mind's not made up. One way or another, with you or not, he'd be calmer. He's wavering.*

Tristan frowned. He wasn't sure Thomas was totally right, but he couldn't say the cat was wholly wrong, either. Thomas observed people better than anyone else Tristan had ever known and had matched his own doubts too well.

He felt, deep down, that Jehan still had a problem about making the sword. Once committed to the task, the smith would pursue it to the end, come whatever might. Tristan was sure of that. The man's earlier vow, and the way he held to it even in the face of the dream, spoke well for that. Tristan had thought he'd secured the commitment he needed. But had he?

He'd better be careful.

Jehan took up his steel and struck a rain of sparks into the pit. A tiny curl of pale smoke reached up toward his face. Scorning the bellows as yet, Jehan blew his own breath upon the flame. The shavings and the kindling took fire. Their crackling seemed loud in the morning stillness.

Tristan made his way to the firepit. He hadn't expected Jehan to begin without even a bite of breakfast, but there was nothing to be done about that.

"Can I help?"

Jehan started out of some private reverie.

"Indeed. Ever worked a bellows?"

Tristan had not, but the task immediately at hand did not call for any great skill. He worked the sheepskins as Jehan poured charcoal into the pit, all about the tiny heap of flame. Tristan's arms began to ache rather embarrassingly soon, but Jehan took over then, the proper amount of charcoal being in the pit at last. When the fire burned well, he said, they would rake it into its final shape. Tristan surreptitiously rubbed his shoulders and was surprised at a blister on his palm. He'd thought his hands were tougher.

"The tinder," he finally asked. "Was that Kinarkan cedar?"

"Aye," Jehan answered, and then said nothing more. Orange flames still licked the lumps of charcoal and colored the smith's eyes. Not till the coals were powdered with white ash did Jehan speak again.

"The woman's cards—you say they showed you the sword you're seeking?"

"Yes—"

"Describe it, then. Be as particular as you can—length, type of guard, and so on. You know much about swords?"

"A little." Tristan's studies with Blais had been extensive and omnivorous. Apparently the smiths of Kinark made several distinct types of blades, though, and Tristan wasn't overfamiliar with them.

"A straight blade," Tristan finally said, closing his eyes and letting the image of the sword-bearing card form on the inside of his eyelids. "Rather thin—it certainly wasn't a broadsword. A plain crosshilt. The grip would have been long enough to get two hands on, but you'd only have used one unless you were making a really hearty slash—or felling trees. A pointsword, more than a slashing weapon anyway. Double-edged— a nice, handy size." Hc was lucky—the sword could just as easily have been a longsword no one but Polassar could have lifted.

"A *skean*," Jehan said. "That just means 'sword,' because

it's a very old type. There weren't any others, long ago. An all-purpose weapon, light enough to be useful to anyone, whatever his size. Because of this."

He turned and burrowed about in his pack, removing at last the costliest ingredient Tristan had bought, except for the Istron water—a silk-wrapped chunk of sky-iron Jehan had personally inspected off and on for two full days before suggesting its purchase.

"*Stoiloh*," the smith said. "Sky-silver." He unwrapped the undyed silk carefully. "Though 'tis not silver. It's iron, right enough, but rare, passing rare. Just as well. A rain of these would kill a man."

"All your swords are made of this?" Tristan asked, awed.

"All that can be. Our days of greatness began when we discovered that this iron made blades that could be thin and strong at once. It's rare, as I say. It falls from the sky. Some of the lesser swords are made with common iron now, using the techniques that we learned from working stoiloh. If the smith is very good, you might hardly notice the difference. But a good smith would never use common steel for a skean. Certainly not for a King's Blade. We were lucky to find this bit, because it's large enough to make a sword. Cobbling two lesser bits together makes for sloppy work."

The iron was the size of a man's head, dull gray and pitted like a rat-gnawed loaf of bread, crisscrossed with bright scratches in places. It looked nothing like a sword. It seemed impossible that it should ever become one.

Crewzel crept in with the last filaments of the morning mist about her, looking no more cheerful. Tristan started to explain to her that he wouldn't be able to join the search that day, but she waved him away, not needing more explanations than the kindled fire and waiting iron before her eyes and not wanting the words.

Using the break her entrance offered, Tristan gathered together a hasty meal, mostly leftover bits of bread and cheese from last night's supper. Crewzel pulled a couple of pomegranates out of her skirts, then poked about, inspecting the fire, the level of ash upon the coals, and the iron, though she dared not touch it. She seemed not to mind continuing her search alone, but she was so skilled at hiding her true feelings that Tristan wondered.

He nibbled at his crust of black bread, noting Jehan's courteous offering of bits of food to Crewzel and his coaxing of her until she ate, even though she mostly ignored him. Maybe, Tristan thought, he wasn't the only one inside the forge suffering pangs of guilt over abandoning Crewzel to her own devices after she'd been such a ready help to them. But might Jehan's feelings perhaps run deeper than mere guilt?

Jehan laid the lump of iron in the fire and left it there till it glowed redder than the coals. He manned the bellows himself, fanning the coals to greater heat. Tristan watched long enough to pick up a few tricks which promised to make his next turn at the contraption less painful, and then turned back to Crewzel, who sat watching.

"You'd think we'd at least have an idea of where he went," he said. "But this city—it's like quicksilver, all change, nothing solid, though it looks so bright and shiny. I sometimes wonder if Delmon isn't simply always at one end of the city just when we're at the other! And there's so *much* magic, I can hardly breathe sometimes. I can't sort out all the influences clearly enough to get any kind of feel of one person. When I was looking for you, I had the same trouble—"

Tristan slapped his forehead suddenly.

"Thomas! What a *fool*! The cats! What do the cats say about him?"

Thomas, snatching a doze in the day's first patch of sun before any noisy hammering could begin, lifted his head and blinked. Crewzel cocked her head at Tristan as if more concerned with the state of his wits than any clue to her son's whereabouts.

"Delmon was fond of you," Tristan pressed on. "It's not beyond reason that there's some other cat in the city who's had contact with him—"

I'm probably a special case. Thomas scrubbed a paw elegantly. *Everyone likes me.* He stood up and stretched, taking time over it maddeningly as only a cat could. *It's a good thought, though. I'm pleasantly surprised at you.*

Jehan gripped the tongs, lifted the iron to the anvil, and took up his hammer once more. The steady sound of blows drawing the iron out began—steady, but far from the continuous, clattering, pounding, Tristan had expected. Rather, short passages repeated over and over, almost musically, until the iron went back into the fire once more. Every third blow struck the anvil alone, rather than the iron, resting Jehan's arm without disturbing the rhythm of his stroke. Tristan helped to hold the iron under the slow, deliberate blows, and turned it as and when he was so bidden.

With many heatings and hammerings, a shape began to emerge. The hotter the iron, the easier it worked; but if left too hot too long, the metal would scale and waste itself, so Jehan brought it along slowly. The more often it was heated and hammered, the stronger it would become, he said.

At first the change was barely discernible, but the pittings disappeared, and gradually the lump elongated until it was a bar rather than a lump and was slowly, slowly teased out until it was far longer than it was wide. The fire was reraked and made narrow and very deep, to heat something as long as a sword properly.

Yet when the iron was a bar, Jehan began to fold it upon itself intricately and then to hammer all into a smooth bar once more. The method had first been tried by smiths working with only small amounts of iron, Jehan said—they forged long, thin rods and combined many rods together until they had enough metal for a blade. Such blades, made of intertwined rods forged solid, were found to be stronger, more flexible than those made by other methods, so the practice was continued and expanded upon, even when more and better iron became available.

The folding and the twisting took two whole days, from sun-up to sun-fall. Tristan added fresh charcoal as the fire required it and cleared the pit of ash and slag each morning and sometimes during the day, if too much had accumulated. If the clay coating the wooden sides of the pit chipped away, he fixed that, too. His eyes burned from the heat, smoke and glare, his ears ached from the continual noise, and he wondered frequently if Jehan's arms were as sore as his own. The smith gave small sign of any such discomfort or even boredom with the slow process. His face was peaceful, almost trancelike sometimes, until some trivial thing should call the shadow back to his eyes.

Thomas' inquiries went slowly, too, since there were many cats in Kôvelir and none of them would talk to a stranger-cat who hadn't the good manners to engage in lengthy preliminary formalities. Tristan did wonder, though, if those formalities must always include interludes of love, as they seemed to. Thomas stayed haughtily mute on that subject.

Tristan was worn enough by the day's labor to sleep without being troubled at all by tired muscles or ears, either, but such wasn't the case with Jehan. He tossed and moaned in the grip of his usual dream—at least Tristan supposed so, when the noise eventually roused him.

Jehan had passed a couple of nights without dreaming. They'd thought the problem ended, or nearly so. But the problem was not so easy of solution, apparently. Tristan pushed himself up on one elbow and rubbed at his eyes. Moonlight poured through the smokehole they'd punched in the roof and onto the smith's contorted face. He wondered if he ought to try to wake Jehan, at least long enough to break the dream's hold. Past experience suggested that would be useless. When the dream came, it came and ended in its own time.

Then Jehan seemed to quiet a little on his own and rolled over onto his face, so Tristan lay down once more and drifted peacefully off. Maybe it had been another dream, then, just a minor nightmare—a normal one.

He woke again when Jehan tripped over him, kicking his leg. Tristan yelled with surprise, but Jehan didn't even turn his head. It was then that Tristan noticed the sword-bar in his hand.

What the—? Was there some arcane virtue to be obtained by exposing the steel to moonlight, maybe?

Jehan carried the blade into the shaft of light under the smokehole, where it glinted dully. The light touched Jehan's open, sightless eyes, too, just as the smith lifted the blade up and smashed it down across the anvil.

Tristan's scream was drowned in the clang of metal. He threw himself toward the anvil without even getting wholly to his feet, tripping on a clinging edge of his cloak, and just managed to lay hands on the sword before he fell.

He'd hoped to dislodge it from Jehan's sleeping grip as he did so, but he didn't hit hard enough. Jehan shook him and the bar as a bull might have tossed an annoying raindrop from its face. Tristan was slammed against the anvil.

He gripped the bar yet tighter, wrapping his arms around it, thankful that it had no cutting edges yet. Jehan let go with one hand, reaching—knowing it was there, somehow—for his great hammer, which leaned against the anvil. Tristan got a purchase with his feet against the anvil's oaken base log and shoved out with his shoulder, pushing Jehan further off balance.

He wrenched the bar free, just as Jehan's fist hit his cheek and sent him sprawling back over the anvil.

Tristan rolled across the floor, trying frantically to keep his body wrapped around the fledgling sword, to shield it from Jehan in any way he could. Jehan, on hands and knees now, swung blindly toward him, his fingers groping ahead of him. His eyes might be empty, but his aim was unnerving. The smith lurched to his feet, and Tristan saw that he'd found the hammer again.

Tristan dodged around the workbench, but Jehan tracked him easily. After one last gasp, Tristan tried to still his breathing in case that might be how the smith had located him. He had to be careful. He daren't use magic—not gripping naked steel in his bare hands! And if the struggle hadn't waked Jehan, what else would? Another toss like the one he'd just gotten would likely knock him out, and there was that hammer too, lethal at close quarters. Tristan didn't like to think what would happen if Jehan hit him with it. He tried edging around the firepit, but Jehan blocked him swiftly. The smith's mouth hung open, his jaw slack. He was panting, the sound loud and ragged in the night, uncanny against the silence. His eyes were still open and without sense. He never even blinked.

"Thomas!" Tristan yelled desperately. "Help me wake him up!"

Me?

Jehan made an experimental swing with the hammer. It didn't miss its mark by much. Tristan jumped back and considered trying to make a break for the door. No chance. Jehan was too close, and the hammer whistled by again, smashing a crockery bowl on the workbench.

"Now might be a good time, Thomas!"

There was a whinny, just outside the door, a scuffling, and then a thudding as hooves crashed against the door. The door held—the bar was strong, and the boards were thick. Valadan might have helped him, but he was too effectively locked out.

Tristan considered tossing the bar out through the window. That might buy him breathing space. Or he might throw something at Jehan, trip him. Only before he could do either thing, Tristan stumbled backward onto a heap of charcoal, turned an ankle as the clods rolled under his foot, and fell.

Jehan turned to face him as Tristan sprawled helplessly, the bar cradled in his arms. The moonlight vanished from the smokehole as a cloud passed overhead, leaving them in utter darkness.

Now I don't even have to shut my eyes, Tristan thought. He tried to get up silently, but his foot turned again, so he let himself fall backward, hoping the hammer-blow would miss. The darkness wouldn't confuse Jehan, who was asleep and working within his own inner darkness anyway.

There was an almighty splashing, suddenly, and much howling and cursing. Water hit Tristan's face, but nothing else touched him.

After a couple seconds of suspense, Tristan fumbled out his crystal and forced a feeble light out of it. He promptly dropped the stone in startlement when its light was reflected back from Thomas' green eyes a mere foot from his own.

Thomas pawed the stone back to him, and it lighted faintly as it touched his fingers.

Good. You're all right. So you can explain to him how he happened to fall into the water trough.

Indeed, there Jehan sat in the slack-tub, spluttering and shaking his head and wondering at the hammer in his hand and the light in Tristan's. Very slowly, Tristan laid the sword aside, got up and put out a hand to help Jehan up.

Catching Jehan between sleeps as it did, Tristan's explanation didn't stick with the man very long. He woke at midmorning and looked frankly amazed at the sights of the wrecked forge and Tristan's bruised face. Tristan had been afraid to sleep again and so probably looked even worse than he felt by then, with his eyes dark circled and rimmed in red. He sat chewing on a bit of willow twig, which took away some of the lingering pain in his ankle. He was just about tired out, now that the night was finally over.

"Sleep well?" Tristan couldn't resist asking Jehan. He spat out a bit of twig.

Jehan's eyes swept the room—the spilled charcoal, the overturned bench and tub, and the scattering of files upon the floor. Finally his eyes came to rest on the sword-bar, lying across Tristan's lap. His hammer was atop the highest rafter Tristan had been able to reach, with Thomas perched watchfully beside it. Jehan paled.

"No," he whispered. "It was just a dream, I didn't really—"

"I wouldn't really say *you* did." Tristan winced a little as speech pulled at his sore cheek. "You were sound asleep the whole time. But we need to talk about this."

Jehan wanted to leave, of course, to go back to Kinark that very day. Then he was all for being securely tied hand and foot each night, but Tristan vetoed that as he had voted down the earlier suggestion. For one thing, it seemed excessively degrading to the smith, even though Jehan himself had suggested it. And for another, he wasn't any too sure it would work. Tristan had no reason to suppose that Jehan couldn't untie knots in his sleep exactly as he'd done so many other unlikely things, no matter how cunningly the knots might be tied. Tristan felt sure he'd never get any sleep, for wondering, so the precaution would be worthless.

And why did the dreams still continue stronger than ever? Thomas seemed proved right about Jehan's wandering intentions, but what man could thus order his own dreams? Yet dreams welled from the inner man and reflected his most secret feelings—unless the dreams came from without, instead.

But from whom, then? Surely no dream resulting from a misdirection of Tristan's sword-seeking spell would lead a smith to destroy that very blade? What would happen if the dreams weren't connected to this sword at all?

Tristan finally suggested that Valadan should stand guard in the forge. They'd be a little cramped for space, but at night that hardly mattered. And Tristan had no doubt of the stallion's ability to control Jehan, even in the grip of the wildest dream. It was almost the only certainty he could still claim.

Jehan accepted the proposal without debate and said little about it afterward. But it needed no great sensitivity to understand his shame at its necessity. Tristan still slept poorly.

Flawed Steel

THE RING OF the hammer on the bar was changed now. Even Tristan's undiscerning ears could make out the difference. The bar was a sword in the making now, no longer an inert lump, and it was beginning to know it.

"That's her point, there." Jehan gestured.

Tristan cocked his head to one side. Sweat ran down his nose and dropped with a sizzle onto the coals.

"How do you decide?"

"*I* don't. It just is, by the feel of it. The sword always chooses. There's no explaining it any better than that."

Jehan lifted the blade, peering at it closely and then pointing at the tip as he spoke. "You want the point steel worked just a certain way, because it has to hold a good edge, while being thin enough to slide between a man's ribs without getting stuck and tough enough not to break if it hits one. You can do more than hack with this kind of blade. With a skean you can kill a man before he knows he's dead and never get a drop of his blood on you."

Tristan smiled politely, if a little forcedly, trying not to visualize what Jehan was talking about.

You don't take a sword seriously as a killing weapon, Thomas

195

said abruptly. *A sword's more than just a fencing toy, you know. It can kill. It's designed to, and whatever he says, not unmessily either. But you don't accept that side of it, and it's the same with magic. You continually ignore what you don't want to see. And until you unlearn that, your effectiveness with either weapon is blunted.*

Tristan swallowed, a little taken aback at the unsolicited criticism. Thomas stalked away. Jehan, oblivious, lifted the bar from the fire again.

"A few more times on the anvil, now," he said. "And then we'll be ready to do something else. Let's have a few more coals, there." Tristan hastily obeyed.

Let's just hope the racket doesn't draw the Watch, Thomas said sourly. He had no appreciation for noise, whatever its cause. Maybe it was just the days of the clatter that accompanied the forging that had put him into such an ill-temper. Tristan hoped the next stage, whatever it was, would be quieter. His own nerves could use the rest.

He supposed Valadan was keeping watch, in case any local authorities did hear the noise. The stallion always did that, even if not specifically bidden to. Tristan wasn't very worried about the problem, anyway—they were in as much of a deserted area as could be found anywhere in the city, yet not so far away from other metalsmiths and similarly noisy craftsmen that the noise would be remarked upon. Crewzel had chosen the spot with that in mind. And wizards would not mess with blacksmiths. Cold iron rendered a smith virtually immune to petty interferences.

Tristan had set up some pretty elaborate illusions, though, aimed at masking both sight and sound of their work. It was important that Jehan be undisturbed. Tristan wasn't sure how well the spells were working—it wasn't possible to tell, from inside the illusion itself, and he hadn't been outside it since he'd set it up. At lest there was no further cause to worry about smoke—happily, charcoal gave off very little. The noise was the greater problem. But he'd done his best and he doubted they'd be bothered, whatever Thomas might think. Tristan leaned closer, ready to assist as Jehan should need him.

The smith's massive shoulders could be best appreciated at such times. He was a bit out of practice after so long a time away from his craft—not that his touch was in any way unsure, but Tristan had noticed Jehan rubbing at tired muscles sometimes, looking perplexed as if he'd never suspected they could lose their tone. Sweat sheened his face. Tristan had shrugged out of his jerkin a long while ago, but Jehan kept his own shirt on, in deference to flying sparks and the unexpected popping of coals. The cloth, dampened, clung to him like a second skin.

The accident was an unhappy blending of mischance and carelessness. Tristan was at the sword's point, holding it steady with the tongs while Jehan worked the metal farther back, at the tang end. He'd lifted a hand between strikes to wipe sweat out of his eyes. Tristan had calculated that he had the moment— by the rhythm of his stroke, Jehan's next blow should fall upon the anvil; and before the hammer touched the sword again, he would have both hands on the tongs once more. Tristan congratulated himself on having mastered the timing so quickly. Now if only his back didn't ache so—

Unhappily, the blow was just a shade out of true, and caught the edge of the blade as well as the anvil. It was a light tap, but the tongs weren't gripping tightly, and the blade started to twist under the blow, sideways. Its edge came up. That was the carelessness.

The mischance came when Tristan realized what was happening and put his right hand back down onto the tongs hastily to steady them. He missed and grabbed the sword instead.

He saw his mistake at the last instant, a moment of perception impossibly suspended, and saw the sword striking up at his bare hand like a snake, but it was too late to pull back. The snake struck, and its bite was both sharp and hot.

Tristan cried out and reeled back. The tongs flew out of his hand and fell into the firepit, but Jehan didn't pause to retrieve them. He dropped his hammer too, and was by Tristan's side as fast as he could intercept him. Thomas had been closing in on him, too, but now leaped back out of harm's way. Jehan flung his left arm about Tristan's shoulders, stopping his movement and holding Tristan's right arm immobile between their two bodies. Tristan was doing his best to curl up around his wounded hand, but Jehan held him upright.

He caught hold of the hand Tristan was cradling to his chest and prised the clenched fingers open.

"Let me see, now. I've got some experience with burns, as you can maybe imagine."

There was little blood, most of it smeared across Tristan's chest. The cut on his palm wasn't deep; the hot metal had

seared the wound partly closed. Tristan forced himself to draw
a deep breath, and was relieved when the room steadied around
him. He was mildly amazed that he still had all of his fingers.

"Have to bind it," Jehan was saying. "You're lucky. I've
seen worse on apprentices. It will scar some, but you'll have
a tale to tell about it anyhow." He pushed Tristan down onto
the nearest bench and left him there while he rummaged for
the necessary rags and salves.

One wave of pain crested and passed Tristan by. It would
be followed by another, certainly, but not immediately, and
the moment's relief gave Tristan space to think.

Even bound up, his hand was going to be impossibly awkward. He wouldn't be able to grip anything with it until it
healed—which meant days of uselessness and probably delays
in the forging, if Jehan had to work alone. No. That couldn't
be permitted—not while there was something Tristan could do
about it. What was he a wizard for, anyway?

It wasn't easy to work a healing-spell one-handed. Anything
fast or showy was prohibitive, but Tristan thought he was doing
well enough despite his literal handicap. He concentrated and
felt the wound close as he made passes and whispered arcane
words over it, felt a healing warmth soak downward, deep into
his palm. The spell would run a few moments before it was
complete, but it was working. Already the pain was lessened.

Tristan lifted his head, seeking Jehan. "Never mind the
rags," he called. "I've got it, I think—" He got to his feet.
The air inside the forge was close, he needed to get away from
the fumes and the smells of charcoal and hot metal. A few
breaths of fresh air could not but speed the healing-spell along.

"Are you daft? That's got to be bound. Sit down."

Tristan waved Jehan off. "It's all right, I tell you. I just
need some air." He started past Jehan.

As he did, it began to occur to him that something was
wrong. The warmth in his hand had developed rapidly into a
fiery heat, nearly as bad as the hot sword that had seared him,
and it was getting rapidly worse. His hand felt twice its normal
size, though it looked no bigger, and the pain pulsed through
it in time with his heartbeat, which was unaccountably rapid.
As he took another step, the forge swung and shadowed around
him.

Tristan realized that he was fainting. He put his good hand
out for the doorjamb, missed, and staggered forward to land

first on his knees, then most painfully on his face. His senses fled, seeped back rather unwillingly.

Jehan was trying to drag him upright, then back through the doorway. Tristan's hazy request to be put down was ignored, or else unheard. His stomach was queasy. When his hand got jostled in the struggle, there were flashing lights in his head, too. His chest ached, straining for air; his ribs were bruised by Jehan's grip.

Water splashed his face. The coolness was welcome, except that it roused him to full awareness of pain again. Tristan groaned, biting his lip. Blood ran into his mouth.

"Easy," Jehan cautioned. A wet rag dabbed first at Tristan's forehead, then tried to offer its comfort to his hand. The scream that the light touch startled out of Tristan was as shocking to him as it must have been to Jehan. Thomas yowled no less frenziedly.

Jehan fumbled a pot of salve open, dipped two fingers in and tried frantically to apply the mess to Tristan's hand. The task was nearly impossible, with the way Tristan was twisting back and forth on the floor. Jehan pinned him finally, but the salve was long since smeared over his clothes and the cat, who kept getting in the way. Jehan thrust Thomas away for what felt like the twelfth time and reached desperately for the tangled mess of bandages. Cover the wound tightly, keep the air out. That was the best he could hope to do, unless he found some poppy to quiet his patient.

The cat was back, crouching on Tristan's chest. He was using his claws both to keep his place and to hold Tristan's right hand down while he pressed his face close to it. Jehan, thinking only of hairs and dirt and an open wound, made to toss the cat aside again.

Thomas had had all the interference he was minded to allow. Spitting furiously as he whirled, he lashed out at Jehan with both front paws, slashing the smith's fingers. As Jehan recoiled, Thomas turned back to Tristan and struck again, his dagger-sharp claws ripping the closed wound wide open. Tristan screamed again, and tried to pull his hand away, but the cat was too quick for him. Thomas clawed him a second time, and this time his paw came away bloodied, but with a bright splinter of metal adhering to it.

Now try the healing-spell, he said.

* * *

His hand was neatly bandaged when Tristan woke to find he could think clearly once again. His whole arm ached, and he felt as if injudicious movement might spark the real pain awake again, but at least for the nonce there was only bearable discomfort.

Jehan propped him up and pressed a cup of wine to his lips. Most of it went down Tristan's chin, both men were trembling so.

"Are you all right? You look as if you've been bled."

"So do you." Tristan managed to get a little of the wine down, though he choked on it. Its warmth in his stomach settled him marginally.

"It wasn't that bad a burn! I don't understand—"

"It wasn't the burn. It was the metal splinter." Tristan swallowed more wine hastily. His voice had begun to shake, and that threatened to set the rest of him shivering too. "Iron and magic don't mix, remember? No one's ever figured out precisely why, but it's demonstrably true, as you saw."

"That little bit?"

"Size doesn't matter. I said a spell over it, to close the cut up. That's all it takes. Iron and magic."

"Then you're an idiot even to touch the stuff," Jehan said uncompromisingly. "I could have hired a helper. Anyone with two hands could have—"

"It's not as bad as all that. Some wizards have worse trouble; they can't ride a horse shod with iron or use even a silver-hilted sword. I'm luckier than most, when I'm not being careless." Tristan glanced down at his swathed hand. "It's a severe lesson, but I think it will stick." He sighed. "Help me up. We've still got work to do."

Jehan swore at him. "No. Have the sense to lie quiet. You could as easily have fallen into the firepit."

Tristan tried to lever himself up onto one elbow and began to think Jehan might just be right, after all. Movement dizzied him and made his hand throb in a warning way. He'd better do as he'd been told, at least for a while.

Something furry touched Tristan's cheek.

"Thomas?" Tristan reached his good hand out, and the cat rubbed against his fingers.

Do you think you could find it in your heart to consider being just a trace more careful? I only have nine lives, and these frights are using them up at an alarming rate.

"I'll think about it. Thanks for the surgery."

Jehan put a cloak over him, being careful of both the bandaged hand and the cat. There were several parallel lines of dried blood across the backs of his hands, Tristan saw.

"You bide here a bit, in the fresh air. Want more wine?" Jehan started back into the stable.

Tristan did, but not the sleep the wine was sure to bring. "No. I'll just rest a little, while you heat the blade again."

Jehan froze beside the anvil. "While I *what*?"

"It's cooled again by now, hasn't it?"

No answer came from the stable—only silence. Tristan tried to sit up and, when that proved possible, got carefully to his feet. His unsteady movements couldn't have been that quiet, but Jehan gave no sign of having heard them. The smith was still standing beside the anvil, staring down at the half-worked blade. The metal was a dull gray, lifeless. The first blood it had drawn was burned off, vanished without a trace.

"That needs to be heated up again, doesn't it? So it will be ready for the tempering?"

Tristan was about to ask if he should blow the fire up a bit—he thought he might be able to manage that, since the bellows could be worked by foot as well as by hands—but Jehan's face arrested the question. The man's lips were parted, and his breath came panting between them. And his eyes—they were as dull as the sword, but black, not focused, yet seeing horrors.

"The dream," Jehan croaked. "It's the dream, come alive."

The nape of Tristan's neck prickled. Was this another of Jehan's wide-awake dreams? He forced himself to speak normally, and not only for Jehan—he had to convince himself that he could stay on his feet long enough to handle this.

"Well, this time you can work it through and then you won't need to dream it again." The air felt too thick for this lungs; he wasn't going to be able to work long, Tristan thought. He ignored the weakness. He had to get Jehan past this crisis, whatever the cost to be paid later.

Jehan seemed still to be in his odd trance, staring at the anvil and seeing who knew what visions. He did not lift his eyes as Tristan spoke to reassure him about the dreams and promised their ending. The smith still did not look up when at last he spoke himself.

"No. This time I will have the strength to stop before someone gets killed. Better never to lift that hammer again than be tempted to use a gift cursed and curdled. This was a fool's business. It goes no further."

"*What?*" Tristan asked, appalled.

"I can go back to Kinark, I think. Not to smith again, and that will be hard to bear, but my penance is best done there— even if they cast me out again."

Tristan could hardly take his meaning in. The air was heavy again, and his head hurt with the effort of trying to breathe it. "But you promised me. You can't—"

"I'm used to breaking vows now. You helped me break one, you'll recall. What's another? Or a third, depending on how you count them?" He looked at Tristan finally. "I know what that sword means to you, but it's not worth your life. Let your king go after his sword himself, if he wants it so badly."

Any words Tristan might have said, whether entreaty or pure anger, stuck fast in his throat. He couldn't move, even to lie down again. He was sure he'd be sick. The wine went sour in his stomach, like his defeat. He wasn't ready to fight this battle again and couldn't brace himself for it.

He kept thinking—as much as he was able to think, with the stable and the world swinging slowly around him—that he should have seen this coming, should have read this end in Jehan's continuing tension. It had only needed this small excuse to find release. And the worst of it was that there had been no need for such an end. Jehan wasn't cursed as he believed. But one moment's inattention and a misstruck blow would have the smith believing that for the rest of his life.

Jehan picked up his pack and put a spare shirt, a loaf of bread, and a water bottle into it. He took nothing else, not even one of his tools. No, of course not his tools, Tristan thought dully. The man was determined he'd have no need of them, ever.

He should be dealing with this. There had to be some way, some argument. But Tristan could barely stand. There were hands on him suddenly, Jehan was easing him toward a sleeping pallet.

"Rest now. Sleep well."

"Do you think *you* will?" He managed to get that out, useless as it was.

"I'll risk it. Maybe this is how the dream ends, when I finally turn my back on it. Maybe we put the wrong meaning on the dream—you because you needed a sword, me because I wanted so badly to forge it. Maybe giving up smithing is what I have to work through."

He was gone, when Tristan opened his eyes.

Tristan thought he might be able to get to his feet again. He found he was wrong.

Thomas crouched nearby, watching with unveiled concern. "Did you see where he went?"

If I did, you're the last one I'd tell. You don't need to be out wandering the streets after him.

"You could have followed him."

Thomas licked a paw. *And leave you here, like that?*

"I'm all right, Thomas." Tristan realized that he couldn't even convince himself of that untruth. He felt worse than he ever had in his life, cold and very sick. "You could still follow him," he suggested. Thomas ignored him, of course.

There was nothing he could do about that, and Tristan found that he cared less and less about it. Pain was snarling his thoughts, making concentration a joke. Mastering it took his whole attention for a long space. Thomas brought him his butterfly box, full of Blais' salve, and Tristan carefully unwrapped his hand and applied a little of the medicine. The wound was messy, half burn and half cut, but he couldn't muster another healing-spell for it yet. He'd have to rely on the salve to deal with the pain and leave the healing for later, when he could concentrate.

Afterward, he had only energy enough to sit quietly, afraid to stir lest he rouse the pain again. The things he ought to be doing eddied through his awareness, plaguing him with guilt but eluding his grasp before he could hope to act on them.

They'd have to leave for Calandra in the morning. There was no use staying, so he might as well go back and face Elisena with a failure so absolute that he could salvage nothing from it. It seemed to be setting a pattern for his life, but Tristan wasn't much worried about being stuck in it. This failure ensured that his life would hold room for but one more. One very final disaster.

It was dark in the stable. The forge fire was barely still alight, and its glow did not pass much beyond the clay-coated box that held it. Tristan had not kindled any other light—since sun-fall he had been busy debating whether more salve would do his hand enough good to offset the pain he'd incur applying it. He looked up at a noise, to find Jehan filling the doorway and blocking out the first stars in the night sky.

"How did you manage that?" the smith demanded.

"Manage what?" Tristan asked blankly.

"You must be more of a wizard than you think. With that hand, I'd have thought you couldn't magic a mouse out of a bellyache." Jehan stepped into the stable, found a candle, and lighted it from one of the few live coals still in the firepit. "It's a nice bit of work, too. Circle and circle, and always I end up back here. Did you enjoy it? You can stop it now—or I'll stop you, I promise you that."

Tristan stared at him, incredulous—or as close as his still half-fogged wits would let him get to that state.

"You think I'm working a confusion-spell on you? _Now?_" He would have laughed if he'd been able to. "Sorry to disappoint you, but I never even thought of it."

Jehan's pack dropped down beside him, as the smith's fingers abruptly released it. He sank down to the floor, maybe to talk more easily, but Tristan saw how Jehan was trembling and realized how hard-held his calm had been.

"There's no way out, then," Jehan whispered. "Not of any of this. I thought it was just you. I told myself that and knew if I begged you, you'd let me go, because you were too decent not to. Or else I was just simply getting lost, I thought—" His eyes were dark as smoke, shadowed all about. Tristan would have spoken, but he was too much at a loss. He didn't understand what had brought Jehan back and knew no way to keep him. He reached out a hand to the man awkwardly.

Jehan looked up at the touch. He was weeping silently.

"I told you I was cursed, and you think you understand that. You think I'll come to my senses, to see that I've judged myself too hard. And I'll forge you your sword, and the dreams will stop, and everything will be all right for both of us. But you _don't_ understand, because I lied to you, to make sure you wouldn't—" He fought for breath and barely found it.

"My brother went out to make his way in the world, and all I could see was that he was deserting me when I needed him most, after I'd taught him everything I knew about smithcraft in spite of the guild laws. I thought he'd always stay by me, you see, be loyal to me the same way I was to him. I put that on him, never considered he might want other than I'd chosen for him, and refused to see how he struggled against it. He was stubborn. When he was old enough and determined enough, we quarrelled for the last time. I said things that could easily have withered steel or hidden a flaw within a blade. I gave him a sword, aye, but I was so hard to him that he had to steal it, the dark night he finally left me. He left while I slept, and I never saw him alive again." Jehan choked a sob back, but not a bitter laugh.

"I may not sleep sound now, but I could still do so then! I let him go, and he died far from home, in a meaningless fight, because he thought I hated him. That blade was only the last part of me to betray him."

Small wonder the man's very dreams rose up against him, dreams of swords that were at once symbol and reality. Tristan tried to say as much, but he couldn't order his thoughts fast enough to break through the sound of Jehan's sobs. The wave of realization almost overwhelmed him.

"I didn't need to vow not to forge another sword. I am not fit to, and all Kinark knows it—even dead metal knows it! I've lost a brother, aye, and that shame will never die till I do, but I've lost something that mattered far more, and there's the curse—that it did matter more, and that I blamed him for it— blamed a dead man for what I wouldn't face."

There was a silence.

"Could a sword forged by a man like that save your kingdom?"

The tears streaking Jehan's face had dropped down to splash the sword's point. First blood, then tears, Tristan thought. *What better tempering?* What else had Calandra's lot ever been?

"Why not?" he answered.

the Quenching

TRISTAN SLEPT, SOMETIMES deeply and sometimes fitfully, but most amazingly through many stages of reheating and hammering, despite the noise attendant on the operation. The sword was in something like its final shape when he saw it next, and Jehan was working at it with a dogged, hopeless sort of determination which suggested he'd worked straight through the night. His eyes were red, but his face was calm, as if he'd found oblivion in his work by refusing to leave it. Forgiveness he would not hope for.

Tristan sat up carefully. He felt sticky, as if he'd had a fever which had broken hours earlier, or as if he'd merely slept overlong. He stretched cautiously, being careful of his hand, but when he unwrapped it, he found he didn't need to be. There was a red line slanting across his palm and a few blisters. Nothing more.

The salve had done its work with dispatch. Tristan dabbed a bit more of it around to finish the job and considered how lucky he was. He might easily have lost the hand.

Serve you right, Thomas agreed.

Tristan wished him a good morning.

It's afternoon. You sleep with more determination than anyone I've ever seen.

206

"I stay out of trouble that way." Tristan reached for the wineskin, hoping for a drop or two to wash the taste of sleep out of his mouth. The skin was empty. He belatedly remembered Jehan pouring the last of it down his throat just before he'd gone to sleep.

After some few moments' search, Tristan found a several-days-old remnant of a loaf of bread, and tried a few bites of that. It was a dismal experience, and he cut his mouth on the rocklike crust, but still he offered Jehan a share. The smith only mumbled something which could have been a comment on the bread or on the weather in Kinark at this season. His hammering went on without pause, even while the blade itself was among the coals—he used those brief intervals to work upon the quillions.

Tristan gave Thomas a puzzled look.

Crewzel, the cat said, bland and unhelpful.

"What? Oh—she *was* here, then? I thought I dreamed that. What happened?"

Not much. She came back just after you'd gone to sleep. Jehan told her what happened to you, but she didn't pay much attention to him. Just looked at you for a long while. Very strange. She was gone before Jehan could climb over his shyness to say anything more to her. She hasn't been back.

"That's not so unusual."

You didn't see her. She looked like a person trying to say good-bye.

Odd as the statement was, Tristan could in no way disprove it. Crewzel wasn't back by nightfall; the later the hour grew, the less reason Tristan had to suppose she would be. By morning he was very troubled indeed.

There'd never been any formal agreement that she'd stay with them. It could have been chance or convenience, from Crewzel's point of view, that kept her with them so long. Tristan didn't think so. Nor did he believe she'd have gone after Delmon alone. If she'd had some lead, she'd have told Jehan, surely. She'd said nothing, though, just vanished.

He wanted, of course, to go after her and did not, could not, any more than he could balance Crewzel's needs against Calandra's. Tristan did what he could—he sent Thomas to continue his quest among Kôvelir's cats, while he prowled the alleys by night. By day, he put on Jehan's too-large work gloves, manned the bellows, tended the fire, and sold all his spare articles of clothing and the tools they had done with to buy food for their infrequent meals.

It was a nightmarish parody of a return to those hopeless days at the Academy. By day, Tristan's back ached, his eyes burned, his hands blistered and bled inside the gloves, and the fire cooked him half silly. At night, after a meal that was more like a promise of one, the dark streets swallowed him up and lured him on till he was nearly asleep on his feet. He never found Crewzel, or even anyone who'd seen her.

He began to wonder if he had any right to look for her, since she'd chosen to leave. Who was he to meddle? The more nights he spent looking, the more prone he was to seeing her leaving as a desertion. He fought with that resentment, refusing to give in to it. He kept searching.

It was a sevenday before Jehan was satisfied enough with the shape and balance of the blade to proceed further. Times without number he let the metal cool enough to handle, hefted it, sighted along it, and made practice cuts and thrusts—then somehow remembered the needed corrections while he heated the iron again and made them, until the balance was right for the sword itself.

Most fine swords were balanced to the hand of the man who'd wield them—a man who could afford such custom craftsmanship. Not so the blades of Kinark. Such was the smiths' art that each was made to one pattern, one sublime design which years had not been able to improve. It took Jehan a week of finicky work, but he achieved the balance he sought, and at last was satisfied.

And in all that week there was no sign of Crewzel, or Delmon, or Thomas.

The cat came creeping back early one evening, thinner than his shadow, as he'd have put it. His fur looked half uncared for, as if whatever he'd been doing had left him no leisure for even that most basic of tasks.

Tristan mentioned that at once, too shocked to be tactful, and startled Thomas into taking a couple of quick licks at his back, but the cat's tongue couldn't cope with the knots and mats that were more than surface deep. He draped himself gratefully across Tristan's lap and let Tristan's fingers tend to them.

That in itself was unusual enough to be worrisome, but a hesitant purr was a little relieving.

"Are you all right?" Tristan ventured.

Do I still have any feet left, or are they all worn off? I think I walked another life away.

"And?"

Thomas sighed and switched his tail. *I know where Delmon is.*

Tristan echoed the sigh, and laid his head on his arm. His hair was as matted as Thomas', and sweat-soaked. He scrubbed at his face with his fingers.

"But I can't find Crewzel," he confessed.

Jehan brought the blade to a white heat, working the bellows continually and adding much fresh charcoal. Then the sword disappeared from sight as he covered it over with more charcoal and left it to work the bellows once more. Some of the charcoal passed into the iron, he said—a little during the many heats of the forging, more now. It made the iron hard outside and tough inside—exactly what a sword needed to be. When the blade emerged from its rest, it would be mere iron no longer, but transformed to steel.

Tristan, too disturbed to sit still, paced in the alley, muttering his thoughts to Thomas.

"This is my fault. I should have gone after her right away, and plague take the sword! I knew I should have; it was the only decent thing to do. Jehan didn't need me all that much. I—"

What do you think you are—superhuman? Thomas, atop Valadan's back, looked exhausted at even the sight of someone else walking. *You've got a death grip on guilt.*

Tristan shook his head wearily. "All right. What about Delmon?"

He's with a troupe of Halbern jugglers—thieves, more like. His magical training ought to come in handy.

"How did you hear?"

They do a cat act. Can you imagine that—cats trained to perform for tossed coins? I'm not surprised that the poor things are so degraded—one of them had a bit of sport with a fisherman's cat, and left her full of kittens and very bitter. Seems he'd promised to take her away with him; she, being dazzled

*by him after her dull life there, used to sneak off to watch his
performances. That's where she saw Delmon.*

"Where are they now?"

*Touring. That might explain why Delmon went with them—
a painless way of traveling free to where he wants to go anyway,
looking for his mother. They shouldn't be too hard to locate,
now we know what we're looking for. Would you mind stroking
me just a bit harder? All that walking has left me stiff all over.*

Tristan lifted him carefully from Valadan's back, and went
to sit near the forge fire, cradling Thomas in his lap.

"I didn't even know you'd left Kôvelir."

*And didn't miss me, I'll be bound! Still, having seen the
life these provincial fisher cats lead, I should be thankful I had
the sense to follow you away from it. A little lower, please. I
think my spine's permanently knotted. I'd forgotten what life's
like on the dirty side.*

"Do you want something to eat?"

*About time you remembered your manners. And you prob-
ably haven't got anything good enough for me. But after three
days of dining on fishheads with road dust for dessert, I'd be
delighted to join you in a meal. Got any cream?*

Tristan settled the cat tenderly on his folded cloak. "If I
have to steal it," he said, and went out.

The time had come to temper the blade. It was later that
night, very late, but they didn't pause. Jehan put the carbon-
steel blade into the fire once more, heated it barely red, and
began to hammer quickly at its edges. Packing, he called it,
to make the blade keep an edge longer. While he was busy at
that, Tristan dumped the Istron water into the trough, thriftily
piling the small bottles up for later resale. When he'd emptied
the last, the trough was filled to a barely adequate depth.

Thomas dabbled a paw in the water. He thought it might
be a good physick for his worn pads.

Doesn't feel magical.

"Jehan is sure it's the real stuff."

Thomas fanned his whiskers, watching his reflection echo
the action. *That doesn't mean it's magic. Legends can grow
up in the oddest ways. You of all people ought to know that.*

The fire was fanned carefully and the blade laid in and
covered with glowing coals for the last time. It had no really
sharp edges yet, of course, only such as Jehan's hammer had

given it, but the unwhetted shape alone was of an unequalled grace, and it made a very fine weapon, even unfinished. When all was done, it would cut spider silk on the breeze.

Jehan seemed to succumb to the spell of the blade at last. He leaned against the doorjamb and gazed at the firepit with a light in his eyes that had nothing to do with the fire's reflection.

"'Tis writ in our books that the metal is fit when it glows the color of the sun rising over the deserts that lie to sunward of us," he said softly. "And the steam that will rise from quenching is gentle as the morning mists of the Istron, for the steel loves that water well, and is not affronted by its touch. It swims there content until it's the color of the robes kings sometimes wear—or like the wine they drink—and then the smith must lift it swiftly out. Then it will move like the stars and cut like the winter wind that blows between them."

Tristan listened in wonder, seldom having heard Jehan say half so many words in a single hour, far less in such a poetic vein. There must be great minstrels in Kinark, he thought, if their swords could move even the smiths to speak so with their tongues as well as their hands.

"Once—a very long time ago—our swords were quenched in the living bodies of men. This is not a thing that's often told." Jehan still watched the steady glow of the fire. "They were prisoners and criminals condemned to die in any case, but there was great shame in those blades, alongside their great strength. They were dark things—I doubt any of them has survived to this day, though it would be well that they did not. They carried a seed of destruction deep within the steel, a hate and a need for more blood like that they were tempered in. Never quiet were they, but always eager for war, discord, and quarrels of madness."

He paused, swallowed.

"So say our legends, but they say true. I know this. Once I craved to make a blade like that, a blade to root out the pain in my own heart. I turned from swordcraft, rather than fall to that temptation, but there was bitterness and danger for me even so, and a mighty darkness that was beckoning ever more sweetly. You led me safe away from it, Tristan, though you didn't understand what you were doing. I . . . think I might be able to face dawn, now, and accept the daylight as my right. I do not know. I may never be as I once was—I suppose I should hope not and learn to be wiser. My debt's beyond repayment, but if this sword will serve you, let it begin the compensation."

"Jehan, the debt's mine. I—"

"No. And I wouldn't take your silver either, if you had it to offer. You don't understand what you've done for me."

No, Tristan thought, and was silent. He'd not suspected this last revelation, for all he'd known that the dreams were only the surface of a sea of agony. All at once he remembered Valadan, that instant before he'd freed the horse from Nímir's spell of binding. It all came back clearly, the taste of hate and the sense he'd been given then of a great power foully twisted and curdled. Tristan hadn't examined the feelings then—they'd overwhelmed him and then passed on; too much had happened after—but he recognized them now, realizing the incredibly innocent thing he'd done in enlisting Jehan's aid and in bending the man's will to his own. It should have been impossible and it would have been if he'd only known more about it. Whatever final outcome this sword helped to shape, there had been an accomplishment beyond dreams here. He might need to remember that. He didn't feel responsible. He felt like a chess piece—a confused pawn who'd won a game he hadn't known he played.

Jehan reached with the tongs among the coals, lifted the blade quickly, and swung it over the trough. The sword leaped like a trout into the water and swam there, as Jehan moved it up and down, along its cutting edge.

The steam came up like a live thing, noise and movement both, exactly as on Crewzel's card so long before. The vapor had a curious smell, nothing like the metallic stink of the hot iron or the woody smell of the charcoal fire. It was a scent like silver or like magic, something at the back of the tongue, too faint to be tasted but not too faint to be perceived as a change— like that first instant when life's scales tip and winter yields to spring.

The mist swirled, cloven by a stray breeze passing the doorway, and Tristan saw Elisena's eyes shining up at him from the water. This was no sending, not a using of the water as the mirror she'd promised. It was just a hint, a memory, gone in that instant of recognition.

"The water!" Tristan exclaimed, understanding. "It *does* change the metal! That must be why the High Mage was able to ensorcell the original sword and bind it to the throne, even though it's cold iron. It never occurred to me to wonder how he did that!"

The blade was barely visible beneath the roiling water, but it had already cooled considerably. Jehan gave it a practiced look.

"The quicker the cooling, the tougher the temper. But we don't want it *too* tough, or she'll be too inflexible a weapon. Better a blade that bends like a willow than one that breaks like a stone, eh?" So saying and waiting for no answer, Jehan lifted the blade out.

Water vanished from the blade rather than dripping, the metal still hot enough to evaporate it before it could run off, though a few drops managed to soak Jehan's hand and sleeve. He held the blade close before his face, inspecting it minutely with an artist's abstraction.

The fire still cast a glow, but nothing to match the sheen of the new steel or the light in Jehan's eyes—a light as pure as ever came forth from a wizard's crystal, as sweet as a summer's dawn. It washed most of Tristan's doubts away. If Elisena could match the magic to such a blade, how could the crowning ritual fail to accept it? His tiredness melted away, along with most of the thirst that had worked inward from his throat to his bones. Tristan smiled and wondered if something was the matter with his face; the change of expression made his cheeks feel odd.

"I can see why we never discussed a fee," he said lightly. "How does anyone ever pay for work like that? A firstborn child wouldn't be enough."

There were sparkles upon Jehan's cheeks, running down into his beard. The light made the tears a benediction.

"You've paid the fee," Jehan said. "Weren't you listening?"

"By making you do what I wanted you to do? That's peculiar logic."

"You still don't see, do you? The parallels? The metal to the fire, again and again, the heat and the pounding, the torture if you will, until finally 'tis pure, and has its final shape. A shape that the metal never could have dreamed of. And finally the water. A sharp and sudden change, it makes the metal stronger. The last thing you'd expect, really. It's so drastic. Rock would shatter, for all it's strong, glass would break, for all it's sharp.

"A drastic cure, and one only a smith can work. You'd be a fair swordsmith, Tristan, if it weren't for that little disaffinity you have for cold iron. Look what you made me do for myself. What other payment could you offer me?"

Trial and Error

TRISTAN SLEPT POORLY, for all his elation over the sword's near completion. He dozed lightly and woke with the sounds of clashing swords still ringing in his ears and an odd fancy that Blais had slipped back over death's borders to refresh his pupil's fencing skills. Yet it was not Blais his thoughts fastened on, but Crewzel.

He heard an hour bell chime faintly. Once. Twice. A third time. Then all was silent—listening, Tristan thought irrationally. He was surprised that his own heartbeat didn't echo inside him.

The sword was nearly finished. So what was he going to do then? Go blithely back to Calandra, with never a backward glance or thought of Crewzel? Thomas was curled by his side, a warm circle of consolation. Tristan wondered if Crewzel was still alone in the dark. That idea was not bearable and was certainly not one with which to woo sleep.

He sat up, hugging his knees. Thomas protested sleepily, then wormed back under the cloak's warmth and was quiet. By the door, straw rustled as Valadan shifted his weight. When that noise ceased, Jehan's calm breathing could be heard once again, deep and restful. Tristan's ears fed him all those messages. The fire was covered too deeply to give off even a glow, and there was no moon to thrust its light through the smokehole or the chinks in the shutters.

For all that, he could see with a pitiless clarity, staring into the dark. Crewzel had used him whenever she could, always, in spite of friendship. And he'd done whatever he could for her—whatever was convenient, or at least not too inconvenient. She was fiercely independent, and it would have half-killed her to be thought of in any other way. Trusting him, she'd let her guard down, and his inability to help her was nothing less than a betrayal.

There was no sense his wandering the streets after her. She'd never come to him. In perhaps as little as a day, he must be gone from the city. Into her life he'd come, wreaking havoc, and then would be gone again, clear of the wreckage. He could twist and turn all he liked, but those facts were no more to be altered than the sword he could sense lying across the anvil.

Like Jehan, he would simply have to learn to face the dawn.

He was up and out before Jehan was even stirring, carrying the bag of empty bottles carefully. The streets were empty as Tristan made his way to the apothecary's.

He had thought, somewhat wistfully, of refilling the bottles with the water left in the slack tub, or from some convenient fountain. Selling so many bottles of purported Istron water would go a long way toward repairing the inroads their purchase had made in his slim purse. Aside from the day's meals, Tristan wanted to leave Jehan with traveling money, at least. Sober reflection had decided him against the tempting course, though. It was far from his basic honesty at work—there might be other folk than Crewzel in the city who could prove out magical frauds, and there could be stiff penalties for being caught.

Tristan couldn't even get coppers for the bottles. The apothecary pretended to be too well supplied with similar items, and then haggled for a half hour before Tristan managed to trade them for a small sack of oats and a fresh egg. Those would barely make flatcakes, and Tristan had spent his last coin for cream the night before.

He reflected upon the dismal state of his fortunes. Polassar had been as generous with money as he'd been able to be, considering that Calandra's king had no treasury to fund even his own travels—and Tristan had been duly careful with the coins he'd been given. But he'd spent some of them on provisions for Crewzel and himself when he first parted from her. The bulk of his funds had gone for tools, the lump of sky-iron, and of course the Istron water. The had trickled away, till now his purse was as flat as his empty belly.

Well, this foraging expedition would just have to be extended a bit, then. Tristan cushioned the egg safely in the middle of the sack of oats and tucked the top of the sack securely through his belt. He'd fed himself in Kôvelir before this—fed four folk and three horses, indeed. Surely he could do so again.

Tristan strode rapidly over the cobbles, taking a perverse pleasure in the twinges the action produced in his legs. He felt as if smithing had strained all the muscles in his body and quite a few belonging to someone else. The mild exercise did a little to brighten his mood.

He came to a cross street and waited while a wagonload of hay passed by. The weather was fair for the first time in a week—as if the mages had suddenly recalled that they were possessed of weather-spells. Good. That would draw folk out, and crowded streets would make Tristan's job simpler. He was anxious to get started, but he still hadn't found what seemed to him a likely spot.

Tristan paused at a bookseller's stall, fingering fine parchment pages and admiring gold letters illuminated with twining vines. Next he glanced at some exceedingly strange bestiaries. Deeper within the shop, scribes worked with chisel-pointed goose quills upon great slanting desks, setting up a busy scratching sound. Tristan smiled. Like so many mice, Thomas would have said.

He'd left the cat sleeping, still worn out from his journey. Perhaps some special sort of treat might be welcomed, when he bought the things for their evening meal, if there was going to be an evening meal. *Optimism!* Tristan chided himself. A very fresh fish for Thomas, or maybe some even fresher asparagus, if there were any to be had at this season, and if Kôvelir was having a spring that was better than that in Calandra. He found it hard to be sure of the season in the city, dwelling far from the gardens of the higher classes in the innermost circles and having spent all the daylight hours in the forge.

He had missed the open air more than he'd realized. Just being out now had improved his temper, though he'd sooner have been in the countryside itself and smelling the fresh scent of the earth. The pit of roasting beef he was just now passing was interesting, but it was only what his belly longed for, not his heart.

He wasn't made for cities, Tristan told himself, nor for crowds, really. He felt pushed and harried if there weren't some moments in the day he could call his own; perhaps that was why he felt so much better now. It was an awkward mood that fell on him, when he could least well afford it—he had no business wasting time thinking of himself at all, with the joint business of Galan and Nímir hanging over him and the matter of Crewzel nagging at him, as well. Action was what he needed, or else a patient purposeful working out of his problems, not moping. Thus resolved, he set out to find a decent spot to begin his morning's work.

Crewzel had taught him that the folk who populated Kô-velir's night paid far better than the honest farmers and merchants he'd find now in the middle of the day. The lesson was a true one. Tradesmen would barely tolerate being diverted from their work, much less welcome it enough to consider paying for the pleasure. Yet nightfall would be far too late for what he had in mind, which was a little income swiftly converted into dinner. A train of double-humped camels passed Tristan, brought all the impossibly long distance from Bokár with loads of rolled carpets and rare spices in huge carven chests which were worth nearly as much as their rich contents.

He had an odd fancy that the city was not as quiet as it seemed and that this meant something. Tristan caught himself looking back over his shoulder, shrugged, and shook his head at himself. Kôvelir was too big to have its mood gauged by any one man. Perchance he'd just happened to wander across the edge of someone's spell and smelled a trace of someone else's nervousness. Back to business.

He needed a spot where folk had some reason to wait, or at least to pause. The passers-by were intent on business, not strolling about in search of entertainment. And finding a decent spot not already taken by some other street magician might prove difficult.

In the end, though, it didn't. There was a queue outside a baker's shop—the new bread was just being taken from the ovens, and not all the customers could be served at once by the baker and his helpers—and no other wizards were about.

The waiting people weren't an especially prosperous-looking bunch, but it was a start. There were a few children waiting with their mothers. That should give him a starting point. Tristan decided to concentrate on them.

He scuffed around in the dust of the street until he located three fist-sized stones. He laid them in a row in front of him, squatted back from them a little way, squinted at them in consideration, and made some neat finger motions.

Instantly the stones began to twitch and were soon leaping over each other in a fine imitation of a band of tumblers. When he got tired of jumping them over each other, Tristan made them balance shakily atop themselves. He heard childish laughter and looked up with an answering grin.

A tow-haired little girl smiled back around the fingers thrust in her mouth, then watched the stones again. She pointed at them, giggling. She was too young for intelligent speech, so Tristan wasn't able to take whatever suggestion she'd made, but he piled all the stones up—without touching them—and swirled dust around them until he'd made a sandcastle shape. He looked up to check the child's reaction.

He saw a hand reach down to catch the small wrist and drag the whole child back to the safety of her mother's skirts. The smiles left the little face as she swiveled her head around, and Tristan started to his feet, fearful the child would be beaten for straying from her mother. The castle dissolved around his boots, its walls crumbling like Crogen's. But as he began to apologize and to explain, he saw that the woman had no intent to strike the child. Her face looked as apprehensive as her daughter's, maybe more so.

He barely had space to register that, let alone ponder it. The woman heaved the child up into her arms and fled. She didn't quite run across the square, but it was a retreat all the same. Tristan stared at her back and at the flapping tails of her apron. A passing gazelle-hound eyed him with sympathy.

Maybe she had some irrational fear of wizards. Maybe she'd been afraid he would steal the child. Were there wizards in the city who would do that? The baker was staring at him, as were all the other customers. Tristan straightened up casually and dusted his pants off. The baker had turned to speak to one of his apprentices—one of the older, larger ones. Tristan judged it time to leave without waiting to have his curiosity satisfied.

He tried a chess game, outside a blacksmith's where women

waited to have leaky pots mended and horseboys brought their masters' fine mounts to be shod. Tristan drew a board in the dust of the street, magicked the playing pieces out of whirls of dust, and made the first move, using the pale horseman. He glanced up, caught the eye of a well-dressed youth who was watching him with some interest, and offered a game with a sweeping gesture at the board. Tristan wasn't particularly good at chess, and the spell required all the concentration he'd normally have devoted to the play, but it wasn't as if he intended to gamble on the outcome. They'd play a few moves, and he could hope for a couple of coppers tossed his way as reward for allaying boredom—the price of a loaf of bread.

The boy suddenly got very interested in flicking a bit of dust from the end of his sleeve and then examining the sleeve for any possible damage the dust might have done. After that, he went to soothe his horse, which was standing placidly sleeping while awaiting its turn by the anvil.

Tristan dismissed the board with an irritated snap of his fingers and walked off. He'd never expected things to be *this* bad. He walked a few blocks, thinking intently. The lower walls of the houses that lined the street were carved with striding figures bearing diverse goods. Tribute bearers, from some long-ago age of Kôvelier's greatness, Tristan supposed. Small good the sight of such carved riches did him.

Aha! What was this, now? a gaggle of ladies' maids were doing laundry at a trough by a circular well. Tristan smiled. Surely *they'd* welcome a bit of diversion. This late in the morning, they had doubtless chewed over their store of gossip at least twice and would happily drop the bare bones of it now, if better entertainment presented itself.

He strode up to the well and seated himself on its broad edge, feeling their eyes on him but not speaking yet. He knew the very thing to try.

With a flourish, Tristan reached inside his jerkin and pulled out the clay pipe he'd borrowed from Jehan. He grinned at the girls then, held up a finger for silence, dipped the pipe into the trough of soapsuds, then put it to his lips.

He produced a half dozen bubbles in swift succession. A girl with a freckled face and improbably black curls giggled at him. Tristan shook his finger sternly at her. A little soap ran down his hand.

The bubbles bobbed in the breeze. The sun picked up rainbows on their sides. They shimmered and twinkled, and all at once the girl gasped as she realized that she truly *did* see a picture inside one—three tiny laundresses bent over a tub the size of a fingernail. The other bubbles echoed the scene, then shifted so that one was full of clothes hanging to dry in the sweet air, another was clogged with irons and the fires to heat them, and the last was the interior of a chest where the folded clothes were strewn with handfuls of dried lavender.

No one could be diverted by watching their own work, especially work that was still to be done. Tristan shook his head. He put out his hand and popped the bubbles one by one, then took up the pipe and blew another, larger sphere. It was full of living lavender, even as it came from the pipe, waving as if the flower stems felt the breeze that wafted the bubble toward a kerchiefed redhead.

Her small eyes widened. Behind the lavender, growing larger as if she walked toward it, was a castle of silver gray stone, its towers impossibly fine and thin, reaching up to prick the clouds that spotted the blue sky. Like a bird, the bubble's view rose toward the castle—toward one tower.

A woman stood there, her unbound hair teased by the wind. It spilled over the balcony she stood upon and seemed about to brush the walls of the bubble. She gazed outward, her eyes bright with tears.

Tristan blew a second bubble. This one held a man, a scholar by his dress, who dropped a book in startlement as he looked up and beheld the other bubble. The spheres floated toward each other and danced about, but did not touch.

The little man waved frantically to the tiny lady, his lips moving. She did not seem to see him. The maids strained closer, trying to read the motions of his lips into a speech. The bubbles circled.

At last her eyes met his. Her lips moved as well; tears started from her eyes and rained down on the marble rail of the balcony, unheeded.

The scholar lifted his hands to her. One of the maids uttered a dismayed sound, as she saw he could not reach his desire, though the bubbles were the closest they'd been. The lady must have agreed. She shook her head, sadly.

Tristan blew gently upon the scholar's bubble, and it moved gracefully as a ship under sail toward the other, bumping it. For an instant the two bubbles shared one common edge—flat, where their other surfaces were perfectly round. Quick eyes might have seen a rosy fog of the same hue as the lady's gown moving between the bubbles, might have seen tiny arms intertwine and miniature lips meet. Then the twinned bubbles broke, leaving a spatter of water droppets on the edge of the trough.

One white rose lay lightly atop a mound of soapsuds. Tristan took it gently and offered it to the red-haired girl.

She flinched away as if it had been a flaming brand. Scooping up an armload of clothes, she dunked them into the trough and began scrubbing zealously, joining the other girls in pretending that Tristan did not exist.

It wasn't just coyness. Tristan couldn't even put it down to his own overactive imagination, coupled as it was with the reactions he'd gotten from his other spells. He stared at the girls—or the tops of their heads, anyway. Something was very wrong here.

One last bubble hung from the upended bowl of the pipe as Tristan made to put it away, somewhat disgusted. Bits of foam dripped down it and spattered on his boots. Colors shimmered and trembled across the bubble's surface.

Abruptly a face shaped itself there. Tristan saw wildly curling red hair first, then high sharp cheekbones. Lastly he saw horrified eyes as dark as sloes; Crewzel seemed to look straight out of the bubble at him, her lips opening in some soundless warning.

The bubble burst, as an errant breeze brushed it too roughly, before Tristan could speak or note anything of Crewzel's surroundings. He heard the tramp of bootsteps—loud, as if there were a lot of boots, but rhythmic, in unison, coming in his direction.

The sound spoke, clearer than any words could have. *The Watch*, it said. And Tristan belatedly remembered one of Kôvelir's laws that he'd run foul of before, a stern decree against street magic without prior purchase of a license for the same. Now the wary, frightened reactions to his tricks made sense. Someone had reported him. Aghast at his own stupidity, Tristan took to his heels, the pipe clattering to the cobbles and smashing, the laundresses staring after him.

Once before, he'd easily outrun the Watch. But that last time, he'd had a pair of advantages he was now caught without. It had been night then, the dark streets easy to hide in. And he'd been given a timely warning by a friendly stranger. This time, he had neither such aid. Tristan had barely gained the far side of the square when shouts told him that his pursuers had him in sight.

Sure of him now, they would doubtless pursue him the more hotly. He should have sat still, Tristan thought, and tried to bluff his way out of the charge. It was too late for such regrets now. Still, Tristan wasn't yet truly alarmed. He was fleet enough of foot, and if he managed to double back once or twice, he was confident that he could elude those bootsteps. His own boots barely seemed to brush the cobbles.

It was a pity that this circle was mostly residential. There were no folk about, to form crowds he might hide in. Tristan went through a garden, snapped at by a tiny dog wearing a collar of bells. A handy flower tub gave him the extra inches he needed to scale the far wall. Beyond was another street, a narrow passageway.

He ignored a shouted command to halt that came much too soon. The sound of running feet was close behind him. Try as he might, Tristan couldn't seem to draw away from it. He had no chance to gain a rooftop, and he found he didn't know this part of the city well enough to double back as he'd planned without considerable risk of trapping himself in the process. Tristan swore under his now labored breath and tried to run faster. The alley twisted sharply, and he was bruised by not turning with it quickly enough.

Was it sensible to keep running? Surely if he stopped, explained, and invoked Cabal's name if need be—? But when they didn't believe him, which they doubtless wouldn't, he'd face hours or days of delay, at best.

He needed shadows to hide in, and the bright day offered none. Ahead, overhanging second stories nearly met each other above the street, shutting out the sun. It would have to do. Tristan sprinted forward and dove into the safety the dimness offered. If he could not double back, at least he might hide in a doorway and hope the pursuit overran him in their eagerness.

Cobwebs brushed his face as he burst through them—except he couldn't break through. The sticky webs stretched tight around him like a net, wrapping around his ankles and snaring his wrists when he flung his hands up to claw the silk away from his mouth before it choked him.

Trapped, Tristan realized too late, knowing he'd been neatly herded to the spot for all his self-supposed cleverness.

He struggled anyway, feeling as if his boots were stuffed with lead and his legs with straw. Then he was either tripped or thrown onto his face.

His mind hit the upreaching blackness long before his body hit the alley's cobbles.

Prisoned

HE WOKE SHIVERING and reached to pull his cloak closer about him. His fingers met first empty air, then something that felt like damp straw, and Tristan knew at once that things had somehow gone very wrong indeed. He opened his eyes.

The room was small, and very dim. He wasn't alone. A skinny boy dressed in particolored hose of dirty pink and a painfully clashing turquoise tunic was crouched on the room's none too distant far side, rifling Tristan's belt pouch.

"Hey!" Tristan started to jump to his feet, outraged, and was rewarded for the movement with a wave of nausea that nearly blacked him out again.

"Don't fret. You haven't got anything worth stealing anyway," the boy said peevishly and kicked the pouch across the cell. It slithered through the straw and hit Tristan's ankle.

Tristan made himself pick it up, though even that slight movement was dizzying. His mouth tasted foul; he swallowed and nearly vomited. His confusion was absolute.

"Thomas?" he asked, hoping for some clue.

"He must have been luckier than you," the boy suggested. "They brought you in alone."

The boy was closer now. He had a tattoo on his face—a

bird, done over his eyelids so that every blink made it seem to flap long-lashed wings. His hand darted out suddenly, to tilt Tristan's head and peel his eyelids back with skillful fingers. Tristan jerked away, but he had nowhere to go and no recourse but to lie there while his eyes were peered into.

"Nice spell, isn't it? Being a wizard, you can appreciate its finer points, I'm sure. Don't worry, you'll be all right soon. It's unpleasant, but it does pass." He let go. Tristan slumped back into the straw.

He waited for the pounding in his head to fade. When it was down to a dull throb, Tristan opened his eyes again—not that he needed to. He had a fair idea of where he was by then. The mere thought made him feel he might be coming apart.

"Does the Watch bring all their prisoners here?" Tristan asked.

"For a while." The boy still watched him carefully. Footsteps sounded beyond the barred door. The boy tensed and then relaxed as the sound stopped a good distance away. He sat cross-legged and spoke conversationally. "What did they get you for?"

Stupidity, Tristan very nearly said, flaying himself in Thomas' place. He patted his pouch, empty except for the box that held his magic stones. He'd lost the sack of oats and the surely smashed egg.

"Trying to make myself more worthwhile to rob." His voice sounded odd, but it got stronger as he used it. "You used to be able to make a decent living with street magic here."

"You still can. You must have been uncommonly careless." The bird beat its wings at him.

Tristan sat up, clasped his arms around his knees, and laid his aching head on them. "I didn't know they took that law so seriously."

The boy hooted. "I thought everyone in the whole world would have heard about the new edicts against street magic; they broadcast them loud enough. But you're the second one they've caught this sevenday claiming total ignorance. It won't do you any good—they didn't let her go either. Don't you know that itinerant street magicians are a pack of thieves and endangering the lives and properties of all right-thinking citizens? Not to mention their pocketbooks?" he mimicked.

Something—the tone of voice, or one of the gestures used, rang false to Tristan. He'd drawn a breath to speak, but said nothing, staring instead. The blue tunic was as tight as the hose on the slim figure. He'd been wrong. The tattooed creature opposite him was definitely female. He could see her ribs rise and fall with her breathing, lifting her small breasts.

"It's not the street magic they're so upset about, mind," she was saying. "Though they claim it attracts rogues and pick-pockets—it's losing the revenues from the license that worries the Council." She threw a glance at the door, belatedly. "Sometimes they'll turn a blind eye to the license, but just now they're not in that vein. Must need the money, or think the city needs the discipline. That will pass, but your timing's off—you aren't one of the fish that will slip the net."

"Is that what you're here for?" Tristan asked. He felt as if he might be able to move without risking sickness now, but he didn't quite want to try. He wasn't really all that curious about the girl's crimes, either, but he felt he ought to say something.

"Me? A conjuror? Hardly."

She stood up fluidly and, to Tristan's complete amazement, did a backward flip as she came to her feet, her heels nearly brushing the ceiling's rafters. As the girl landed, she tucked forward and rolled that way, ending up standing in front of Tristan once more, not even breathing rapidly.

"I'm Kitri, the dancer. Maybe someday you'll have heard of me, if we both live that long."

"Dancing's against the law here too?" Tristan's eyes widened.

"No." Kitri laughed bitterly. "But it's folly to deny your favors to your patron, if he's a powerful man who loathes to be gainsaid. He says I stole a ring of his—he planted it on me so he could have me arrested as punishment. If he wants to punish me badly enough, he'll have them hamstring me." She sat in front of Tristan again. "When I'm sufficiently chastened by my experience, I'm supposed to go crawling gratefully back to him." Her tone was matter-of-fact.

Tristan gaped at her. She couldn't have been much past fourteen years old, yet her audacious manner put him very much in mind of Crewzel. A street background must breed such foolhardy nonchalance.

Kitri tossed her head, fluttered her eyelashes. "I'm still a fool. I gave you my name and never demanded yours in trade. Will you work a spell on me now, sorcerer?"

She laughed before he could reassure her.

"You can't anyway! They have this place superbly well protected. You try any magic here and you'll be sicker than you were before—if not dead. I saw a demonstration of that right after I was brought here. A big man he was, but not when they took him out of here."

Tristan shrugged. He supposed he should be grateful for the warning, but he felt little inclination toward working magic just then, anyway. That could be either the aftermath of the spell the Watch had taken him with or the effect of the ensorcellment used on the cells, but whatever it was certainly seemed to be doing its job. His head still felt thick.

"I'm called Tristan," he said, remembering that it would be polite to exchange names.

"Delighted. Wish it was in better circumstances—for me if not for you."

A small pail in the corner held water and a dipper. Kitri offered it to him, and Tristan drank. The water tasted of iron, but he made himself swallow it. He wondered how long he'd been there. Had Jehan missed him? Or Thomas?

Neither of them would have any idea where he'd gone. He hadn't said anything about his plans for the day, expecting to be gone a few hours at most. Stupid, Tristan thought furiously. He felt feverish, his thoughts floating in a dark pool of grief and disaster. He wasn't sure if he'd fallen into it yet, or if the danger merely threatened, despite his present circumstances. Was his life to be just one mischance—and of his own making—after another?

The novelty of talking to him having worn off, Kitri got up and began a vigorous program of stretching exercises, bemoaning cramps in her legs which she swore would never have begun if she'd had her woolen leg wrappings when she was taken. Yet she was graceful enough despite that. Tristan found himself fairly well entertained, enough to forget his own miseries briefly. He could always dwell on them later.

"Four days they've kept me here," Kitri was grumbling. "I'll never dance again, even if they *don't* hamstring me." She pirouetted on her toes, stirring the straw. Something green and gold caught the torchlight that filtered through the bars and into the cell.

Tristan idly reached for it and saw that it was not the dropped bauble he'd supposed. It was an oblong of parchment or thinnest ivory, with a pattern painted in greens and golds and scarlets on one side. The reverse side was dark.

His fingers knew it before his eyes, for he'd seen it mostly in the company of its mates, but his fingers had handled Crewzel's cards singly as often as in the pack.

Tristan's sight came and went in his excitement, and his hearing seemed to do the same. He had no voice for several moments. That didn't trouble him. He could hear—in very recent memory—Kitri's voice saying, "You're the second one they've caught this sevenday. They didn't let her go either." *Crewzel!* No wonder she hadn't come back. All the wasted anger he'd spent on her— He would have been shamed by it, but he was too anxious to bother with that just yet.

"Kitri?"

"Yes?" She paused in her exercising, breathing lightly and rapidly. Her cheeks were sheened with sweat, and her hair curled damply about them, brushing the bird wings.

"This card—" Tristan held it up between thumb and forefinger. "You said there was someone else brought in, because of street magic. Was this hers? A red-haired woman?"

Kitri's eyes narrowed speculatively. "That looks like it might be worth something. What is it? Is that gold on there?"

"Do you know where they took her?" Tristan put the card quickly behind him. "Please. It's important."

"To me or to you?" Kitri asked, abruptly withdrawing her interest. She raised one leg nonchalantly high, clasped it at the ankle and pressed it to her face so that her foot pointed straight at the ceiling. The action put her back to him, and she kept it there.

Tristan persisted.

"If you've been here four days, you must have been here when she was. Do you know where they took her? Or even when?" Maybe, if it hadn't been too long ago, her trail would be cold, but not dead.

Kitri bent slowly to the floor, her fingers sliding down her leg. Tristan felt an urge to shake her until the answers dropped out of her mouth, but he was sure force would be useless. And he had nothing else to offer.

He moved around the cell's edge till he faced her.

"Look, the card's not worth anything. And she's not worth anything, except to me. I'm not trying to do you out of anything." Yet plainly he needed to make some sort of offer.

Kitri was moving only one foot now, rotating the ankle in slow circles, pointedly not looking at him, even though he was right by her face. Tristan went on desperately.

"I need to find her. You know I don't have anything to pay you with or much prospect of getting any money. I don't know what's going to happen when they take me out of here, but I promise that I'll do whatever I can to help you. I've got a friend here at the Academy; surely he can do something—"

Tristan knew he sounded a lot more confident than he felt. But if things worked out in such a way that he couldn't put in a small word for Kitri, then he'd be in no position to look for Crewzel either. He couldn't think about it that way. It was best that he tend to one thing at a time. That was all he could efficiently worry about.

"Kitri?"

She lifted her face to him. Her lashes and the bird's wings fluttered.

"What's to stop you just leaving me to rot here? Not that you'll get out of here at all." She tossed her head. "If you *did* have a friend among them at the school, you wouldn't be here now."

Tristan shook his head. That hurt. "What have you got to lose? You'll have to trust me, but you're getting a bargain."

It wasn't working. All he was doing was passing the time for her. Good enough, it kept him from uselessly fretting as well. And there was a more than even chance that Kitri couldn't tell him anything helpful anyway, other than that Crewzel had been in the cell.

He could always try later. Apparently he'd have plenty of time for it. It would be nice if some food were to appear somewhere along the way. Tristan wasn't hungry yet, but he thought he might be later. Maybe he could bribe Kitri with a part of his share. But more likely she'd take all of it, and laugh in his face. And probably she'd be the one to get out of this prison, not him. Tristan pounded a fist into the straw.

"If I tell you," Kitri said abruptly, staring at her pointed toe, "will you really get me out of here?"

Tristan lifted his head and gave both Kitri and his conscience a long look. "No," he said reluctantly. "I won't promise you that." He dared not, however desperately he wanted to. What was it Crewzel had accused him of? Disappointing himself with promises he couldn't make good? "I won't lie to you. I don't know if anyone will listen to me. I pledge you my word that I'll try, but that's all I have to offer."

Kitri stared in amazement. "You *do* have an honest face," she whispered. "They're so out of fashion here, I was thinking you were just simple. All right." She waved a hand at the card. "She was here when I came and one day after that. Then they took her away to be tried and they didn't bring her back. That's all I know, I swear."

"Was she all right?" Tristan thought of Crewzel as he'd seen her last, prey for almost any madness. And there had been fear in her eyes in the vision of the bubble.

"As right as you can be when you're *here*." Kitri stamped a foot on the paving stones. "We didn't talk much, but I liked her."

"Where do they usually take prisoners? What's the sentence?" He might need to know for his own sake as much as Crewzel's.

"In—what's it called? Indenture? Apprenticeship for ten years to one of the mages—one of those on the Council. Spelled so you do only his will. Someplace far away from here. They take all the convicted ones in a train, under guard. I've seen them. That's what will happen to me." Kitri shivered. "I've heard it said that Lord Avendil's building a pleasure garden on his country estate. Maybe he'll want dancing girls, once the wizards are done building it for him. Or maybe he'll just have me killed."

"I swear I'll do my best—" Tristan touched Kitri's wrist reassuringly. Her bones were light as a cat's. He couldn't believe she was in any great danger—but then he hadn't believed that the edict against street magic would be taken seriously either.

"Is she your wife?" The bird wings fluttered at him again. Tristan's mouth curled as he considered what that suggested union would have been like.

"No. Just a friend." A thought of Elisena brushed him, like a whiff of lavender or the touch of a cool raindrop on his lips, her face seeming to hang before him in the air. No, that wasn't quite right, but he sensed her near; he felt that he could touch her if he stretched out his fingers in just the right way—

All at once there was a considerable increase in the light

and noise outside the cell. The door opened gratingly. Six men carrying torches stood without. A seventh, who carried no light, jerked a thumb at Tristan. Kitri's face had gone gray. She let one breath out now and drew another.

"You. Now. You're to be questioned."

the Council of Nine

THE GUARDS' LEATHER armor was rune-incised, so thoroughly that the carving swallowed the torchlight as it fell upon them and gave nothing back—not even a faint glitter. The strength those sigils afforded their wearers made steel armor seem a laughable frivolity. Tristan went very quietly. He could feel Kitri's astonished eyes on his back the whole way.

The intervals between torches decreased. When the whole of their way had been well-lighted for more than twenty paces, his guards dragged Tristan to a halt, thumped upon a round-topped oaken door, and thrust him through the portal when it had barely opened. Two of the guards remained. The rest marched off, their bootsteps echoing gloomily.

A young man sat behind a stained table littered with papers and curling parchments. At his right hand a little cauldron of sealing wax bubbled over a blue flame which melted the wax and yet conveniently left the table beneath unharmed. By his left hand, a pot of ink balanced beside a couple of reed pens, none of them very far from the table's edge.

The youth's lips thinned, and he barely glanced at Tristan and the guards.

"Is this the last?" He scarcely waited for one of the guards to rumble something indistinguishable before initiating a search through the litter before him. "Ah, yes." Apparently he'd found what he sought.

Tristan had, during his time in the Library, learned how the color of a man's robes marked the grade a wizard of Kôvelir had attained. This man, only a little older than Tristan, looked more a clerk than a judge, and his brown garb so marked him. He was an acolyte, nothing more, and with no more power.

Doubtless he'd had the smaller nuisance cases pushed off onto him to spare his betters excess work. He was probably empowered only to pass sentence, not to release prisoners—if a prisoner's possible innocence should even occur to him. Having his guess confirmed by the man's expression and his peevish hasty reading of the particulars of the case, Tristan determined not to cooperate in the slightest way and to make as much of a fuss as he possibly could about it. Hopefully, such intransigence would force his case up to some higher authority.

He sensed that if he showed the slightest fear or uncertainty, he'd be lost. So Tristan put on the same sort of arrogance that Howun both used and inspired—oddly thankful for the useful memory—and prepared to face his judge down.

"You are charged with—"

Tristan interrupted the recital briskly.

"Is it customary for a wizard to be tried by those ranked lower than himself? I should have thought the Examinations counted for something, still."

The acolyte glanced up in startlement, and Tristan smiled inwardly with relief. He hadn't been certain precisely how one passed from one grade to the next among the mages here, but some sort of ritual test had seemed reasonable. Apparently he'd guessed rightly. Toadstools! Now if his luck only held—

The acolyte tapped the parchment with one of his pens. It looked as if he chewed upon the other end of the reed rather frequently. "*Street-magic-without-license*, it says here. Those cases come to me."

"*Street* magic?" Tristan curled his lip scornfully. "Really, there are more wholesome ways of earning a living here." He stepped forward, too swiftly for either of his guards, and turned the parchment around. One guard reached him then. Tristan glared over his shoulder at him, but haughtily forbore to shake the man's hand from his arm. He fixed his gaze back on the parchment.

"There's not even a *name* on this," he protested, his astonishment no longer just a part of the role he played. "How are you sure you've attached the right papers to me?"

The acolyte looked rattled again and glared at Tristan's escort.

"Except for the dancing girl, he's the only one left in that block," the guard nearer the door supplied helpfully. "We cleared all the rest this morning."

That news made the acolyte bolder and therefore nastier. "Of course there's no name on this writ," he snapped, snatching the parchment back. "It says here you tried to escape arrest and had to be rendered unconscious. And you had no papers of any kind on you. Most particularly the license in question. And that's the charge. Case closed."

"For all you know, I may be guilty of nothing more than falling in with bad company in a wine shop." Tristan pretended to lose his patience, which wasn't altogether difficult. "You have no authority over me. So I suggest you produce someone who does, if you intend to carry this charade any further."

All he hoped to gain was a few minutes' speech with anyone whose face showed a vestige of intelligence and a willingness to listen to his story. The quicker he could become a person again, and not merely a blank writ, the sooner Tristan would feel easier. But just behaving highhandedly wouldn't be enough.

He didn't want to waste any more time with underlings. They could, if he let them, shuffle him back and forth for many hours. And having little idea how long he'd already been locked up, Tristan felt he could ill afford that.

He remained adamant and intractable. And after a few more minutes of attempting to read the charges and having them continually challenged, the acolyte gave up and sent for help. They waited for it.

Footsteps sounded in the corridor. Tristan relaxed, but he kept his back straight and his nostrils flared, still feigning anger. Red robes swept through the doorway as it opened. Good. An adept would certainly have acquired some sense in the course of his advanced training. Surely, Tristan thought, he'd be free of this mess soon. If he acted outraged enough, maybe they'd even buy his silence with a pouch of silver.

Tristan stood quietly, facing the door. He found himself staring right into the adept's narrowing eyes.

"*You!*" Howun spat.

* * *

Despite his surprise, Tristan's reflexes served him truly. His hands moved almost of their own accord; since none of his guards suspected a common street magician of possessing such a puissant ward, he was able to complete the personal-protection-spell easily and well ahead of any action they or Howun could take to stop him.

And then, for good measure and having observed Howun's starting of a counterspell, Tristan raised his right hand again and signed the ward with Cabel's personal rune, leaving it glowing in the air before him.

He knew the sign perfectly, having observed it often enough on his own hand, after Cabal had put it there to grant Tristan free passage to the Library. Howun recognized it too, plainly. He hesitated before launching his own spell, though only for the briefest instant.

The spell shattered itself against Tristan's ward, and nothing else Howun or the others did was even slightly more effective. Tristan couldn't relax his spell, and it didn't permit him to move quite freely enough to leave, but so long as he kept up the magic, no one could lay a hand on him—at least no one Howun felt safe to summon.

. He might, Tristan thought, have overreached himself. He'd been put in a room to wait again—after hasty conference, many examinations of the rune and himself, many finger-pointings and jabbings, and consultations of other adepts. He was going before the Council now, the highest ranked mages of the city.

That wasn't precisely what he'd hoped to accomplish. Getting free of the Council itself might well be more than he could manage. Tristan shrugged. He hadn't had much choice, and there was no going back. He set himself to wait once more.

That was more difficult. He'd done too much of it. Tristan realized that he was angry to a much greater extent than he'd been at any point during his exchanges with the clerk. Perhaps it was just being free of the inhibiting-spell Kitri had said was used in the dungeons. Or possibly the earlier spell, the one they'd captured him with, had only just worn off. Maybe the protection spell had something to do with it. At any rate, Tristan's indignation was rising.

He seethed for a while, till his galloping rage stumbled over a moral block. The charge he'd been arrested on was—at least in letter—false. But was outrage justified simply because he hadn't gotten so much as a single notched copper for any of his spells? He'd intended to gain by them—that he hadn't was no doing of his, and no proper defense, which the Council would easily note.

Tristan decided he'd best settle for leaving with a whole skin and let go of crazy thoughts of revenge and recompense. He stopped pacing about. Those ideas belonged to the role he'd used to bring him this far—he could drop it and them now— and had better. He hadn't been hurt, really. It would be best just to concentrate on getting free. That would be fine indeed.

He slumped down into a chair, wishing he dared to sleep. He hoped fretfully that he hadn't already made more fuss than was healthy.

He was grateful for the chair. The room lacked windows, a fireplace, or even a brazier, and there were still a half dozen guards outisde its door, but at least there was a rug and the chair, and the place was quiet. Tristan could think and be reasonably comfortable as he did so. He'd best use the respite.

There was no point in trying to clean his clothing. Aside from the dungeon filth he was smeared with, most of his things looked as if he'd been dragged through half the streets of Kôvelir in them. He probably had been.

His appearance might, Tristan supposed, even win him some welcome sympathy from the Council, if they felt he'd been treated badly. He certainly wouldn't scorn favorable feelings from that or any other quarter.

Contemplating his appearance led him down some other interesting avenues of thought. Tristan recalled the glamour Elisena had cast over him to awe Galan. He understood the heart of that spell, which was the key to the job. He might cast a similar spell himself, armed with that knowledge. The question was—presuming his success with the spell—should he appear as a fearsome foreign mage, full of righteous kingly wrath, or should he try to look even more humble and harmless than he normally did, so they would be moved to let him go? Either extreme might be equally effective—or equally disastrous.

His heartbeats ticked by. Tristan had been given to understand—rather rudely—that it would be some while before all of the Council's prior business was transacted and they'd have time for him. He didn't doubt they'd see him in the end. Apparently his use of Cabal's rune was something they couldn't ignore. He was lucky to have hit on it.

He hadn't wanted to drag Cabal into this. He still didn't want that, nor did he want to be forced to tell the Council's members who he was and then explain his business in Kôvelir more fully. Scant help any of the mages other than Cabal had given him on his quest for Allaire and little did they care what became of Calandra. His business was none of theirs, Tristan decided stubbornly.

Of course, he might not be believed. Tristan knew he wouldn't have accepted the tale himself, if it hadn't happened to him. That had to be considered, as well. This wasn't going to be easy.

A flicker of movement drew his eye. Across the room, a white cat slipped behind the carven legs of a second chair. Its ice-green eyes had a familiar look about them, but all Tristan thought was how he wished Thomas were with him.

The Council hall was walled with leaded glass. Part of the group of buildings at the hub of both the mages' Academy and the city of Kôvelir itself, it had small need of sturdy walls for its protection. The many panes were mostly clear glass, giving watery views of the gardens, but toward the roof a design of trailing vines took shape, and the bits of glass were colored in lifelike shades of green, brown, and soft rose. Tristan wondered uselessly if the glass were painted or blown to those colors.

The floor was partly glass, as well—heavy opaque tiles of it at the center of the room, shaped like those of the windows, only bordered with mortar rather than lead, making a vast circular design of leaves and flowers. Nine chairs sat loosely grouped upon the pattern, and a mage sat in each, all of the them black-robed. Some of the robes were neatly edged with runes of silver.

The Council watched as Tristan entered among his guards, his back carefully straight and his pace studiedly unhurried. Curious, he scanned their faces as he walked across the room to them.

They were of middle years mostly. Which meant something different than the ordinary usage in a wizard. No longer in their first youth or early maturity, they had arrived at an intermediate stage which could last for scores of years; with luck, while magely powers were at their full. Tristan suspected a few were a great deal older than they appeared to his first glance—there were signs of strain about the eyes of those; if the texture of one mage's skin did not hint at unhealth, then it spoke of appearances kept up skillfuly but at dire cost.

As the mages viewed Tristan's progress across the broad room, Council business was yet being transacted. One mage leaned from his chair to speak to a brown-robed clerk over-burdened with rolled parchments. After the exchange, the aco-lyte juggled his way to the room's edge, where a gray-robed youth waited with a quill pen. At the acolyte's direction the pen began to move, first to the inkpot and then upon a scrap of paper.

The distracted mage turned his attention back to Tristan. He lifted a hand, revealing a rich golden lining beneath the sleeve slits of slits of his gown, and spoke.

"Know that this matter is worthy of our attention only be-cause of our regard for Master Cabal. You shall have the hear-ing you demand, but you will be brief and consider the value of this Council's time and the shortness of its patience."

His appearance was hardly the most distinguished of all the Council's members, despite his rich clothing. He had an or-dinary face, marked by nothing more unusual than rather heavy brows, darker even than his small beard. His face was a trifle heavy; none of the features were remarkable enough to call attention to themselves singly. But from his assurance, there was no doubt that this man was the accepted, unquestioned spokesman for his fellows. And the firm set of his mouth left equally little doubt of his feelings on the matter in question.

"I presume you are aware of the nature of the charges against you, despite your obdurate refusal to hear them read?"

Tristan forced an easy smile. "My lord, I have a reluctance to hear false charges read against me, particularly when there are no witnesses to it but myself and my accusers." He was relieved to discover that he could hold his voice steady.

"Do you question our justice, sirrah?" The mage's face reddened.

"On the contrary, my lord. I've gone to extraordinary lengths seeking it." Meekness would probably win him nothing. The man had convicted him in his mind already. Tristan glanced at the faces before him, to judge the effect of his words on the others. Reactions were mixed—boredom, curiosity, and ner-vous interest. The spokesman simply looked angry.

"You are now before the highest authority in this city," the mage said coldly. "You are charged with the illegal practice of street magic. We have the authority to try you—a point you have insisted upon. So speak to us now. That is your right. But I warn you, the evidence presented against you is straight-forward and complete. Trading on some fleeting acquaintance with Master Cabal will avail you naught."

Tristan felt his own temper flaring. He scrapped his carefully thought-out plea and spoke what was in his heart.

"My lord, I am in this city on a quest of great importance. Because I choose to earn my bread rather than live longer on Master Cabal's hospitality or your charity, you've brought me here. I suppose you have proof enough of your charges. But can you hold me guilty of breaking a law I was ignorant of?"

An eyebrow raise answered him.

"Unless you'd have us believe you a half-wit, such protes-tations of innocence hardly become you." The mage gestured broadly at a sheaf of papers lying at his feet. "These writs have been read throughout this city. You could hardly be unaware of them."

"I have but recently returned to the city." It was all Tristan could do not to grind his teeth. At all costs, he must hold on to whatever was left of his temper—if it wasn't already too late.

"On quest, you say?" This mage had sandy hair, pale brows, and light eyes. His features were strong, but his expression was not. "What manner of quest?"

Tristan knew then he should never have mentioned it. He should have known they'd ask and he dared not answer. Even a half-truth would be useless. He had learned enough of the Council already to know he'd get no help from them and he could guess at the hindrance they might offer, even benignly. If they chose to openly oppose him—

"I am not at liberty to name it, my lord," Tristan said. Out loud, the words did not seem so diplomatic as they had in his head.

"Not at liberty?" the spokesman asked, incredulously. "What arrogance is this? You're not one of ours."

And so much for Cabal's offer, not so very long ago, of a place for Tristan at the Academy. The statement might have been intended as a dismissal, but Tristan chose to regard it as a question. He drew himself up straighter, wishing he had his cloak with him. It might have lent him an air of respectability, which he suspected he rather badly needed.

"No, my lord. But my master was one of you." He said it respectfully, managing that somehow.

"Then he should have brought you to us for registry," the spokesman snapped. "If he were a mage trained here, he'd have known that."

Tristan wondered if that were true. No one registered the wizards of Calandra; there was no formal organization among them. If matters were different here, as they plainly were, Blais would surely have known of it. Had his master simply forgotten? Tristan doubted that. Probably such a registry simply hadn't been practical. Blais had never intended him to come to Kôvelir, after all.

"He didn't have time for such things, my lord. He was murdered rather unexpectedly. I realize that he wasn't able to finish training me." Tristan gestured vaguely at himself. "I'm very conscious of that, but I've done my best to keep to the course he set for me. That's why I'm here." He was back to the plea he'd come intending to make, but the time for it was probably past.

"Then you contend you're something more than a back-street conjuror and are worthy of special consideration?" Nine pairs of eyes glittered at Tristan, but only one mouth was doing any serious questioning, and its owner wasn't going to be diverted, it seemed.

"What proof can you offer? How are we to know that you are what you say you are?" Another mage spoke now, and then looked as if he wished he had not. He had gentle eyes and weak hands. Even if his question had suggested sympathy, which was by no means certain, his support would be of little practical use. Tristan knew well enough by then which of the nine he had to deal with. He considered a further moment before answering.

"My lords, I think the fact that I stand before you now offers more proof than any words I could say."

There were sounds of derision. At this point, Thomas would certainly have inquired as to Tristan's sanity. Tristan could half hear him doing so.

As he'd have done with Thomas, Tristan waited for silence and then went on.

"Wouldn't a 'back-street conjuror' be aware of this law? He would know it better than anyone, and whether he could flout it safely and avoid the Watch? If I'm a thief, I'm a remarkably poor one, by your own admission, and I'm sure this conjuror we're discussing would long since have turned to honest work to keep from starving!"

The silence fell thick as a winter cloak. Tristan swallowed hard. This wasn't working at all. Where had he ever gotten the idea that he could talk his way out of anything?

He squared his shoulders again. He might have to tell them about the sword after all. There seemed no other course. He tried one last stratagem first.

"My lord, there's more I can say, but this is not for the ears of many, even so small a group as this. Are you the head of this Council? The High Mage?"

"This Council has no head," the Council's spokesman said.

He was perhaps about to explain smugly that the Nine ruled jointly and spoke with one voice when another tongue spoke up from the doorway with admirable clarity.

"And thus no brain? Did any of you perhaps think to check his story, or to consult with me, instead of merely gaping because he knows my naming-rune?"

Tristan whirled, astonished. Cabal stood in the doorway. The old mage leaned heavily upon his yew staff, but he had put on his black robe once more, and his beard was carefully dressed.

"It would have been simple enough, Gannett," Cabal went on. "I am hardly difficult to locate and I do not move swiftly enough to avoid you. In any case, I'm amazed that no other of you remembers Tristan. He's been about the Library for many days, with my mark on him all the while."

Tristan felt both relief and concern sweep over him. He saw Bleyvr behind Cabal now, his long face furrowed with worry; yet from his posture, he was seemingly resigned to this. Tristan wondered what arguments or sheer stubbornness had won Cabal this far from his sickbed.

The nine mages looked uncomfortable. If Cabal's stern address made them so, surely that boded well? Yet Tristan felt odd—not rescued and not alarmed, but somehow detached, as if this were all a dream from which he could depart at will.

Cabal ignored eight of the members of the Council, and glared at the one he'd named Gannett. He planted his staff with a firm thump upon the tiles.

"Well? I have said that I know this man and that I vouch for him. Does my word now count for nothing?"

Gannett cleared his throat. He remained seated, though courtesy would have bidden him to rise, so long as Cabal stood before him.

"My lord, you have been gravely ill. Indeed, it surprises me that your physician approves your presence here. So while this Council rejoices to see you once more, I must ask you, my lord, for your own sake and for the love and respect this Council bears you, to leave us to our work. We would have you well again."

Cabal snorted into his beard. "Well again? To offer you a service you ignore, as you ignore me now? No. I shall stay. This matter concerns me, since it was my rune that was used. And Tristan deserves one voice to speak for him."

With a peeved frown he didn't trouble to conceal, Gannett rose, signing an apprentice to bring another chair, and stood before it while Cabal settled himself.

Tristan didn't know if Cabal had ever held a place upon the Council, but it was clear that this present Council held him in a great deal of respect. At Cabal's insistence and over Gannett's protests, the previous proceedings were reviewed minutely. Every word and every smallest point was examined. The writ was read, twice, and Tristan was finally permitted to speak.

He told the precise truth, while carefully not mentioning Jehan, the sword, or anything that touched on his past, except to say that he came from Calandra. He did not exactly become more hopeful—one look at Gannett's face was enough to stop that kind of nonsense—but his stomach settled down.

Cabal meditated a moment, glancing slowly at each member of the Council in turn. More than one of them could not long meet his eye. At length he spoke.

"I am informed—yes, my lords, there are still those who do me the courtesy of keeping me informed of events—that since the new edicts were issued, the prisons have been filled day and night and that the acolytes can barely hear all the new cases brought before them. I am told that the streets are quiet as new graves and folk move like shadows, even at noon. They fear that the trade in magical properties and supplies may be proscribed to those unable to purchase licenses. I am told that already trade has fallen off because of the restrictions placed upon it, though the decline is as yet slight. And of course we profit from the service fines. A tenth of Kôvelir's citizens may be forcibly apprenticed to us." Cabal shook his head.

"Is that worthwhile, my lords? Have our coffers grown so thin that we are reduced to a practice of extortion efficacious now and surely ruinous in years to come? Have we examined what the results of these edicts will be? Shall we cleanse the city by scalding it to death, and take a profit from the outrage as well, all in the name of government?"

"My *lord*—" Gannett began, and shot a venomous glance at Bleyvr, who feigned blindness to him. Cabal waved a hand as if at a troublesome insect.

"This Council scarcely works as one, whatever you may say, Gannett. And that is well, for it keeps the others from a too close examination of the policies you command, does it not? By the time they have ceased their petty squabbling and the carving out of comfortable niches for a secure old age, you shall have achieved your ends long since, shall you not?" Cabal sighed. "Well, I am old. It matters not to me. Ruin yourselves." Cabal swept his eyes over the rest of the Council once more. "Gannett could do nothing without your willing, knowing blindness. Do as you will, but remember my words. And release me this man."

"This is a civil matter, gentlemen," Gannett said coldly. "It hardly seems necessary to turn it into a general indictment of Council policy. My lord Cabal has made his views well known to us in the past; they need not be repeated. You know well the incidents that led to the edicts and respect the sense that limits street magic to accredited members of the Academy. And as for this man—he seeks to cloud his own guilt, nothing more. The law is plain, as is our duty."

"Guilt?" Cabal scoffed, and seemed about to say more, but he mastered himself. "No matter. I would not for all the world challenge or mock the lawful edicts of this Council. What words I have on the subject have indeed been spoken several times before this—and before this body—without discernible result. However, I submit that, under your own cherished laws, you have no case against this man, and he has done well to drag the matter into the daylight. I don't imagine that was easily done. My lords, he was taken without a single copper in his pockets; your own writ says so. Can you truly convict him of unlicensed magic for profit? How has he profited, save by a night's free lodging in your jail?"

Gannett stood with a swish of his robes meant to damp any wavering sympathies among his fellows.

"And are we then to accept the word of any vagabond thief who wanders through our streets spouting nonsense about a quest—a quest he will not name? This passes understanding. Do *you* know what this quest of his is, Cabal?"

Cabal shook his head. "No. Nor do I require to know. It is not my quest."

"Yet he requires your help with it—your protection, and the use of our Library."

Tristan felt himself sinking into a morass of legalities. He should have resigned himself to being shuffled by underlings—it might have been quicker. It was all he could do to stand still, and he only managed it so as not to provoke his guards. He was half frantic with an irrational need to get to Jehan at once. It was not quite a premonition—he had no sure sense of any harm coming to Jehan or any danger involving anyone but himself, and yet... foreboding raised goosebumps along his arms. The air felt chill, despite the lamps and braziers.

"No book is harmed by being read, Gannett," Cabal answered. "And Tristan has been helping me seek an apprentice of mine, who seems to have vanished under mysterious circumstances. Scant help have I received from anyone else in this matter. As for protection, he has asked for none till now."

"And while he purportedly seeks this missing apprentice, he wanders the streets playing at magic?" Gannett snapped. "Why has be been so discreet about this quest, Cabal, and not open even with you, his friend? I submit that he has lied to you and I think the Watch has done better than they know in bringing him to us. There is more involved here than street magic."

Tristan felt as if he'd been plunged into iced water. He suspected he was about to be accused of spying, or something a lot worse. Gannett didn't appear to need proof of any sort for any charges he might care to make. And the Council would back him.

Cabal spoke again.

"Considering how you treat his honest answers, Tristan does well to keep his secrets close. I know nothing of the nature of this quest of his, but it can be nothing injurious to this city. I do not doubt him."

"There are those of us who do. He's a cheat and a liar. Let us so deal with him."

It was not Gannett's voice this time, but it might as well

have been. The words were his—if not spoken at his direction, then gauged to curry his favor.

Was Nímir's hand to be seen, when a stranger changed suddenly and implausibly into an implacable enemy, or when ordinarily sensible and sane men lost all reason, doing it so mildly and consistently that the average man would never mark the change? Kôvelir was a great stronghold of magic—perchance the last such in all the world—so Nímir would hardly try a frontal assault on it, complete with showy glaciers and dramatic blizzards, Tristan realized. The mages of Kôvelir were neither so safe nor so independently secure as they fancied themselves. Perhaps their false beliefs were fostered elsewhere—a far colder elsewhere.

The image was so fleeting that Tristan could barely track it as it passed across his thoughts. He wanted to cry the Council a warning, but at the same time he knew that such an action would be bitterest folly. They'd never listen to him—to him least of all—even without Nímir's prompting.

By this same means Nímir had depleted Calandra's wizardry, causing little mistakes and trifling madnesses, and preying ever on pride, ambition, and misguided heroics. Had he now turned to Kôvelir, having let centuries pass to lull their sense of self-preservation and soothe their memories? Tristan's lips twitched, and his fists clenched till his knuckles whitened, but he forced himself to remain silent. He knew the Council would never heed him.

Gannett spoke again, plainly resigning himself to lengthy dealings with Cabal, now that the mage was proved determined to meddle in what had promised to be a simple affair.

"My lord Cabal, is it not possible that this man has indeed deceived you with his words, as he seeks to mislead us? Is the only proof you can offer us that which he told you with his own lips?"

Cabal's hands trembled badly on his staff. Was it from weakness or simple indignation? Tristan couldn't tell. He kept seeing images of ice and cold in his mind's eye, and they held him frozen, unable to move. Cabal was very old and gravely ill. If he collapsed now—Tristan was under no illusions as to his own probable fate.

"Let him be truth-read, then!" Cabal cried, and his voice at least was strong. "Grant him that, before you condemn him." He slumped forward in his chair, clutching at the staff for support. Tristan took a step toward him, alarmed and hoping no one on the Council would try to stop him, but not really caring if they did, for they'd never succeed.

His mind whirled. A truth-reading was the last thing he wanted, if he hoped to keep his quest a secret. And with visions of Darkenkeep flitting before his eyes and glints of ice visible behind the glances of the Councilmen, that secrecy seemed suddenly imperative.

"Truth-read him!" Cabal's voice was nearly gone, and he was going to need more than his staff to keep himself upright in a minute, Tristan saw. He had a hand on Cabal's shoulder by that point, feeling dry cloth over dry bones. He was afraid to grip tightly enough to support Cabal.

"Truth-read him," Cabal croaked again.

"That won't be necessary," the voice of Reynaud said. "The tale is true. But he's left out the most interesting bits."

Cabal's Passing

TRISTAN STRAIGHTENED AND turned slowly and deliberately. He felt the blood leaving his face; his breath deserting his lungs.

Reynaud inclined his head toward him.

"Well met, wizardling."

Tristan's dry lips parted. He started to breathe again, but very shallowly, as if a deeper intake of air might provoke some more baleful interest from Reynaud. If Reynaud was recognized and joyfully greeted by any of the Council, or if there was any sort of outcry at his entrance or his words, Tristan did not hear it. His ears as well as his eyes had wholly focused on Reynaud, to the exclusion of all else.

The red and yellow tracery on Reynaud's garments looked to be made of gems this day. The lines of the runes glittered under the light like thousands of rubies and yellow diamonds, transformed to myriad glimmering points. Tristan lifted his eyes slowly from the dizzying display to Reynaud's face.

Reynaud smiled at him, a flash of white amid the pointed blackness of his beard.

"I hardly thought to find you here, my lord—it seems this journey has been more productive than I might have dared to expect. Is there some sort of trouble here?" It was an unnecessary question. Reynaud would never have entered the room without knowing exactly what was taking place inside it.

Gannett might have been annoyed or might have mistaken whom Reynaud had addressed. But if he did answer, Tristan couldn't hear and couldn't drag his eyes from Reynaud to see if Gannett's lips moved. He must have said something, for Reynaud was turning to him.

"Yes, gentlemen," he said. "I believe I can offer you a great deal of interesting information. You will be astonished."

Tristan watched with stiff lips and empty eyes as Reynaud was welcomed by the Council—welcomed like a brother, and not a chance-passing stranger who happened to follow the same calling that they did. They seemed like a flock of crows, Tristan thought numbly, listening now to the shrill greetings and seeing black robes flapping as arms lifted and gesticulated. No, Reynaud was not unknown to the Council.

Tristan's mind churned. If only he had a sword, or even his table-knife . . . But that would be useless against Reynaud, as every defense he could hope to summon against the man would be. And if Reynaud were not powerful enough alone, he plainly had friends in plenty here.

Something moved under Tristan's hand, which he realized still rested on Cabal's shoulder. Well, he wasn't quite alone here himself, then—but that didn't seem to make much difference.

The old mage had risen to his feet and seemed to be leaning less upon his staff, though Tristan, who could see Cabal's hands at close range, knew that for a careful deception. Cabal also watched the Council and Reynaud. He didn't seem to need to ask who the newcomer was.

It wasn't natural to be so afraid, Tristan tried to tell himself. But even if Reynaud had encountered him only by chance, even if the master of magic hadn't tracked him all the way here at Galan's command, Tristan still wasn't safe. Reynaud would not be slow to profit from good fortune—and if what profited Reynaud did not happen to have anything to do with Galan or his politics, still there was grave danger for the object of Reynaud's attentions.

Cabal's lips moved. At first, Tristan took no notice. Any sound the old mage made was only a rustling deep within his beard; there was no sound left over to travel even the short distance to Tristan's ears. As Cabal spoke, the fingers of his right hand moved in subtle patterns upon the shaft of his staff, and the fingers of his left sought to match or mirror them. Shadows lifted and recombined, as if a cloud swept across the glass ceiling of the hall. Delicately, the chamber altered.

At any instant, Reynaud would turn back toward them, denouncing Tristan for a would-be usurper of Calandra's throne, and shout out whatever he might have guessed about Tristan's business in Kôvelir. Or perhaps only Gannett would act, pronouncing sentence and calling the guards back at one and the same time. Tristan stiffened his back. They would not take him without a fight, but he had Cabal to consider. He could not involve the mage in a duel of magic, especially one he was almost certainly fated to lose—not that fate had much to do with it. Tristan's own uncertainty and inexperience would surely suffice; destiny need not stir to lend a hand in his destruction.

He might, Tristan thought, manage to weave some sort of ward about Cabal, enough to shield him from random harm. That should do—no one would strike at the old man intentionally. Surely even Reynaud would not stoop to that. Tristan turned over the pages of Blais' grimoire in his mind, seeking the spell he needed. He must—

Of a sudden, Tristan felt very odd indeed. His sight blurred and his ears deadened. He swallowed hard, to clear them, then swayed on his feet as the room seemed to tilt under his boots.

Cabal's staff prodded him.

"Come. This will only last till one of them touches your seeming, which they are like to do soon. You must be well away before that can happen."

Tristan stared in amazement, after a couple of rapid blinks had restored his sight. He and Cabal stood at the room's edge, hard by one of the glass walls. The glazed flowers were close enough that Tristan could mark every bubble the glassblower had left to texture his artistry. At the room's center, more dwindled by distance than it seemed right they should be, sat the Council, with Reynaud just beginning to address them formally.

In front of them, the object of Reynaud's explanatory gestures, Tristan saw himself, with Cabal standing at his elbow, leaning heavily upon the yew staff.

A confusion—Tristan automatically identified the spell almost absently. Kin to the glamour, it was another artful rearrangement of light and shadow—but even more deceptive. He had never seen it done on such a scale, before so many witnesses in a well-lighted room. Tristan stared as his other self answered something Reynaud had said to it—answered with real spirit, too, to judge by the way its head came up.

Someone plucked at his sleeve—Bleyvr. He too looked impressed by the working of the spell, but plainly was less awed by it than Tristan was.

"Please. Help me get him back to his rooms. I don't think he'll come unless you do." Tristan saw that Cabal sagged against Bleyvr's arm. But there, across the room, Cabal still stood, still seemingly well.

He and Bleyvr half carried Cabal down the corridor, one supporting each arm. The sumptuous black robe might have been draped over a sack of loose bones. Tristan found that he was trembling all over. He'd thought at first that it was only his hands. He could hear his own heartbeat, too, loud over the swish of mage's robes.

Their progress was too slow. At any instant someone might see through Cabal's deception. Reynaud was sure to, if he gave his surroundings any interest at all. And how long could the spell hold up, even without close scrutiny, now that Cabal had left the room? Tristan kept hearing cries of discovery in his mind. He tried to hurry their steps, at least so far as a concealing bend in the hallway. Bleyvr frowned at him.

"Have some sense. Or if not that, pity," Bleyvr said.

Tristan stole a look at Cabal and felt himself color with shame. The mage's face was a waxy yellow, as if his skin had gone transparent and let the color of the bones of his skull show through. His eyes were shut. With no more ado, Tristan lifted Cabal up and carried him the rest of the way. It wasn't difficult. He was middling tall, and Cabal seemed to weigh almost nothing.

They reached Cabal's rooms.

"I heard you . . . before I went in. Facing them down. Blais would have been proud." Cabal's fingers wandered on Tristan's forearm, clutching without any force. "I'll be proud in his stead." His words were puffs of air with no force behind them. Bleyvr drew the bedclothes down, and Tristan lowered Cabal onto the sheets.

"It's cold," Cabal said.

Tristan was sweating. Bleyvr moved about the room softly, lighting candles and kindling the brazier. Tristan was relieved to see he'd locked the door and barred it.

Reynaud was here in Kôvelir! Tristan ran all the things that could mean through his mind, nearly paralyzed with possibilities, but keeping his face smiling at Cabal all the while. After a minute, he let the thoughts drop, and turned his full attention to the old man on the bed.

Beads of sweat dotted Cabal's face now, like drips on a tallow candle, but the mage had strength enough to smile his thanks as Tristan drew the embroidered coverlet over him. Tristan set the yew staff down gently in a corner and glanced at Bleyvr.

Bleyvr shook his head. Tristan crossed back to the bed, hooked a stool with one foot, and dragged it near enough to sit.

He tried to speak. At first his voice failed. His throat ached, and he could force no words through it.

Cabal's fingers squeezed his briefly.

"You should go."

Tristan shook his head and forced a smile, as if the movement of his lips could assuage his throat. "No. Not yet. I think it's time I told you what Blais' quest was. He would have wanted you to know."

He told it all, to the sound of Cabal's labored breathing— the search for Allaire, her last ring, and how those two were at last and so strangely found. Tristan told the tale well, each bit in its proper place, as if it had been some saga passed down from mouth to mouth over ages. He included even the faintly embarrassing bits about his own kingship, and Cabal took it all in without comment but with the perfect understanding that only another mage could share.

Tristan spoke of the troubles in Calandra and the discovery of the need for the sword. He mentioned Crewzel's cards, and how he'd sought her, found her, and lost her again.

"I think Delmon's all right, though. We did find him for you. That was no lie."

"None of it was," Cabal breathed. "Those fools . . . you gave them the only thing they could never believe—the truth. And they wondered why you would not name your quest."

Tristan would have known neither Cabal's voice nor his face, and he entered the room unprepared at that moment. He could hear Bleyvr moving about the room behind him, but dared not even glance that way. No herb the healer could choose now would make any difference, unless to speed events which were moving rapidly enough. Tristan made haste to complete his story.

He spoke of finding Jehan, their labors in the city, and the hopes he had for the sword Jehan was even now completing. He wanted desperately to have Cabal's advice on whether he dared believe the makeshift sword would suffice. Not having consulted even Elisena in the matter, Tristan badly needed another opinion, and Cabal's would have been invaluable. But that was never to be.

Cabal had listened without further interruptions or response, until Tristan wondered if he accepted the tale as truth at all, despite what he'd said, or if he thought it merely a fiction cobbled up to divert his ears. Cabal's breathing was steady but shallow. The wavering candlelight made the rising and falling of his chest uncertain. Tristan interlaced his fingers with Cabal's once more.

He traced the naming-rune upon the back of Cabal's hand carefully. "If I could have chosen—"

Cabal's eyes were only just visible, slits that the candlelight glittered upon, but Tristan thought there was sense and understanding there still.

"If I could have chosen, I would have stayed here, when you asked me to. I would have been your student gladly." Tears blurred Tristan's sight. He blinked them away and felt warm drops spill down his cheeks. Somewhere some student was practicing a wind-charm upon a flute, repeating phrases and variations endlessly. The sound wound through the moment, stretching it, then died away.

Bleyvr touched his arm once more. Tristan let himself be drawn to his feet, away from the bed. He glanced back. Cabal's eyes were closed now. There was a faint, faint smile yet on his lips. Tristan started to speak, then stopped. He faced Bleyvr.

The lines on Bleyvr's face could betray no further sorrow, but his eyes glittered as he lifted up Cabal's staff and laid it upon the fire. At first the flames did not accept the wood but held back from it, quivering and shying away. Bleyvr spoke sharply and the blaze flared up till it licked at the mantelpiece. The mage paid that no heed. He held the blaze and kept the flames high.

Tristan felt the tears dry, leaving his cheeks sticky. He stood trembling, wanting to look anywhere except at the bed or at the fire and the green flames crawling over the yew wood.

Bleyvr thrust a leather pouch into Tristan's hands. His fingers inspected it automatically, without interest. By the feel, there were coins in it and maybe a little compact food. Bleyvr stood at the door, lifting the bar and making complicated hand passes.

"To the left out this door, two more left turnings, and the next right," he said. "You come to a half-door. It gives onto a quiet street where no one will see you. Try to get out of the city. Go now, my lord."

Tristan went.

A Task Completed

THE NIGHT WAS full of peril, and every shadow was a danger, but Tristan paid that scant heed. He twisted his way down the Academy's corridors, making the turns automatically. He could hear sounds of groups moving about, searching for him almost certainly, but they weren't very close. He ignored them. Meeting Reynaud alone would have been disastrous, but it didn't happen. Tristan arrived at the final door.

He might, if he had been worrying, have considered that it might require a Word of Opening, and not receiving such, give an alarm. But there was not even a keyhole, just a plain bar which he lifted easily, and then the postern swung open.

Still his luck—the good fortune of the uncaring—held. There was no ambush, no sudden flare of torches, no chance cry of discovery. He was in a cobbled courtyard, slipping on its damp stones. There were rounds carpeted with moss at intervals, and gnarly black trees planted among them. Tristan staggered into one, and pressed his cheek against the wet bark, making it wetter still. A bitter scent of crushed moss rose around him.

Drops of water hung from the branch tips, catching and magnifying the faint starlight until the drops shone like new-made stars. Tears, Tristan thought them. The whole world was weeping for Cabal, and he was not ashamed to join. He could have done nothing else.

He moved like a ghost through the dark streets, starting now at every noise. He stumbled often; tears distorted what little vision he had. He couldn't think about anything. If there was a pursuit, he eluded it without conscious design by aimless wandering. A sane man would have fled the city. Tristan went deeper into it.

There was a wind behind him, scattering the rubbish in the streets. If he had been sure that it was the Hounds, he would have turned and waited for it. But the wind was only wind, not punishment or absolution.

He trod on something soft, and a horrible noise tore through the night. A cat ran off, still squalling, as Tristan fought for balance, lost, and fell to his knees. He stayed there for a long while, not caring if he never moved again.

There was a puddle of water on the cobbles. Despite the stars in a clear sky, there had been rain sometime during the night or late the previous day. Tristan dipped his hands, washed away the tears, and then went on.

After a long time and many wrong turnings, he staggered down the proper alley at last and heard Valadan whinny a relieved greeting. Tristan looked up. Only one bright star burned, low on the horizon, and there was the beginning of color in the sky. It was nearly morning. He stroked Valadan's neck, while the stallion blew warmly into his face.

All is well, now that you are back. As if to prove the point, Valadan moved from under Tristan's hands and began to tear at the grass he was tethered in. A moth fluttered away from his teeth.

Tristan sighed. He hadn't considered that Jehan might have moved in search of him. He hadn't considered much of anything, and his relief at Valadan's reassurance came as a guilty surprise. A faroff keening reached his ears—one of the wind-towers in the hills outside the city, Tristan thought. The pre-dawn stillness of the air permitted the sound to carry for miles. No bells tolled yet at the center of the city, but Cabal's death was not unmarked. Tristan's throat ached cruelly, but he could not swallow the lump.

The stable door gave him pause—it was barred from within. Tristan dredged up a word of opening from somewhere deep in his memory. It was fortunately a simple spell, and the memory was accurate. Tristan carefully held the bar after having lifted it, though the effort at the end of the long night was nearly too much for him. He nudged the door open and slid through.

Thomas blinked at him. At least the cat's glowing eyes vanished for a heartbeat, then reappeared.

Nice of you to drop in.

Tristan swore and caught the bar with his hands as the spell let go of it. He still nearly dropped it, and one end of it cracked him hard on his knees. He heaved it back into place on the closed door, wondering why a man with the strength to use such a log to bar a door would bother to bar that door at all.

Thomas stood reluctantly. *Even I don't come in this late. Better to stay out all night. It's an awful time to be waked up.*

"Sorry." Tristan tried to tell himself that Thomas was right, that everything was properly at its lowest ebb at this hour— the night, the tide, and his spirits. It didn't help. The darkness was like velvet, embroidered by Thomas' shifting eyes. After a while, Tristan could see a bit better.

Jehan was fast asleep, rolled tightly up in his cloak and Tristan's as well. The forge fire was out, the unneeded smoke-hole covered, and what light there was crept in through the cracks in the shutters. Tristan knelt down and touched the smith's shoulder.

"Jehan?"

Jehan came awake with explosive swiftness, like a banked fire suddenly granted air. He rolled over and out of the cloaks in one motion, a knife popping into one hand and leveling itself at Tristan's throat.

Tristan froze, his eyes wide.

I should have mentioned, Thomas said, *that he wakes up in a nasty temper.*

Tristan merely wished he could be sure Jehan was awake.

The knife dropped. Jehan rubbed at his eyes with the back of his empty hand.

"Oh. Where were you, anyway?"

Tristan drew a deep breath and let himself sag sideways until he was sitting on the floor. "In trouble. Toadstools, that was stupid! I should know better than to wake you up like that." He was starting to shake. Jehan had triggered the reactions he'd been so carefully repressing.

Jehan sat up beside him. "What kind of trouble? Where?"

"In jail." His teeth kept hitting together most unpleasantly. "No, don't bother with a light. I'm all right."

"You don't sound it."

Jail?

"Jail?" Jehan echoed, unaware of Thomas' query. "What did you do?"

"Made a little miscalculation. I'm truly sorry I woke you." Tristan rubbed at his neck. He had a headache, which made it difficult to think straight. "It would have kept till morning."

"By the First Fire, it would not!" Jehan kicked the rest of the way free of the cloaks and stood up. "You were gone two days! We looked everywhere."

Well, not quite, Thomas suggested. *Obviously.*

Jehan struck a light. Tristan flung a hand up to shield his eyes from the glare, but not nearly in time. His eyes watered fiercely, even though he'd shut them. Jehan swore again, apparently regretting his hasty action.

You look terrible, Thomas informed Tristan helpfully.

"I imagine you could do with a bite of supper," Jehan said more gently. After some rummaging about, he thrust a cold meat pie into Tristan's hands and set a wine jug beside him.

Tristan stared, tears drying on his cheeks, wondering if the room was going to start spinning in a moment.

"Where did you get these? We were flat out of food and money. That's why I went out—to try to get some of one to buy the other." He bit into the pie without thinking about it; his mouth and empty belly took over for his sluggish brain.

Jehan uncorked the jug for him.

"While I was looking for you, I ran across a smith who'd let his helper go early on a slow day and then got busy after the boy had drunk himself silly celebrating his holiday." Jehan grinned through his beard. "He said it was fine having a helper who could do more than hold a horse. I could have got myself apprenticed with no trouble."

Tristan swallowed the last of the pie and took a quick swig of wine. He hadn't given food a thought until Jehan mentioned it, but it must have been two days since he'd eaten. He licked busily at his fingers.

"It's late, but I can try to get more if you want it. Or there's bread—"

Tristan waved him off. No more wine for him either, though there was plenty and he wished he could get drunk. He'd be crying again in a minute if he drank more or thought about Cabal.

There was still the problem of Reynaud, too, needing his immediate attention, but he simply couldn't manage it. Valadan would surely warn him if Reynaud managed to track him here. Tristan yawned till his jaw popped. Jehan leaned close, looking concerned.

"No, I'm fine. I just—" Tristan yawned again.

He was probably asleep long before Jehan eased him to the floor.

"Thomas? Cabal's dead."

I know. You talk in your sleep worse than Jehan did.

Tristan breathed a spell upon his brass knife, trying to put a sharp edge on it long enough to shave. It was a common spell, though he didn't use it often. No wizard would ever use an iron knife, since an instant's carelessness or mischance could cost him a few fingers and most of his magic. Brass was safer. But the spell wouldn't take this time. The knife stayed dull; it was just as well, the way his hands were trembling.

Now you're going to tell me how it was all your fault. Have a good wallow in guilt.

Tristan laid the knife aside carefully and made no answer. Thomas knew him altogether too well.

Jehan has the sword done. The whole thing.

"Oh." He was still thinking of Cabal. He'd heard no tolling of bells, but surely that would come soon. He wouldn't have slept through it.

Just oh? After all these weeks of rushing about and toiling and fretting yourself half to death? Your enthusiasm quite overwhelms me.

With an effort that seemed to require all of his strength, Tristan got up and fetched Jehan's razor. Thomas had sense enough to keep quiet then. Shaving seemed to take hours, between the way Tristan was feeling and his therefore acute need for caution; but by the time he was done, he was surprised to find that he felt much better, if only from having successfully dared the cold iron.

Jehan didn't voice his relief at seeing Tristan somewhat

recovered—the man didn't need to. He'd gone out for fresh
bread, but now he didn't politely wait for Tristan to eat before
he began to pry. Tristan swiftly tired of answering questions
singly and in endless succession, and told Jehan everything
without prompting, through mouthfuls of his breakfast. At last
he stopped, brushing bread crumbs away.

"Ah." Jehan had needed to light a pipe, the better to listen.
"Think they're still looking for you?"

"I doubt it. They'll expect me to have run farther than this.
But I can't stay here much longer. Nothing fools Reynaud for
more than a little while." Tristan took a swallow of ale and
wiped his lips on his hand. He did feel better. The night had
gone, and with it most of the shadows, except for those which
would always lie across his heart.

Jehan blew a spear of smoke and followed that with a slowly
expanding ring. He stood up.

"You won't have to. The job's done." He drew a length of
cloth away from the anvil. The folds caught briefly at the hilt
of the weapon that lay there, then slid to the floor at Jehan's
feet.

The sword was finished indeed. Files, grindstone and more
fine files had done the last of their work. Its edges were whetted
sharp, leaving the blade so burnished that the iron was nearly
indistinguishable by color from the silver wire intricately binding the hilt. A scabbard lined with shearling lamb lay beside
the blade. Jehan had, as it happened, got it from a cobbler, in
exchange for the repair of some leather-working tools.

He slid the blade into the scabbard for Tristan's approval.
It moved freely as a sighing breeze. Tristan remarked on that.

"Aye. You'll have no rust to worry about—this is fine steel,
and the oils in the wool will keep it so. Mountain-sheep wool.
Best there is. The cobbler balked a bit when I named my price,
but then his tools will never again have such an edge as I put
on 'em."

"Do I need to say you've surpassed yourself?"

Jehan bowed slightly, and offered Tristan the sheathed sword.
"You do not, my lord."

It took a moment for the shock to finish reverberating through
him, for Tristan's blood to race through his veins, and for his
eyes to find Jehan's.

"Did you think I didn't know?" Jehan was smiling at his
discomfiture. "It took me a while, of course, to be sure. It was

after you cut yourself—you wanted to go on right away, even though you could barely stand up. You needed that sword so badly; no one would have looked the way you did on someone else's behalf. A king can command a lot, but not a look like that."

"I must say, you're taking this better than I did myself."

"Ah. A smith stands equal with anyone, you see. Don't you want to hold your sword, m'lord?" Jehan proffered the blade almost tenderly. Tristan's reaction was nearly timid—he clasped the hilt but lightly and only drew the blade because Jehan pulled the scabbard away.

It was the first time Tristan had touched the sword since it had become more than a metal bar. He didn't quite know what to expect it to feel like; with most of his stronger emotions currently worn away, Tristan was even less certain than he might otherwise have been. Would there be some hint of the sword's latent power—a bright thrill running through the muscles of his arms, from his fingers to his heart? Might the blade glow? What could he expect, halfway between the forges of Kinark and the throne of Crogen?

The only apparent thrill was the joy of holding a finer weapon than any he'd ever imagined. The balance was so nearly perfect that the silver-wrapped grip seemed glued to Tristan's fingers, the blade obedient to his slightest whim, with no will of its own to conflict. It would probably be impossible to drop such a sword in battle. Tristan stared at the sword and tried to imagine that moment when he would thrust its hilt into the socket of Crogen's throne. That was the ultimate test. He went cold all over, just trying to think about it.

He looked at Jehan, able to smile with his lips, if not with his eyes. "It's perfect. There's not another smith in the land who could have done this." Tristan swallowed, finding his throat dry. "And I can't even pay you properly. Bleyvr slipped me some money, but it will never be close to enough—"

"Kings are notoriously poor risks." Jehan clapped him on the shoulder. "They tend to pay with prestige instead of gold. And I told you—making me do this was payment enough, though I don't expect you understand that yet. Truly, my life's changed."

Jehan coughed, then fixed Tristan with his gaze. "There's more I have to say. You have your sword. And I hope it's rightly done. It's as right as it's in my power to make it." He lifted his hand at Tristan's beginning protests. "There's something else you should keep in mind. I know what you're planning this sword to be and what you're going to do with it, and I'd be no friend if I didn't warn you now. No two smiths handle metal with exactly the same hand. And no two bits of iron are the same. Far from it! But from what you told me, if there's one small eccentricity in the cooling pattern of this steel, if I made one tiny mistake in the forging or the tempering, if the balance is off a hair or the point's a touch heavier than it should be—come to that, if the magic you use on it's not exactly right—then this blade will be as much use to you during that crowning as an icicle in your hand."

Tristan nodded and felt his breakfast rearranging itself in his belly. "I know." He noticed that his voice was a bit choked, despite his attempt at normality.

"Aye. You would, I suppose." Jehan twisted a nail between his hands, bending it double. "I just wanted to be sure you realize how great the risk is."

Tristan paced across the room, aimlessly as a trapped moth. He *felt* trapped. But he'd known the risks and had accepted them when he set out on this course.

"It's our last chance. If I *don't* try, there won't be much reason to live, anyway." He forced a smile again, banishing visions of ice. "Don't look so glum! This should be a time of rejoicing for you."

The nail sailed across the smithy and pinged against the bricks.

"Not if another of my blades causes the death of someone I care about!"

"Without you, I'd have no chance at all. Look at it that way." Tristan dragged a saddlebag over and began stuffing gear into it.

"You're going to go today?"

"I think I'd better. I might be able to give Reynaud the slip for a while longer. If I can't, at least I won't be dragging you into the mess."

Tristan was amazed to notice articles flying out of the pack faster than he'd tossed them in. Closer inspection revealed Thomas inside, arranging things to his own taste. Tristan sighed and regrouped his thoughts.

"Will you go back to Kinark now?" he asked.

Jehan retrieved a bag of cooking herbs that Thomas had

rejected. Tristan motioned him to keep it, knowing Thomas would only toss it back again. The cat must have decided that the trip home would be too brief to require meal-crafting.

"I don't think so. I'm still forsworn."

"I wouldn't say so."

"Aye. But it's true all the same, by the letter of the law there. And what I said about having changed—I do not hanker to slip back into the old habits. The world's a wide place. I could see a lot of it before I settle again."

An idea sparked again in Tristan's brain.

"Would you like to see Calandra?"

Thomas' head popped up, and Tristan took advantage of the distraction to slip a couple of bundles into the pack as he spoke.

"Crogen's falling apart. It could use a resident smith. If you don't want to work weapons, there are still gates, door hinges, and lanterns. Magic can only do so much—the place could really use you. And if I've got to put up with being crowned king, at the very least I can hire myself some congenial workmen. Will you come?"

Jehan ginned. He looked younger now, Tristan thought, despite the daylight throwing shadows into the lines of his face.

"You tempt me. But just at present, I've other matters to attend to."

Tristan glanced about the stable. The forging apparatus had been partially disassembled.

"You mean all this? Pack it, sell it, or leave it. There's nothing here I can't find you another of."

"No." Jehan twirled his hammer between his palms, his thoughts patently on anything but tools. "No. Crewzel."

Tristan stopped in midthought. "Oh."

"I'm not ready to give up on that woman just yet. I think maybe I can find her. I have the time now and I'm the patient sort."

Tristan knew he should have been saying the same thing; he should have offered first. Oh, he'd spent days looking for Crewzel, but that didn't matter. He'd gotten what he wanted from Kôvelir, with Crewzel's great help, and now he was going to desert her.

Thomas took one look at his face and made a disgusted noise.

"I don't mean that as a reproach," Jehan said. "If you stay

to find her, you may wait months, and your duty's elsewhere now. You've done all you can. But *I* haven't."

Tristan was surprised. He tried to recall what Crewzel and Jehan had been like together. Obviously he'd underestimated the depth of Jehan's feelings about her and the man's determination. He supposed he ought to be grateful for both. Reaching inside his jerkin, Tristan drew out the card he'd found in the cell.

"This is hers," he said. "It may help you find her. And if you do, she'll want it back. I found it in the dungeons, and there's an excellent reason to believe Crewzel was there till just a couple of days ago. A dancer I met there saw her."

Jehan took the card.

"It's blank?"

"Yes. But there's not another pack like this anywhere, so far as I know. You can use it; maybe it will even draw you to her. Prisoners here are sentenced to a sort of magical indenture—cheap labor seems to be a favorite device of the Council. Kitri—that's the dancer—said that one of the mages on the Council is building a pleasure house in the hills outside the city. They may have sent Crewzel there, if it wasn't just a rumor."

"Then what's wanted is a bit of discreet eavesdropping."

"Mmmm. And your best bet for that is either near the Academy or from the street magicians who've gone to ground in the city. I'm sorry I didn't pay more attention to the talk."

Jehan looked cheerful. "A smith hears a lot of gossip. It's wonderful how the sight of someone else working loosens folks' tongues. And a traveling smith has reason to travel *anywhere*, especially where there's building going on. What about her boy, then? Any luck with that?"

Tristan related what Thomas had discovered. "He may have joined the jugglers as a simple way of traveling around while he looked for his mother. By what Thomas learned, they're not mistreating him, and juggling skills will certainly do his magic no harm! You should be able to find Delmon when you're ready to."

"When I've found Crewzel."

"I wish you luck."

"And when the matter's settled, I'll think about coming to Calandra. You're not this easily rid of me."

"I thought it was always you that wanted to leave." Tristan grinned. "I'll be watching for you."

They shook on that.

Kitri's Ransom

IT STILL FELT wrong to go, an easy way out of a tedious situation. Tristan didn't much like himself for going. Yet it was only another choice that really wasn't his to make.

He forced his thoughts back toward Calandra as resolutely as he'd bent them in the other direction weeks before. He reminded himself that he wanted very much to see Elisena again—needed to desperately. Now that the meeting was only a day away at most, he could bear to think of that. Valadan clopped over Kôvelir's magic-mortared cobbles, taking him nearer to her.

They were reflected in an ornamental pool now, a legless horse sailing smoothly as a swan above the masonry hemming the water, his rider apparently serene on his back. That reflection was no more his true self than Cabal's seeming of him had been, Tristan thought, as his varied emotions left him anything but calm. He saw Thomas' head pop up out of the reflection of the pack.

"Take a good look. We won't be back."

That's what you thought the last time.

"This time, I'm sure. And maybe glad. I don't think I can deal with this place's memories."

Unbidden, Crewzel's face rose in front of him—on a length of silk embroidered with the form of some foreign tree-goddess that hung from a draper's window. Tristan started, so closely did the sight match his thoughts, till he saw that only the flame-colored hair truly resembled Crewzel's. The cold majesty of the stitched face really had nothing to do with her.

Thomas had not missed his lurching back in the saddle. *You're still being a little hard on yourself.*

"I don't much like having to let my friends down," Tristan retorted defensively. "Or abandoning them, or realizing that I feel a little relieved when someone else is going to deal with the mess." He ducked as they passed under a rug hung for display over the street. Its owner claimed the power of flight for it. Tristan saw the glint to sunlight on fine wires and doubted the claim.

Thomas fanned his whiskers. *Don't underestimate Jehan. He'll find her. And if you're insistent on punishing yourself, you can always be sick on the ferry.*

"I probably will be, anyway, if we get there. I think we made a wrong turn."

Valadan snorted offendedly. But the street they were on *did* slope steeply upward, and they needed to cross no hill to reach the Est and the ferries there. Tristan pulled at the reins, but Valadan paid no attention to him.

Evidently, this must be another way to the docks. Good enough, but Tristan had chosen his route with extreme care, to avoid having to ride through the whole of Kôvelir. It was long past sun-high, but the sun had not yet set and there was plenty of light. Mixing with crowds by daylight meant the risk of discovery. He'd hoped to leave the city quietly. So why had Valadan chosen his own course?

The street steepened, and the buildings along it vanished, replaced by a stone railing on either side. It was a bridge, Tristan saw; but rather than spanning some diverted branch of the Est, it crossed a broad street below.

From this height, the whole city was spread out at a traveler's feet. Tristan looked with interest, seeing the city strewn like a living, breathing map. There, far off to his left, the buildings of the Academy and Library sparkled, their roofs— even the glass one of the Library—golden. Pools of water within the Inner Circle shone like sapphires.

There were no other travelers on the bridge, so Tristan could gaze to his eyes' surfeit without impeding anyone. He had left the rumble of carts and the cries of merchants behind, or else most of the city was busy at its evening meal. In the quiet air, sound carried.

From the Academy, Tristan could hear a chant of many blended voices, plaintive and almost unbearably lovely as it swelled to fullness.

Somewhere below, the funeral rites for Cabal had begun. Ill-informed on the custom as Tristan might be, there was no mistaking the significance of the chant. Even the words of leave-taking came clearly on the breeze.

Tristan's eyes misted, but not with sorrow for Cabal—not for a long life well lived and now peacefully ended—but for his own dreams. The golden music in the golden city was a reminder of what he had once thought Kôvelir to be and what it once had been. He gazed over the matchless sweep of the city and thought of the smallness of the Council, not even worthy to be called a nest of spiders lest that demean an honest spider toiling at some lowly spot in the city.

A procession wound solemnly about the Academy walls. Another wove through the streets below, though it was a while before Tristan, wiping at eyes and nose, marked it.

There was no chanting there, only the soft stirring of many footfalls, most of them shuffling, and the grumbling of the brown-robes who guarded and guided the column.

Their charges seemed to have little need of guarding—most of them shambled along more blindly than Jehan had done while sleepwalking. The brown-robes had only to step forward sometimes to ward off a stray dog or pig which threatened to disrupt the march.

Valadan snorted. Tristan patted at his neck.

"It's all right. I think that's just the latest bunch of the Council's prisoners, off to wherever some councilman needs a bit of free work done. I'd have been with them, if not for—"

He stopped speaking. At the line's tail, as if he'd conjured her there, he'd glimpsed a flash of Kitri's turquoise, and now he saw pink there as well.

The straggling line moved around a turn of the street and out of view. He wasn't sure, but there wasn't time to waste on a second look. Their course would bring the prisoners under this very bridge in a few moments. Tristan slid out of the saddle and ran across the bridge, trying to discover where the street ended.

It reached a square quite soon, and he could see the Est from here, too. The square led to many alleys; if he bore always to sunward, he'd stumble upon the ferry easily enough. Fortunately that course would put the sinking sun in any pursuers' eyes. Tristan ran back to Valadan.

He put his face close to the stallion's.

"I'll meet you by the ferry. You might want to create a diversion." It didn't seem necessary to tell the stallion more. Valadan had not brought him up here by accident.

Thomas, however, was confused. He gave a frenzied howl as Tristan straddled the bridge railing and began to lower himself down the other side.

Tristan paused, gripping the railing with both hands.

"It's all right, Thomas. I'm just keeping a promise, for a change."

Thomas wailed again as Tristan disappeared entirely. Then Valadan began to move, carrying him out of sight of the bridge. They headed for the Est.

Tristan heard the hoofbeats moving away. He understood fleetingly why Polassar always seemed happiest in action and just how miserable the man must be at Crogen. The mere prospect of a physical, positive solution to a problem cheered him mightily, despite the risks.

He counted seconds, but didn't have to do that for long. The column's leaders came into sight and passed under him without glancing up. Tristan was thankful that Kitri was at the end of the line. Had she been anywhere else, this contrivance—it was too hasty in conception to be called a plan—would have proved impossible. He might still have tried, but matters would have been far less simple.

He wished he had a rope. Even hanging from his hands, the drop would be too great; he'd risk breaking a leg . . .

The answer swung before his eyes. One of those humble spiders he'd had such considerate thoughts of a few minutes before dangled in front of Tristan's face, still spinning busily.

He hooked an elbow around one of the railing's supports and grasped the silken thread gently between thumb and forefinger. The fingers of his other hand wove about as nimbly as a spider running about its web. "Your pardon, little sister," Tristan said. He tucked the spider safely into a crevice underneath the edge of the bridge.

He was not "one of theirs" to the might mages of Kôvelir. He was a vagabond, a mere back-street conjuror. He snorted, smiling without humor as he worked a transmutation upon the spider thread.

He let go of the bridge, dropping down toward a blur of turquoise among the brown and other somber colors. As he fell, the thread thickened between his hands, strengthened, and brought him up short and safe. With more presence of mind, he might have grabbed Kitri and hauled them both back to the bridge, baffling or at least delaying pursuit, but the spell dissolved as his boots touched the street.

Still, the surprise of the maneuver was all he could have wished. Tristan had grabbed the arm of an astonished Kitri before any of the acolyte guards had even turned a head, and they had time to run foward past the whole column before a single shout was given.

He might have expected Kitri's tranced state to give him some trouble, but his abrupt touch seemed to rouse her. Maybe the docility-spell didn't apply firmly to those who didn't follow magical arts, leaving a dancer mostly immune. At any rate, Kitri's eyes and mouth both opened wide, and her legs obeyed instantly when Tristan began to drag her forward.

They darted under the bridge, out of the street shadows, into the light of the square, and then into an alley. Kitri ran well, her dancer's legs seeming longer than his, though her height was less. There were shouts behind them now; but, if Tristan had calculated rightly, all the guards could not leave the other prisoners, even ensorcelled to docility as they were, to pursue one fugitive. There had been only three guards—at most two would come after him.

"Didn't think I'd see you again," Kitri panted at his ear.

"My meeting with the Council didn't work out." Tristan swung her around a sharp turn onto another street. "I had to leave in a hurry." Could they stay ahead of the acolytes all the way to the ferry—and would Kitri want to leave the city if they did? Fine time to think of such things, as Thomas would have been swift to point out.

There was a horn blast somewhere behind them. Kitri tugged at Tristan's hands.

"That calls the Watch."

And it ended any hope of escape. Unless—

Alone, nondescriptly dressed and not clearly seen by any of the surprised guards, he might just make it to the ferry if he went straight—but not trying to elude pursuit while running and dragging a brightly dressed dancing girl behind him. Ahead, a fountain splashed. In its midst was a sculpture group of dancers and musicians, the water spouting from the horns and flutes of the latter. There were five dancers. There were about to be six.

Tristan sprinted through the water. The statues stood on a small flat base, but fortunately it was above water. He motioned Kitri onto it.

"Can you stand like that?" He gestured at a statue that had its hands poised above its head and one leg raised so that its toe touched the calf of the other leg.

"I'm a dancer!" Kitri flashed at him.

Of course. "And for how long?"

"Forever," she declared proudly, assuming the stance.

"That's good, because as soon as you move, this illusion will end," Tristan said, stepping back through the water. The wind had swirled debris at the base of the stone. He gathered a handful of dust from the cobbles. "Stay still till dark, if you can, or at least till the Watch goes by."

"Light and shadows," he intoned in his mind as he flung the handful of dust between the falling sprays of water. His words lashed out behind it, settling upon Kitri even as the dust did. She blinked once, but otherwise had no time to react.

"There's a Kinarkan smith called Jehan, who'll be in the Second Circle for the next day or two. If you find him, I think he can get you a place in a traveling juggling troupe. There's sure to be a vacancy. Good fortune, Kitri," Tristan said to the sixth statue and strolled away with feigned nonchalance.

Black Ice

TRISTAN WAS OUT of breath by the time he reached the quayside. Even when he'd stopped hurrying, he felt no better—his nerves were too taut. The wharves were busy and crowded. Where might Thomas have hidden Valadan? A familiar-sounding *meow* sent him a good way in the wrong direction before an indignant neigh corrected his course. The tethered dray horses looked rather relieved whan Valadan left their midst.

In moments they'd made their way past the grainships beyond the fishing smacks. Where the piers dissolved to a raggedy collection of individual docks in varying states of decay and neglect, Tristan found the smaller boats he sought. He didn't see any he much liked, but he was in no position to be choosy. The fishermen were just starting to come in. None would put back out for a single passenger, with night coming on. Even the bargemen who would do that were only the most desperate.

Tristan selected the likeliest prospect and at once found his barely achieved calm sorely tested. The Watch reached the docks just as he began to dicker with the ferryman. He permitted himself but one glance, eyebrow casually raised, and quietly went on negotiating his passage. If he could maintain nonchalance, he stood a good chance of being away before the Watch reached this far down the docks; but if he showed the slightest anxiety, he would either be detained or be asked a price he couldn't hope to pay, depending on the honesty of the ferryman.

Eying the man warily, Tristan knew which end he ought to most fear and guessed he'd be overcharged anyway. He argued only enough to thwart the suspicions his too ready agreement would have raised.

Price finally agreed upon, Tristan led Valadan carefully onto the small barge—which seemed *much* smaller, once the horse was on it. Valadan shifted his feet cautiously and snorted his disapproval. Tristan looked back at the city.

The Watch was just reaching the spot they'd launched from, but that no longer mattered. The city receded, and Tristan had leisure to note the waterfront buildings.

Cross-chop hit the barge, rocking it. The motion made the cityscape heave, as if it were embroidered upon a cloth blowing in a gentle breeze. Tristan had no time for such poetic musings, though. He was being cruelly reminded of the peril at which wizards dare to cross running water. The world spun around him, and his stomach heaved even harder than the boat did. He tried to sit down and would have gone overboard if he hadn't been detained by his grip on Valadan's reins.

Not that you couldn't use a bath, Thomas said, washing his paws and maintaining his balance easily. Tristan thought it unfair that familiars shouldn't suffer just the same as wizards did—at least for so long as he could think at all.

The ferryman made to engage Tristan in conversation, noted his green-tinged face, and put a bucket handily by him instead. Apparently he'd carried wizards before and recognized the signs and symptoms.

It's not that hard to do, Thomas pointed out. *Try to stay awake, just so he doesn't get the happy idea of robbing you and dumping you in midstream to save himself half the trip.*

That was probably meant as a joke, since Valadan wouldn't let any such thing happen, but Tristan was too ill to see the humor. The idea that the barge might sink before it could be poled across the river hadn't weighed all that heavily before, with the Watch so close behind him—now drowning was starting to seem like a pleasant alternative to the journey, promising relief of a sort. The boat heaved again. Tristan moaned and nearly bit through his lip.

He couldn't guess if the rest of the voyage would be eventful. Tristan expected it to take a long while. The Est's mouth was wide, and there were many islands in it to be avoided. The swift-running current made ferrying still more difficult. Soon all self-congratulatory thoughts about Kitri were gone. The trip already seemed to have taken half his lifetime; he couldn't remember much that had happened before it began. He probably wouldn't have noticed if a water-monster had risen up before them and attempted to devour ferry, ferryman, and passengers at one gulp.

All he could see was water. So Tristan shut his eyes, and then all he could *smell* was water and all he could hear was the slap of waves against the barge's low sides. His heart was still racing from all that running; it had never seemed to settle down to a normal rate. The air tasted thick. The whole boat shivered violently as the waves hit it—whenever it wasn't plunging and lurching about like a frightened horse.

Tristan put his face in his hands and moaned again, glad that he'd probably never be able to return to Kôvelir. Nothing could ever force him to do this kind of traveling again.

Do you suppose this is why the Council gave up posting wizards in Calandra?

Tristan didn't dare unclench his teeth to answer. *Why* had he let Jehan coerce him into having a quick meal before he left? He stumbled to his feet, reaching blindly for the bucket.

As he did, the ferry hit something solid, with a horrible amount of crunching and grinding following the initial shock. Tristan sprawled across the deck, a snorting Valadan trying to catch his own balance without trampling him.

Wonderful, Tristan thought. *We're sinking.* Valadan's knee banged into his cheek as he sat up.

He was soaking wet—the ferry was more leak than boat—but they weren't going to drown. There was no dock on the Esdragon side, at least none that lent itself to such a small, illicit boat, so they had run up on a graveled beach, some way downshore from the tall wharves where the grainships docked. The ferryman lifted Tristan up, dusted him off a bit, and took the pouch Tristan wordlessly thrust at him. It was the pouch Bleyvr had given him, and there was more than enough silver there, Tristan knew. He didn't care how much more.

He was boosted into Valadan's saddle and somehow avoided toppling right over the other side of the horse. The Est was crossed—Tristan hoped for the last time.

Valadan's back rolled worse than the water, though he walked very carefully until Tristan had roused enough to hold on. That was only after they had gone some way inshore, into the gathering night. Thomas remarked that there hadn't been this much trouble crossing *into* Kôvelir, but Tristan, who could scarcely think as yet, couldn't remember.

The air was very cold. That, more than anything, revived Tristan eventually, and he started to look about. There wasn't much to see—just a deserted road, which Valadan proceeded along with thoughtful slowness.

Welcome back.

Tristan didn't know if Thomas meant to Esdragon or to the living. He ignored the cat.

"Where are we?"

Valadan provided precise references and mentioned a storm as he quickened his pace. Tristan looked in the direction they were galloping and felt what little blood had returned to his face leave it.

The land was dark, but the sky still held a residue of light, through which the first stars showed dimly. Some few leagues ahead, the road disappeared. The sky there was a dingy gray-white and it had lowered until it met the ground. Even as Tristan watched, the boiling wall was sweeping closer.

"That's a storm?" Its speed and size passed belief. "Are you sure we're going in the right direction? That looks more like a sea fog."

Valadan snorted. *A sea of Nímir's making, then.*

"Can we get around it?" Tristan stood in the stirrups, trying for a better line of sight, but slipped before he could get one.

Not if we wish to reach Crogen.

Tristan dismounted and quickly put his gear in order, strapping everything down tightly and making Thomas comfortable in the saddlebag before he laced it shut. There was no chance of shelter in this deserted spot. And where could he hope to shelter safely from Nímir's wrath, unless at Crogen?

A storm like this wasn't something they'd been expecting and prepared for. Tristan's clothes and cloak were barely adequate for a normal winter, and Valadan had nothing at all to keep his blood from freezing but his speed. They had braved the Winterwaste so once, but the experience hadn't been pleasant. And this time, Tristan suspected, they would be far more sternly tested. There was no question of defending himself with any sort of magic—neither Tristan nor the sword was ready for that.

Valadan went at speed. This storm couldn't be trusted to blow itself out if they delayed, even if they found marginal shelter. The wind coming past the stallion's neck was so cold that Tristan wondered at first how he'd recognize the storm when they reached it; but there was no question about it when that time came. He huddled lower over the reins, but that didn't help much.

For a long time there was only the wind, steady, invisible, and cold. Capricious gusts hit them side-on sometimes, but Valadan ran steadily, ignoring the buffeting. Tristan had only a little trouble keeping his seat. His fingers were numb, but he had them wrapped so tightly in the reins that he thought there was no question of his losing his grip and falling. No snow was falling yet, he noticed thankfully when he was able to blink the tears out of his eyes. He couldn't see a road anymore. Valadan might have left it, if it meandered too much.

They had run a long time. The sky was a mass of clouds, so black that Tristan almost looked to see stars; but overhead were only twisting cloud edges and forks of lightning, arcane and awful.

Valadan faltered, snorting, and Tristan hoped the horse wasn't lost. He straightened in the saddle. They were on the lee side of a hill now, in the midst of what looked like an apple orchard. Valadan raised his head, searching for a pattern to the wind. Tristan guessed they must be about to change directions and to make directly for Crogen, leaving even the pretense of roads behind.

Well, if Valadan was hesitating, it was probably out of consideration for him, nothing more. Tristan tried to pat the stallion's neck to signal that he was well enough. He was grateful for the rest. The going ahead was apt to be worse than anything they'd been through when the jaws of the storm snapped shut behind them. They might not find another such sheltered spot to collect themselves.

Then even this haven was ripped from them.

The wind wailed around them, keening and depositing ice on the leaves and branches overhead. Underfoot, the grass glistened like fractured diamonds, revealed by lightning flashes out of the dark sky. Then the grass shattered, and the fragments flew up in a choking cloud.

Ice covered Tristan's face. He tried to wipe it away, but found his hands were tangled in the reins and Valadan's mane and iced over. He couldn't get free. Leaves, freighted with more than their own weight of ice, fell from their branches and whirled away, tinkling like dropped wind chimes. The branches from which they'd broken groaned, wind-racked.

Valadan fought the wind, twisting about to keep it at his back, turning like a demented weathervane. A frozen sea gull, carried an unthinkable distance by the storm, smashed to earth by his feet and shattered. Tristan's sight blurred. He was looking at the world through lashes clogged with ice. His hands were too frozen to rub at them, and he was effectively blinded.

There were heaps of fallen branches on the ground, so that Valadan stumbled whichever way he turned. A sound began, like stones falling on the earth, but it was neither stones nor hail, as Tristan first guessed. Frozen apples—the remains of last year's crop—rained from their boughs, some of them nearly the size of a man's fist. Ice and snow creaked in mad orchestration.

The ice-sheathed branches were further laden until they broke and came crashing down, tearing trunks asunder in the process, and ripping whole trees out when the branches tangled. Valadan sidled indecisively. Lightning split the sky again. A branch narrowly missed Tristan's head, and a frozen apple smashed into his cheek. He'd have fallen from the saddle if he hadn't already been frozen to it. Hot tears of pain unstuck his eyelids.

He was able to see clearly again and half wished he couldn't. Through the gloom, the almost solid wall of snow was moving toward them. Tristan's throat worked soundlessly, and he began to be truly afraid. His eyes froze shut again, as the snow hit them.

The darkness was terrifying. Unseen, the snow cut at exposed skin like knives of glass. It had gone so far beyond normal cold that Tristan's senses could not even accept it as snow. He sobbed with pain; then he considered that his tongue might freeze to the roof of his mouth and forced his mind back into control.

Valadan's ribs heaved between Tristan's knees, as the stallion struggled to draw breath. He seemed afraid to move—all the ground was ice, except for that exactly under his four hooves; if he so much as stirred, the wind would slide him along it and ultimately hurl him from his feet.

The wind swirled, rather than blowing straight against them, circling for a kill. Tristan imagined a wall of frozen snow whirling about them. It would be packed as solid as rock when they moved at last and smashed themselves against it. He couldn't see, even when he got his eyes open again by biting at the inside of his cheek until blood and tears flowed.

In the dark, the wall was real, whether created by the snow or merely his shriveling mind. This storm was Nímir's work, and it left him unable to trust even his own thoughts, which the Winterlord might have played with.

Tristan thrust the doubt away, as once he had shoved away the Guardian's spell. He would assume the wall to be real, though incomplete. That incompleteness might explain the redoubling of the distracting cold. Nímir was trying to buy himself time.

Tristan shoved his boots deeper into the stirrups and slapped the reins on Valadan's neck with a tinkle of smashed crystal.

"Get us out of here! *Now!*"

Hold on, the stallion warned. Valadan leaped forward as if he hoped to gain the sky, through falling branches and dangerously daggerlike icicles. For an instant, in the confusion of dark and wind, Tristan lost all notion of the direction in which the ground lay, and felt himself falling. He clasped the stallion tighter with knees and hands, sobbing.

The footing was treacherous. Branches and icy trunks of trees wove a tapestry of death, Nímir's ultimate creation. With his cut cheek pressed to Valadan's neck, Tristan could feel the slipping and sliding of the stallion's hooves as clearly as if the steps had been his own. And they might as well be. If Valadan fell, neither one of them would have a chance to rise again.

The trees were a trap, a promise of shelter twisted into a tangle to catch their legs and hold them there for the wind's pleasure. Valadan moved always on disaster's ragged edge, leaping from one icy spot to another, without hope of catching his balance, and then leaping again, somehow. A claw of wood with icy nails scraped Tristan's back, but he was too desperately trying to become a part of his horse to be dragged off by its grasp.

He was more terrified that something might snag the sword's hilt, and thankful that he'd thought to strap it flat to Valadan's side. If it had still been on his own back, as it had been during the ferrying, either it or he would long since have been lost, grounded and more vulnerable to the storm's tender mercy than ever.

There was a change in the wind. It blew straight past them, no longer swirling. They'd reached open ground at the top of the rise. It offered no shelter, but gave them relative safety.

Valadan quivered between Tristan's knees. *I think this is how he made the Winterwaste. First the black ice and then the snows.*

Tristan cringed as thunder boomed. The ground around them looked as flat and black as the sky. A finger of wind shifted, probing at them.

"Our best hope is to get to Crogen and Elisena." Tristan had to shout to be heard and was troubled over what else might hear. Suppose the Hounds—

We are safe from them here, at least. They will not venture into this, Valadan said. *They have no need to, and nearly as much to fear from it as do we. This storm recognizes neither us nor them—it simply destroys.*

Nothing personal, then, Thomas said. *How comforting.*

It was, in many ways, much worse than the Winterwaste. That was an old and mostly passive evil, but this storm was both young and actively malignant. It recognized life, but only the better to destroy it.

Its winds harried them like an unseen wolf pack, opposing, probing, testing, teasing, sometimes chasing, and sometimes catching them despite Valadan's speed. A gust caught Tristan's cloak, though he'd shoved it through his belt to keep that from happening—first lashing it across his face to smother him, then ripping at it so violently that the clasp left bruises on his throat, before the metal snapped and released the cloth. The cloak whirled away, lost forever, but Tristan scarcely missed it. He didn't think he could possibly be much colder; in wind like this the cloak had offered scant protection. He couldn't feel Valadan under him any longer, and he was hearing noises in the wind—raucous music he was sure couldn't be there. He suspected his ears were freezing and knew that if Valadan didn't reach Crogen soon, they never would.

The wind-swirled music *did* play to Valadan's ears, though the stallion laid them back tight against his neck to keep out the noise as much as the cold. The winds circled to the music's tune, winding tighter and tighter about him, trying to force him to turn. Spots on his belly and back, where once a brass pole had pierced him, burned with cold.

Yet this time he was able to resist the ensorcellment and scream an effective defiance at the storm and its master, for he did not fight alone or for his own sake only. Valadan no longer carried an empty saddle.

They ran from the storm. There was no question of fighting and no valor attached to dying uselessly, crusted over with ice like a taffied apple, even in defense of a dying Calandra, however strongly instinct might so call.

A lifetime later, Valadan told his half-frozen master that they had reached Crogen.

Homecoming

VALADAN CLATTERED OVER the icy cobbles of the courtyard. Polassar loomed up out of a puddle of yellow torchlight, dressed in what seemed impossibly bright colors to Tristan's fogged eyes.

"*Wizard!* How did you win through the army? I heard no fighting!"

Tristan slid down over Valadan's shoulder and threw an arm across the saddle to keep himself from falling when his knees buckled. "What army?" he asked dazedly. He knew he must have voiced the spell that had opened Crogen's gate, but he couldn't remember doing it. The wind had slammed the portal shut behind him.

"Are you hurt? Hark, there's blood on your face—" Polassar gestured, sending someone running for help. There were loud footsteps and then a crash as the man slipped on the ice and fell.

"I don't know," Tristan answered truthfully. He could barely feel his fingers, and he'd thought his face was too frozen to bleed. "I don't think so." He doggedly took hold of the sword, abandoning his other gear, but it got tangled in the girths and he had to devote what attention he had left to getting it and himself free and forget conversation. It seemed a monumental task, quite beyond his present very diminished capacity. Tristan tugged at the straps, started to overbalance, and had to grab hastily for the saddle again. His fingers slipped on the slick leather and he felt himself falling.

Polassar took hold of him by the shoulders.

"*Wizard?* What's amiss?"

Valadan swiveled his head around, concern burning in his eyes, but a great measure of pride as well. The whole front of his face was white, and every hair was frosted as if with age. He sounded amused.

I did warn you. You did well—not many men have tasted my full speed and stayed with me.

"I didn't have much choice," Tristan mumbled. Polassar jogged him upright and queried something. Tristan couldn't hear; the wind still made too much noise. Or was that rushing only inside his head?

"You! *Boy!* Fetch me brandy from the guardroom and be quick about it, or I'll flay your hide!"

Tristan wished Polassar wouldn't shout so, just when his ears cleared; he didn't like to be deafened. He leaned against the man, quite happy not to have to rely upon his own legs for a while. After a moment, he did try them again, but Polassar was pouring a heroic draught of brandy down his throat. After warming his belly briefly, the liquor coursed downward to eat away at his knees. The brandy did something to his head, too, making it whirl, and sending the black and white walls of snowbound Crogen reeling around him.

"Not much better, eh?" Polassar's voice asked out of the confusion. "Best get you into the warm. Let go of that, now. The horse will be all right. I'll see to him, once I've settled you. The boy there can take him into the stable now, if you'll let go of him."

Tristan kept on fumbling at the saddle, almost blind with exhaustion and drink. He had fastened the sword down so securely that he couldn't loose it now—either that, or his concentration was so poor that he could scarcely recall what he was doing long enough to attempt it.

"Here, what are you about? Can't you let that be? Come on, now." Polassar's voice gentled. "Wits froze like your ears?"

Tristan finally tugged the sword free. It came loose suddenly, and he staggered backward as the straps released it into his hands and stumbled into Polassar with a small jolt which he really didn't feel.

Polassar whistled, a sound long, low, and probably painful to his cold-cracked lips. The pain didn't seem to deter him.

"You got it, then? I expected this to be a night of wonders, but I took your getting here to be the last of 'em." His eyes ran up and down the sheathed blade with admiring awe.

A cold wind rattled past, and Polassar gave himself a shake. "Come on then, Wizard. They'll have the fire going by now. You can go straight to bed. If I keep you standing here longer, the Lady will have my hide for boot soles, and rightly." He glanced again at the sword, which Tristan was having an awkward time managing. "Want me to carry that for you?"

Tristan shook his head dazedly and tightened his clumsy grip on the scabbard. He was even more reluctant to be dragged away from Valadan. There was something else he needed besides the sword, somthing equally important. He couldn't remember what it was. Polassar led him away, calling instructions to his men—or to the flake-filled air, for all Tristan knew.

The next thing he was aware of, the next sound anyway, was Polassar furiously poking up the fire. It needed more air, not more poking, Tristan thought hazily. He turned his head, and the linen pillow under his cheek rustled crisply, releasing a strong scent of lavender. He recognized objects in his line of sight—the brass lion-dog incense burner, a tottery stack of books, and a pile of creamy wool with Elisena's drop spindle lying beside it, the little birds carved into the clay whorl catching the fire-thrown shadows. This was their room, then, but no one else was in it besides Polassar.

"Where's Elisena?" he asked Polassar's back. His face must be starting to thaw—his cheeks felt very odd when he moved his lips.

"She's on her way, Wizard. I sent to tell her you were back safe. She won't waste time, depend on it." Polassar was grinning at him, as if something he'd said was extremely amusing.

Tristan didn't get the joke. Frowning, though, would have taken a quantity of will which he no longer possessed. The bed was piled thick with sheepskins and pillows, and he was starting to remember what it was like to be warm.

A blue, yellow, and white feathered blur erupted over the foot of the bed, and Tristan heard Minstrel's chirps of joy and thanksgiving. He rubbed the bird's breast ever so lightly with his forefinger and felt the tiny head rubbing a frantic caress on his own neck in turn as the bird chirped further welcomes. Minstrel had come through his moult in fine shape, and his coloring was more striking than ever.

Tristan whispered compliments on that, his eyes moist. He hadn't realized the bird would miss him so much when he had Elisena to love and care for him. Nor had he noticed, till this moment, how he'd missed the bird and how homesick he'd been.

Then Minstrel removed himself to the windowsill, and the canary's throat began to swell with the first song he'd sung since months before when he'd begun moulting, even though the hour was late. And what was Tristan to do then but courteously and happily listen? He relaxed back among the sheepskins, grateful for their warmth and for the song that was a distillation of summer mornings . . .

Suddenly the room was very still, and quite dark, save for the candles and the shining crystals in Elisena's hair.

Tristan pushed himself up on one elbow. Thomas was curled by his feet, and he could see a headless-seeming puff of feathers on a wall perch which would be Minstrel, sleeping. The room was very warm, perfectly quiet. The sword leaned in a corner, candlelight dancing on it. Someone had washed his face and tended to his cut cheek.

It was kind of Polassar to let me out of the saddlebag. I imagine you slept easier knowing I was comfortable.

Tristan's mouth dropped open in surprise. So that's what he'd forgotten!

"Thomas—" he started to apologize, horrified, but Elisena shook her head slightly. Maybe Thomas hadn't been overlooked for as long as he might like to pretend. Tristan reached out and stroked the cat's back. Thomas certainly seemed comfortable enough. His fur was warm to the touch; he'd been inside a good while. Tristan wondered what had happened when Polassar opened the saddlebag. Maybe he owed Polassar more of an apology than he did Thomas.

I was well behaved, as always. Otherwise you'd hardly have slept through it, I assure you.

"You almost did sleep through supper." Elisena shifted slightly so that Tristan might see a little past her and pointed to a tray covered over with white linen. Her movement made the tray rock a little with the bed's motion. "Thomas says everything's just the way you like it. He ought to know. He tasted all of it."

"I'm sorry." And certainly embarrassed as well. "Not to stay awake long enough to talk to you—" Things had happened too fast again. Tristan cast his mind back over the past few hours, dazedly scanning all their whirling events. Images spun like leaves before his eyes in an evil dream. He was half unsure he wasn't dreaming still. At any moment, he might wake to find Jehan shaking him, asking what was amiss that he'd begun dreaming, too.

Elisena's touch reassured him; it and she were both so undeniably real. She wore a gown of velvet, its color like blackberry wine in a goblet held up to firelight. Its sleeves fitted closely at the wrist and grew full as they reached her slim shoulders, making many hills and valleys for the candlelight to explore, as Tristan's fingers longed to. Her crystals caught the light, and turned to rubies. The gown was worn in places and faded in others, but the candlelight was kind to those minor blemishes.

"Look. I've got roasted chicken here, and new bread come straight from the bakehouse. Baked apples to delight your sweet tooth. And I'm very glad you did sleep, because things were hectic for a while here, and this is the first moment I'd have had free to talk to you, anyway. This way, there are no hurt feelings. Mind you don't burn your fingers."

They shared the meal right there on the bed. The food left Tristan sleepy once more, but only pleasantly so. The warmth and the wine Elisena had brought fostered an odd fancy that he might let his body drop off while his mind stayed alert and interested. It seemed like a fine way of managing his conflicting desires, and he slid into it willingly.

Such contentment could scarcely last. Anxieties intruded even through Elisena's smile. There was so much he had to tell her, all of it mortally urgent.

And yet, where to begin? The list of his failures, his misadventures, and his makeshifts seemed beyond Tristan's power to order. Should he start with Cabal, Reynaud's unnerving appearance in Kôvelir, or his own reasons for abandoning the search for the true sword and having a replacement made? Suppose she said that act had been his greatest error of all?

Should he ask about the storm? Had Nímir raised it specially to keep him from reaching Crogen, or had his usual ill-luck

alone caused him to blunder into the mess? Elisena had done
something to shelter them from the storm, Tristan was sure.
Those winds which had hammered Crogen's walls behind him,
screaming in thwarted fury, had not abated of their own will
while he slept. Now the air was still, and Elisena looked very
weary under her happiness at having him safely home. She'd
said she'd been busy; that must have something to do with the
storm.

Her touch—just a finger lightly brushing his—banished all
his fears. Tristan began to speak, as much with his heart as his
tongue.

Elisena could have learned all she wished to and answered
her every question by consulting with her magical rings, but
she let Tristan talk and even drew him out a great length. He
must explain himself, for his own sake. In speech he'd lose
much of the strangeness of his homecoming and the disorientation produced by their weeks of separation and the storm,
put some order to his thoughts, and gain some understanding
of what the events of his journey had been and meant. Out of
confusion came that order, at last, as welcome as the lights of
Crogen after the storm. The tale was done, and already Tristan's
face looked less drawn. And it was good to hear his voice
again.

Elisena's fingers worked in his, gently, blindly, the way
Tristan's own fingers often moved in Thomas' fur while his
mind was elsewhere. Tristan had no words to express his gratitude for that small comfort, which had given him back himself.

Elisena spoke then of little happenings during his absence
from Crogen—things of no moment at all and no cause for his
concern, but only for his present entertainment. Tristan was
thankful for that gentle consideration, too. She laid worries
aside so easily, putting him at liberty to do the same.

Elisena caught him watching her, a sad half smile lifting
one corner of his mouth.

"What is it?" The half-told tale of Minstrel's protracted
quarrel with a sparrow flock was forgotten.

Tristan shrugged, tilting his head a little to one side.

"You're so very lovely," he said shyly. "I'd forgotten. I
don't—" He searched for a proper expression of his feelings.
"I don't fit you."

"Oh? Are you so ill-favored, then? I hadn't noticed." Her eyes were laughing at him. Her nose crinkled.

Tristan looked away, his face still sorrowful. "That's not what I mean. So *ordinary*—a failure most of the time, sometime a disaster. You deserve something better—a hero, a Polassar of your own."

Elisena threw up her hands in amazement. The tray skidded perilously close to the bed's far edge. She paused long enough to halt it with a gesture, but the tiny interruption did nothing to divert her.

"What would I do with a Polassar?" The crystals jangled. Minstrel lifted his head from under his wing and cheeped softly in protest. "Always stamping about and shouting—it would drive me mad! You've absolutely no conception of what it was like here without you. I remember thinking frequently that whatever faults you might have, at least you were quiet to have around. There's a lot to be said for that."

Tristan started to open his mouth, as if to disprove her statement. Elisena held his lips shut with one beringed finger.

"You aren't always looking for some noisy way to prove how brave you are. When I think of the hours I spent keeping Polassar and his army here, instead of his dashing about the countryside, trying to get you crowned by the force of his arm at whatever cost—which *he* wouldn't count—it makes me droop with weariness. And I happen to love you, as you'd surely know if you could bring yourself to believe it."

"You love me?" Tristan asked, bemused. This was the sort of conversation one had in dreams, when painfully personal things might be discussed remotely, safe from oneself. The wine must have been stronger than he'd thought. He was mildly amazed. That he loved Elisena went without saying—how could he not? But for the feeling to be returned, to be something more than the necessity he'd assumed and the affection he'd hoped for—

"How can I explain it better? I don't think you quite believe me, no matter what I say."

"I just don't understand it," Tristan said wonderingly. Not after all his failures, especially the fresh ones he'd just told her about.

"Hasn't anyone ever cared? Don't you know what it's like?" Elisena's voice was softer all at once, her body warm and close to his. She'd switched to teasing now, he thought, but was serious underneath.

"Not that way." He thought of Crewzel, Jehan, even Polassar. None of them seemed to feel quite this way toward him, friends though they were.

"Not even Blais?" She touched his cheek gently.

"That's different," Tristan responded scornfully. "He raised me."

"He certainly didn't have to. He could have left you wherever it was he found you," Elisena told him.

Tristan smiled and joined the game in earnest. Otherwise, he might just weep. His emotions were treacherous still. "Ah, but you didn't know him. That man would take anything in, no matter how much a misfit it was. We had a five-legged sheep for a while. Looked very funny when it ran."

Elisena stopped his recollection with a bit of bread popped deftly into his open mouth.

"I think I like you better than a five-legged sheep."

"How about a two-headed calf?" Tristan asked, chewing. "We had one of those, too, but even Blais said a cow with two udders would have been so much more useful—certainly more use to him than I ever was," he added.

"*Tristan!* He never said that!"

"No, of course not. *I* just did. But nonetheless, it's true." Such had been his darkest fear all his life, it seemed.

"It's not true, and it's worse that you say it about yourself, as if you think you have to, before someone else does. I'm going to put you back to bed. You're terribly cranky. Oh, stars! Couldn't Polassar have taken your boots off, at least?"

Tristan was somewhat taken aback at her outrage. Hadn't they still been teasing? He elected to stop the talking and fussing for another while himself, and did it without recourse to bread, though some few crumbs were trapped between their lips, hopeless of escape.

Elisena lay against him, soft and warm and tranquil, making Tristan feel protected and safe from all harm. The feeling was welcome. Whatever might have happened to the storm, all seemed quiet outside.

Tristan stared at the single candle still burning beside the bed, watching the steady burning of the flame, and feeling the beat of Elisena's heart next to his. He wondered how long it had been since he'd really looked at such a simple thing, acknowledging all its overlooked wonder and significance, as Blais had taught him to long ago. How long since events had permitted that? How long since he'd had a life, not merely a string of events?

The flame twinned, reflected in Elisena's newly opened eyes. Her words might not even have come from her lips, but Tristan heard them without difficulty and knew they came from her heart.

"In all those lives Nímir forced on me, I never once gave myself to a man. Oh, I was taken sometimes, that being the nature of life, and a keener torture which Nímir must have delighted in. I never could let myself love or hope, for Nímir would have snatched me away from any joy I dared reach for openly. I learned to guard myself and hold back. I waited for the man I could love—the king I was promised to and who was promised to me. The High Mage only made me that promise when he betrothed me. He never told me the king's name—and assumptions can be mocked."

She laid her face against his neck, and Tristan felt the warmth of a falling tear running from her cheek to his. "I love you. Accept that. It is a rare offering. Think on it, when you or any other question the right of your kingship. Hold onto it, though the world goes dark around us." Her words made almost an oath. "It's all either of us truly has, and more than most can hope for."

Beside them, the tiny flame burned warm and true, saffron and white, undisturbed by any chill draft.

Appraisals

"WE'VE RECEIVED PROVISIONAL promises of support, Wizard," Polassar said, as they finished an inspectional tour of Crogen's defenses. "The provision being that we beat Galan first."

Tristan shrugged. "So much for good news."

You're learning. Thomas trotted businesslike beside them, intent on seeing everything. Tristan had never suspected the cat of having such a military turn of mind.

The ice storm had left vast quantities of wreckage in its wake, but nothing that could conceal the numbers of the force Galan had mustered for his attack. Nor could the tense faces of Crogen's defenders conceal their situation—Crogen was under siege. Tristan marveled afresh that he and Valadan had passed through Galan's army without noticing it, even given the storm's shielding. Maybe Valadan *had* noticed.

"Since he encamped those, no one else has gotten through. Not that anyone was trying. I was summat surprised to see that *you* made it, though likely I shouldn't have been." Polassar squinted a practiced eye at the banners, searching for new arrivals.

"I never even saw them. And I still don't see siege engines out there. Shouldn't there be catapults or something?" Tristan thought about the awesome engines of destruction some of Blais' books had pictured.

"Happen he doesn't think he'll need 'em. He knows the supplies we could bring or gather are running dangerously low, and he can read the weather as well as any of us. Neither Galan nor we can wait out a long siege."

Tristan followed Polassar's glance to the sky. It was an ugly color, almost like a fresh bruise. One storm had passed, but it wasn't traveling alone. Another one was building.

"We lost part of the sunward wall last night," Polassar reported gloomily. "It's been heeling over for weeks, but the wind finished the work." He spat onto the frosted ground. "Always was a soft spot, so I never put stores in the buildings near it, but 'tis hard to plug a hole that size."

Tristan nodded. He would look at the wall later. Maybe he and Elisena could shore up whatever bits were left.

"Who else is out there?" he asked. "Besides Galan?"

"Danac of Westif's with him—mark the Falcon banner. And Baird of Amrein, not too close to Danac. There's bad blood there, Wizard, from some very ancient feuds. Andrayne of Heil with his brother Geraint. And if that banner's a mace and not a wand . . . Can you make it out? That would be Kerrgis of Josten, then. A newcomer. He wasn't here this time yesterday. After that storm, he may wish himself still elsewhere!"

The lords' banners were ripped nearly to shreds and some were no longer raised at all, though their bearers had not quit the field. There was a bustling in the camp as repairs were effected. A long string of mounted knights was circling about. The encampment was much closer than Galan had dared settle previously.

"Ye did well to slip through them, Wizard."

"I can't take the credit. I truly never saw any of them."

"No? Then there's truth to the tales of the Warhorse. There'd better be—we'll need all the help we can snatch at, magical and otherwise."

"That's about as we expected," Tristan said. He shivered deeper into the patched cloak with which he'd replaced the lost one. The storm had gone, but the cold remained, and the sun hid itself behind the leaden clouds.

"I'd hoped to do a little better by you, Wizard. It's a woeful commander who can't even raise an army." Polassar's face was grim under the bear-helm.

Tristan looked at his commander sidelong. "I hope you're not trying to resign. In the first place, I'll simply ignore it; and in the second, no one could have done more. It's just a bad situation."

"Aye. Trouble is, you're an unknown, Wizard. You don't even have a military record. If others follow us, 'twill be because some other they trust or owe fealty to has already joined us. Unfortunately—"

Polassar's spread hand indicated the mostly bare sweep of Crogen's battlements. Despite all he and Elisena had been able to do—and that had been a great deal—their numbers were still pitifully few, even if not contrasted with Galan's still-growing horde. They couldn't even muster a watch on all the walls at one time.

"The only matter likely to prosper us is that they're not properly allied at all." Polassar brooded. "Baird would as soon cut Danac's throat as spit, and if the tale I heard about Geraint despoiling Kerrgis' sister is true, there's little love lost there, either. Fighting you is all that holds 'em even this much together; they can't bear the idea of anyone else taking the prize they've been squabbling over all their lives. They're spoiling for a fight, but Galan will have a precious time working with 'em."

"Well, we knew just gathering an army wouldn't be enough—" The sky looked darker. Tristan wondered if that was wholly his imagination.

"That was when I thought we *could* gather an army! Wizard, I've failed you—"

Tristan leaned out over the battlements, trying to estimate Galan's numbers and not sure he really wanted to know them accurately.

"Polassar, just pray I haven't failed all of us and that this crowning will do what Elisena expects it to."

Tristan's thoughts went naturally to the sword, which Elisena was even now inspecting and working with, deciding how best to bind the crowning spells to it, if indeed that could be done with any reasonable hope of success—or at all.

She was by no means sure of it. Elisena had recognized the blade as a counterfeit at once and had been both perplexed and wary. Tristan had related all his struggles and searches to her, explaining his certainty that they could never hope to find the true sword. He'd taken every precaution to ensure as exact a replica as possible; beyond that they could only trust to fate, he insisted. His finding Jehan had surely been no accident.

It was a gamble worthy of her own devising, but Elisena balked at it. If the process of sword-forging was imprecise, as Jehan had said, then the process of spellcasting was hardly less so. They would be chancing all on the hope of perfection of effort, and they had no means to check their work until it was put to the ultimate test. There would be no second chance. She could not have hidden her concern from Tristan had she chosen to try.

But Elisena was cloistered now with the blade, while Tristan listened to Polassar's accounting of their strengths and all too numerous weaknesses. The crowning would need to take place very soon, Tristan thought, with just a trace of nerves. The twin sights of the dark sky and Galan's army reinforced the desperateness of their situation. He and Polassar descended from the battlements and crossed a narrow courtyard running between stables and a barracks that had once served cavalry and now housed most of Polassar's men. Footsteps sounded as a man approached, treading briskly.

He looked at least a score of years older than Polassar, but was dressed somewhat similarly, as might befit the lord of a small holding with rank but no especial wealth. Tristan didn't think he'd met the man before among Polassar's men.

The stranger greeted Polassar, who in turn spoke to Tristan.

"My lord, this is Canfors of Darlith, a convert to your cause."

"My lord," Tristan said politely, inclining his head, and saw Polassar wince. Evidently he'd been too casual or too subservient—probably the latter—since he was in fact this man's lord. But Canfors was old enough to be his grandsire and surely merited all the respect Tristan could offer him—if only because the man was here. Either Canfors was an exceptionally honorable man or he felt he had nothing to lose by this alliance. As their sole ally, he was to be closely cherished.

Canfors looked pleased, if Polassar did not.

"Where is Darlith, anyway?" Tristan asked, watching Canfors' straight back and unbowed head as the man went off to tend some matter involving the posting of guards.

"Esdragon. Top o' the Promontory. He brought us twenty-five men."

"Tw—" Tristan's word ended soundlessly, as his mouth opened wide. Galan probably had more men than that assigned to guard his cockatrice banner.

"Aye. Bright picture, isn't it, Wizard? Of course men will flock to us like ravens to battle if we beat Galan off, but we won't need them then, and I'd mistrust that kind of loyalty."

"No," Tristan answered thoughtfully. "Why should they feel any other way? We've got to see this the way they must. Canfors' coming surprises me a lot more than all the lords who didn't."

The wind felt colder than ever as they mounted another wall. Tristan looked out over the field again.

"Some of them are certainly just trying to protect their own ends, but a few of these lords may genuinely be doing what they see as the best thing for the people they're supposed to be responsible for. They're good stewards. I'd trust them later. If there *is* a later."

Tristan found Elisena in a little octagonal courtyard which he'd finally remembered as a favorite of hers. After only three false searches, he'd located it, and watched unseen as she knelt by a wind-riven tree, stroking its bark delicately and brushing snow crystals away.

Her rings gave off a gentle glow, guiding her inspection of the jagged crack in the wood. Elisena's fingers began to make what looked almost like stitching movements, pushing and pulling at the tree, molding it as if the wood had become malleable clay. She was whispering, too, but Tristan was too far away to catch the spell.

The glow increased, flowing from her hands and limning the line where the crack had been. It seemed to soak into the bark, and Tristan could imagine he saw the light rising like sap through the branches and out to the smallest twiggy tips. Just above Elisena's head, a tiny knob of bark swelled and greened and then opened into a pear blossom.

"Oh, no, little one." Elisena touched the fluttering petals tenderly. "No, not yet. But live to see another spring, the true spring, my friend." Somehow, the petals folded inward—Tristan could have sworn that he saw her tuck the bud back beneath the surface of the bark.

Elisena rose and turned to see him waiting. Her fingers pushed her hair back and set her crystals dancing. She looked tired and discouraged.

"Well?" Tristan was loath even to broach the subject, but otherwise he'd simply have to stand there and stare at her till he thought of some other reason for having disturbed her. "How does the sword look?"

Elisena sighed. "It's a fine weapon. Your Jehan is a master, whatever else he may or may not be. I wonder what Crewzel's cards will show *him*? As to whether a blade that's merely like the first without actually being the same will serve—I cannot tell. Swords—Kinarkan swords—are like living things. No two can ever be alike. I might find another man of your height and coloring, but he would never be you—and were he ever so like, still I would know the difference."

"But can the throne be that selective?"

Tristan wanted desperately to hold her close, to warm her hands and comfort her doubts. Yet he didn't move toward her. Her anxieties he could understand and share, but her pain was beyond his reach. His question seemed inane, on the face of it. He was sorry he asked it, sorry he'd come at all so impatiently, breaking in on a time Elisena probably desperately needed to spend alone.

She lifted one shoulder slightly. "I came here to think, and my mind is as bare as that tree. It was never meant to be attempted, but there's a tiny wild element in any great magic, and strange things can happen. A prophecy's meaning can shift, a kingship can fall upon the unsuspecting. I can't answer you. There's only one way to know—and I only wish it didn't have to come so soon."

"Soon?" Tristan hated the comical surprised tone his lips put on that word. He couldn't still be hoping to avoid the crowning, could he? Not with the signs of its necessity all about him.

"Very soon. That ice storm you came through—I can't tell you if it followed you here or if you only crossed its path by mischance, but it was not the first such little greeting Nímir has sent to Crogen. Now he is massing another storm, beside which that little collection of wind and freezing rain is like—" Elisena's eye fell upon Minstrel, who was busily teasing a loose thread out of Tristan's collar.

"Like comparing Minstrel to the Guardian of Darkenkeep," she finished, lifting her eyes to Tristan's. "The snows are gathering in Channadran, and soon they will sweep from one end of this poor land to the other. We will move before that begins. With the sword you brought . . ."

Those words still sent shivers down his spine the next afternoon. Sometimes, Tristan thought, he tended to forget the awesome powers Elisena's rings contained and the fearful duties and prophecies heaped upon her.

It was only just past sun-high, but he'd had to light two candles to gain enough light to read the grimoire. The frozen-looking cloud cover was thicker than ever, and Tristan was just nerving himself to do something about it.

If there was any branch of the magical arts that he could generously be said to excel at, certainly it should be weather-witching. He and Blais had earned their living so for years, and Blais' spell-book was stuffed with applicable formulae. All Tristan needed to do was choose a proper one, based on his experience, and he felt well qualified to do so.

Any break in the building weather front would be welcome, however brief. Just one glimpse of the sun would do more than raise spirits among Crogen's defenders—and if it flawed the pattern Nímir wove, it might be days before his powers could conjoin properly again and come to bear on Crogen once more. Or so Tristan hoped. Just one very little spell, like a grain of sand dropped unobserved into a pot of polishing ointment, to flaw all it touched. . . .

Tristan inspected his tools with care. He didn't require many. The simpler the spell, the less the chance of its being detected during its execution. Just the grimoire, a bit of stone containing reflective flakes of mica, and lighted candles should suffice. Tristan stretched his fingers, licked his lips, and began.

The chant was simple—sounds suggesting warmth, spoken slowly and sleepily. All the while the stone was being moved nearer and nearer the candleflame so that the light grew upon it the way the sun would seem to move nearer as the mists about it thinned and vanished. When the sun shone, it would grow much warmer, warm as Tristan's fingers upon the stone. He spoke the cantrip carefully, over and over, as regularly as the sun rose each day, tracked across the sky, and shone down warmly upon the land. The stone circled closer to the flame. Outside, the sky grew lighter. Tristan did not need to watch to know that this was so.

The window-hanging was only a square of tanned leather, barely heavy enough to keep most drafts out, but with the sudden force of the wind behind it, it hit Tristan harder than a falling wall might have done. He was too startled to cry out, even as he was knocked off his feet and flung onto and over the table. He hit the floor before he could realize that something had happened. He blinked twice, beginning to feel the pain of a bruised leg.

Thomas blinked back at him. The cat had kept his feet firmly on the floor by digging every one of his claws into the floorboards, but all his fur was standing in the wrong direction. For once, he was speechless.

Tristan started to sit up, pushing against the floor with shaking hands, and discovered that he was lying in the middle of a sizable snowdrift. Bits of his golden stone powdered the top of it. The grimoire, its ensorcellment-protected pages straightening themselves, lay against the far wall.

Thomas still said nothing. Neither did Tristan. For the moment, there seemed to be very little to discuss. Tristan debated starting over again, if he could figure out where he'd gone wrong. Maybe the stone had been flawed inside—

Elisena burst into the room, her face limestone-pale. She stopped, panting and clutching at the doorframe.

"Are you—"

Tristan groaned. "Toadstools! I've scared you again! No, I'm not hurt, except for what little was left of my pride. I was just—" He stopped. The scattered apparatus made what he'd been attempting generally plain to anyone with Elisena's experience. "I was just trying to help. I should have tried just taking a nap. I'll get this mess cleaned up." He got to his feet, forcing himself not to wince.

"Tristan—"

"No, don't bother. I'm not going to try it again the minute your back's turned." He had to stop himself from taking out his anger on her—anger and frustration at having only dragged

her away from her work while trying to lighten it for her.
Tristan picked up the grimoire and put it carefully on the table,
smoothing the cover closed.

"The sun came out," Elisena said, still breathlessly. "I was
grinding herbs in the stillroom, when all at once every one of
my rings lighted up and the sun broke through the clouds,
bright enough to cast shadows outside." She lifted the edge of
the window curtain, spreading it out slightly. It was badly split
for nearly half its length.

"You almost broke Nímir's hold on his clouds, with nothing
more than a stone and a bit of candle," Elisena said, letting
the curtain fall. "Small wonder he was angry. I wish I thought
I might learn to fail as spectacularly as you do."

the Vigil

It took a full day to assemble the Regalia, put it in working order, and prepare the throne hall with burnt herbs and complex spells. Polassar had wished to serve notice of the time of the crowning so that any waverers who chose might attend, but Tristan pointed out that this came rather close to inviting an attack at a moment when all their attentions should be focused elsewhere. The lines of allegiance had been clearly drawn some time before, when Elisena had first issued a proclamation that the king would be crowned at Crogen. They had already seen which lords would heed it, and in which way.

Polassar was undoubtedly doing some other sort of military scheming, but Tristan had seen very little of him. His own part in the preparations had been rather mundane. He'd stayed in Elisena's stillroom, grinding herbs to powder and freeing Elisena for other pressing tasks.

He had worked steadily, reducing little bundles of leaves till they were fine enough to float about even in quiet air, whispering a specific cantrip over them with each motion of the pestle. Grace notes on the land, Elisena had called them, the little herbs that everywhere covered the ground, even under the snows. Speedwell, plantain, lion's tooth and mint gave the room a fertile smell of spring. Tristan supposed they must serve some like purpose in the spell Elisena planned to combat Nímir's storm with after the crowning. Optimistic of her, Thomas had said.

Tristan still smelled of the mint, though he'd been bathed, barbered and anointed with a lot of stranger-smelling herbal concoctions, before being dressed in linen undergarments and a lightweight wool robe marked with a golden sunburst on the chest. Tristan shivered. The clothing was more ceremonial than practical, and he was going to have to keep a night-long vigil in it. A vast room like the throne hall would certainly be plagued with drafts. The wool was scratchy about his neck.

The purpose of the vigil Tristan had been told was to imprint him with the sword and the sword with him as fully as was possible. It would be, if nothing else, a tangible link between him and all the kings who'd gone before. But those kings had contemplated their swords—or whatever the ritual trappings of their ceremonies had been—with perfect confidence, something Tristan couldn't begin to share.

The torches were lighted all around the hall. The great tapestries were hung, and the odds and ends that remained of the Regalia were arranged in their proper places.

Elisena stood beside him, though it was nearly time for her to quit the hall and leave him to his chilly wait. She spoke softly.

"It's not too late, you know."

"Too late?" Tristan frowned, called away from his scrutiny of the room.

"To change your mind."

"I can remember—it seems a very long time ago—promising you that I'd try this. I work very hard at keeping my promises. I won't back out now, never fear."

"I wish you would." Elisena had her back to one of the candlestands. He couldn't see her eyes, but Tristan realized that her suggestion had been neither a last-minute misgiving about his dedication or a challenge of it.

"What? I thought we were agreed. There's no other way—"

"I think we should try to find one." Elisena took his hand, and candlelight washed her face gently as she moved, but her eyes stayed shadowed. She faced her own lonely vigil this night, Tristan thought. "Tristan, this frightens me. I don't think you've accepted what a risk this sword truly is. I'm sure Jehan warned you of all the variables involved in making a sword, but have you stopped to consider the impossibility of *exactly* duplicating a spell that relies so much on delivery, on voice inflections, and doing it well enough to compensate for a sword that may not be everything it should be?"

"There's no one better qualified to speak those spells than you," he assured her, knowing it to be the pure truth.

"All right," Elisena said impatiently. "I've invested this sword, and, so far as I know, it's flawless. But that's just the point—we *can't* know until it's far too late for you. That sword and the other—they *aren't* alike, any more than two snowflakes are alike, however similar they seem. If it matters, you'll be dead before we know about it. And there'll be nothing at all I can do."

Tristan wondered if Jehan had felt this way when he began to forge the sword—plunging into the task wholeheartedly one moment, lost in the work as it went forward, and the next instant doubting it to its very core and tortured by answerless questions. Working with a divided will and cautious heart, there was no chance for success at all. Sometimes you simply had to give yourself up to the task and dare the outcome.

"If I don't try, it's too late for all of us," Tristan insisted doggedly.

"Not necessarily." Elisena paused and bit her lip. "Suppose that I augmented that storm instead of trying to quell it or turn it from us. My rings have that power. I could use it to scatter Galan's forces and buy us time to study that sword further—"

Tristan took her hands again, gently, firmly, but in haste, before she could say one word more.

"Thank you. I understand what you're trying to do for me. But if you augment that storm, aren't you in effect granting Nímir admittance here? Aside from that being exactly the opposite of what your rings are meant to be used for, can we be sure we'll be able to get rid of Nímir when we want to, having invited him in? You'd never be able to turn back the full weight of his winter after that. No. You don't invite the wolf to sit down at your table and then ask him to mind the baby afterward."

"I can control the storm," Elisena persisted. "I—"

"*No.*"

"I should be counting myself a widow already!" Elisena snapped, wrenching her hands away. Then their eyes met. He'd never seen her face actually crumple before, whatever calamity befell.

"Tristan—"

"Trust me."

"You trust *me* too much. I'm not perfect, whatever you think. I'm not incapable of making a mistake, and now I've lost my nerve. It was bad enough to see you hurt because of my ignorance. I can't bear to see you die because you trusted me. Use your own eyes, too." She searched his face desperately. "I don't think you heard me at all."

Tristan took her hands again. Her rings felt hot, though Elisena's fingers were cold.

"I think in some things our fate's not our own at all," he said. "The most we can do is try."

She shook her head violently. "No! How can I make you understand—"

"It's you who doesn't understand!" Tristan finally lost control of his temper, though he didn't fully realize why until the words were on his lips. "We've gone too far to back out now. Cabal's dead. Crewzel's in prison, and I left Jehan wandering around in a strange country, trying to find her. All that just to get *this* sword! Polassar's lost Lassair, and if this castle is taken, he's likely to lose his life as well. Not to mention what *you're* planning to do, taking on Nímir single-handedly! Am I the only one not permitted to risk anything? What does that mean— that you don't think I'm good enough? Could I just carry the guilt for all this around instead? If I *don't* try this, I don't think I can live with the results. I don't think I want to try. I can hardly live with the things I've had to do to get this far and to get this sword." He stopped, breathing as if he'd been running, trying not to gasp obviously for air.

Elisena was trembling, but she said nothing for a long while. Tristan thought he'd won. He was awed at her distress, considering her uncanny calm at what had seemed to him worse times.

"I *can* stop you, you know." Her eyes locked with his.

Tristan shook his head. "You won't. Because, as you said, I trust you too much."

A tear spilled from Elisena's left eye. Tristan put a finger out and gently traced its course down her cheek, ending at the corner of her mouth.

"Whatever happens tomorrow," he began, finding his breath unexpectedly choked in his throat. "Whatever happens... coltsfoot, there doesn't seem to have been much time, does there? We've hardly had a chance to get to know each other. And you were something I never expected to find, never dreamed to have. I never wanted any of this, but whatever happens tomorrow, it's been worth it. For this. For you."

Outside the light of the four torches flanking the throne, the world seemed not to exist. An occasional crackle of the flames was the only sound except for Tristan's rapid breathing, and the light dazzled him just enough that he could see nothing beyond it. Flame shapes like marsh-lights flickered before him even when he looked away from the torch flames.

The stone flags under his knees were solid, real, and very cold. There was no danger that he'd doze off. Tristan knelt before the throne and stared the sword into his brain.

He wished he knew how he was supposed to feel and what this vigil was really meant to accomplish in him. If he knew what to expect, he might be better able to help things along. Would he know if he succeeded?

Torchlight limned the blade as it lay upon the dais before the throne, making it impossible to ignore, like some of the other things praying on Tristan's uneasy conscience now.

He was sure he'd have been able to approach the crowning with more confidence if he could have seen his right to the throne free and clear, but self-doubt was a strong habit, a constant of his life. And his right of blood was so easily doubted, despite Elisena's rings. As for his having some personal knack for governing—

I wish I could feel there's been one person in my life I haven't let down, Tristan thought miserably. *Just one.* But he'd failed them all, starting with Blais and moving right on down to Kitri, whose fate he couldn't even guess, optimistic though he might be about her. Crewzel he regretted most of all. He couldn't be what people needed him to be, or even what they wanted him to be. He tried. But things never worked out. Maybe through his personal fault, some flaw—

Nobody's perfect. At least among humans.

Tristan started violently, then shivered. A shadow trotted purposefully toward him, flicking in and out of the puddles of torchlight.

"Thomas, what are you doing in here? I'm supposed to be keeping a vigil. *Alone.*"

Sometimes there are advantages to not being human. Thomas stretched luxuriously. *I doubt anyone would even bother to object to me. And cats excel at watching.*

It was good not to be alone, really, but there wasn't much Thomas could do to assist, except to settle down beside Tristan and watch the sword with him. When the cat said nothing more, Tristan's thoughts tended back to Crewzel again, pulled as by a dismal lodestone.

He knew, in his mind, that he'd done, if not the right thing, the only possible thing. Jehan knew as much as he did about where Delmon was; if the smith managed to find Crewzel, there'd be no problem. And if Tristan had stayed in the city even another two days, looking for her, he would not only have risked arrest, but would certainly have been too late getting back to Crogen. His urgency at that point might not have been wholly his own, and he could certainly justify it.

But by leaving, he'd undeniably deserted Crewzel when she needed him and he had to accept responsibility for that. And he'd also left Jehan unpaid and alone in a strange city, looking for salvation and a woman whose feelings toward him were uncertain at best.

Then there was Cabal. That hardly bore thinking about.

So many guilts, so little time, Thomas grumbled.

Tristan wished he could see it that way. But the point was, he didn't feel the least bit worthy of the sword. Even if it was right and true, *he* wasn't. He knelt before it, and the sword seemed to look straight into his heart and know his unfitness. He wouldn't be at all surprised if it chose to fail him as he seemed to have failed so many others.

I killed a dragon once, Tristan thought, as if a past act of heroism could justify him to the sword. It had happened so long ago that the incident seemed almost accidental. He couldn't remember now if it had been deliberate or not. The pale memory had no meaning for him, anyway.

An hour had crawled by, measurelessly, when Tristan heard a whisper of sound behind him and saw the torch flames waver and steady the way they might if the smaller outside door of the hall had been opened a crack, letting fresh air in to stir them.

Tristan stiffened, knowing himself to be excruciatingly vulnerable here, caught like a moth in the torchlight while the rest of the room was thick with concealing shadows. And he remembered that Galan and Reynaud were just outside such walls as Crogen had, and that Reynaud had breached those walls once before, undetected. The urge to turn about was nearly unmasterable, but he refused to yield to it.

Instead, Tristan set a spell in his mind, one that would snuff the torches at his word and even the odds a bit. He reminded himself that the sword was at hand, conventionally useful as a weapon, even if it proved to be nothing more.

The room was silent. Maybe he'd been mistaken. His nerves must be very bad, worse than he'd thought. Tristan turned his eyes and attention back to the sword.

"My lord—"

Tristan jumped, then controlled himself with an effort and left the torch flames burning. Surely no assassin would call him so courteously by title.

He looked around and could just make out a figure in the shadows beside the door. He couldn't see it clearly, but the sight and the slightly familiar voice led him to realize that it was Dickon—Dickon of Falkerry.

"Are you still here?" Tristan asked wearily. He didn't feel nearly as relieved as he should have, somehow.

Told you so. Thomas turned about and wrapped his tail about his paws.

Dickon spoke in a rush, as if he greatly dreaded interruption, moving jerkily across the room. He didn't want to have to shout, so he must come close, yet he feared to approach his king too closely for fear of offending.

"My lord, I'm sorry to disturb you, but this is the very first time I've been able to find you and speak to you face to face. Your men wouldn't let me see you or accept my service in your name. I've been turned away every time, so I had to come to you myself. I know it's not done, but I—"

He stopped as if shot with a crossbow bolt when Tristan turned enough to let the torchlight touch his face.

"*You?*" Dickon whispered.

"I'm afraid so." Tristan got up from his knees, turned about, and sat down on the edge of the dais with a small moan of relief. His knees were very stiff and unbent protestingly.

"But why didn't you *tell* me?" Dickon staggered a couple of steps closer before halting again. "You *knew* what I wanted. I told you, first thing when I got here. And you never said a word."

Tristan sighed, wishing he could dodge the subject—a subject he'd assumed was safely closed. "I hoped you'd given up and gone home, back to your farm, alive and in one piece."

The boy colored. "You think I'm not good enough," he said, outraged. "Because I'm unproven. But if you'd just give me a chance—I didn't come empty handed. I've got my own sword—" His desperation overrode even his anger and any notion he might have had of the proper way to address his king.

"You're persistent, I'll give you that. I just can't understand why." Tristan rubbed wearily at the bridge of his nose. His eyes were aching from the uncertain torchlight, and he was tired of thinking. He'd searched his heart to its roots and found only a confusing tangle of roads leading to other searches. "Get out."

Dickon didn't move.

"Out, I said!" The words cracked out like a whiplash, and Tristan turned away, recognizing the embarrassment fueling his anger. He was trying hard to do the right thing, and to be seen here, quaking in the dark . . . He was no king, either by breeding or background, and it was a hard charade to play out, even in front of himself. To have a witness was proving to be unbearable. His failure would be seen soon enough, come dawn.

The anger could be used, though, to send Dickon from the hall with his ears blistering, so fast he'd be halfway to Falkerry before he could pause to think. And Tristan thought he'd feel better for the release of tension, even if only briefly. He opened his mouth with the words ready.

The look on Dickon's face stopped him. The boy looked as green-sick as if he'd already had the incipient tongue-lashing, expected and accepted it, but wasn't going to budge till he'd had his petition heard.

"My lord, you need every man you can get! Give me my chance. Let me prove myself to you." It didn't seem to matter to Dickon that he'd already been refused and then further insulted by not being told of it.

"I'd rather not have you on my conscience," Tristan mumbled, belatedly hoping that Dickon was still too far away to hear.

There were probably boys even younger in Polassar's company, or among Canfors' men. But they would have grown up familiar with weapons, trained in their use and in the other skills vital to survival in battle. Dickon probably barely knew one end of his sword from the other. He didn't move like a fencer, though there was nothing the matter with him beyond an untrained awkwardness. He'd surely be more at home tilling the ground than bleeding all over it, or herding sheep rather than following them to slaughter.

The torchlight flared at Tristan's commanding gesture, washing over the boy, who blinked rapidly, dazzled. Tristan took a good long look at him, before he let the flames die down again.

Dickon was as clean as it was possible for a person to be, but his hands and nose were red, and he looked cold, not just nervous or excited. He had no cloak—only his heavy shirt, breeches, and rough home-cobbled boots. He didn't look the least bit like a knight or a gallant soldier, despite the scabbard strapped to his side; Tristan saw that it was fastened wrong, anyway, so that he could never have drawn the sword from it. He didn't look the least bit like a knight, though such had doubtless been his intention. The sum of all his preparations had so much the opposite effect that Tristan might have been moved to laugh if the boy hadn't been so deadly serious about the business.

As it happened, Tristan didn't feel the least bit mirthful. He might have been regarding his own mirrored self, not that long ago, setting blithely forth on his quest for Allaire, wearing clothing so threadbare that it held together more out of luck and loyalty than anything else, without a copper in his pockets, and with an old man's dying commands about an impossible quest circling like crows in his head. They weren't so very different, he and Dickon. Was that why he felt this inconvenient mixture of pity and responsibility toward him?

"Why do you want to serve me so badly?" Tristan asked, baffled. "You don't even know me. I can give you half a hundred reasons why you'd be better off turning around right now and going home. If the lords want to play power games, that's fine; at least they know what they're getting into. But

you don't have their background for any of this. You weren't
brought up with your head stuffed with history and legends.
It's not your fight. You're all that's going to be left when this
whole glorious, doomed enterprise finally shakes itself apart,
and yet you're begging to get shaken apart with it. You're a
farmer, not a soldier. Go home and grow something, so at
least everyone won't starve to death when this is all over!"
Tristan turned away. The room seemed darker than it had been;
he must have been looking right into one of the torches unawares, half blinding himself. "You want to serve me?" he went
on. "Go home. You can do that for me."

"We have the legends," Dickon said unexpectedly.

"What? After all this time? Still, they're only legends. They
can't possibly mean much to you."

"You're the rightful king," Dickon repeated doggedly. "The
legends say so."

"If you'll excuse my being so blunt, what difference does
that make to you? It's nothing to you one way or the other
who's king." A cold draft licked at Tristan's ankles. He shivered.

"It could be. I believe that. I can have dreams too." Dickon's
mouth settled into stubborn lines. "I want to fight alongside
you."

"You don't even know what I'm fighting for," Tristan
snapped. "Would you give your allegiance that blindly?"

Their gazes locked briefly. Dickon swallowed hard, and
lifted his head higher.

"You're fighting. I know that. And I choose to fight by
your side, whether you'll have me or no. It's better than freezing in the dark. You can't stop me. I've been working here in
your kitchens for months, waiting, and you never knew I was
here. I can lose myself again and still fight for you. You won't
know, but I'll be there."

"And die for a legend?"

"You sound like my father." Dickon smiled, an unexpected
lightening of his face. "My father says that when the legends
come to life, that's a good time to lie down and hide till they
go away, because otherwise they'll trample right over you."

"Your father sounds like a sensible man," Tristan said,
reflecting upon the many ways his own destiny seemed to have
trampled him.

Dickon took a fast half dozen steps across the room into the torchlight and knelt down so quickly that Tristan had no chance to stop him.

"My lord, it's the night of your crowning. I've heard that kings must grant right-hearted requests then. Maybe that's just another legend, but I feel it should be true. My heart is right; all I ask is that you let me prove it to you. Can you refuse me so simple a plea?"

"Anyone in this castle can tell you that I'm no more a king than you are a soldier," Tristan said, his annoyance overriding his pride. "How would I know if that bit about not refusing requests—I believe they're called boons—is true? I'm not overfamiliar with the customs of royalty. And neither are you."

Dickon looked at him, not even reproachfully now. He just looked.

The night was wearing away. Tristan thought again unexpectedly of how glad he was not to be alone here—and how futile it was to think he was anything but alone. Because neither Dickon nor Thomas was going to have to plunge the hilt of that sword into the hollow of Crogen's throne and learn in a flashing instant whether he was going to rule Calandra or die in the attempt. The idea terrified him. He wanted to beg Dickon to stay, as fervently as he'd tried to turn him away. The room was crowded with ghosts, its own and his own, and the dark between the torches crawled.

He'd like to do just one decent, right thing before his life ended, as he was certain it would in the morning. He wanted one last chance to atone for past guilts, past lapses, and bunglings. Do right by just one person. Maybe this was that chance. But what was right for Dickon? To grant his request and probably take his life? Or to send him home, having crushed his spirit and killed his hopes, both surely worth more than a mere body?

The sword wouldn't make him an answer. It wouldn't speak to him until the morrow and even then might choose to be silent. And Thomas, his green eyes unwinking as twin gibbous moons, had no answers either.

The torches crackled and spat like angry cats. Tristan watched the flames, irresolute. They burned so brightly, though for such a little time. Bright, beautiful, deathbound, no different from truly living things like Dickon and like himself.

"You have to understand," Tristan began to explain, haltingly, his voice hoarse. "I'm very new to all of this. I've spent almost my whole life in a peasant cottage with my master and my books. I never saw anyone so important as a knight, much less a king—there weren't any kings to see, anyhow. I know how to deal with farmers and fishermen and I don't always get cheated by shopkeepers, but beyond that I'm lost. I don't have any idea of how to go about this. You'll have to help me—that can be your first service. I don't suppose you know the formalities of offering and accepting fealty?"

Dickon was still tangled a few words back.

"My first service?" He looked as though he hardly dared hope he'd heard rightly.

"I'd as soon not have to call Polassar in," Tristan said reasonably, "though I'm sure he could help. I'm supposed to be holding a solitary vigil, after all! So you'll have to think of some way to manage this—some proper way that's not too ludicrous. Any idea how this kind of thing is handled?" He felt like some sort of conspirator.

Get in practice. There's sure to be a lot of this after the crowning, Thomas suggested.

Dickon knotted his brows, thinking dutifully.

"I've heard it spoken of as offering one's sword. I know when you take service with one of the lords, you just see his swordmaster or the captain of the guard—but yours wouldn't see me."

"I know. That's my fault." He'd have to see about removing that spell now, Tristan supposed. Though he should be pleased that it had held up so well.

Dickon registered a little surprise, but mastered it. His tongue-tip protruded a little from his mouth as he worked further on the puzzle of the protocol.

"I think I just offer you my sword," he finally said, gravely. "And all you would have to do is touch it in acceptance and hand it back. Say a few words if you want, but that's the gist of it."

Tristan nodded. "That certainly sounds simple enough. You've got a sword, I believe you said?"

"Yes, my lord!" Dickon eagerly unbelted the scuffed leather scabbard that hung at his side. The buckles were fastened so awkwardly that the procedure took him some time.

"It's very old, but the metal's sound as oak. I've kept it oiled and polished, and the edge is true. It's a good sword." His ardor was still spilling over.

"All right." Tristan got to his feet and positioned himself directly in front of the throne, in lieu of sitting upon it, which he didn't think would be at all wise. Dickon knelt bolt upright before him, the sword and scabbard lying across his palms.

Tristan coughed.

"For a start, get up. I can't for the life of me imagine why people think I want to see the tops of their heads! If you're good enough to be my soldier, then you're more than good enough to look me in the face. Now. You have something to offer me. Stand up and be proud of it." He strove not to feel ridiculous, carrying out this makeshift ceremony in the ruined, time-raddled throne hall.

Dickon got up slowly. Tristan could almost watch the questions churning in his mind as he tried to remember or invent the ceremonial words.

"My lord, I offer you my sword. In—" Dickon paused and thought, licking his lips nervously. "In token of my life and service, which I place in your hands."

He raised his palms a fraction higher, and Tristan realized he was to reach out and take the sword now. He resisted an urge to clear his throat before he spoke.

"Dickon of Falkerry, I accept your service, and all rights and responsibilities attending to it. Let my acceptance of this sword be token of that pledge."

Creative of you.

But in the murky hall, the plain words took on a richer meaning, as if Crogen recalled days of ancient glory and added its own resonance to the words of fealty whose like it had heard so often. A whisper of an echo ran about the room. Tristan unsheathed the sword, curious to see what sort of a weapon would come out of a Falkerry farm.

The blade was indeed very old, and had seen hard use, but Dickon had cared for it as well as he'd claimed—every hint of rust had been carefully teased away, and the silver wire binding the grip was bright as a candleflame. Torchlight ran over the blade as easily as water over smooth stone, flashing into Tristan's eyes. He blinked and shifted his hold on the hilt, turning the edge out of the light. The grip felt good to his hand, nestling trustingly against the palm like a live thing sheltering there. The balance was sweet and true as a dream. The steel hung almost weightless. A fine weapon. Passed down from better days, surely, but a fine sword then and a fine sword still.

The torchlight touched the blade less blazingly now, but Tristan felt his breath leave him as he looked at it, and his heart staggered with surprise. Less dazzled, seeing the sword clearly, he realized it was a twin to the one Jehan had forged, the blade that lay now before Crogen's throne. But *this* blade felt alive in his hand, as the other never had. Tristan was powerless to understand the feeling, the unexpected deepening of his senses. Just experiencing it took all his attention. Blood crashed and surged in his ears till he was uncertain of what he might be hearing—whether shouts or sourceless music—and the torches seemed to pulse in time to the sound in an almost silent dance. Crogen's hall had altered. Tristan could have sworn he and Dickon were no longer alone. He was reminded of the glamor Elisena had cast, with the shadows regrouping to her ordering. There was magic at work here, or he knew nothing of the art.

Radiance dripped down the blade and over the hilt as light should not have done, spilling over onto Tristan's fingers. He kept blinking his eyes, but his sight wouldn't clear. Tristan clung to the sword hilt, watching the silver glow limning the veins of his right wrist and presumably traveling onward up his sleeve. The King-mark on his palm flared fitfully; the sword hilt was in the way, but Tristan could make out a bluer light joining the silver, spilling out around the hilt.

Dickon thumped down on his knees, bonelessly. Thomas made an almost human gasp, the oddest sound Tristan had ever heard come out of the cat. But he couldn't stop to wonder what it was they saw or what he must look like to them. It was all he could do not to whirl and plunge the sword hilt into the throne right then, the blade wanted that so badly. Tristan closed his left hand around his right wrist, and held on till his knuckles went bone-white and sweat stood out on his forehead.

He was beyond surprise by then, but still not sure he could beat the thing. The blade's will was as strong as its steel, and he was only bone and quivering flesh. The sword's need was stronger than his certainty of its prematurity. Yet Tristan fought.

He told the blade, over and over, that its time had not yet come. And in return, he received a staggering flood of images—swords flashing, ice flashing, jewels flashing, banners waving, gold and candles and armorplate, mouths opening with shouts of battle, castle gates opening, the circlet of a crown, a silver ring flung away, and a flashing circle of silver.

It was the ring that saved him. Tristan recognized it, and recognized at the same time the recurring pattern in the images the sword sent him, a pattern of openings and circles beckoning to him, once all the flaring and flashing had stopped. Behind their shadows was doubtless hidden the silver light of the rune-circle on Crogen's throne, waiting for him when he reached out for one of the other treasures. Greatly as the sword desired it, it was not yet time for the meeting between them. They must wait for Elisena, Tristan insisted. The worn silver upon the hilt burned like flame under his fingers.

Finally the sword seemed to recognize his authority and the struggle ceased. The light about the blade was only torchlight now, and Tristan could see again the shadowy hall and Dickon's white face before him. He found he now held the sword reversed so that the hilt lay against his chest, shaking in time with his heartbeat. For a moment the only sounds in the hall were the whisper of Thomas' fur settling down flat again and the hiss and crackle of the torch flames.

"Where did you get this sword?" Tristan asked, barely recognizing his own voice, but he scarcely listened to Dickon's tale of a sword passed from father to son, hung high on a wall like a trophy, hidden by smoke, soot and shadows, neglected by peace-loving farmers, yet never discarded because of lingering memories that once it had been cherished or valuable, though it had no present utility.

Tristan would have kicked himself, if he hadn't already felt so bruised from his mental battle with the sword. All this while he'd been so fatally certain that his sword-seeking-spell had failed, because the sword had not presented itself to him in the manner he'd expected! He'd been impatient and expecting a spectacular conclusion to his spell—and there had been no fanfare of trumpets, no flash of light, no magical trappings of any kind. There was just one threadbare boy from nowhere who wanted mysteriously and obsessively to be a soldier and had brought his own sword along for the purpose.

Tristan had run off to Kôvelir, seeking a blade which all the while was in Crogen, where it had dutifully come to his call by the best means it could. His own spell to make Dickon be unnoticed had probably hidden the blade from him, along with Dickon. Tristan started to lean sickly against the throne, then recovered himself. It seemed the room's due, if not the sword's.

"I will accept your sword, Dickon of Falkerry," Tristan said finally, formally, wanting to laugh or weep and wondering what Dickon would think of him if he did either. "And I offer you in turn my own sword to seal our pact, lest you be deprived of a weapon. I offer that—and a thanks you may never fully understand."

He bent and put Jehan's sword into the boy's hands gently, amused at Dickon's wondering, then incredulous, then doubtful expression as his eyes touched the perfect edges of the blade—utterly perfect, since they had never yet met with another blade—and the heavy silver and satiny wood of the grips. Tristan felt the same sense of wonder about the sword in his own hand, but for a better reason.

"It's a good sword," he assured Dickon. "Maybe the finest to come out of Kinark in recent years. But this seasoned blade is better suited to me, believe me." He stroked the sword he held tenderly. "It's been in the family, you might say."

the Crowning

TRISTAN KNELT BEFORE the throne and the sword again, but now that the sword he watched was another blade, the darkness of the room was neither oppressive nor haunting. Rather, it was comforting, warm and safe as sleep, and a great aid to concentration. Tristan slipped into it gladly.

He kept his vigil in earnest then, and time passed swiftly as he contemplated the blade and felt its history and the history of the realm soaking into him. Years and events flowed over and through him as he gazed, marveling. He seemed able to be both passive observer and active participant at once, without the least trace of confusion. It was certainly an improvement over the close-written, often tedious scrolls.

The sword shone like a candle before him. It gave off a most restful light, peaceful and sure of itself. Tristan was grateful. He had been feeling anxious about something, but now he couldn't remember what had so troubled him. He sighed and relaxed, swaying a little on his knees. He felt as if all his bones were melting, but it was a good feeling. The sword was more than strong enough to support him through the dark hours.

Outside Crogen, a murky dawn was hesitantly beginning to break. Galan's captains were astir, readying men and arms.

Today at last their strength had reached its crest; all the expected lords were in attendance, all damage done by the storm had been repaired, and their commander had assured them that he would finally launch his oft-postponed attack upon the ridiculously indefensible heap of stone that sprawled before them. Today, his sources had promised Galan, attention within the castle would be divided. Galan had plenty of efficient spies, even though his fearsome master of magic seemed to have vanished, and the news had spread throughout the camp.

Anticipation ran high. There were tales that this usurper king had found means to unlock Crogen's hidden treasure vaults, which doubtless was the reason behind Galan's decision to lay siege to this laughable stronghold. Well, if Galan was not disposed to be generous, neither did he enjoy complete control of his allies. There'd be rich pickings, whatever. Those great clouds on the horizon only foreshadowed Crogen's fall. And then they could all go some place out of this cursed wind.

A faint light limned the windows of the hall, picking up spectral colors from the tapestries.

Tristan shivered. With the obvious advent of morning, he began to feel vaguely alarmed and trapped. He trusted this sword with his whole heart. But this crowning seemed to have stolen upon him too quickly, before he could think it through or think about it at all, and now he was reverting to his truer self, his other preoccupations all having been settled. He struggled in panic against the pull of the sword and of the magic night, even as he argued with himself.

It wasn't Elisena who'd trapped him. That was utter nonsense, since she would no more have trapped him than she would have chosen him for this, if there'd been any other choice. That cursed destiny of Crewzel's speaking had dropped this on his shoulders, apparently, and the fact that he and Elisena chanced to care for each other was simply an inexplicable kindness on the part of that destiny. Tristan shivered again, realizing how truly bleak his future might have been.

I hope you're not going to be sneezing and sniffling all through the ceremony.

Tristan reached out and ruffled Thomas' fur, glad to be called back to himself. He still wasn't sure he wanted to go through with the ceremony at all—but he had to. There wasn't any way out; his choices had defined the problem too closely for that. Maybe at the very beginning, with perfect foresight, he might have made a change, but not now. He thought through it all once more, moment by moment, and decided he probably hadn't had a choice then, either. He turned back to the sword, yielded to it, and lost himself in it again.

Tristan managed it so thoroughly that second time that, when an apprehensive Elisena came to ready him for the ceremony, she found him more prepared than she could ever have hoped to make him, so raptly bound to the sword that she could barely force him to take note of anything else.

She led Tristan out of the hall gently, wisely doing nothing to break the spell, and robed and gowned him with her own hands and fitted the special slippers on his feet, all the while trying to convince herself that this was nothing at all like readying a body for burial. Tristan's unfocused eyes did not reassure her. From the hall, she heard muffled commands as Polassar's men carefully unrolled the great scarlet carpet.

Allaire appeared in the doorway, arrayed in a white samite gown with hanging sleeves that drooped low enough to brush the ground by her slippered feet. She knelt and bent her silver-gilt head hastily to Tristan, who didn't seem to see her.

Her blue eyes widened like morning glories opening as she took in his pale, grave face.

"Is he all right?" Allaire's head turned toward Elisena as she spoke, but her eyes stayed on Tristan.

"I think so." Elisena touched his shoulder gently. Tristan drifted slowly about to face her. She looked at him closely. "It's part of the spell—we don't really exist for him right now. I could rouse him a little, but there's no need, and it's kinder not to." And he was much easier to dress, she thought wildly, as she fastened the great cloth-of-gold robe at his throat. He hated having his clothes fussed with. Allaire would have been shocked, could she have heard the thought. Tristan would probably have laughed.

Tristan was aware enough to know that the heavy robes fitted perfectly, their weight distributed so that he could move easily. There was some magical art at work there, he was certain, for surely all the Maristan kings had not been of a size? That was not possible, for some of them had been notable warriors, which he certainly was not. Surely they had been bigger, taller men? Tristan thought he could see the threads of the cloth drawing closer together. The robe shimmered, but that might have been only a stirring of the candles which lit the room, and in any case his eyes were not to be relied upon.

He had plenty of leisure then to ponder the question of his family, as time seemed to stretch like the robe for him. He'd casually wondered about them as a child, though without much urgency, since there'd never been any way of proving speculations. Blais had known nothing and could tell Tristan only that he and an ancient, rust-pitted sword had been discovered beneath one of his apple trees when Blais came to speak a Midwinter's Eve greeting to the trees. It might have been just a story, but likely it wasn't. Always swords, Tristan thought.

And look what that started.

Thomas?

Who else?

Where are you? Tristan tried to bring his surroundings into focus but found he couldn't.

Under the robe. It's all very well for wizards to immerse themselves utterly in magic for a ceremony that hinges on magic, but if you'll excuse my saying so, you want looking after, even when you have all your wits firmly about you. The state you're in now, you need me more than ever.

Well, Thomas always had had a feeling that it was his birthright to do and go as he pleased. Doubtless he'd mount the throne right alongside Tristan, and that was fair enough. Thomas had done as much as anyone to get him into this. Let him share the work, Tristan thought, with a strong sense of the justice of it.

Elisena offered water from a fragile silver goblet. Tristan gulped it greedily, having had nothing all night. Fasting was considered necessary for an effective vigil, but his throat was dry, and he felt empty as air. He took a little note of what Elisena was wearing—in bits and snatches as she crossed his line of vision.

Not white—that was forever Allaire's province, it would seem—but silver, like her rings, and that silver worked all over with runes, so that Tristan got a fresh reminder of magic whenever and wherever his eyes lighted upon her. Elisena's silk skirts were full but soft, so that they flowed about her without a whisper of sound—at least no loud rustlings such as Allaire's gown made. He'd never seen her dressed in fabrics that draped and shimmered. The change was intriguing.

Her face looked different, too, when she put it near his. She'd swept her tumbling hair back from her face and secured some of the curls with silver pins, though most of them still hung free. There was something Tristan thought he was supposed to tell her, something important. Let Thomas out of the saddlebag? No, that wasn't it, surely. Something else, something she'd be glad to hear. It slipped away from him. Elisena's lips were moving, but Tristan didn't hear and didn't need to. It was enough just to see her.

"Come, my lord. It is time." Formally, she spoke as if they were strangers again. Tristan smiled at that. She had never been that formal when they *were* strangers. A bright rune on her sleeve lured him off into contemplation of a spell once more.

He couldn't know what Elisena was thinking—couldn't guess how the haste of this ceremony both repelled and attracted her till she scarcely knew right from expediency.

Patience was a virtue she'd been forced to cultivate. The years and endless seasons of her captivity at Nímir's hands had not been passed in oblivious sleep as the more fortunate Allaire's had. Elisena had lived, wide awake every moment, waiting for rescue while the hope of it dwindled year by year, wizard by wizard. She'd been hidden in many bodies, in vastly differing life situations that yet had vaster, broader similarities. There had always been the brightly hopeful beginning, passing slowly into the despair of an aging body and the bitterness of chances perhaps forever past. She had watched herself age, again and again, anticipating time's familiar changes, wondering if *this* time she would be permitted finally to die, knowing that the small power she inherently, irrevocably possessed made even that small mercy beyond her hope. Then would come a darkening, and that bewildering shift to a new body, to begin the cycle yet again. There was the early frustration of thoughts and movements trapped in a body too young and weak to express them, then the years of impatient growth, until she was old enough to speak and be listened to. Yet there too lay pitfalls, for there were some things she must *never* express. And still the wizards searched, dared Darkenkeep, and died, and the Winterwaste spread in her heart as well as over the land, until her hair, whatever color it might once have been, grew as white as the Winterwaste's snows. Sometimes Elisena wondered if it might be *her* cries of anguish which haunted the winds there.

She had learned her lessons most thoroughly. Many lives could teach many useful things. Yet now all that wisdom was barely sufficient to prevent her dissolving into tears.

Elisena ignored the nagging knowledge that in this body she no longer had time to wait, even if she still laid claim to the patience. This was certainly her last enfleshment, locked as she was to her present body by Tristan's reforging of the tenth ring. She could no longer wait out eternity with dumb patience and unreasoning hope.

That was fate—her fate—and she would not shrink from it, or turn aside. But what of Tristan? What had she led *him* to?

Valadan waited like a witness in the hall. Draped with the black and scarlet of Esdragon, in silks that trailed to the stone floor, he stood out with impossible solidity in a chamber filled with mist wraiths, whose tinny voices Tristan barely comprehended.

He was not to be ridden, though. Tristan's robes made that an impossibility. Valadan merely headed the procession, walking between the ranks of men-at-arms to stand with Polassar and Canfors before the throne. It was fitting. Valadan represented a rank that had too long been unseen in Calandra.

Someone nudged Tristan's elbow, and Thomas stung his ankle with a well placed claw swipe. Prodded, he moved after Valadan. A shaft of scarlet light stretched endlessly before him, and he walked along it.

Outside, there was a whistle of wind, and Elisena looked up sharply once, but Tristan didn't react to it. At the end of the red path was the throne, flanked by the great candletrees, each aglow with a dozen flames. It wasn't seemly for him to look about on his way to the throne, but the hall struck Tristan as being awfully crowded for the number of people he knew to be inside it. He had an odd impression that there were more people behind him after he'd passed by the thin ranks on either side. Shadows or optical illusions, he thought skeptically. So many folk could never keep so silent.

His feet met the first step, then the second. Tristan ascended them without trembling or stumbling. He turned about and seated himself between the carven lions that framed Calandra's throne.

Galan armed himself, proud that despite his small handicap he could still dispense with an armor-bearer. Baird of Amrein was no longer that agile, though Baird might fancy that his sword arm still smote like a thunderclap.

Galan was, he prided himself, the only lord in his whole command who was both old enough in experience and young enough in years to be suited to lead the others. There might be squabbling beneath him—Baird seemed able to get on with no one—but there was none *with* him, which was what counted. His authority was absolute. This victory, now—he doubted the outcome not for a moment—would set a gilded seal to his leadership.

Galan draped his cloak carefully over his armor and fitted on his helm. The design of it was his own and fairly ingenious. There was no need to leave an opening for an eye which no longer existed, and much need to protect the side of his head which had no eye to detect attacks, so the left side of the helm was all enclosed, like a mask, artfully sculptured into a replica of his old profile which would both deceive and disconcert. Already there were rumors running that his sorcerer had changed his whole body to bronze, and that thus he was invulnerable. Galan did not discourage such beliefs, though he did not care to be reminded of Reynaud.

Galan still smarted over the wizard's hasty departure and parting sneer that he'd fulfilled *his* part of the bargain and was scarcely accountable for the bungling of Galan's men.

Galan cast the memory away and made a final adjustment to his helm. He thought the portrait flattered him, even without Reynaud's agency. The day was uncommonly chill, despite the sun which should have risen by now. Galan snugged his cloak closer about him and drew on his gauntlets. He couldn't count on the battle to warm him—he didn't expect there would be that much fighting. And just to be sure, Baird would command the van and bear the brunt of any resistance, sparing Galan's personal troops. He easily had the combined forces necessary to overwhelm Crogen, whatever defenses Polassar and that changeling witch had brewed up between them. Galan had given orders that they were to be taken alive for his future pleasure—Polassar, the girl, and that upstart peasant.

That jumped-up wizardling was more a personal than a political matter—but one Galan would relish taking personal care of, all the same. Polassar's machinations—who'd have thought that oaf had the wit for this game?—could be easily dealt with, but would not afford half the pleasure Galan anticipated when Tristan was before him at last.

The snowclouds flowed like a river over Channadran, steadily, efficiently. No wind dared tear at them, though one wind ran before them like a herald and another followed behind like a sheepdog.

The clouds had begun as wind themselves, warm, moist, and tender, moving over fertile ground and a sunlit sea, before Nímir had summoned them, commanded them, and dragged them to the chilly heights of Channadran, where they were condensed by force into their present form and impregnated with his snows. They carried the seeds of glaciers within them and might have relished the knowledge as their master did, could they have understood it. Some might have fled from the truth, but others would surely have rejoiced at their new importance.

First the snow and then the cold, the winds whispered to them, and perhaps the black ice again, when all defenses were down, to seal in the snow and the cold, to turn blood and sap to rare crystals, and to turn stone to powder.

But first, now, the snow.

Galan flicked a star-shaped flake from the back of his gauntlet, and cursed. Snow might turn the ground at the base of the walls to a quagmire, hindering his army, though perchance the ground was too cold to readily produce mud. And if not, he could always hope the fight would be swift. The sky above him was as gray as the metal of a spear blade.

Sleet was being hurled against the roof and through the windows of Crogen. The torch flames blew raggedly as Elisena, impassive or perhaps fatalistic, mounted the dais with a circle of glowing silver between her hands. She spoke a few words which might have been ceremony or magic, then advanced a further step. The circlet swam nearer, the air about it shimmering with the spell so that the crown itself was difficult to see. Tristan lowered his head slightly, obeying some well-drilled command or wisp of spell.

When he lifted his face once more, it was with a slight sense that something wasn't right. There was something else he needed to do.

The rune-circle inset on the arm of the throne caught the light and drew his eye. He couldn't look away.

The sheathed sword lay across his knees, and its hilt glittered in the same way the circle did. Obviously they were kin. Something to do with the pattern the silver on each made. Certainly they attracted each other.

Elisena was speaking, words which struck Tristan as being silver as well. He looked up at her, concentrating on her face instead of her weaving hands with some effort, and received a smile and a nod. Her eyes looked tenser than her lips.

The sword's grip molded itself to his palm, and he drew the blade free of its scabbard with an easy motion. It seemed mist-light in his fingers—with no effort at all, he held it upright before him. Then he gently seated the pommel inside the circle of silver.

For just an instant, Tristan thought he knew what it must be like to be inside Valadan's eyes, not looking out but living what lay within. Images fragmented around him, suffused with light. He couldn't distinguish anything with much clarity, but the barely glimpsed pictures were still familiar enough to shape themselves in his mind, triggering memories. Banners swirled and flared, hoofbeats drummed, a thousand spells rose and chanted and sang around him, swirling like droplets of colored ink agitated in water.

Tristan saw things even the chronicles he'd read had barely hinted at and knew them for truth. He heard spoken as for the first time great spells which had been only legends for generations. He understood every spell woven into his royal robes, and felt them working in him.

He saw Crogen's stones rising one upon the other, moving by magic, and saw workings of law as well as spell. In the land's other far corners more wonders took place—castles sprang up like mushrooms, roads were spun between them, and bridges thrown across a thousand streams. Orchards were planted and the twigs grew to fruitful trees in what seemed a single heartbeat. On the coast, seawalls provided safe harbors where none had existed, and fishing became an important trade. Everywhere between the sea and the forests the land was green, or gold with grain, a tapestry stitched with rows of apple trees whose fruit glowed like rubies.

It was a Calandra fair and beautiful as it had never been in Tristan's lifetime, but as the sword remembered it and as the throne promised it could be again. That might be half the purpose of the spell, Tristan realized—to ensure the king a clear vision of what he fought for, lest memory fail that service over the long, barren years.

He felt the flow of power as strong as a river current, running from the throne through his body and into the sword. He received it gladly. The sword's light was as nothing else on earth, save for the rings on Elisena's hands. Its magic and their life-magic were the same.

Tristan's eyes shut on the glory finally, unable to register more. He swayed on his feet and had to lean upon the sword for a moment. He couldn't have said when he'd come to his feet at all, or when he must have removed the sword from the throne. Gradually the sounds ringing in his head faded until all he heard was Minstrel, singing.

Calandra's king opened his dazzled eyes and looked out at his people.

. . . and in Channadran, slow realization dawned, or was pricked awake. An unthinkable thing had happened. Ten rings were reunited, and a lost sword was found. Long had it been since that joining was more than the fleetingest of possibilities. At first this new danger seemed hardly real. But when a storm vanished, its purpose of destruction unfulfilled—that passed belief. Yet it had happened, and the thing must be studied, so that Nímir might learn how this impossible thing had come to pass. It was time to take a more active hand, perhaps, and depend less upon his winds' terrified reports.

This new storm besieging the south should *not* vanish until its deadly work was done!

An Open Invitation

"HAIL THE KING of Calandra! All hail!"

The shout reverberated almost unnervingly. Tristan was so startled that he could only blink once more.

Yet the hall wasn't as crowded as the noise made him expect. The group clustered about the throne was small—only Polassar and some of his men, Canfors, Elisena, Allaire, and some perplexed peasants dwelling near Crogen who'd decided to shelter within the walls and had come to watch the scene being played out. Behind them, the hall still seemed strangely peopled, exactly as it had when Tristan passed through it on his way toward the throne. Whether with shadows or memories, Tristan was hardly sure. He didn't think anyone else could see them—at least no one was paying them the slightest attention—but it seemed to him that all Calandra's past kings were in attendance. Some of them looked pleased.

Of all the faces, Tristan sought only one. She was not shouting. Tears of relief wet her face, catching the swordlight and the torchlight.

Tristan cursed himself for a fool. He'd never told her about Dickon's sword! He'd let himself be so utterly caught up in the sword's spell that he'd never remembered that Elisena was ignorant of its true nature and had no way of discovering it unless he told her. So, of course, she'd still been half frantic, expecting that he'd be dropped dead at her feet. He could have spared her that, at least.

Tristan put his thoughts together and moved toward Elisena. He hadn't noticed yet, though she had, that the throne behind him was softly glowing, as if it were hollowed alabaster filled with fireflies.

He knelt down before her and reaffirmed the pledge he'd made her once in Blais' orchard, as if his being here were not enough fulfillment in itself of the promise. And then, hands joined, they spoke to each other ancient words of bonding that were hardly needed between them, before all the witnesses in the hall. Minstrel still sang somewhere, bright and shrill, but Tristan's head hummed with the love and support he felt flowing through him. He barely heard the bird. Elisena's rings tingled against his intertwined fingers, and the sword glowed between them, for he couldn't bear to sheathe it yet. Thomas purred.

For just a space, that light shielded them. Reality did not extend beyond its glow, and nothing entered the magic circle to disturb them. For just that moment, they were as private as in their own chamber. Then Tristan lifted one of Elisena's hands to his lips, smiled conspiratorially, and turned with her to receive their people's homage.

They stood before the gently glowing throne to do so, their hands joined in visible token that they hoped never to be parted in life. Tristan sheathed the royal sword carefully, and let his empty hand rest lightly upon its time-worn hilt.

Polassar was first to approach the dais, as was fitting, beyond any dispute of protocol. He had drawn his own great sword and knelt with its hilt upraised before him.

"My sword and sword arm I pledge to my liege lord, and to his kingdom." Polassar's voice boomed out impressively—in a suitable setting for once—and in a tone which suggested that everyone else within hearing would do very well to emulate him. "And my life, should king or kingdom require it." He kissed the sword hilt and offered it. Tristan touched it in acceptance. If he was able to do this now without fumbling, and even with a certain grace, then he had Dickon to thank for the rehearsal as well as a lot else.

Polassar stepped back, giving space to Canfors. As he did,

the tall doors of the hall opened, crashing back on their hinges. A sentry stood between them, breathless with running from his post.

"My lord! Galan's army marches!" Trumpets blew distantly in punctuation.

Another force marched as well, and drew first blood. A wind tore past the sentry, ripping the flames from the torches and hurling the man off his feet with a crash. The door swung crazily, almost unhinged.

"Man the walls!" Polassar bellowed. Snow-laden wind circled his ankles like a cat, depositing a little drift before the throne. Allaire looked at it and shrieked, stepping away. Thomas gave her a withering glance as he broke cover and sprang to the arm of the throne for better vantage. Polassar stepped forward, snapping out further defensive orders.

"No," Tristan said, in a voice that made itself heard, though he did not raise it against either turmoil or wind. Heads turned toward him—eventually, even Polassar's.

"Galan's men are our people too," Tristan said. Elisena gestured beside him, and the torches obediently sprang to life again. "We have to believe that, or all this is meaningless mockery. We can't just abandon them to die in the storm. Open the gates and let them in."

The sword pulsed gently in his hand. He didn't remember drawing it—perhaps it had drawn itself.

Polassar gaped in astonishment.

"What?" His incredulity must be great; the word was hardly more than a whisper.

"Open the gates. And let no one stand in their way. I don't want fighting. They'll be looking for me—let them find me." Tristan gestured broadly at the room.

Polassar met his eyes, still perplexed. Then an understanding dawned. He smiled craftily.

"Aye . . . and they find us as well! If we douse the torches, let 'em be blinded in the dark . . . if you've the stomach to stand fast for a bit, we can lure them straight in—"

"No!" Tristan cried out, too horrified to remember to sound commanding. "Not an ambush. No tricks, but an honest welcome, open-handed."

Polassar snorted with disgust as he turned away. "Wizard, they'll cut you down where you stand!" Polassar was only half attending to him by then. He'd begun to check his armaments, and loosen his longsword in its scabbard, dismissing his king entirely. Plainly, war was his proper business and none of Tristan's.

"If they do, if this is all a lie, then we'll do better to die quickly and have it over," Tristan persisted. "Open the gates."

Polassar's men looked at him wall-eyed, but didn't move. Nor would they, not in the face of Polassar's refusal.

Tristan glanced over the dim room hastily, seeking one face, any face he could count upon to obey an order of his, feeling himself caught up in a nightmare of frustration. What good, to be crowned at last, if no one listened? He spotted Dickon finally, very far back in the small crowd, his new sword belted on crookedly.

"Dickon! Get those gates open!"

The boy ran, eagerly. The spell upon him had worn off partially, but Tristan had had no time to lift the remainder. Polassar turned as if he thought he saw something, then wiped a hand across his eyes, frowning. He turned back to Tristan's side. He met his king's eyes again.

Tristan didn't know what his commander saw there. Maybe more than he intended. Polassar gave a fatalistic shrug.

"Wizard, I hope you know what you're about, for all our sakes."

Do you? Thomas' whiskers twitched.

Tristan wished he knew, himself. But he had best behave as though he did, while he waited for further inspiration to strike.

"Give the order," he told Polassar. "Call in the guards. No trouble, no fighting. Let them simply come in." He saw it done, finally. The word passed from man to man, and Polassar's garrison trickled in from the walls.

Nothing happened for a while. Doubtless whoever was leading the vanguard of the army was wary of traps, and this could hardly look like anything else. Tristan's back ached with tension; his hands and feet were cold.

Fear had nothing to do with his discomfort. Sleet still slashed through the windows, and what had melted upon the floor had frozen once more. Elisena ordered the shutters closed and sealed them herself. Tristan stared, his mouth drying, as the wood grew together until there was not the least line between the leaves, as a living tree heals a scar.

There was a clatter outside the hall. Valadan snorted, and his ears pricked alertly.

"No one is to lift a hand," Tristan said firmly. "Let them come in unhindered."

A pikeman was first through the door, closely followed by Andrayne of Heil, who'd been considered expendable by his betters, though of course he didn't know of the consideration. He hesitated, sword drawn, and took in the ranks of armed men formed up about the throne, weapons at rest but ready.

Andrayne's eyes easily found the gleam of the sword. He thought it flickered like a mirror in a dark room, drawing him closer.

Now, Tristan thought, reaching deep within himself and shutting out all but Andrayne's face. How is it you want to handle this? Really want to, not just play-acting, not what Polassar would have you do, or what Thomas might suggest, or the accepted military way, or even what Elisena might counsel. The whole chess game hinged upon him, the humblest of pawns, and it was his move. As with this man, so with all the rest. Tristan reached into his own heart, where the sword had sunk its roots.

Could what felt right truly *be* right? With the question came an acceptance of the answer. He knew it to be true, as if the sword were a light for seeing with the heart rather than the eyes. There was no decision to make. It had already been made, long since, and rightly made.

"Enter in peace," Tristan said. "And live to leave so." This was the test of the sword. The throne had been nothing. If the tales weren't true, or were only exaggerations . . .

Tristan was amazed to discover how easily he tossed off such trivial fears.

Andrayne advanced slowly, and Polassar's men parted for him at a wave of Tristan's hand. He was a youngish man, hard in his armor, hot-eyed, and now perplexed.

"You are welcome here," Tristan said calmly, and held Andrayne's eyes. After Polassar, it was almost easy.

Apparently it was that and the incredible strength that had to back such an audacious speech that won Andrayne over. He let his sword drop until its point tapped the floor before he noticed it; when he raised it, it was only to sheathe it. His hand dropped in puzzlement, and the battle fire in his eyes turned to smoke, as he stood before Tristan and his amazed friends.

When Andrayne didn't reappear, a question was called from outside, asking why he didn't report.

"Who asks?" Polassar shouted, as if happy to deal with something he understood.

"Baird of Amrein," came the muffled reply.

"Tell him to come in out of the cold," Tristan called clearly enough to be overheard outside. "And to put up his weapons— there's no fight to be had here." His sense of command, at the sword's prompting, was astonishing even to himself. He didn't argue with it, but rode it as one rode Valadan, unquestioning.

Don't push your luck, Thomas cautioned nervously.

Baird sent a whole company of archers in first, before risking his own person. Tristan raised the sword slightly, and watched notched shafts wilt like tallow dips at midsummer. Polassar's jaw imitated them. Baird was no different when at last he ventured in, though he blustered more before capitulating.

The atmosphere in the hall was tense, despite that success. The sword did not convey perfect peace, at least not without an effort. Tristan felt the strain keenly as he tried to watch the whole hall at once without any unseemly twisting of his head.

It seemed to him that the tension must break out into blows at any moment, but somehow it did not. There was an almost continual flow of men into the hall, in companies and singly, behind their bold commanders or leading them. Polassar's eyes were fairly starting from his head by then, when Geraint's men of the Red Lion were closely followed by Kerrgis of Josten and twenty mounted knights. Some of the latecomers were armored with considerable quantities of ice and snow as well as metal plate.

Tristan didn't wonder that he knew the lords' names, their strengths, their loyalties, and their hates. It was another gift of the sword, accepted without question as the sword itself must be accepted—something that simply *was*. He cataloged them mentally, one by one.

"Nímir's power forced them to fight without real cause," Elisena said softly in his ear. "The sword frees them from that, but beware the habits they've formed. Those may be stronger than Nímir."

Tristan agreed. His control was not perfect, at least not so solid that he could remain inattentive to it. Some dispute either broke out or was remembered between Baird and Geraint, even as Elisena spoke. Swords were drawn, and men moved swiftly to their lords' defense.

Just then came an almighty crash as the doors blew open again, and the horses screamed in fear. A drift of snow forced its way in, and the door was shut on it only with the combined efforts of all the fighting factions. For a moment, that cold wind had seemed fully capable of stopping hearts.

The hall became breathlessly silent. When a man did breathe, that breath froze upon the air.

"The hart had better learn to lie down with the lion," Tristan said pointedly, looking at Baird and Geraint's badges respectively. "If either one of you wants to see spring again—or daylight, for that matter." There was silence once more.

When the doors opened next, it was to admit Danac of Westif with his tall proud sons; mixed among the falcon banners of his company were many silver cockatrices. A shivering wolfhound trailed them.

The yard behind them was a swirl of white, and the far wall of the court could not be seen. Tristan hated to think what conditions were outside Crogen on the open ground, if the wind blew so here, with walls to break and turn it.

"Is there anyone else out there?" Tristan called. He almost hoped not. The hall had barely breathing-room left between its walls.

One last figure struggled through the door, which was then shut with another vast combined effort which further united sworn enemies. He was so snow-covered that nothing could be seen of whatever badge he bore, but the ranks somehow parted to let him pass through. He staggered right to Tristan's feet and would have dropped there, had there been space for him to fall.

"There's no one else, my lord. No one I could see." The man's voice was raspy from the cold, and his face was bone-colored for the same reason, save for the right side which looked bruised, as if he'd been struck. He probably had. Dickon whispered through frost-bitten lips that he'd been manning the gate after nearly being trampled in the first rush of entry. There was nothing, he added, to be seen beyond the walls now but the snow, and even retracing his steps to the hall had been nearly impossible.

The floor was tightly packed. Tristan relaxed a trifle—they didn't have *room* to fight now, even if they chose to. A horse neighed and stamped, and the wolfhound whined. Tristan scanned the room from the useful height of the dais. There were badges in plenty, and frosted tunics blazoned with the highest heraldries in his realm, but not the one that mattered most.

"I don't see Galan."

"Don't let it grieve you." Elisena looked up from tending Dickon. Her attitude was hardly surprising, Tristan supposed.

A blast of wind rattled the stone walls, and shook down shreds of old banners from the raftered ceiling. Elisena got to her feet slowly, glancing up.

"Is it time?"

There was no need to wait upon her answer. The chill in the air was . . . different, and told Tristan all he needed to know.

"Time and past." Elisena took his hand. "I'll need your help."

the Quelling

THEY STRUGGLED ACROSS what Tristan suspected was one of the inner courtyards. Which of those it was, and whether its location had any sense or significance, he couldn't guess. A wall bulked dimly ahead, then beside them before snow obscured it once more.

He was glad he'd thought to belt the sword on over his robes, holding them closer to his body; he'd have been blown off his feet long since if the wind had been able to get a real hold on that heavy cloth. As it was, Tristan staggered when the robe tangled tight about his legs from knee to ankle and he was barely able to steady Elisena as she too stumbled in the growing drifts. Tristan glanced back. He couldn't see the doorway they'd come through, or mark their passage by their footprints—those vanished even as his eye fell on them.

Black tree branches waved wildly, clattering against each other. Surely they were still inside Crogen, though. They had not struggled far enough to have left its perimeters. Tristan tried to remember which of the courtyards had trees. Not that it mattered.

Elisena stopped. Tristan knew she would wait for the white heart of the storm to reach them—such was the only way she could be certain of aiming a killing stroke with a single blow.

In the meantime, they must not freeze. They might as well have been right out on the open plain for all the shelter Crogen gave them, but Elisena was not long at a loss. She lifted her hands, and with airy gestures and much bespeaking of a ring whose silver curled and looped about itself a dozen times before finally circling her finger, she worked her magic to build them a shelter and grant them respite.

The air close about them shimmered and formed of itself a large bubble—large enough to encompass the two of them from head to foot, at least, and an arm's-span outward—forming an effective shield. Though the winds raved like maddened wolves and hurled sleet like a rain of daggers, testing her unceasingly, they could not break Elisena's power. They tried, relentlessly. Elisena ignored the wind, and pushed the edges of the bubble back a little further, to perhaps the distance of a pace.

It was still cold within the bubble, though the air was calm. Tristan's face burned with it, and Elisena let her hands fall, gasping at the strain, but thrust off all his efforts at support. The spell held, and gradually the air warmed till it was breathable. Tristan let his hands drop helplessly to his sides.

"I wish the High Mage had left some *written* word concerning these rings he made!" Elisena cried, as another blast rocked them even through the bubble. "He left too much to chance, and we can't afford to grope now. This is not the time for discoveries!" She began to kick at the snow, clearing it away to bare the ground beneath.

"What can I do?" Tristan asked, desperate to be of some use. His teeth were chattering with the cold. He bit his tongue in the middle of a word and tasted blood.

"Help me clear the ground. We have to find soil." Elisena glanced down at his feet, in the ridiculous pearl-embroidered slippers. "I wish you had your boots."

At least. You'll catch your death of cold if you survive that long.

Tristan jumped. "Thomas? How did you—never mind how, but go back now! It's not safe here—"

Go where? the cat asked. Nothing farther away than their own feet was visible in any direction. *I'd be happy to accept any reasonable suggestion.*

"That's immaterial," Elisena said sharply. "He can't get out through the shield, and I wouldn't want him to, now. He'll have to stay."

Thomas must have stayed under the robes, Tristan thought, running along by his feet the whole way, his curiosity getting the better of him. If the cat regretted that now, there was just no help for it.

Tristan knelt, his fingers unfastening his swordbelt as he did so. He dragged the scabbard free of the belt, took the sword out and laid it carefully on the ground. Using the scabbard's flat edge, he swept snow from the ground between himself and Elisena. It piled up at the invisible edges of the bubble, looking so odd that he might have laughed had matters been arranged less seriously.

At last, a show of initiative. Thomas began to scrape with his own little paws as well. *I thought that crowning had done something permanent to your wits.*

They reached soil. Elisena gestured for Tristan to stand up and back while she inspected it. She drew a finger across the dirt several times, as if attempting to write upon it. She shook her head.

"Too hard. It froze deep before the snow fell. Let me see then . . ." Elisena glanced at the sword lying by her feet. "Perhaps—"

By the sword—and under it when she lifted it—there were no crystals of frost upon the ground. "It's little enough but it will have to do," Elisena said. She handed the blade back to Tristan. "This is your work."

The grip seemed warm under his fingers, warmer than a weapon lying on frozen ground should have been. But Tristan had little time to wonder as he began at once to follow Elisena's directions. He drew a pentagram with the sword's point first, large enough to take in all the space they had within their transparent walls. He inscribed other figures within it. Some he knew so well that their names were direction enough, but others he did line by line, following right behind Elisena's instructing fingers. When the designs were done, he could recognize most of the unfamiliar ones as belonging to her rings.

When he had finished the last crescent moon, the final triskelon, and the ultimate interlacing of patterns, Elisena motioned him back and drew a leather bag from inside her left sleeve. She teased its fastenings open, and reached two fingers in. A fresh smell tickled Tristan's nose, and he recognized the herbal powder he had helped to grind. Carefully, Elisena dusted the sword-graven lines with the powder.

The powder vanished into the soil as she did so, like water soaking into thirsty ground. Elisena nodded at it, satisfied.

"Stand behind me now, but link your arms through mine," she further directed Tristan. "I need to draw on the power of the sword, but your hands must be on it as well."

The top of her head nestled just under his chin, and she was pressed tight against him the whole length of her body, but it was hardly the moment to appreciate such niceties. Little eddies of snow were creeping closer to their feet, sneaking under the bubble's edge, and the cold of the storm must be beyond belief by this time. The sword's metal was burning Tristan's fingers.

"Hold tightly, close your eyes, and think of the springtime," Elisena said. "We reach for the land's very roots."

Tristan remembered how easily Nímir had slapped his earlier spell away, and wondered how much use his help would be. Would matters stand the same now, even though he held the sword?

That might well be. But whatever his other shortcomings, he could at least remember spring, though the last one he'd seen seemed many lifetimes away. He could remember. Tristan shut his eyes. It was less easy to shut out the whistle of the wind and the cold touch of it. The bubble would be dissolving gradually, since Elisena could hardly cast a spell through it. He would be colder yet, if he let himself dwell on it. He did not.

Spring! Tristan imagined the little herbs thrusting themselves up through the soil, through the soggy hay of last season's grasses, and through at last the tough crust of winter's last snowfall. They were tiny and fragile, yet unrelenting. Beneath the snow, the purple runners of mint would be questing outward and the buds of coltsfoot pushing upward to mimic the sun they awaited. And the crust of snow should be collecting diamonds of melt, turning to lace, to glass, and then to water that nourished the infant plants.

The silver circlet on his head pressed icily against his temples, hinting at a coming headache, until Tristan longed to reach his hand up and tear the metal away. He resisted the temptation, because to act upon it he'd need to release the sword. Rather than do that, he'd bear the discomfort.

Elisena began to speak. At her words the powder was activated, and a strong perfume of herbs rose about them. Tristan thought of spears of new grass rising through the snow. He thought determinedly of the sun's tender warmth on those leaves, battling the cold and breaking winter's grip.

Elisena's hands lifted, and shone with a light that penetrated his lowered eyelids, painting pictures there. Tristan could feel snowflakes striking his cheeks, but he was sure none dared touch either rings or fingers, so swiftly did they move. And as they moved, so would the stormclouds.

The clouds roiled about, not yet amenable to Elisena's control but affected by it nonetheless. The wind forced Tristan's eyes open. He saw the sky above churning. Lightning flashed.

Tristan held the sword firmly point down to the ground, at the center of the patterns they'd drawn, as a focus for Elisena's power. And focus it Elisena did, with a gesture of magic graceful enough to take his breath and nibble at his heart with an emotion that surpassed professional jealousy.

Yet it wasn't quite enough. The storm resisted. It still held vast reserves of snow and ice, contained winds yet hungry for the warmth of the world. It refused to die or be dismissed and disbanded. It sought to turn all thoughts to contemplation of its strength and thence to despair.

Could a blade of grass or a leaf of mint despair? Tristan didn't know. He was trembling.

Elisena flung her words of power into the sky as a gentlewoman might toss an unhooded hawk, and the syllables were as shrill and proud as the cries of a stooping falcon. The storm winds swallowed, drowned, and tore the spell, but she spoke it again, dauntless, and lifted hands that were like flowers of light, their slender petals waving on command, ignoring the wind.

Elisena drew the storm to her, seeking dominion, and the winds circled inquisitively at her unfamiliar, irresistible touch. Sleet first soaked, then flayed, when the wind came forcefully behind its frozen needles. Tristan kept Elisena in the shelter of his arms and of the heavy robe as much as he could manage, and was thankful for the weight of the cloth-of-gold. Without its heaviness and the incorporeal but nonetheless real weight of the spells woven into it, Tristan felt he must long since have been lifted clear of the ground and swept away.

He remembered the numbing cold of the spells of Darkenkeep's Guardian and knew those had been naught compared to this. Though he had fought them successfully, that victory meant nothing here and now. The wind's roar confused Tristan, tangled Elisena's spells, or whipped them from his ears so that he had no hope of seconding them. He supposed his fingers were still rigid on the sword, but he could barely feel the hilt between his palms.

The metal—the silver at least—was moving as he glanced at it, writhing and coiling in rhythms quite alien to the storm's— answering, maybe, Elisena's unheard words. Tristan hoped so. At least the sword's tip was plunged firmly into the magic-soaked soil of Crogen itself. Surely that should be of some help. The land knew other things than winter and knew them firmly, ready to answer Elisena's call.

She needed his help, though, to find her full voice. Reach for the land's roots, she'd said. Yet somehow, against the full night of Nímir's storm, those little springtime magics Tristan had used to defeat Darkenkeep's Guardian seemed trivial and futile, and he didn't know what else to try.

He could feel the cold sinking into him. He'd fail her— that was becoming certain, as his heart seemed to shrivel within him, afraid even to beat. He didn't know how to fight back.

But the sword knew. Tristan reached blindly for *its* memories, the heat of its making, the fires and the forging, the glowing of charcoal and the white heat of the iron. And the memories of the quenching were there as well, when the heat of the iron had changed Istron water to miniature clouds that swirled, even as those overhead did. Strong, those memories were, even now. As strong as the magic bound into the rings by the High Mage and somehow, Tristan fervently hoped, able to blend with it.

The blade flashed white down its whole length. The glowing stopped at the hilt, so that Tristan was not burned, but he felt his knuckles blistering in the heat that rose from the blade. Its point, he thought, must have reached a deeper source of magic than Crogen's throne—maybe whatever spring that power welled up from. Here, somehow and probably by accident, he'd contacted it directly.

He had no idea what the sword was or could do, and there was no time to learn. Unpracticed instinct might not serve, but Tristan didn't have time to worry about that either. Such haste would at least simplify whatever was left of his life. Tristan reached desperately for the summer the sword sought. His hands felt suddenly empty. There was a piece missing from the spell, and he couldn't find it. Anguished, he reached out yet farther.

The heat was so great, Tristan feared the blade itself might be unmade. And all the while Elisena's hands lifted and fell and twisted just above his own, and her voice came and went in his confused ears, strong and proud, insistent. The spell reached its climax and ended with a crash of sound, and then silence.

Had they stood upon stone, it might have melted, but the earth was more resilient, and the lines Elisena had made upon the ground protected the spot where they were. Tristan drew a sobbing breath and opened his eyes.

There was a whiteness everywhere, as before. No spring, no green, just whiteness. Tristan's head sagged, as if he expected the cold to dispatch him with an axe stroke. His throat closed, so painful with tears that he felt dying would be easier than breathing. This had to be his fault. Whatever he had done or reached had not been enough. The sword hadn't been enough. Despite it, underneath it all, he was still himself, still flawed, and his failures still predictable.

A weight of grief settled damply over him. He held no hope for any future—Elisena would be exhausted from casting her spell, incapable of any further action without rest. The spell's failure ensured that she would never have time to regroup their forces. Hope was gone. Tristan wished he weren't dragging so many others down with him.

If only he'd been stronger, or had prepared himself better... Tears scalded his face, too hot to freeze at once, though surely they would soon enough. Tristan fell to his knees in front of the upright sword, his arms still wrapped around it and risking cuts—cuts that wouldn't matter. He pressed his wet cheek against the flat edge of the blade.

He heard his name called. It was a moment before Tristan could lift his head, and he did so reluctantly. He could face his failure, but he didn't want to look at it again. He just wanted to die and have done with it.

Elisena stood frowning at him, her lips parting with either a question or an understanding.

Her eyes reflected the sky back at him, exquisitely. For a space there was nothing between her lashes but that sky—dawn colors, pale rose and sea-foam green. Then her hand lifted, silver-ringed, and brushed the tears out of Tristan's eyes. At last he looked about him.

The snowdrifts about them were melting. The snow and ice upon Crogen's walls had thinned to a tracery that made the crumbled stones whole and sound once more. In the windows of the hall there was rainbow glass where the ice had been.

Far away, the spent snowclouds sagged to the ground, and a fog settled on Calandra, to turn to gold as the sun touched it. The air was appreciably warmer, and beginning to smell of growing things. Tiny green spears of grass were poking out, and the trees bore the first hint of new leaves.

Deep within Channadran, there was a mighty crashing as a glacier was riven from its bed by Nímir's wrath. Bits of it fell toward the valley below, yet never reached the ground. The coldness of the air alone shattered the ancient ice until all that remained was a sparkle smaller than snowflakes, too light to fall to the ground. The bones of the mountains cringed, and still Nímir raged.

Such rage was best expressed upon the underlings whose failure had occasioned it, but those were less than even the snow-sparkles now, vanquished utterly, and beaten by one small woman and one nearly frozen manling who dared not even name himself wizard!

The stones of Channadran continued to shiver, as blacker clouds formed about their highest peak. No more ice fell, but Nímir's enshrouding of his mountain boded no good, even for things as incapable of fear as the rocks were. Among them the Hounds cowered, not daring to howl or even slightly whimper lest they attract their master's ire upon themselves.

No one ventured from the hall yet—if the cessation of the winds after one disappointed shriek that had risen to escape hearing had been marked yet, it had not been trusted. But Elisena laid her cheek against Tristan's chest and permitted herself one tiny sigh of relief.

"And it was written—never mind where—that a sword would be forged, and its light would shine for all to see. It is fulfilled!"

Tristan held her, still weeping. He didn't know what he'd done, or how, or if the sword alone had acted to save them, and he cared less. He might, if fate were disposed to permit it, willingly stand here for the rest of his life holding Elisena, her soft hair against his cheek, smelling of lavender.

"Our battles are not done," Elisena said. "But we have a proof we did not have before, to go with our hope. The rings work as the High Mage meant them to, and you may be more even than he expected."

Tristan held her to him. Just now, he wanted to hear no more nonsense of prophecies and ages-old plans. It was enough to feel the sun on his skin.

Someone in the hall made bold to try one of the windows. A panel was cranked open. Instantly a blur of blue, white, and yellow shot out. Minstrel cut the air like an arrow, flying high. He found a breeze and rode it until he was a mere speck against the bluer sky; he might have been able to see as far as Kôvelir, for all Tristan knew, wanting to ask: Would Jehan still be there, still seeking Crewzel? Or might he already have found her?

Minstrel could not answer. He was too busy with his song and his flight even to note the question. Tristan dropped his eyes back to Elisena.

"I'm still not sure I like this task you've set me. It seems you've upped the stakes, and I never was much for dicing. As for the sword—swords have a nasty habit of dissolving in my hands." He touched her tenth ring lightly. "If you recall."

Elisena's smile was warmer than a candle's flame. Her fingers closed about his, being careful of his blisters.

"You keep your promises well. I have no doubts. I never have."

He's got enough for both of you, Thomas said to Elisena.

"You mean I'm well and truly stuck," Tristan said. "And now I've got a whole throne hall full of mortal enemies that I've got to send home full of the conviction that they've each gotten exactly what they wanted today."

He glanced around the shining courtyard, down at his somewhat bedraggled royal robes, and back at Elisena. "I'd hate to be the chronicler who tries to write a conventional history of *this* reign."

Over Crogen the sun shone, if only briefly.

About the Author

SUSAN ELIZABETH DEXTER was born in July of 1955 and has always been delighted that NASA should schedule such important events as Moon landings and the telecasting of *Viking* Mars photos on her birthday.

She was born in western Pennsylvania and has spent her whole life to date in that area, except for shopping trips to New York and side trips to World Fantasy Conventions. She had an uneventful education until high school, when she enrolled in a three-year commercial art course at a local Vocational-Technical school. She has been employed as a fashion illustrator, layout and free-lance artist for the past eleven years.

An interest in illustration led her to adult fantasy, via its many award-winning cover designs, but the roots of her interest go far deeper. In childhood her main literary interests were fairy tales and horses, and as she grew up she moved into historical fiction and the occult. From there the next step was logical, and she's still unsure at what exact point she crossed into Fantasy.

Her interests include omnivorous reading, fencing, herbs, macramé, weaving, soft sculpturing, and fine arts. She loves Richard III, Fafhrd and the Gray Mouser, unicorns, canaries, King Arthur, carrousel horses, books, pizza, birds of prey, wolves, and silver rings.